The Life and Times of
Tommy Travail

A Drop Of Truth

David G. Groesbeck

iUniverse, Inc.
Bloomington

The Life and Times of Tommy Travail
A Drop Of Truth

Copyright © 2009 by David G. Groesbeck

All rights reserved. No part of this book may be used or reproduced by any means, graphic, electronic, or mechanical, including photocopying, recording, taping or by any information storage retrieval system without the written permission of the publisher except in the case of brief quotations embodied in critical articles and reviews.

This is a work of fiction. All of the characters, names, incidents, organizations, and dialogue in this novel are either the products of the author's imagination or are used fictitiously.

iUniverse books may be ordered through booksellers or by contacting:

iUniverse
1663 Liberty Drive
Bloomington, IN 47403
www.iuniverse.com
1-800-Authors (1-800-288-4677)

Because of the dynamic nature of the Internet, any web addresses or links contained in this book may have changed since publication and may no longer be valid. The views expressed in this work are solely those of the author and do not necessarily reflect the views of the publisher, and the publisher hereby disclaims any responsibility for them.

Any people depicted in stock imagery provided by Thinkstock are models, and such images are being used for illustrative purposes only.

Certain stock imagery © Thinkstock.

ISBN: 978-1-4502-9410-2 (sc)
ISBN: 978-1-4502-9412-6 (hc)
ISBN: 978-1-4502-9411-9 (ebk)

Printed in the United States of America

iUniverse rev. date: 08/29/2011

ACKNOWLEDGEMENTS

I would like to thank the people who have helped me discover The Life and Times of Tommy Travail. Together, we have been on an adventure ride of the spirit. Their support, encouragement, and friendship have made this a rich and rewarding experience for me. I hope they enjoyed the ride as much as I have; and, I hope they are as excited as I am about our next adventure.

The one person, who has shared more of this excursion with me than anyone else, is my loving and understanding wife, Betty. Tommy Travail would have never come to life without her daily support and encouragement. She has made many sacrifices to give me the time I needed to spend in Tommy's world. Her reflection can be seen throughout The Life and Times of Tommy Travail and I love her for it. She is the one that makes me feel special.

TO

Kevin, Nhan, Tyler,
and, the always,
adorable,
Haley

Contents

ACKNOWLEDGEMENTS..v
Prologue..xi
Chapter 1   The Rubber Band War 1
Chapter 2   Crime and Punishment.......................19
Chapter 3   Family.....................................34
Chapter 4   A Box of Memories and a Locked Door 44
Chapter 5   The Key....................................55
Chapter 6   An Act of Defiance 66
Chapter 7   Carla......................................77
Chapter 8   The Road To Cantwell 89
Chapter 9   The New Castle and Registration 102
Chapter 10   Historical Problems........................114
Chapter 11   Results and Consequences...................125
Chapter 12   Rules and Code of Conduct..................135
Chapter 13   Return to Cantwell.........................147
Chapter 14   Whitelace's Mission........................161
Chapter 15   The First Day of Classes 171
Chapter 16   A Drop of Truth and the Rules of Racing....188
Chapter 17   The Second Day of Classes..................199
Chapter 18   The Hazards of Cross-Country Racing........218
Chapter 19   New Castle Town............................229
Chapter 20   The Plan...................................239
Chapter 21   The Depths of the Well 252
Chapter 22   The Room of Destiny 265
Chapter 23   The Cavern of Contemplation................278
Chapter 24   Dragona and the Pit of Perpetual Pain......295
Chapter 25   Friends, Family, and a Few Things Most Familiar ..309

Prologue

Tommy Travail is an ordinary young boy whose life is about to become full of mystery, magic, and mayhem. The decisions he is about to make will challenge his understanding of reality and cast him into a land of fantasy and enchantment. The adventurous Life and Times of Tommy Travail is just about to begin, won't you come in?

Chapter One

The Rubber Band War

A breeze came across the classroom from an open window and brushed across Tommy's face. It had the cool warmth of an early summer's day. Tommy raised his eyes and peered out the open window. He gazed across a vast lawn sprinkled with several large oak trees. Tommy could see the rough hewn back side of large granite stonework that stood along the main entrance to the administration building. Although he could not see the front of the stonework, he knew that, unlike the back side, the front side was flat and polished with gothic letters engraved into it. It said, "The University of Brookfield." The building he was in now had a much smaller version of that stonework next to its entrance that said, "The University of Brookfield Preparatory School for the Gifted."

"Gifted? Ha Ha," Tommy thought.

"**Five** more minutes ladies and gentlemen," the voice of Professor Schroder rang out from the front of the classroom. "You should be starting to wrap things up."

Tommy turned his attention back to his paper and wrote, "In conclusion: The forces applied to the X and Y axis, as shown in the formula above, cancel each other out. Therefore, the object remains motionless." And with that he was done, done with physics, done with classrooms, done with school for a whole glorious summer. And, what a summer it was going to be. His best friend, Michael Woden, was going to be staying at the school all summer. And, as Tommy stayed at the school every summer, it was going to be great. Tommy lived with his grandfather, Professor Layton Galloway, who is the curator of the University's museum and the head of the archeology department. His grandmother, however, had died before he was born. Some time ago, because the museum was busy all year long and other circumstances, the University's Board of Governors decided to provide a residence for its curator. As a result, Tommy and his grandfather lived in a modest sized stone cottage behind the museum. It was connected to the museum by a wide covered breezeway. Halfway across the breezeway sat two stone benches facing each other on opposite sides of the walkway. This was one of Tommy's favorite places and it was where he had agreed to meet Michael as soon as class was over, in… in, **four and a half minutes!**

"There must be a law somewhere in physics," Tommy thought, "that says that the speed of time is inversely proportional to the degree of anticipation of coming events." This had been one of the longest days of his life. It seemed to him that the clocks had been running slower and slower as the day went on and now he was sure that they had come to a complete stop. Four minutes, three minutes, two minutes, one minute, one minute, one minute; "Come on," Tommy thought. Finally Professor Schroder stood up and announced that time was up and directed everyone to turn in their papers. It was here. Summer holiday was here at last.

Tommy grabbed his papers and his back-pack and headed to the professor's desk. He placed his papers on the professor's desk and thanked the professor. He wasn't quite sure why he had done that, but maybe it was because it had been an interesting semester. Or, maybe it was because he thought that he had just aced his physics final. Or, maybe it was because he was so happy to start the summer holiday that he just wanted to thank the whole world; no, the whole universe. All he wanted to do now was get back to the cottage, check in with his grandfather, and meet up with Michael.

He headed out the side door of the building and eyed the long traverse to the museum. He knew a shortcut, but that would take him dangerously close to the Delta Epsilon Pi fraternity house. The Delta Eps lived to torment Preps and Tommy knew it. All the Preps knew it. It is said that the Delta Eps once overheard a Prep refer to them as the

"Dips" so they barbequed and ate him. Tommy didn't believe it, but all Preps believed they were capable of it. Tommy weighed his options, and, since school was over and the University classes had ended the previous week, he thought it was worth the risk. So he decided to take the shortcut and headed off. The shortcut would take him across the street, down one pathway, then down another pathway and bring him out at the sidewalk that went right across the front of the Delta Epsilon Pi fraternity house. Tommy made up his mind that when he got there, he would break out in an all out run. Tommy was about average height and weight for a twelve year old, but he could run pretty fast. He figured he could get past the frat house before they knew he had ever been there.

As he walked, Tommy thought about his friendship with Michael. The first time they met, almost four years ago, they didn't get on very well; no, not very well at all. In fact, the first time they met, they had a fight, a fight that left Michael with a black eye and Tommy with a fat lip. It took almost a month for Tommy's lip to heal and left him a slight scar on his right upper lip. On the day they had met, Michael was looking for a fight with anyone, for any reason. He desperately wanted to vent his anger. His mother and stepfather had just dropped him off in front of the administration building without so much as a fair-thee-well. His mother just said, "Bye." And his stepfather said, "I better not get any bad reports on you, boy." That was it, and off they went. Tommy, on the other hand, was trying to deal with the loss of both his parents and he was in no mood to take anything from anybody. Tommy had fairly straight, light brown hair, but he had one curl that when unmanaged fell down across his forehead. As the two of them waited in line at the registration desk, Michael started teasing Tommy about the "cute little curl" hanging down on his forehead. Tommy ignored him at first, but Michael persisted. When Michael said that he was far too cute to be a boy and that he must really be a girl, Tommy said, "I'm a boy," and took a swing at him. Fists flew and both boys wound up in detention before school even started.

Michael continued to call Tommy, "Tommy I'm a boy" for quite a while. That eventually changed to "Tommy Boy." And, he still calls him "Tommy Boy" occasionally. Even though they didn't like each other very much when they started out, they soon found that they had one thing in common. That one thing would keep bringing them together. Neither one had a "gift." They were just two ordinary boys. They did not have a special gene somewhere that had exploded to leave them with a special skill or talent; nope, just two ordinary guys. They were the only ordinary kids at The Brookfield Preparatory School for the Gifted. In fact, they may be the only two ordinary kids that had ever attended The Brookfield Preparatory School for the Gifted. There were kids with extraordinary abilities in mathematics and science. There were kids with special talents in art, music and languages. There was one girl who could speak sixteen different languages by the time she was five. But not so with Tommy and Michael, for them there was no special "gift." Michael was there because his stepfather, John Zeigler, was one of the richest men in the country and Tommy was there; well, because of his parents and his grandfather.

For three hours a day the "gifted" kids would go off somewhere and do whatever it was that they did. Michael and Tommy were assigned an extra study period and two free periods during these three hours. This put Michael and Tommy together a lot. It didn't take long for them to see that they had more in common than they had first realized. They found that they both really liked video games. Michael liked war games with strategy, tactics and lots of shooting, while Tommy preferred adventure and role playing games. But video gaming is video gaming; and a gamer is a gamer. Another thing they were to discover they had in common was the schooling itself. Since they were in a school for the gifted, everything was advanced; advanced math, advanced science, advanced theory of this and advanced theory of that. It was hard work and they were thankful for their extra study and free periods. They needed them to keep up with the workload. It didn't take long for the two of them to become the best of friends. Tommy learned to put up with Michael's moodiness and explosive temper, and, Michael learned to put up with Tommy's bouts of depression over the loss of his parents.

Deep in his thoughts about Michael, Tommy had lost track of where he was and suddenly realized he was on the sidewalk in front of the Delta Eps house. He started to run, but it was too late. Three frat brothers had come off the porch and they were now headed right for him. The one in the middle was tall and lean. The other two, although shorter, were huskier and a lot more muscular.

"Hey! You, Preppie," the tall one called. "Just what do you think you're doing? I didn't see you salute our flag. You know we can't have anybody disrespecting our flag. Dean, did you see this Preppie salute our flag?"

"Nope," said the unshaven one on his right.

"How about you, Bobby, did you see a salute?"

"Nope, I didn't see a salute either," said the one on his left.

"I'm sorry," Tommy pleaded. "I just hadn't got to it yet," he lied and immediately snapped to attention and smartly saluted their flag.

"Too late," said the tall one. "There must be a penalty for this offense. A fine, I think. Yes, a fine. The fine will be, let's see, ah yes, it will be one Euro."

"But I don't have any Euros," Tommy exclaimed. "Where would I get any Euros?"

"Oh," said the unshaven one. "Failure to pay a fine is an even a worse offense than disrespecting our flag. You are really in trouble now."

"Hey, James," a voice came from the porch of the frat house. "You better take it easy on that one. He's Professor Galloway's grandson."

"Is that true," the tall one said to Tommy.

"Uh, yes sir," Tommy responded.

"You don't sound too sure of yourself," the tall one said. "Are you, or are you not Professor Galloway's grandson?"

"Yes sir," Tommy responded again.

"Well," said the tall one. "In that case maybe we can cut you a little slack this time. What do you guys think? Shall we cut this Preppie a little slack? I'll tell you what," he continued without waiting for an answer. "Since you did salute our flag, I think we'll let you pass this time, but the next time we see you, you'd better have that Euro you owe us. Now get out of here."

Tommy didn't wait to be told twice. As he started to run, he could hear the three Delta Eps break out in uproarious laughter, but he didn't look back. He ran the rest of the way to the cottage. When he

David G. Groesbeck

reached the front door of the cottage, he paused to catch his breath. After a moment, he opened the door and called to his grandfather.

"Grandpa, Grandpa, I'm home. I think I aced my physics final." But, there was no answer. "Grandpa," he called again, and still, no answer.

"Oh well," he thought. "Grandpa must still be at his office in the museum."

Tommy set his back-pack on the sofa next to Mister Buttercup, Tommy's enormous long haired tiger-striped cat. One day a few years ago, Mister Buttercup appeared on the breezeway. He was somewhat sickly, but he was just a baby. He couldn't have been more than a few weeks old. He was so young and tiny that he could fit in the palm of Tommy's hand. It is very difficult to tell if a baby kitten is a boy or a girl, but he was such a cute little ball of fur that Tommy was sure he was a girl and named him Buttercup. Then he started to grow, and grow, and grow. He became extremely large for a house cat and his long fur made him look even bigger. In time, Tommy realized that Buttercup was a boy and, in order to give him the respect he deserved in the cat world, especially given his size, Tommy "corrected" his name to <u>Mister</u> Buttercup.

Tommy reached down and scratched Mister Buttercup behind his ears. Mister Buttercup raised his head, grunted out a purr then put his head back down between his front paws and appeared to go back to sleep. "Cats really know how to live," he thought. "They do what they want, when they want." Since his grandfather wasn't there, he figured he might as well go out to the breezeway and wait for Michael. As he went through the kitchen towards the back door, he paused at the refrigerator and grabbed a soda, then headed out to the breezeway. He walked down the breezeway to the stone benches, sat down and took a long drink of his soda. When his mother was alive, she used to sit here with him and tell him stories of the great societies of the past. His mother, Sara, was a professor of anthropology at the University and his father, Steven, like his grandfather, was a professor of archeology. His father had met his mother while she was helping her father, Tommy's grandpa Galloway, at an excavation site in Egypt. They fell in love right away and, with Grandpa Galloway's approval, they were married a year later. A year after that Tommy was born.

During the summers, Tommy's parents would go on archeological digs and, most often, they would take him along. It was exciting. And suddenly, it was over. They were gone. He really missed his mother and father. Oh, his grandfather loved and cared for him, but he missed the tenderness of his mother and the strong warmth of his father. He never met nor did he know anything about his father's parents. His father never talked about them. Tommy could feel himself slipping down that slippery slope and he was getting depressed. Just then, Michael arrived.

"Hey Tommy Boy," Michael said. "Why the long face? Did you blow your physics exam?"

"No," he said looking up at Michael's thin maturing face. Michael was changing into the man he was to become and looking less like the boy he had been. Suddenly a big smile broke across Tommy's face. "I think I aced it," he said, "Grandpa's going to be really happy."

"I'll bet," Michael responded.

"So," Tommy continued, "what do you want to do? I can't wait to get at it."

Michael didn't hesitate for a moment. "I want to go to the University Store," he said. "There's a new video game out. It's called; <u>The Last Soldier</u> and I want to take a look at it. Then I'd like to go over to the recreation building and, if the University guys are gone, I'd like to see if I can get some time on one of the snooker tables." The two of them had spent many hours watching the older guys play snooker and, for a young guy, Michael was actually a good player. Snooker is a lot like pool or pocket billiards, but it is played on a larger table with smaller balls and smaller pockets. It can be a little confusing to watch if one doesn't know the rules, but it's really not complicated. There are fifteen red balls called "cherries" and six numbered balls, numbered 2 through 7. The object is to pocket a cherry and then pocket a numbered ball, then pocket another cherry and follow that with another numbered ball and so on until the player fails to pocket a ball, then it's his opponent's turn. Numbered balls are spotted back on the table immediately after they are pocketed, but cherries are never spotted. A player gets one point for each cherry and gets the number of points that corresponds to the number on the numbered ball. So if a player sinks a cherry and follows that with the 7 ball, he would get eight points. When all the cherries are gone, the remaining numbered balls are pocketed in numbered rotation, 2 through 7. The game can be played until the table is cleared or to a predetermined point total. The key to the game is to "snooker" your opponent. That is, when you lose your turn you want to leave the table in such a way that your opponent has no clear shot. Michael liked the game because of the strategies that come into play. And, Tommy liked the game because, like all billiard games, it was a game of geometry. Tommy really enjoyed trying to conceive a possible shot when there were no apparent shots.

"Say, Michael," Tommy started. "Do they have a currency exchange at the University Store? I need to get a Euro."

"I don't know," Michael responded. "What do you need a Euro for?"

"Oh, it's nothing. I'll tell you later. But, I'm not going to the rec hall if there's any Delta Eps there."

"I'm not afraid of those Dips," Michael boasted. Michael was six months younger than Tommy. He had been about the same height as Tommy until a few months ago when he started on a growth spurt. Now, he was six inches taller than Tommy and, apparently, starting to feel it.

"You better not let them hear you call them that." Tommy advised. "You know what they say."

"Oh, you mean that barbeque stuff, you know that's a bunch of baloney," Michael replied.

"I don't care. I'm one of those people who believe that those guys are capable of almost anything. I wouldn't push my luck if I were you."

"Ah, to heck with those guys," Michael started. "I want to go the store and the rec hall. What do you want to do," questioned Michael.

"Hey, it all sounds good to me. But, I have to check in with my grandfather first and he wasn't at the cottage. We'll have to go up to his office and see if he's there. Then, what do you say we stop at the cafeteria on the way to the University Store and get something to eat. I'm starved. If Grandpa will let me stay overnight in the Dorm, we'll be able to play video games until dawn."

"Okay. Let's go," Michael said.

The two boys headed down the breezeway to the museum. The museum was quite a spectacular place. The Museum building, in part, was very old. The first story of the building was made of stone that had been constructed as part of a military outpost over two hundred years ago. Legend has it that the outpost itself was built on an even older site. A fire in the early nineteen hundreds had gutted the structure, but left the stone walls intact. Around that time there was a brilliant grad student studying architecture and engineering at the University named Phillip Worm. Worm had been an equally brilliant undergrad student, and in his senior year, he designed a building for the site. After he graduated, he returned to the University as a grad student. He spent most of his graduate years petitioning the Board of Governors to tear down what remained of the old structures and build his building. But, it wasn't until after the fire that he finally got the approval to build the new structure. Naturally, rumors spread that Worm himself had set the fire, but nothing was ever proven. Worm designed the current building using the original stone walls. He added two more stories to the height of the structure made of iron, steel and glass. He added a large glass dome in the center of the roof. In the interior, he created two mezzanines that went all the way around all four walls so that the center of the building was three stories high and in the area covered by the dome it was almost four stories high. Offices and other assorted rooms were on the mezzanine levels. There were conference rooms, bathrooms, storage rooms for precious documents and rooms where ongoing research was conducted. All the glasswork made the interior bright and perfect for displaying the treasured items the University had collected. The University had been collecting items from around the world for a long time. And, Tommy was proud that his parents and his grandfather were responsible for discovering or acquiring quite a few of the items on display.

When they got to the museum door, Tommy took out a key and unlocked the door. The two boys entered the museum and Tommy turned around and relocked the door. Professor Galloway's office was directly across the museum, but all the way up on the second mezzanine. Worm built an open air elevator in each of the four corners that went up to the mezzanine levels. The elevators were of the cage type. The cages were made of wrought iron with ornate scrollwork and shapes. They sat diagonally in the corners so that each cage was triangular in shape. They had an outer gate and an inner gate that was part of the cage. On the side of the outer gate was a call button to call the elevator if the cage was on a different level. Inside the cage was a box with two buttons. One was labeled with an arrow pointing up; the other button had an arrow pointing down. Worm had designed the elevators and their mechanisms so precisely that, in all their years of service, only a handful of parts had ever needed replacing. He also devised a whole array of safety devices that made them safer than a modern elevator. Halfway between the corners of three of the walls, Worm had built spiral stair cases that also went up to the mezzanine levels.

Halfway between the corners of the fourth wall, the wall that was directly across from the boys, Worm built a fifth elevator. This elevator was different from the other four. It was the only one not in a corner, so it was square. It was still of the cage type, but it sat back in a niche in the wall. Like the other elevators, it had an outer and inner gate and a call button mounted on the wall next to it. However, as one entered the cage, there was another gate on the left side. In the corner between the two gates, Worm had installed a pedestal with a key pad on top of it. It had sixteen ivory keys and they were mechanically connected to the elevator's operating system. The keys were arranged in a four by four square and there were no identifying marks on them, one just needed to know what keys to press and in what order to make the elevator work. Tommy knew which ones to push. He and his grandfather might be the only ones who did know the correct sequence. His mother and father, of course, knew the sequence when they were alive. They used the elevator frequently. When the elevator reached the second mezzanine, the gate on the left opened to a rustic oak door that led directly into Professor Galloway's office. That door was quite often locked and, as far as Tommy knew, his grandfather had the only key. His grandfather almost always used this door to enter or leave his office, but Tommy knew that he was not supposed to use that door. Instead, he had to exit through the front gate and go down the mezzanine a little ways to the official entrance to the Curator's Office.

The Life and Times of Tommy Travail

The shortest route to the Professor's office was to use that elevator. Michael started off in that direction, but Tommy caught his arm and stopped him. "I don't want to use that thing," Tommy said.

"Oh you say that all the time," Michael chided. "Your grandfather uses it everyday."

"I don't care," Tommy continued. "That thing creeps me out. It has that weird vibration and the noises it makes worries me.

"Come on, Tommy Boy. It's shorter," Michael insisted.

"No," Tommy said emphatically. With what the short route had gotten him into earlier, he wasn't going to take any chances.

They went to the nearest corner elevator and took it to the second level mezzanine. As they walked around the mezzanine to get to the Professor's office, Tommy peered over the railing. It really was a wonderful view with all the museum displays spread out across the floor below. There were a few people down there looking at one display or another. Tommy thought about the floor below and wondered if there really were tunnels below it. For a history paper near the start of the school year two years ago, Michael had been studying some old military documents from the days of the old outpost, when he found a single reference to catacombs below the outpost. When he told Tommy about it, they began musing about what could be down there. Before they knew it, they had treasure fever. The more the two of them talked about it, the more excited they got about it. Tommy had evidently inherited his parents' curiosity for the unknown and unexplored. That's when Tommy realized what his parents must have experienced when they were preparing to go on an expedition. The boys spent most of their free time that year trying to find out more about the catacombs. They searched all the documents that they could find at the museum and library but were unable to find any other reference to tunnels or catacombs. When Tommy finally asked his grandfather about the catacombs, his grandfather told him that he thought that there had once been tunnels under the structure, but that they had been filled in when the reconstruction was done after the fire. That hadn't stopped the boys and they continued until they had searched every inch of the museum for some type of entrance. Having been unsuccessful in that, they finally gave up. Occasionally one of them would bring it up and they would talk, but in the end, they decided it was a lost cause.

They turned the corner of the mezzanine and were on their last leg to the Professor's office. "We'd be there by now if we would have used the other elevator," Michael quipped.

"Ahh, we're almost there," Tommy responded.

The section of the building that encompassed the Professor's office was the first section that Worm completed. The Professor's office was originally built by Worm for himself. It was from there that he directed the reconstruction of the building. He could see nearly everything that was going on with the reconstruction from that high vantage point. He had installed the elevator for his own use. He also built the cottage that Tommy and his grandfather now lived in for himself. It took nearly three years to complete the project. After the building was finished, Worm became the museum's first curator. With his keen interest in mechanical design, he collected many ancient and odd mechanisms for the museum. The museum has a whole section devoted to his collection. He continued to live in the cottage and maintain his office in the museum for the rest of his life.

The boys finally reached the door to the Curator's Office and went in. There was an outer office area with a desk and filing cabinets where the Professor's secretary worked. There was no one at the desk, but Tommy instinctively looked to see if there was a note for him on the desk, and there was. Tommy picked up the note and read it. It was from Wilhelmina Woodword, the Professor's secretary. It told Tommy to wait in his grandfather's office and that his grandfather would return soon. The two boys went past Miss Woodword's desk and through the door into the Professor's office.

The Professor's office was a reasonably large room with two large windows that overlooked the front grounds and the main entrance to the museum. In front of the windows was a large oak desk that had originally belonged to Phillip Worm, which, of course, Worm had designed. There were several things on the desk including a name plate with Layton Galloway written on it. Several books were stacked in one corner on the chair side of the desk, and a stack of papers filled the other corner on the chair side. An odd looking mechanical device filled one of the front corners. It was and old device. Worm

The Life and Times of Tommy Travail

either found it or built it. There had originally been two of the devices on display in the Worm section of the museum, but one of them had gone missing. Ever since then, his grandfather kept this one on his desk. The interior of the device was mostly exposed. It was full or gears of various sizes. It had a movable platter and a covered roller. The finish had dulled considerably over time and it was a bit rusty, but there were three shiny surfaces deep in its interior. They would have gone unnoticed, except that they would occasionally twinkle when struck by sunlight. Tommy's grandfather always left a small piece of paper on the platter of the device. He felt the paper was appropriate as the device appeared to some type of ancient printing machine. Tommy had fiddled with it many times, but could never get it to work.

A black high-backed leather chair sat behind the desk and two overstuffed low-back leather chairs were in front of the desk. A series of bookcases which were overflowing with books and papers ran along one wall. A long credenza stretched along another wall. It had two lamps on it near each end and in the center was the mounted skull of a saber-toothed tiger. It had been a gift from Tommy's mother to her father for his fiftieth birthday. On the wall above the credenza were two framed Egyptian papyrus reproductions. The museum owned the original papyruses, but they were far too expensive and delicate to be wall decorations, even in the curator's office. Worm once had two drafting tables along the walls now occupied by the bookcases and the credenza. In the remaining wall towards the corner, was the door to the elevator. Diplomas, degrees and certificates of varying sizes in thin black frames covered the rest of the wall. It represented a lifetime of achievement and excellence for Professor Galloway.

Tommy went around the desk and sat in his grandfather chair. Michael plopped himself into one of the overstuffed chairs. Tommy surveyed the desk. In addition to the books, papers and ancient printing device, the desk had a green shaded desk lamp on it. There was also a blotter and an assortment of notepads and writing tablets along with several pens and pencils. Tommy noticed two new boxes of rubber bands and picked them up. He put them on his lap so that Michael couldn't see what he was doing. He opened one of the boxes and took out a rubber band. He stretched the rubber band from his index finger, raised his hands and fired the rubber band at Michael, striking him right in the middle of the forehead.

"Hey man, that hurt," Michael exclaimed.

"Tommy threw one of the boxes to Michael and said, "One to nothin', the first one to twenty-one wins."

The war was on. Rubber bands soon filled the air. In no time at all, rubber bands were everywhere. They hung from the lamp shades and littered the desk and floor. They covered the chairs, credenza and bookcases. One hung from a corner of one of the framed papyruses and one was dangling out of the mouth of the saber-toothed tiger like some long shriveled tongue. A few of the Professor's framed diplomas had been knocked askew. The score had run up to nineteen to twenty, Michael's favor. Tommy had to do something quickly. The desk had a set of drawers on each side and a foot well in the center. Tommy figured that if he could get into the foot well he would be protected on three sides and might be able to catch Michael with a double whammy when he came around to get him. Tommy jumped for the foot well and quickly got himself set. He pulled out two rubber bands, looped one over his index finger and one over his baby finger, and stretched them back. He carefully watched both sides for any sign of Michael's attack. Michael, however, quietly climbed on top of the desk. In one quick move, he leaned over the desk and fired his shot. At close range, the rubber band struck Tommy on the cheek with a pop.

"Ouch," Tommy hollered. A raspberry welt immediately began to appear and he rubbed his cheek. In his crouched position, he let himself fall over fainting death. As he did, his shoulder hit the inside wall of the foot well and a hidden door popped open.

"You have to watch out for the sneak attacks, Tommy Boy," Michael said with victory in his voice.

"Hey, look at this," Tommy replied. "There's a hidden compartment under here." Tommy swung the door all the way open and looked inside. There was a book and a conductor's baton. Tommy reached in and pulled out the baton. It was warm to the touch and was different from the other conductor's batons he had seen, and, he had seen a few. For one long semester, both he and Michael decided that they were going to be rock stars, so they signed up for band classes. Michael took up the drums and Tommy tried several different instruments. In a band full of musical prodigies, Michael and Tommy didn't have a chance, and in no time at all, they realized that they had made a mistake. They decided that it was just another example of how "ordinary" they were and moved on. Tommy crawled out from under the desk so he could take a better look at the baton. It wasn't like the wooden one that Professor Noteworthy had cracked across his head on several occasions in band class. It wasn't made of wood, Tommy was sure of that. The shaft was black and appeared to be made of very fine fibers woven together that made the shaft more flexible than Professor Noteworthy's baton. Its handle was white and wrapped in what appeared to be finely braided gold bands. The butt end of it had a round, marble like, crystal protruding from it.

Tommy took the baton and started. "Remember old Professor Noteworthy," he said. "Okay, ready? A one and two and three and four," he said mocking Professor Noteworthy as he waved the baton through the air. However, something very strange happened. As he waved it through the air, the tip left faint blue traces. The light blue streaks just hung suspended in the air for a moment, then thinned and vanished.

"How'd you do that," Michael inquired.

"Don't know," Tommy responded. "I just waved it."

"That is definitely cool. What else is in that compartment?"

"A book," Tommy replied.

"Well let's have a look at it."

Tommy crawled back under the desk and retrieved the book. It was a black leather bound book with a closing strap and a gold clasp. It looked more like a journal than a book. Then the hair on the back of Tommy neck stood up as he saw the gold engraved initials, SPT, those were his father's initials. Simultaneously, both boys heard the clank of the elevator.

"You better get that stuff back in there," Michael advised. "Your grandfather's coming."

Tommy jumped back under the desk, put the baton and the journal back in the compartment and closed the door. He crawled out, pushed the chair back to the desk and both Michael and he went around the desk and sat down in the two overstuffed chairs. It was at this point that the two boys first notice the condition of the office. There were rubber bands everywhere and there was no time to clean up. They were going to be in serious trouble.

"Act natural," Michael said. "Act like nothing's wrong. We can say we found it like this."

Tommy gave Michael that "you've got to be kidding me look." Just then, the door knob turned on the elevator door. The boys sat straight up and, as hard as they could, they tried to look innocent. However, the best they could do was to get that innocent look that says, "I'm guilty," more than it says, "I'm innocent." Professor Galloway entered the room with his head down. He turned around to locate the door knob and close the door. He was muttering to himself, as he occasionally did, saying, "I've got to call Rayburn. I've got to make a note to call Rayburn." The Professor turned around and looked up. "Oh my," he exclaimed. "Oh my indeed!" As the Professor walked towards his desk, he paused a couple of times to straighten the few diploma frames that had been knocked askew.

The Professor was tall just like Tommy's mother. He was trim, fit and he gave the appearance of good health. His hair was gray and on the longish side. It stuck out in all directions as if he had just given himself a vigorous head rub. However, Tommy knew that wasn't the case. His grandfather's hair was always mussed up like that. The Professor had a slightly roundish face with a brightness that gave him a warm and friendly look. He wore a pinstriped three piece suit with a white shirt and tie, although his shirt collar was unbuttoned and his tie had been loosened. Over this, he had on a plain black professor's robe that was open in the front. The Professor approached his desk and sat down. He took his reading glasses out of one of his breast pockets and placed them on the tip of his nose. He grabbed a pencil and a scratch pad and said, "Call Rayburn" as he wrote.

The Professor then looked up and eyed the boys. "Would either of you boys care to tell me what happen here," the Professor inquired with a sterner than usual look on his face.

Michael spoke first. "It was a war Professor, a bloody war."

"And, who won this war?" the Professor asked.

"Michael did," Tommy answered. "It was a sneak attack," he added as he rubbed the still red welt on his cheek.

The Life and Times of Tommy Travail

"Ah, yes," the Professor said. "The old sneak attack. You've got to watch out for those sneak attacks," and a slight smile broke across his face.

Tommy knew at this point that everything was going to be okay.

"And, besides making a mess of my office, what are you two up to?

"Michael and I want to go over to the store and rec hall," Tommy responded. "Then we'd like to go over to Michael's dorm. Can I spend the night at the dorm with him?"

"I'm afraid not," his grandfather responded. "Not tonight," he continued. "I have to go out of town shortly and I won't be back until tomorrow, around noon," he added. "I've arranged for Miss Woodword to check in on you this evening and again tomorrow morning."

"Well, in that case, can Michael spend the night at the cottage with me," Tommy inquired.

"I don't see why not," the Professor answered. "But, you must be back to the cottage for the night by nine o'clock, that's when Miss Woodword will be arriving to check on you. If you're not there it will send her into a panic, and we wouldn't want that."

"No sir, I mean, yes sir, I mean, we'll be there," Tommy stammered.

"Have you boys eaten," the Professor asked.

"We thought we'd get something at the cafeteria on the way to the store," answered Tommy.

"Well okay," the Professor said. "Off with the both of you before Wilhelmina gets back and sees this mess."

"Oh," Tommy said as Michael and he stood up. "You don't happen to have a Euro I can have, do you Grandpa?"

"I don't know," his grandfather responded as he reached into his other breast pocket to retrieve his wallet. "No, sorry I don't. What do you need a Euro for?"

"It's nothing. I'll tell you later," Tommy responded.

"By the way, how'd you do on your physics exam?" his grandfather inquired.

"I think I aced it," Tommy said as the boys headed for the door.

"Very good," his grandfather said with a big smile starting to appear on his face, "very good."

David G. Groesbeck

As the two boys passed through the doorway, they met up with Miss Woodword coming the other direction.

"Has your grandfather returned," she asked Tommy.

"Yes ma'am," Tommy replied. "He's in his office."

Miss Woodword passed them by and entered the Professor's office. "Oh my word," the boys heard her shriek. "You boys get back in here right now," she called after them. The two boys broke out into a run and didn't look back.

Chapter Two

Crime and Punishment

The boys exited the museum and headed for the cafeteria. On the way, they joked and laughed about their rubber band war and the narrow escape that they had. Neither boy, however, was quite ready to talk about the contents of the desk's secret compartment. They reached the cafeteria and continued their discussion as they entered.

"Well…I'm telling you, Michael, if you hadn't cheated with that sneak attack, I'd have gotten you with my double whammy and won the war," Tommy was saying.

"I don't think so, and since when is a sneak attack cheating? I won and that's all there is to it," Michael responded emphatically.

"Yeah, I know it," Tommy said with a big smile spreading across his face. "But it was close." They both laughed and headed for the pizza bar.

They filled their plates and stopped at the soda fountain to get drinks before looking for a place to sit. Since this was the end of the school year, the place was near empty, but both boys knew they wanted a little extra privacy. There was a table in the far corner and simultaneously they both went off in that direction. They sat down and started eating. Neither boy said anything for quite a while.

"Well, what do you think that stuff was," Michael finally said as they neared finishing their meal.

"That book, that book, it had my dad's initials on it. I think it's one of his journals. I've just got to get back there and take a real look at it. And man, I really don't know what to make of that conductor's baton."

"That was really something, I mean really something. Did you see how it left those blue traces? Did you see that? You did see that, right?" Michael questioned with a slight hint of self doubt.

"Yes, of course I did. You should have felt it. It was warm to the touch and when I waved it felt funny."

"Really? Funny? How so?

"I don't know. It, it was weird, really weird. You know, I was thinking, what if it's not a conductor's baton at all? What if it's a wand?"

"A wand," Michael questioned. "You mean like in magic wand?"

"Yeah," Tommy answered intriguingly.

"Snap back to reality, Tommy. Don't you think that's, as they say, a bit over the top? I mean, magic? Come on."

"You didn't feel it and I did. And, I got a really close look at it and I'm telling you that there's something unnatural about that thing."

"So what are we going to do about it?" Michael queried.

"Well, let's go to the store and I'll think about it," Tommy answered. They emptied their trays and left for the store.

They arrived at the store and split up. Michael went to look at video games and Tommy went to see if he could find a currency exchange. Tommy went to the cash register and asked the clerk if they had a currency exchange machine. The clerk told him that there was one end of isle four. Tommy set off in that direction. In the meantime, Michael had found <u>The Last Soldier</u> and started reading the back cover. Tommy found the currency exchange machine and inserted his University Card, pushed the button for one Euro and a brand new Euro came rolling out. Tommy folded it and put it in his pocket. He then started off to find Michael. That wouldn't be difficult to do as the two of them had spent a lot of time looking at video games in the store and he knew right where to go. He was feeling a whole lot better now that he had that Euro in his pocket. When he rounded the corner of the video game isle, he spotted Michael right away.

"Does it look any good?" Tommy inquired.

"Yeah, it looks really good," Michael replied without looking up.

"Gonna' buy it?"

The Life and Times of Tommy Travail

"Man, I'd like to, but I'm going to have to wait. I don't have enough money." Michael's stepfather may have been one of the richest men in the country, but he had Michael on a very tight budget and he'd have to save for weeks to but something extra.

"What you say," Tommy started. "How about we skip the rec hall and head back to the cottage?"

"Sounds good to me," Michael responded.

Michael put the game back on the shelf and they left the store. They arrived back at the cottage. Tommy didn't know if his grandfather had left yet, but when they went in, they found a note from Tommy's grandfather. It just said, "See you around noon tomorrow. Sorry! Love, Grandpa." Mister Buttercup was still curled up on the sofa and paid little attention to the boys' arrival.

"So," Michael said. "Got any ideas about that stuff in your grandfather's desk?"

"Yeah, but we gotta wait until Miss Woodword comes and goes. You want to play some video games until then?"

"Okay," Michael responded. "How about we play some of," he paused for affect "The Last Soldier," and raised his shirt to reveal a video game stuck in his waist band.

"Michael," Tommy started, "I thought you didn't have enough money to buy that."

"I stole it," Michael said proudly.

"But I saw you put it back."

"I guess this is just one of those times when two came off the shelf, but only one made it back," Michael snickered.

"You've got to take it back," ordered Tommy.

"I'll do no such thing. It's mine now."

"Come on Michael. It's not right. You gotta take that back. What if someone saw you? What if you had gotten caught?"

"Nobody saw me and I didn't get caught… Did I?

"How do you know," Tommy mused. "What if they're out there looking for you right now and just haven't found you yet?

"Well," Michael started. "I hadn't thought about that… but no, they're not."

"Look, how would you like it if it was yours and somebody stole it?"

"I'd track them down and beat the living daylights out of them," Michael said boastfully.

"So you're saying that it would be okay for the University Store to hire someone to track you down and beat the living daylights out of you? I don't think you'd like that very much."

"No, but no, I guess I wouldn't like it," Michael responded. "But, I can't take it back. I won't take it back."

"I'm really going to be mad at you if you don't take it back," Tommy said sternly.

"Ah, come on, man," Michael pleaded.

"I'm not kidding, Michael. What if my grandfather found out?"

"Well, maybe I will take it back. Maybe I'll take it back tomorrow, especially if you're going to be really mad, and all."

"Hey, don't do it for me. Do it because it's the right thing to do. Man; Michael, right is right and wrong is wrong."

"Okay, okay. I'll take it back tomorrow."

"No," Tommy said looking at the tall grandfather clock that stood in one corner. "If we go now we can get back to the store before it closes and still make it back with plenty of time before Miss Woodword gets here. We'll take it back right now, right?"

A rather flat sounding "Yeah," was Michael's only response.

Tommy quickly got his stuff together and got ready to leave, but Michael was dragging his feet and Tommy had to prod him along a couple of times. "Say, Michael, have you ever stolen anything before," Tommy asked as they finally exited through the kitchen and out the back door.

"A couple of times, nothin' big, just a couple of candy bars. But… man… that… my stepfather! He's got all the money in the world and he won't give me a little extra spending money. He hates me, him and my mother both. They got no use for me."

Tommy didn't think they hated him, but maybe they did. From what Tommy did know, they didn't seem to have any use for him. That's exactly why they had him enrolled at the school. It got him out of the way. Michael's mother, Joanette, had been rather ambitious when she was in school. She always wanted to have a lot of money and travel around the world. Michael's biological father, Ted Woden, was just an average sort of guy that had some reasonable success as an athlete in school. Michael's mother thought he might be the one that would be able to give her the lifestyle she wanted. Unexpectedly, Michael was born while they were still in school. His father's athletic career fizzled and he wound up working in a factory. He was okay with that, but his mother was not. It wasn't long after that Michael's mother left his father. His father had since married and now had a new family of his own. His mother tried very hard to forget that early part of her life, but Michael was a constant reminder. Not too long after she left his father, his mother met his stepfather and eventually married him. Michael's stepfather made his feelings toward Michael very clear. He refused to adopt Michael, saying that he wanted his own child to be his heir, even though he didn't have any children of his own.

Tommy knew it was trouble to get Michael talking about his mother and stepfather. The subject would sometimes set him off into a rage that could last for hours, or sometimes even days. "Look," Tommy said trying to get back on the subject of the video game, "When we get to the store…"

"How about I just slip the game back onto the shelf," Michael suddenly interrupted. Tommy could tell Michael was also trying to avoid the subject of his mother and stepfather.

"No, I don't think so. If they see you, they might think you're trying to steal it. Plus, they might already know it's missing. I think the best thing is to return it. Tell them you took it and you're sorry and you want to return it."

"Man, I don't know if I can do that," Michael replied.

"You can do it. I know you can and I'll be there for support," Tommy reassured him. "Us ordinary guys got to stick together, right?"

"Yeah, but…"

Michael was still protesting a little when they got to the store. "Come on and get in there," Tommy said as he pushed Michael through the door. "I'm right behind you."

Michael walked across the store to the cash register, "Mister Clerk, sir" he began when he got there.

"Yes," said the clerk.

"Uh, uhm, I want to return this video game," Michael said setting the game on the counter.

"Is there something wrong with it?" inquired the clerk.

"Uh, no. I uh, accidently carried it home with my books. Ouch." Tommy had poked him in the back and the clerk looked at him suspiciously. "I mean," he continued. "I took it...by, uh, accident and I want to return it." Tommy knew that Michael wasn't going to be able to admit that he had stolen it.

"Well," said the clerk. "Has it been opened?"

"No," Michael answered.

"Well that's good. Thank you for being so honest."

Michael turned to leave when the clerk called to him, "Say, why don't you boys pick out a couple of candy bars as a reward. What would you like?"

Michael turned around, smiled and said," Okay, but what you say I <u>buy</u> a couple of candy bars. Give me two of those toffee bars," and he pulled the last of his money out of his pocket and set it on the counter. Tommy patted him on the back.

"Okay, I think I understand," said the clerk. The clerk then took Michael's money and handed him two toffee bars along with a small amount of change.

Michael handed one of the toffee bars to Tommy and they left the store. On the way back, Michael admitted that he hadn't felt right about taking the game and that he was glad that Tommy had insisted that he take it back. By the time they got back to the cottage, they were laughing and joking and the whole incident was ancient history.

When they got back to the cottage, they set up the video game system and started playing <u>At Death We Part,</u> a one on one combat game. They ate their candy bars and had a soda or two. They were playing for quite a while and lost track of time. Michael was slaughtering Tommy, as usual, when a knock came from the back door. Tommy got up and went to answer the door. When he opened the door, he was surprised. It was Miss Woodword, but Tommy had never seen her like this. Just about the only time Tommy ever saw Miss Woodword was when she was working at his grandfather's office. She normally wore a woman's business suit with her hair in a bun and her reading glasses on her nose. But, her hair was down now. It was long and blond and had a curl to it. Her glasses were gone and he could see her bright blue eyes. She was wearing tight fitting black and white polka dot dress. Tommy thought she was really attractive, for an older woman. Of course, to someone Tommy's age, every girl over eighteen was an older woman.

Miss Woodword came into the kitchen area and Michael came in from the living room to join them. "You boys know you're in for the night," She started.

"Yes ma'am," they both responded.

"You boys behave yourself tonight," She continued. "I'll be back tomorrow morning at eight o'clock sharp and I want you boys to be ready to go." The boys looked at each other with curious looks on their faces. "That's right. The Professor has decided that you two should spend the morning cleaning the gum from under the desks and tables in the museum's study room on the first mezzanine level."

"My grandfather decided?" Tommy interrupted.

"Well, yes. Well, no. I decided," she corrected, "but, you are under my care until the Professor returns, and, you *will* be cleaning the undersides of those desks and tables."

Tommy now knew why his grandfather had written "Sorry" in his note. He had originally thought that his grandfather was just apologizing for having to leave.

"Hey!" Michael exclaimed. "You can't…"

"There will be none of that Michael Woden," she said cutting Michael off. "I'd hate to have to write a letter to your stepfather. The two of you will be ready at eight tomorrow. Do you understand?"

"Yes ma'am," they responded disappointedly.

Suddenly Miss Woodword didn't look quite as attractive to Tommy as she had when he had answered the door. Miss Woodword bent over and gave Tommy a little kiss on his cheek right where the still apparent red welt was from Michael's rubber band. "I'll see you in the morning," she said and left.

Tommy still had his lips buffed out with disappointment, but he thought it must be true what they say about a kiss, he'd swear that his cheek didn't feel quite as sore as it had a moment ago.

"Well that stinks," Michael said. "I guess we didn't get away with the rubber band war after all, but, I still won."

"Yeah, but you cheated."

"I didn't cheat," Michael exclaimed. They looked at each other, grinned and smiled. But, Tommy's thoughts were still on that kiss.

"So what's the plan?" Michael inquired.

"What? Oh yeah. Okay," Tommy said snapping back to the moment at hand. "We've got to get back into the museum. That won't be a problem. I have a key to the museum door and my grandfather keeps an extra set of office keys in his drawer. However, not getting spotted by the security patrols, that might be a problem. At night there's a security guard stationed at that little desk by the front entrance. You know the one I'm talking about?"

"I think so," Michael responded. "The one the ticket lady uses in the daytime?"

"Yes, that's the one. Anyway, that guard takes a walk around the museum about once an hour. We're going to have to see where he is and stay away from him. We'll have to go up one of the staircases. That will be the hardest part. If we make any noise, that guard will hear us no matter where he is."

"We can go in without our shoes. That ought to help," Michael suggested.

"Good idea, we'll go in our stocking feet. Once we get to Grandpa's office, we can close the door and we should be okay, as long as we keep it down." Mister Buttercup had come into the kitchen and was now sitting by the back door. Tommy instinctively went over and let him out. "Okay, I'll get Grandpa's keys and we'll go."

Tommy slipped off his shoes and went to his Grandfather's bedroom to retrieve the keys. Michael took his shoes off, went into the living room, turned off the video game and television and grabbed his soda. He returned to the kitchen, took a big drink and thought, "This is going to be fun."

Tommy returned to the kitchen spinning his Grandfather's keys around his index finger. Together, they exited out the back door. They crept down the breezeway path trying not to be noticed, but at the same time trying to look nonchalant so that if someone did see them, it wouldn't look like they were up to something. When they got to the door, Tommy inserted the key and unlocked the door with hardly a sound. They opened the door and slipped in. It would be difficult to spot the guard, but once they found out where he was, they could make their move. Tommy grabbed Michael's arm. He knew Michael, and Michael would want to move in quickly. They sat in a squatting position for what seemed like forever. Finally, they heard the guard cough. He was all the way across the museum at the little desk. The museum was huge, but at night the smallest sound could be heard, sounds echoed and seemed to magnify as they bounced around. Tommy motioned to Michael and pointed in the direction of the little desk with a questioning look on his face. Michael knew Tommy was looking for confirmation of where the sound had come from and nodded in the affirmative. Tommy pointed toward the staircase that was the closest to them and the two of them slowly and quietly moved in that direction. When they reached the staircase, they cautiously started up. They were about halfway up to the first mezzanine level when Tommy stepped on a step that gave out a squeak. It wasn't loud, but it was definitely noticeable. They could hear the guard slide his chair back and stand up.

"Who goes there," the guard said, and he started off in the boys' direction.

From where they were, they could now see the guard. Both boys shivered as they realized that, if they could see him, he could see them.

"Meow, meow."

"Mister Buttercup? Are you in here again," the guard called. "I'll be darned if I can figure out how you get in here." With that, the guard turned around and headed back to his desk.

"Thank you, Mister Buttercup," Tommy thought.

"Meow," Mister Buttercup responded like he could read Tommy's thoughts.

The boys continued on their way. Michael took extra precaution to avoid the step that had squeaked under Tommy's foot. They continued up without further incidence, and finally arrived at the Curator's Office. Tommy let them in by unlocking the outer door. Once inside, they slipped past Miss Woodword's desk, went into the Professor's office and closed the door behind them. The anticipation of what they were about to do suddenly hit them. It was like a rush of adrenalin. Tommy went over and moved the Professor's chair away from the desk. He crouched down and gave the inside of the foot well a thump, but nothing happened. He thumped it again, and again nothing happened. So Tommy crawled into the foot well and tried to recreate the position he was in when he first opened the secret compartment. It took a few minutes, but Tommy eventually realized what he had done earlier. When he fell over pretending to die, his shoulder had struck one side of the foot well, but simultaneously his left foot had struck the other side of the foot well. Tommy took both of his fists and rapped both sides of the foot well at the same time. The secret compartment popped open.

Michael, who had been watching Tommy, grinned and said, "Let me see that baton, or wand, or whatever it is."

Tommy didn't care about the wand; he wanted to see the book. Tommy grabbed the wand and handed it to Michael. He then turned back and pulled the book out. He sat there under the desk just looking at it for a while. He noticed something that he had not noticed the first time he saw it. In addition to the gold letters of his father's initials, on the spine were the roman numerals XIV also in gold lettering. "Fourteen," he thought and wondered if that meant there were thirteen other journals. He could remember his father making notes when they were on expeditions, but that had been so long ago now and he was so young. Eventually, he crawled out from under the desk, pulled the chair back to the desk, set the book on the desk and sat down. He hadn't been paying any attention to Michael, but he could now see that Michael was waving the wand about quite vigorously.

"I'm bummed out. This thing isn't doing anything," Michael said angrily. "Here you try it," and he handed it to Tommy across the desk.

Tommy took it and again it was warm to the touch, it also gave him that strange tingly feeling in his hand. Tommy waved it, and it traced light blue streaks just as it had before.

"What are you doing to make it do that?" Michael queried.

"Nothing," Tommy said. "But I still don't like it. It creeps me." Tommy tossed it back to Michael and returned his attention to the journal. Michael began waving it again, but still nothing happened.

Tommy grasped the journal, unfastened the clasp and opened it. It was handwritten in what appeared to be his father writing. His father severely damaged his arm and writing hand when he was younger. It left him with restricted mobility in that arm and hand. The limitation caused his writing to have a peculiar slant to the letters, which made

The Life and Times of Tommy Travail

it distinctive and easy to indentify. The writing wasn't in English and Tommy didn't recognize the letters, but he was sure they were letters. As he looked at it, the letters seemed to move. They weren't really moving; they just seemed to squirm on the page. It felt like it was more in his head then actually on the page. As he scanned his eyes down the page, his brain seemed to squish back and forth like it was made of shaken gelatin, and, he started feeling nauseous. The more he studied the squirming letters, the more sick to his stomach he felt. Finally, he had to turn his eyes away from the journal. He felt as if he was going to throw-up.

"Hey, Tommy, you look a little green behind the gills," Michael spoke up.

"I think that pizza is coming back to haunt me," Tommy responded. "Give me a minute. I think I'll be okay." Tommy sat back in the chair and rubbed his face with both his hands. In a few moments, his stomach settled down and he was all right.

"I still can't get this thing to do anything," Michael complained. "Are we going to be here for a while? I'm getting tired and if we're going to be here for a while, I'm going to take a nap."

"Yeah, go ahead. I'll wake you when I'm ready to go." Tommy turned his attention back to the journal. He picked it up and began to thumb through the pages. It was all written in that unknown language, but there were a few little handwritten notes in the margins written in English. Tommy decided to write down all the notes he could find. He grabbed a pen and a scratch pad from the desk top. He started on page one. There weren't many notations, but he copied them exactly as they were written. He found that every time he stopped and looked at the still squirming letters in the main body of the journal, his brain squished and he would start getting nauseous again, so he ignored the main text and just checked the margins of each page.

Tommy opened his eyes and he was face down with his cheek on the desk. He blinked his eyes a couple of times before he rose up. Early morning sunlight was coming in the window. It took a couple of minutes before he realized where he was and what happened. He had fallen asleep. He looked across the desk and Michael was sound asleep with his head tilted towards one shoulder. His mouth was open and a drool of spit was leaking from the corner of his mouth.

"Michael! Michael, wake up," he called out. "Michael, wake up. What time is it?"

Michael raised his head and vigorously rubbed his head with his fingers. His longish straight black hair stuck out in every direction. For a moment, Michael reminded Tommy of what his grandfather must have looked like when he was young, before his hair turned gray. Michael rubbed his eyes and wiped the spit from the corner of his mouth. "Say what?"

"I fell asleep. What time is it?"

Michael looked at his watch and said, "It's twenty to eight."

"Holy cow!" Tommy exclaimed, "We gotta get out of here." Tommy grabbed the wand, and in his rush, he picked up the journal before closing the clasp. As he did, a folded piece of paper fell out. He could see the folded paper was pink stationary, but there was no time to look at it now. He carefully tore the page from the scratch pad that he had been writing on the night before and folded it. He then put it with the pink stationary and put them both in his pocket next to the Euro. Tommy then hurriedly closed the clasp on the journal, stowed the wand and journal back in the secret compartment and closed the door. They briskly went out of the office and onto the mezzanine. They cautiously looked over the railing and searched for the guard, but there was no sign of him, so they quickly went down the staircase and out the still unlocked door. Tommy meant to stop and lock the door, but he forgot. They ran down the breezeway to the cottage.

Once they got back into the cottage, Michael stretched and said, "I need a cup of coffee. Nothing like a good dose of caffeine to get you kick started."

Tommy wasn't much of a coffee drinker, he preferred tea, but that morning a cup of coffee sounded like just the thing. He grabbed a couple of cups, filled them with water, stuck them in the microwave and hit the timer for three and a half minutes. "Make us both a cup of coffee when that water's hot. I'm going to the bathroom to wash up a little."

"Your wish is my command," Michael quipped as he sat down at the kitchen table.

When Tommy returned to the kitchen, Michael was sitting at the table sipping his coffee. A second cup sat on the table emitting soft swirls of steam vapor. "Be careful," Michael said. "It's hot." After a pause, he continued, "I think I'll go wash up a little too." He got up and went towards the bathroom as Tommy sat down. Tommy sat there and drank his coffee thinking about the journal. Michael returned after a few minutes looking somewhat refreshed.

"Darn it," Michael said. He wasn't sure why he said that, but it was probably because he never got that wand to do anything. "Did you get anything out of that book?" But, before Tommy could answer, there was a knock at the back door.

Tommy went to the door and opened it. It was Miss Woodword and she looked more familiar to him. She had on a brown business suit and her hair was up in a bun. The glasses were still missing, but she definitely looked more like the Miss Woodword that Tommy was used to seeing. She had two buckets in her hand and in each bucket was a putty knife. Tommy knew what they were for. Mister Buttercup slipped in unnoticed.

"Good morning. Are you boys ready to go," she asked.

Tommy looked at Michael. Michael nodded and the two of them joined Miss Woodword for the walk to the museum. When they reached the door to the museum, Miss Woodword pulled out a key and started to unlock the door, but the tumbler didn't turn. She grabbed the door handle and pulled. It opened. "That's funny," she said. "This door was already unlocked. I wonder how that happened." The boys just took a quick glance at each other.

"Don't know," Tommy lied. "It's always locked."

They went in and took the nearest elevator. When the elevator stopped at the first mezzanine level, the boys got out.

"Now you boys know what to do," Miss Woodword directed, "and, I'll see you in the office when you've finished. Remember to bring your buckets with you, and they better be full." Miss Woodword closed the gate and went on up to the second mezzanine level.

The boys turned to the left after they got out of the elevator. "You know," Michael said, "I got a pretty good look at that baton last night before you fell asleep…"

"Before I feel asleep," Tommy interrupted, "You fell asleep before me!"

"I did not. You fell asleep before me," Michael said enticingly.

"Did not."

"Did so."

The two boys looked at one another and smiled. Tommy knew Michael was baiting him, but that was okay. "Anyway, I did get a pretty good look at that thing," Michael continued as they approached the door to the study room, "and you're right. It's not made of wood. That's for sure. And that handle, with the gold braiding and the crystal on the end," Michael's eyes suddenly got very big. "I got it," he declared. "I got it," he said just as Tommy opened the door to the study.

"Oh, oh, oh my goodness," Tommy said.

"Oh, gee," Michael added.

The room was filled with desks and tables, considerably more than was normally in the room. "Do you think Miss Woodword had all the stuff brought in here just for us," Michael asked.

"I doubt it," Tommy answered. "She didn't have time, I don't think. They probably brought them in here while they start summer cleaning somewhere else. But," he continued, "you can bet she knew they were here. Well, how shall we go about this?"

"Wait, wait. I know why that baton reacted for you, but not me," Michael said impatiently. "You were wearing your school sweater both times you handled it, right? And I didn't have my sweater on either time, right?"

"Yeah," Tommy responded, "So?"

"So...static electricity. You probably gave it a little charge when you grabbed it. I'll bet that's what it was, static electricity."

"Maybe," Tommy responded. "I hadn't thought of that. But, somehow I don't think so. I think there's more to it than that."

"No, I'm sure," Michael appealed. "That would also explain why it felt funny when you touched it. I'll bet it was the static electricity."

"Well," Tommy said. "You might be right. But I'll tell you one thing for sure."

"What's that?"

"I wasn't the first one to fall asleep."

"Was too."

"Was not."

The two boys set about their work. In short order, they became experts in used gum. They found that if a table or desk had a lot of gum stuck to its underside, it was simply better to turn the whole thing upside down. But, if there were only a few, it was easier just to crawl under it. They discovered that relatively new gum was very messy. It would come off in sticky strands that would then stick to everything and it would goo up the tips of their putty knives. They also found out that old gum was practically impossible to get off, and some of the stuff they found was really old, like ancient. They had to hammer and chip away at the old stuff, and then it would only come off in little chips. There was, however, the gum that was just the right age, and that stuff would just pop right off. So for the next two hours they chipped, scrapped and pried until they finished. They got their buckets and putty knives and went to the Curator's Office. When they got there, Miss Woodword was seated at her desk. They put their buckets and knives on her desk. Miss Woodword looked into the buckets to see how full they were and she was apparently satisfied. She said, "Now, I hope you two have learned a lesson here. The next time a staff superior calls to you, you'd better not take off running."

"Yes Ma'am," Tommy said and he finally got it. They weren't being punished for the rubber band war; they were being punished for not going back into the Professor's office when she had called to them. "Life can be funny sometimes," Tommy thought.

"Okay," Miss Woodword said. "You have a couple of hours before the professor gets back. You can do whatever you like. But you, Tommy, better check in with him when he returns."

"Yes ma'am," they both said and left the office. They took one of the corner elevator's to the first floor and exited out the back door on to the breezeway.

"So, what do you want to do?" inquired Tommy.

"Oh I don't know," Michael replied. "I think I want to go back to the dorm and check my E-mails, and I want to stop by the cafeteria and get something to eat. We haven't had breakfast and I'm starved."

"Okay." Tommy agreed. "You do that. I'll stay here and get something to eat, and then I'll meet up with you at the dorm after my grandfather gets back."

"Sounds like a plan to me," Michael replied. "See you at the dorm later."

Chapter Three

Family

The two boys split up. Tommy headed down the breezeway to the cottage and Michael took off in the direction of the cafeteria. Once Michael got to the cafeteria, he grabbed a tray and went over to the breakfast buffet. Even though this was officially the start of the summer, the cafeteria still had a reasonable selection of food. Michael started filling his tray with eggs, sausage and bacon. Just as he was about to spear a pancake he was startled by a voice behind him

"Hello Michael. I see you're still here too."

Michael turned around and it was Sally Ann Vickers. "Uh, yeah. Hi Sally," he said. "Are you staying here all summer?"

"No," she replied. "I just had to finish up on a special project I'm doing. My parents are picking me up tomorrow. You want to have breakfast together?"

"Sure," he said. They filled their trays and found a table. Sally was one of the gifted students, like everybody else, except him and Tommy of course. Sally had this incredible talent for remembering everything she had ever read. You could pick up a book that she read two years ago, turn to a page, any page, ask her what the third sentence was, and she could recite it back to you word for word. Michael thought she was rather cute and he thought she liked him a little. But Michael was not ready for that boyfriend/girlfriend stuff. He had too many of his own unresolved issues to be getting involved in all that. The two of them had a pleasant breakfast together. They talked about the past school year and made some predictions about the next year. When they were finished, Michael walked her part way back to the girl's dorm. They said their good-byes and promised to meet up in the fall when classes started again. Michael then headed back to his own dorm.

*

Tommy went into the cottage after he and Michael split up. He fixed himself a bowl of instant oatmeal along with some toast and a cup of tea. He had just started eating when he remembered the notes he had made the night before. He reached into his pocket to get the note and the folded piece of pink stationary fell out. He had completely forgotten about that. He set it on the table and carefully unfolded it. He went flush and got a little weak in his legs. The note was in his mother's handwriting. It was to his grandfather and it said, "Dear Dad, Now that Steven has found the wand, he'll be leaving to go see his mother. I know you're not going to like it, but I have to go with him. I'm sorry. I hope we won't be gone long. Please take care of Tommy until we return. With all my love, Sara.

Tommy looked at the date on the note and got even weaker. He knew that date. It was forever burned into his mind. It was the very last day he saw his mother and father. On that day, he and his is parents had stood in the middle of the breezeway. His mother had hugged him very tightly and told him that they had to go away for a while. She said that he was to mind his grandfather while they were gone, that they loved him very much and that they would see him when they got back. Then, both his mother and father gave him a kiss and they went into the museum. It wasn't unusual for them to do that. They were always going to one archeological site or another, but this time they never came back. After a number of weeks went by, his grandfather told him that his parents had died in some kind of accident and their bodies hadn't been found. Tears began to well up in his eyes as he thought about his parents. His parents hadn't died going to an archeological site; they were going to see his father's mother, his grandmother. Nobody had ever told him anything about his grandparents on his father's side and he really hadn't thought much about it.

Just then, the back door started to open. It was his grandfather. He quickly folded the note and put it back in his pocket. His grandfather came in and smiled broadly when he saw Tommy. "I stopped at the office before coming down here," he started. "I hear you boys did a good thing today."

"I don't know how good it was," Tommy replied. "But we got the message."

His grandfather chuckled and then said, "So you think you aced your physics final? I'll be anxious to see the grades when they come out. See, Tommy, you *are* special."

"Oh, don't start that, Grandpa, I'm not one of those special kids and I know it. I'm just an ordinary guy…and I'm kind of proud of it."

"Oh, but you are special. You just don't realize it because of the other kids around you. You are light years ahead of other kids your age in the public schools."

"That's just because they work us to death," Tommy retorted.

"Yes. Yes indeed. But you don't just get along, you excel."

"It's just hard work, Grandpa… So you're back early," he said. He desperately wanted to change the subject.

"Yes. The meeting went well and it ended early. The museum is trying to procure a new piece, and, well, it's all hush-hush you know."

"Say Grandpa, have you got some time to spend with me?"

"As a matter of fact, I do. I told Wilhelmina that I was coming down here to see you and have some lunch. I told her I wouldn't be back until one o'clock. What can I do for you?"

"I," Tommy started nervously "I want to know about my dad."

"Well Tommy my boy, your father was one of the finest men I have ever known."

"Yeah, I know that. You've said that before. But, I want to know *about* my father. Where was he from? Where was he born, was he born around here? What were his mother and father like?"

"Listen Tommy," his grandfather stopped him. "Those are questions that would best be answered when you're a little older."

"Why," Tommy protested. "Why do I have to be older to know about my father?"

"It's complicated," his grandfather said. His grandfather knew this day would come and he had been dreading it for years now.

"Your father never told me where he was from." Tommy knew his grandfather wasn't telling the truth. His grandfather wasn't a very good liar and he could always tell when his grandfather wasn't being completely truthful with him. And besides, his mother's note seemed to indicate that his grandfather knew more. "As far as your father's parents goes," his grandfather continued, "well, he didn't talk about them very much."

"Well, when did you meet my father?"

"Tommy, believe me, this is best left for another day."

"No," Tommy said emphatically. He had never said anything to his grandfather with that tone of voice. "I want to know… and I want to know now, not when I'm older."

His grandfather knew that Tommy wasn't going to leave this alone and, although he didn't want to, it appeared that he was going to have to tell him some things about his father. He was afraid that it could ultimately harm their relationship if he didn't answer at least some of Tommy's questions, "Okay Tommy, let me make myself a cup of tea and I'll tell you how I met your father."

Tommy's grandfather put some water in the tea kettle and put it on the stove. His grandfather insisted that tea made the old fashion way tasted much better than boiling a couple of tea bags in the microwave. Tommy couldn't tell any difference. While his grandfather was making his tea, Tommy headed to the bathroom. On his way, Mister Buttercup brushed up against his leg.

"Mister Buttercup," he said loudly. "Say," he then whispered. "Thanks for last night. You really saved our butts." Tommy rarely picked up Mister Buttercup because he was really heavy, but this time he did. Tommy scratched him behind the ears and said, "You really are a pal, you know that." Mister Buttercup had the most pleasant personality. He seemed to take to everybody. Tommy had never seen him get mean or try to bite or scratch anyone. He then set Mister Buttercup back down on the floor, patted him on the side and proceeded to the bathroom.

When Tommy returned from the bathroom, his grandfather was seated at the kitchen table with his elbows on the table and his head in his hands. Tommy entered the kitchen and sat down at the table.

David G. Groesbeck

"You know Grandpa," he said cradling his cup of tea, "I really have a right to know about my father."

"I know you do," his grandfather said as he raised his head. "But sometimes in order to understand the ways of the world one needs to obtain a certain level of maturity. When we are young, a misunderstanding, or a misinterpretation, of people's actions or events can have a profound and lasting negative effect on who and what we become as we grow. That is why I'm hesitant to answer your questions. It's not that I don't what you to know about your father, and your mother for that matter, it's that I want you to understand them. Your father and mother were complex people and it takes that level of maturity to understand them."

"But Grandpa," Tommy interrupted. "I need to know them. I really do. I feel like a part of my spirit left me when they died. Trying to live without them is really tough. I think losing them has matured me some and I think I can understand them, at least, I want to. So please, tell me about them."

"Well okay, let me tell you how I met your father. It was almost fifteen years ago. The first time I ever saw your father he was sitting right there," his grandfather said pointing out the kitchen window to the benches on the breezeway. "I was leaving the cottage to go to my office one morning and he was sitting on that bench, the one on the right. He was bent over with his head between his knees and he was holding a small black book in his hand." Tommy's grandfather paused for a moment. He hadn't meant to tell Tommy about the book. "He had been sick and was throwing-up," his grandfather continued. "As I approached him, I asked if I could help. He was incoherent and I couldn't make out a word of what he was saying. The poor man was pale and weak looking. He seemed confused, but even though I couldn't understand what he was saying, I could tell by the manner in which he spoke that he was a man with a notable amount of education and social upbringing. I invited him to come with me back to the cottage. By the time we got into the cottage, he began speaking clearer and seemed to be much less confused. I made us both a cup of tea. After we drank some of our tea, I asked him what had happened to him. He said he wasn't sure, but that he thought he might have gotten some food poisoning. I asked him if he wanted me to call someone. He said no, then indicated that he was feeling quite a bit better and that there wasn't anyone to contact anyway... He said his name was Steven. When I asked him what he was doing at the University, he said that he was new to the area and he must have gotten lost when he started getting sick."

"How old was he then?" Tommy interrupted.

"Oh, I'm not sure, but he was probably around twenty-five, I'd guess," his grandfather answered, then continued, "He told me he needed a place to stay. By then I was taking an interest in your father. There was something about him that intrigued me. Since Sara was in Greece at the time doing her doctorial work, I invited him to stay here at the cottage for a few days until he found more permanent lodgings. He accepted and I suggested that he rest awhile. I left for the office and wasn't able to return until early evening. When I did get back to the cottage, he was gone and I didn't see him again for about a year."

"Where did he go, Grandpa?" Tommy inquired.

"I don't know and he never told me. But about a year later, he showed up at the office. He thanked me for my kindness the year before. He said he was an archeologist. He said he was looking for work and produced some fairly impressive credentials. I told him that the only vacancy that I had was that of a museum staff assistant and that he was much too qualified for that position. But, he took the job and worked very hard. It wasn't long and I was sending him out to archeological sites to do reviews and send me progress reports. Sara was on staff by then and between excursions to archeological sites, she taught a few classes.

For the first year your father worked for the University, as chance would have it, when he was here at the University, Sara was gone and when she was here, he was gone. We, the museum that is, had finally gotten all the permits to begin the dig at the Valley of the Kings in Egypt. I wanted all of my best staff people there, so I directed your mother and father to meet me there to begin the dig. That's when your mother and father first met. I don't think they liked each other at first. It was probably professional rivalry, I suspect. In time though, they fell in love and, as you know, got married a year later. And,... you know, Tommy..., I think that's enough for now."

"But Grandpa, what did my father do before he came here, I mean before he came here the first time?" Tommy asked.

"I really think that's enough for now. We'll talk more later." His grandfather responded. "I want to freshen up from my journey and fix myself something for lunch." Tommy could tell by the tone of his voice that it was over for now, and there wasn't any use in protesting it.

"Okay, Grandpa," Tommy said reluctantly, "maybe this evening?"

"Maybe, Tommy, maybe," his grandfather now said reluctantly.

"I'm going to go over to Michael's dorm then, if it's okay."

"Okay, but don't forget your cell phone," his grandfather directed. "Now that classes are over, you're on the two hour schedule. Make sure you call Miss Woodword every couple of hours and let her know where you're at and what you're up to."

"Sure Grandpa." Tommy said. He got up and went into his bedroom to retrieve his cell phone. When Tommy came back, his grandfather was at the sink rinsing out his oatmeal bowl and tea cup. "Thanks, Grandpa," he said when he saw what his grandfather was doing. "I'll check in with Miss Woodword every couple of hours. See you later."

"Be back at dinner time, say five o'clock."

"Okay," Tommy responded. "I'll see you then," and he headed out the door.

On his way to Michael's dorm, Tommy thought about what his grandfather had told him. But, he thought more about his mother's note to his grandfather. It raised many questions. His parents were going to visit his paternal grandmother when they died. Where did she live? Did she still live where his father grew up? What was his father like when he was a kid? On the other hand, Tommy knew a lot about his mother. She attended the Brookfield prep school. Yes, his mother was one of the "gifted". She had an extra ordinary talent for being able to assemble a fairly accurate image of something from just a few of its parts. She could do a 500 piece gig-saw puzzle in a matter of minutes. Once she graduated from the prep school, she attended the University for her undergraduate and graduate work. After receiving her doctorate, she went to work for her father and the University. Tommy approached the side door to Michael's dorm. It was the door closest to his room.

There were only a few students moving about. During the school year, the dorm was a busy place. Kids would be coming and going to and from classes. There would be untold activities going on in the rooms. It all combined to give the place a sort of low rumble. But, now it was quite. The few sounds of someone going up the stairs or closing a door seemed to be amplified. Tommy went to Michael's room and the door was open so he went in. Each student had his own room, but every two rooms shared a single bathroom. The students generally got together and figured out a bathroom schedule. Tommy could see Michael's bathroom schedule taped to the bathroom door. There was a single bed in each room with a desk, a chair and a small work table. Tommy noticed that Michael's laptop computer was open on his desk and it was turned on. There was a flat panel television on the wall that broadcast the University channels. There were channels for video classes and entertainment, and there was a special channel for University news. Michael had connected his video game console to the television although the University frowned on it and he was now sitting on his bed playing a video game.

"Hey Michael," Tommy said as he entered. "What you playing?"

"The King's Shield," Michael replied. <u>The King's Shield</u> was one of Michael's favorite games. It was a medieval war game in which the player fought for the King against the CPU controlled Dark Lord. Tommy could see that Michael had his army all set for attack and it looked like he had the advantage. Tommy walked over, sat on the bed next to Michael, and watched the screen. He waited for Michael to make his move, but nothing happened. All of a sudden, Michael threw his controller across the room. It just missed the television and struck the wall so hard that it shattered into pieces, sending parts flying everywhere.

"I'm sick of it," Michael yelled angrily. "I'm sick of all of it. My life stinks. Get out," he ordered Tommy. "I don't want to talk to anybody right now. Not even you. So go on, get out." He then got up, went into the bathroom and slammed the door.

Tommy had seen Michael like this before. Michael kept so many emotions bottled up inside of him that he would occasionally explode in a fit of rage. Tommy got up to leave and once again noticed Michael's laptop computer. He went over and saw that it was displaying an

David G. Groesbeck

E-mail from Michael's mother. It said, "Michael, Just wanted to let you know you're going to have a baby brother or sister. It's too early to tell which. Mom." Tommy thought that should have made Michael happy, not angry; although, it was written in his mother's flat and uncaring way. Still, Tommy would have loved to have had a little brother or sister. Tommy knew what he should do, so he left the room and went to the break room. He put his University Card in the soda machine there and bought two sodas. He bought a Liquid Lime for himself and a Berry-Poppin'-Berry for Michael. "There's nothing so good for one's spirit," he thought, "than two guys sharing a soda," and he headed back to Michael's room. The door was closed when he got there, so he knocked. He heard Michael stir in the room, but the door didn't open and Michael didn't answer. Tommy tried the door knob, but it was locked.

"Come on, Michael," he said. "I know you're in there. I heard you." But, the door didn't open. "Okay," he continued. "I'm going to sit here all afternoon, if that's what it takes."

Tommy sat down and leaned against the door. He suddenly remembered the notepaper he had in his pocket, the one that contained his father's journal notations. He reached into his pocket and pulled out the Euro, his mother's note and the folded notepaper. He put the Euro and his mother's note back into his pocket and unfolded the notepaper. At the time he had copied them, he hadn't thought much about what they said, he was too busy just trying to copy them exactly as they were written, word for word.

Tommy looked at the first item on the notepaper. It said, "Page 1, right margin: Worm knew about the chamber, he must have known about it even before he designed the museum. Found the clue in his drawing for the elevator." Tommy then looked at the second item. It said, "Page 1, left margin: The mirror must be in the chamber." The third entry was the letters of the alphabet arranged in three rows and three columns. It said, "Page 2, left margin: A-B-C—D-E-F—G-H-I" That was followed with another series of letters arranged the same way "Double Tap: J-K-L—M-N-O—P-Q-R" And, then there was a third series of letters, similarly arranged: "Triple Tap: S-T-U—V-W-X—Y- Z-Blank" Then it was added: "Ignore first column and last row" The fourth entry said "Page 2 right margin: WORM DOWN, at bottom, SIDEWAYS" The final item on the notepaper said "Page 3 left margin: Worm never found the wand, must have driven him crazy." Tommy couldn't remember if that was all there was in the journal, or if he had fallen asleep before he had finished the whole journal. He was going to have to take another look at the journal. He began to ponder what it all meant when the door opened behind him and he fell backwards into Michael's room.

"So you're still here," Michael said. "You might as well come on in."

"I got us some sodas," Tommy started. "Wanna talk?"

Michael lay down on the bed and Tommy sat at the desk, folded the notepaper and put it back into his pocket. They drank their sodas and talked. Michael told Tommy that if his mother had a baby with his stepfather, his life was over. He said that they hardly cared about him now and if his stepfather had a child of his own, his heir, he wouldn't care if Michael lived or died. Michael said that he believed his mother still loved him a little, even though she was cold to him. But, he said, if she had a new baby to love and care for, what little love she had left for him would be gone.

Tommy sympathized with him and said, "Well you always got me. I might not be much, but, friends for life, right?"

Michael smiled and said, "You bet, friends for life." Tommy could tell that this episode was over for now.

Chapter Four

A Box of Memories and a Locked Door

"Listen," Tommy said. "There's something I want to do, but I have to check in with Miss Woodword first." He took out his cell phone and called Miss Woodword. "Hi, it's me," he said when she answered the phone. "I'm still at Michael's dorm. We're playing video games, so I'm going to be here for a while longer. By the way, Miss Woodword, do you know where they keep Phillip Worm's original drawings of the museum? Are they at the museum or are they at the library?"

"They're at the library, I believe," she responded. "Why?"

"Oh just a research project I was thinking about working on," he answered. "In that case, I think Michael and I are going to go to the library for a while."

She reminded him to stay in touch. He said he would and they said their good-byes.

"I want to go to the library," he said to Michael. "Wanna come?"

"Yeah, might as well, I can't play anymore video games until I get a new controller."

"What about your other controller," Tommy inquired.

"Oh, I smashed that one too," Michael responded. "And, I was just about to defeat the Dark Lord. I know I was."

"I've heard that before," Tommy quipped, and the two of them set off for the library. On the way, Tommy told Michael about his father's journal notes. When they got to the library, Tommy asked

The Life and Times of Tommy Travail

the librarian where he might find the Phillip Worm drawings for the museum. The librarian told him that they were in the restricted section and he had to have permission to get into the restricted section. Tommy told her that he was doing something for his grandfather and that his grandfather was supposed to call. She told him he hadn't called, but Tommy reminded her that they were talking about his grandfather. Knowing that the Professor could be absent-minded at times, she eventually led the boys to the room that housed the restricted section and helped them find the drawings.

"Are you looking for something specific?" she asked.

"The elevator drawings," he said.

After sorting through several drawers, the librarian brought out a set of drawings and set it on the table. "Here you go," said the librarian. "Let me know when you've finished." And she left the room.

Tommy took out the notepaper and unfolded it. "See here," he said. "My father said he found a clue in the *elevator* drawings, not the drawings of the *elevators*. And, I know which one he was talking about," he said as he flipped through the pages of drawings. "Yes, this is the one," he said as he folded the pages back. "It's the one by my grandpa's office. You know, the one I don't like."

"Yeah, I know," Michael said. "You've put an extra hundred miles on my legs because you won't use it."

Tommy started examining the drawing very closely. "Look, I think I found it. Look here," he said pointing to one corner of the drawing." It was a sketch of the elevator as it stood in the niche on the main floor. In the corner was a tiny arrow pointing down with a 'dn.' printed next to it. Someone had circled the arrow and the dn. in pencil. Tommy bet it was his father. "See here," he said. "That thing goes down from the main floor."

"Wow," Michael exclaimed. "What do you make of that?"

"The tunnels, the catacombs," Tommy declared. "Remember the catacombs?"

"Of course I do," Michael responded. "But I thought your grandfather said they filled them in."

"Apparently not," said Tommy. "We got to go down there."

"But you have to have a code to make that elevator work," Michael remarked.

"That's it," Tommy declared. "Michael you're a genius. That's what these other notes are that my father made. It's how to figure out the code. I've got to go home and study this. Let's go."

The boys left the library after letting the librarian know they had finished. On their way to the cottage Michael pondered, "How are we going to get down there even if you can figure out the code? If we go into the museum at night, the guard will hear us, especially if we try to use the elevator. And, in the daytime, Miss Woodword, or somebody else, might notice what we're doing."

"I don't know," Tommy said as they approached the cottage. "I'll have to think about that."

"Listen," Michael said, "I'm getting hungry and I want to go to the cafeteria. Then, I think I'll go back to the dorm for the evening. Can I borrow one of your game controllers?"

"Sure," Tommy said, "as long as you don't smash it against a wall."

"I won't," Michael replied sheepishly.

"Promise?"

"Promise," Michael said reassuringly.

Tommy gave Michael one of his controllers and Michael left for the cafeteria. Tommy took his cell phone out of his pocket and called Miss Woodword. He told her he was at the cottage and that he expected he would be there until his grandfather came home. He made himself a cup of tea and sat down at the table. He took out the notepaper and unfolded it. He thought about his father's journal. Had he gotten all the notations before he had fallen asleep? He wasn't sure and he knew he had to see the journal again. He tried to picture the journal in his mind, black with gold lettering. He suddenly remembered something. His mother had taken a photo of his father shortly before they died. His mother had surprised his father in his study with her camera. His father, who had been writing in his journal, looked up and jokingly pulled his journal up to cover his face. His mother snapped the picture just as his father started to lower the journal and peer over it. Tommy wondered if it was the same journal that was now in his grandfather's desk.

Tommy got up from the table and went to his bedroom to look for the picture. He rummaged through his drawers, but couldn't find it. Then he remembered a box of stuff that he kept in the closet. He retrieved the box and opened it. The box contained a number of items. Tommy sorted through the stuff. There was a ribbon he had gotten for his third place finish in a spelling bee when he was five and a necklace with a medallion attached to it that his parents had given him for his seventh birthday. Tommy picked up the necklace and when he touched the medallion, it was warm to the touch and it gave him that fuzzy, tingly feeling like the wand had given him. Now he remembered why he never liked to wear it. But, he held on to it and studied it. It was made of gold and the back side of it was smooth and highly polished. On the front side, it had the same kind of writing around its edges as the writing in his father's journal, and the letters seemed to squirm about just like the writing in the journal. Tommy knew the letters themselves were not moving, they just appeared to be moving in his head. In the middle of the medallion was a coat of arms. It looked like a shield with two crossed swords, there was a heart in the upper left hand corner of the shield, and a triangle in the upper right hand corner. In the lower left corner, there were three small starbursts side-by-side, and in the lower right corner, there were two small teardrops. He started to get nauseous and set the necklace and medallion back into the box.

    He spotted a few photos on the bottom of the box. He took them out and began sorting them. There was a picture of him when he was about five years old standing next to his grandfather on the breezeway. There was another of his mother and father at the dig site at the Valley of the Kings. And, there was the one he was looking for. There was his father seated at his desk. He had his journal up to his face covering everything from his nose down. Tommy looked at the journal, but couldn't quite make everything out, so he got up and went into the living room to find his grandfather's magnifying glass. He found it on the table next to the sofa. He turned the table lamp on and sat down on the sofa. He leaned toward the light and, looking through the magnifying glass, studied the picture.

    Tommy could see the journal very well with the magnifying glass. He was sure it was not the same one he had seen in his grandfather's office. It was very similar, but different. His father's initials were on the cover, but they weren't in the same style. Tommy looked closer at the binding and he could make out the roman numerals XXXII. This was journal number thirty-two. The one in his grandfather's office was number fourteen. That set Tommy thinking. Tommy had assumed that the journal in his grandfather's office was the one his father was writing in at the time he died. But now it appeared that, although he may have made the notations in the margin shortly before his death, that journal may have been the black book his grandfather had seen in his father's hand the first time they met. He returned the photo to the box and put the box back in his closet.

Tommy went back into the kitchen and sat down. He studied the note, which was still on the table. He looked at the part with letters arranged in three-by-three rows and columns, and the notation disregard the first column and the last row. Tommy was sure his father must have been writing about the key pad in the elevator. It had keys arranged in a four by four pattern, but if the first column and last row were deleted, it would leave the three-by-three arrangement. Each key could represent a letter of the alphabet for the first nine letters; then, if the keys were tapped twice, they would represent the next nine letters. Finally, a triple tap would represent the final eight letters of the alphabet and the last key when triple tapped would make a blank. Tommy knew three codes to operate the elevator. One would take the elevator to the first mezzanine; the second code took the elevator to the second mezzanine; and, the third code would return the elevator to the main floor. However, as he thought about the codes he knew, he realized they contained some key taps that were either in the first column or in the last row.

He decided to compare the codes he did know, to the key pattern that his father described in his journal. He thought that, maybe, Phillip Worm had added extra key strokes to lend further confusion to his secret code. As he started to transcribe the codes that he knew into the alphabet arrangement, he skipped any key punch that was in either the first column or last row. The first code he transcribed was the one to the first mezzanine level. The code yielded the letters: TWO, the next code yielded: THREE and the final code yielded: MAIN. "That's it," he thought. "If the main floor is counted as the first floor, the codes fit with the elevator's destinations." Tommy wondered if his father had run sequences on his computer to crack the code. His father didn't like computers very much. He thought they were a useful tool, but he felt they were becoming too pervasive in our daily life.

"Mark my words," his father used to say. "It won't be long and they will be running us instead of us running them."

The fourth entry on his notepaper said, "WORM DOWN, at bottom, SIDEWAYS" This must be the code to get the elevator to go down into the catacombs. Tommy took some time to calculate the key taps that were necessary to spell out, WORM DOWN, and, SIDEWAYS. He then committed them to memory.

Tommy was sure he now had a way into the catacombs, but he wondered how he could try to use the elevator without being caught. He realized that the only people he had to watch out for were Miss Woodword and his grandfather. "Tomorrow is Sunday," he thought. He knew the museum is generally busy with visitors on Sundays. If he could avoid being seen by Miss Woodword or his grandfather, no one else would probably pay any attention to what he was doing. So, he worked out a plan and decided he'd get a hold of Michael in the morning and tell him about it.

"Meow… Meow," Mister Buttercup called.

Tommy turned around and saw Mister Buttercup sitting next to his empty dish. "Oh my," he said. "I forgot. I'm sorry big boy." Tommy got up, went to the cupboard, and took out several cans of cat food. "What will it be?" he asked. "Kitty-Kitty, Salmon flavor, or Giorgio's Tiger Food, Tuna and Liver flavor, or how about this one Chicken Charlie's All Chicken Gourmet Cat Dinner, Seafood flavor?"

"Meow," Mister Buttercup called.

"Okay that's it. Chicken Charlie's tonight."

Tommy opened the can, and it wasn't one of those little bitty cans either. It was a big full size can, more like a dog food can rather than a cat food can. But then, Mister Buttercup was a big cat. Tommy filled Mister Buttercup's dish and patted him on the side. "Sorry buddy," he said, "Tommy was a bad daddy today."

Tommy's grandfather came home shortly after that. They fixed dinner together and had a pleasant meal. Tommy didn't bring up his father and somehow he could tell his grandfather appreciated it. They cleaned up the dishes after dinner and spent the evening playing a board game called, <u>The Romans: Builders and Destroyers</u>. In the game, each player is a General with his own Roman Legion. The game is played with the Generals conquering the lands of the Roman Empire, destroying towns, villages and cities in the process. The General would then rebuild the cities using the resources from the lands they were conquered. The game ends in one of two ways. If all the lands have been conquered, the player with the most land and riches wins. However, the game can end at any time if one General defeats the other while trying to conquer the same territory.

They had been playing for quite a while and the game was nearing the end. Tommy had his troops spread thinly along the border of the last territory, but he knew that with any reasonable draw he would be able to conquer the last territory, and that would give him enough to win. However, his draw forced him to have to wait for another turn while his troops were resupplied. His grandfather pulled out a hidden attack card and attacked Tommy from the rear. Tommy's troops were devastated and his grandfather won the game.

"Well Tommy," his grandfather said. "That's twice in two days you were defeated by a sneak attack." He reached over and rubbed Tommy's cheek where the welt from Michael's rubberband had been.

Tommy looked at his grandfather with the scowl of loss still on his face. Then he started to smile; then laugh. His grandfather started laughing with him and they laughed, and laughed. They laughed so hard that Tommy almost fell off his chair. After they gathered themselves together, they put the game away. Tommy let Mister Buttercup out and they retired to bed for the night.

The next morning, after his grandfather left for his office, Tommy called Michael and they agreed to meet at the cafeteria. Tommy asked Michael to bring along two flashlights. They met at the cafeteria and Tommy told Michael of his plan. When they sat down to eat, Michael showed Tommy the flashlights. After breakfast, they went to the rec hall. The boys played some snooker and pinball. At eleven-thirty, they left for the museum. Tommy's plan called for them to be at his grandfather's office by the start of the lunch hour. With any luck, Miss Woodword and his grandfather would go to lunch at the same time and that would be their chance to try the elevator. They got to the museum and it was busy, as Tommy had expected. Security

The Life and Times of Tommy Travail

was busy watching the visitors and the lady at the little front desk was busy letting people in and out. The museum staff were so used to seeing Tommy and Michael there that they paid no attention to them. They went directly to the Curator's Office. When they got there Miss Woodword was not in the office, but there was a note on her desk for Tommy. It said that his grandfather had a lunch meeting with Professor Rayburn and that he would be back at one o'clock. It also said that she had taken an early lunch and she would be back by twelve-thirty. It was twelve o'clock. That gave them a half hour. Tommy thought about taking a few minutes to look at his father's journal since both Miss Woodword and his grandfather were gone, but decided against it. The elevator had to be their priority. They might not get a chance to use the elevator again soon, but he knew there would be other opportunities to look at his father's journal. So they decided to give it a try.

They went out onto the mezzanine and headed to the elevator. It was on the main floor where his grandfather had left it when he left to meet Professor Rayburn. Tommy pushed the call button and, after a moment, the elevator started to rise. In short order, it was at their level. They opened the gates and got in. Tommy tapped in the code for the Main floor. The elevator shook, vibrated and moved down to the main floor.

"Well," Tommy said. "Are you ready for this?" Michael nodded and Tommy tapped the code in, WORM DOWN. The elevator shook for a moment, then the false floor that covered the opening below the elevator swung open and the elevator started down. When they started to get down below floor level, Michael pull out the flashlights gave one to Tommy and turned his on. Tommy followed suit and turned his on. They went through a layer of concrete followed by a thick layer of rock. What first appeared to be a cave began to open in front of them. But, it wasn't a cave, it was a tunnel cut through the dirt and rock. Both boys shined their flashlights down the tunnel as the elevator came to rest at the bottom. They could see that it traveled for some ways and then appeared to turn to the left. The elevator was still in a recessed area of the wall. There were stone walls on three sides of the elevator cage and the tunnel in front of them.

David G. Groesbeck

Michael, with his 'charge right in' mentality, grabbed the gate to open it. Tommy took a hold of Michael's arm and stopped him, "No Michael, wait," he said. "I don't think that's it, there's another code."

"Okay," Michael said. "So, enter it."

Tommy tapped the final code in. The wall to their right started to rumble and it pulled back. The boys shined their flashlights down the exposed opening. They could see a set of small railroad tracks stretching off into the distance. The elevator cage started to shake and four clamps in the corners at roof level snapped and released. The top of the cage with its cable attachment became disconnected and the cage then started to move down the track. As they moved, the vibration knocked some dirt and stones loose from the walls, which crumbled down. They were now looking straight down the track. They shined their flashlights and began to get a glimpse of a stone wall ahead. The cage got closer and closer to the wall. For a moment, the boys thought they were going to hit the wall. But, just as they got to it, the cage stopped. The boys looked at each other. There, behind and to the left of Michael was a rustic oak door, just a couple of paces away from the cage.

"Look Michael. Look… behind you," Tommy said. Michael turned around and saw the door. "It's just like the one that goes into my grandfather's office from the elevator." Tommy moved past Michael and opened the gate. He stepped out and reached for the door handle. He grasped it and tried to open the door, but it was locked. Tommy shook the door handle a couple of times and tried to force the door open, but it was no use. The door wasn't going to open.

"That stinks," said Michael. "We finally get down here and there's a locked door."

"I wonder," Tommy said, "if the key that opens my grandfather's office door would open this one too."

"Maybe," Michael replied, "Maybe."

"Come on," Tommy said. "We got to get out of here. The two boys got back into the cage and closed the gate. Tommy tapped in the SIDEWAYS code. The elevator shook for a second then stopped. Tommy tapped the code in again. The elevator shook again and then stopped again.

The Life and Times of Tommy Travail

"I don't like this," Michael said. "We can't get out of the cage on the tunnel side, there's no gate on that side. The cage is trapping us in here. You would have thought that Worm would have thought of that."

"Maybe he did," Tommy said nervously. "Maybe this is a booby trap of some kind."

"Are you sure you're tapping the right code?"

"Yes," Tommy responded, "Well, yes I guess. But, there could be another code that I don't know about."

"Try all the other codes," Michael directed.

Tommy tapped in the code for MAIN and nothing happened. He then tapped in each of the other codes and each time nothing happened.

"Look," Michael said, "if I get out and slide this thing sideways down the track a little I can get behind it and push it back down the track. Let me see if I can move it." Michael opened the gate and got out.

"There's a problem, Michael. When we get this cage back to the starting point and if that wall closes… Well, if it closes as quickly as it opened, it could crush you, or trap you behind it."

"Since there's a gate on the side I'll be pushing on, you'll just have to open it as we get there and I'll have to jump in."

Michael leaned down and grabbed the frame work of the cage to see if he could move it. "Hold on," Michael suddenly exclaimed. "I think I found our problem." Michael got down on his hands and knees near the track side of the cage and removed a reasonably large piece of rock that was wedged in front of the front wheel. "Must have fallen off the wall," he said as he held it up.

Michael reentered the cage with rock in hand and closed the gate. Tommy tapped in the SIDEWAYS code. The cage shook and started to move. The cage traveled back down the tracks to its starting place. When the cage arrived, the stone wall moved back into place rather quickly. The clamps refastened the roof and cable connections to the cage.

They were back looking down the original tunnel. Michael opened the gate and said, "I'm going to see what's down there."

David G. Groesbeck

"No Michael, don't," Tommy said. "We don't have time and remember…booby traps."

Michael looked at Tommy quickly and closed the gate, and then he said, "Let's get out of here." Tommy tapped in the MAIN code and the elevator began to rise. In a few moments, they were back on the main floor.

Chapter Five

The Key

The effects of what the boys had just been through began to settle in. When they opened the gate to exit the elevator, their legs didn't want to move. They forced them to, but their legs were like rubber and they kind of waddled across the museum, exited onto the breezeway and went into the cottage.

"I think I need a cup of coffee," Michael said.

"Yeah," Tommy said. "I think I would like a cup of really strong tea."

They made their drinks and sat on the sofa. They talked for a bit about their experience. "We got to find a way to unlock that door," Tommy said after a while, "and I'm betting that my grandfather's office key will open it. However, I'm pretty sure there's only that one key and my grandfather keeps it with him almost all of the time. It's very old you know," he added. "I believe it was Phillip Worm's own key."

"We could go to your grandfather's office when he's not there and see if we can figure out some way to pick the lock," Michael suggested.

"I don't think so," Tommy replied. "If Worm designed the locks, then there's not much chance of us picking it."

"You're probably right," Michael concluded.

"This is going to take some thinking," Tommy said. "What do you say we go to the cafeteria and get some lunch?"

"Sounds good to me," answered Michael.

"I got to call Miss Woodword and check in. She's probably back at the office by now." Tommy called Miss Woodword and she was back at the office. Tommy told her that he and Michael were going to the cafeteria to get some lunch and that he'd check back with her in a couple of hours and they left.

When they got to the cafeteria, they got hamburgers, fries and malted milks to drink. They found a secluded table, sat down and ate heartily. "Can you get a hold of your grandfather's key," Michael started, "even if it's just for a few minutes?"

"Probably, why," Tommy asked.

"I've got an idea," Michael said. "If we get some modeling clay from the University store we can make a mold of it."

"Yeah. And...," Tommy urged him on.

"Well, if we make a mold of it, we can maybe make a key."

"Out of what?"

"We could use epoxy and pour it into the mold. It wouldn't be as strong as metal, but we could experiment. It could work. What'da ya think?"

"It might," Tommy responded. "After we finish lunch, let's go to the store and see what they got. I still have some of this month's spending money on my University Card."

They finished at the cafeteria and went to the store. They bought a couple of packages of modeling clay and two tubes of "Super Jaws Rock Hard Mending Epoxy," that, "bonds, welds, glues and forms to any surface for a rock hard and long lasting patch, wet or dry." The epoxy came in a three barreled syringe type container that mixed the epoxy and squirted it out the end. They thought it might be perfect for filling a mold. They figured they'd buy enough to make several experimental molds and keys. After some discussion about what key they might use for making the sample molds, Tommy remembered his grandfather's tool box. It was an old wooded thing that had been handed down to his grandfather from his father. It had a lock to it, but his grandfather never locked it. The key was always left in a tray inside the tool box. It was an old style key, similar in design to the office key, but slightly smaller. They thought it would make an excellent sample key, especially since they would be able to test it on the tool box to see if it fit and was strong enough to turn the tumblers.

The boys went to the cottage and retrieved the tool box and key. They spent the rest of the afternoon at the cottage making test keys. They made ten altogether. All the keys needed some trimming, and they found that a finger nail file worked well to trim and shape them. The last two they made worked. By the time they finished, their finger tips were encased in a crust of hard epoxy. Every time they touched something, their fingers would "click" on its surface. Michael even had a hard dab of epoxy on the tip of his nose where he had accidently touched it. He occasionally pick at it. They decided that the best time for Tommy to make a mold impression of the key was while his grandfather showered in the morning. As it was getting on about dinner time, so Michael left for the cafeteria and his dorm.

Tommy's grandfather came home and they had dinner. After dinner, they watched some videos until bed time. The next morning Tommy arose before his grandfather. He didn't want to take any chance that he'd miss the opportunity to make the impression of the key. It went off well. Tommy was able to get the key from off his grandfather's dresser. He took it to his room and carefully pressed it into the clay. While the key was still in the clay, he smoothed the clay and trimmed the excess. After he removed the key from the clay, he thoroughly cleaned it and returned it to his grandfather's dresser. He returned to his room and cautiously placed the clay mold in his top dresser drawer.

Shortly after Tommy's grandfather left for the office, Michael arrived. "How'd it go," he asked as soon as he got in the door. The tip of Michael's nose was red. He had spent considerable time that morning scrubbing the epoxy off it.

"Excellent," exclaimed Tommy. "All we need to do is fill it with epoxy." The boys got the epoxy out along with the key mold and carefully filled it.

"I think we should let this set up real good before we try to take it out," Michael suggested.

Tommy agreed, so they decided they would go to breakfast and then to the rec hall until around eleven. They wanted to be back in time to try the key during the lunch hour, if they could. Tommy called Miss

Woodword and told her about their breakfast and rec hall plans, and the boys set off. They talked about the possibility of the key working while they ate. When they finished, they went to the rec hall. They didn't do much while they were there. They sat and picked epoxy off their finger tips while they watched some university guys play snooker. At eleven, they went back to the cottage.

They removed the key from the mold, trimmed and shaped it with the finger nail file, then cleaned it. "How does it look compared to the original," Michael asked.

"Pretty good," Tommy replied. "I mean, it doesn't really look like the original key, but the working part sure looks right."

"Cool," Michael said. "Shall we go give it a try?"

"Let's go," Tommy answered.

They entered the museum and went directly to the Curator's Office. Miss Woodword was at her desk. She raised her head and smiled at them as they entered. "Is my grandfather in his office," Tommy inquired.

"No," Miss Woodword answered. "He had a ten o'clock meeting and he hasn't returned. I don't know for sure when he's going to be back.

"Well, will you tell him I was here," Tommy asked. "Tell him Michael and I are going to lunch and that I'll check in later."

"Sure," she said. "My, is it lunch time already? I thought I was getting hungry." She opened one of her desk drawers, took out a brown paper bag with her lunch in it, and removed a sandwich and a bowl containing fruit. "Thought I'd bring my lunch in today, a girl's got to watch her figure you know," she added.

Tommy was upset. What was he going to do now? There wasn't any reason for him to go into his grandfather office. He thought fast and an idea popped into his head. "Come on Michael," he said. I think I'll take grandpa's elevator today."

"What," Michael exclaimed. "You never…"

Tommy poked Michael in the ribs to stop him. "Yep," he said. "Today's the day I start getting over my fear of that thing." Michael looked at him inquisitively. "Come on," he added. "See you later Miss Woodword," and they left the office.

The Life and Times of Tommy Travail

"What's going on," Michael asked when they got out on the mezzanine.

"I was thinking. We don't want to try the key from the inside anyway. We can call the elevator and try the key from the elevator side. But, I thought if Miss Woodword heard the elevator, she might think it was my grandfather and go into his office. If she goes into the office, she might hear us. You stay here and watch Miss Woodword and I'll go push the elevator call button. When you hear the elevator stop, if Miss Woodword doesn't leave her desk, come on over to the elevator and we'll try the key."

"Deal," was all Michael said and Tommy went to push the call button.

Tommy pushed the call button and with a clank, the elevator started to rise. In short order, the elevator was at the top and stopped with another clank. Tommy could see Michael and after a moment, Michael started in his direction. Tommy turned, opened the gates, and went inside. Michael arrived and stepped inside. Tommy turned to the side gate, the one facing the Professor's office door, and quietly opened it. He took two paces after he exited the elevator. He knelt down and gently inserted the key. He tried to turn it, but it wouldn't turn.

"It won't turn," he whispered to Michael.

"Try jiggling it," Michael suggested. "Try jiggling it while you try to turn it."

Tommy did as Michael suggested. It wouldn't turn. Then there was a "crack." "Uh oh," Tommy exclaimed. "If this thing breaks off in there, we're dead." He removed the key very gently and examined it. A tiny piece had chipped off a corner part of the key blade. It didn't seem to be broken anywhere else, so he carefully reinserted the key. He tried to turn it again and this time, the key turned. The tumblers moved with the kind of smoothness that one would expect from a lock designed by Phillip Worm. One small click and the door was unlocked. Tommy opened the door a tiny amount to make sure it was unlock, then reclosed it. Tommy then turned the key in the opposite direction, with the same smoothness and little click, it locked. Tommy tried to open the door and it was indeed locked. He turned to Michael and smiled. Michael was already smiling. Tommy reentered the cage and closed the gate. He tapped the code in for MAIN and the elevator descended with a clang.

When the elevator reached the main floor, they exited the museum and went to the cottage. Both boys were beaming. "Now," Tommy said. "We've have to find a way to try this key on the door in the catacombs. This is going to take some thinking. You wanna go have some lunch?"

"I'm starved," Michael said. "Let's go."

They had their lunch and spent the rest of the afternoon at Michael's dorm trying to figure out a way to get back into the catacombs. They run through a number of scenarios, but found fault with them all. The lunch time scenarios seemed to have the best chance, but they were dependent on Miss Woodword and the Professor to be gone at the same time, and they didn't know from day to day if that would happen. Finally, as it neared dinner time, they decided to call it quits for the day. Tommy left and returned to the cottage.

Michael had dinner and spent the evening playing The King's Shield. Tommy had a nice dinner of fresh fish with his grandfather. Afterward, they played another game of The Romans: Builders and Destroyers, this time Tommy won.

The next morning Tommy was sitting at the kitchen table when Mister Buttercup jumped into his lap. Tommy petted him and scratched him behind the ears. "Got any ideas," he asked Mister Buttercup. Mister Buttercup just purred. Tommy's grandfather came into the kitchen preparing to leave for the office, mumbling to himself as he occasionally did.

"Meow," Mister Buttercup sounded off catching his attention.

"And a good morning to you too Mister Buttercup," Tommy's grandfather said. "Oh, oh my, that reminds me. I promised Professor Rayburn I would stop by at eleven today and go over the big cat genealogy with him. That'll take a couple of hours for sure. Thank you Mister Buttercup. I had completely forgotten about that. And, what are you going to do today, Tommy?"

"Oh I'm not sure grandpa, but I'll bet it will be some kind of adventure," Tommy teased.

"Well, okay just keep up with your check-ins," he said as he left for the office.

A plan started to develop in Tommy's mind. He called Michael and they agreed to meet at the cafeteria for breakfast. Tommy told Michael his plan and after breakfast, they came back to the cottage.

"I still think it's kind of risky, Michael said.

"I know it is, but everything's got some risk to it," Tommy replied. "We can wait in the museum until my grandfather comes down the elevator to go to his meeting with Professor Rayburn. As soon as he is out of the building, we can jump in the elevator and take it down. Miss Woodword will still think it's my grandfather and won't pay any attention to the elevator sounds. Miss Woodword probably won't leave the office until the lunch hour, if she leaves at all."

"But, what if she does," asked Michael.

"Well that's the risk. But, if she does, she probably won't notice the elevator anyway, Tommy replied.

"I don't know, that's a lot of probablies," Michael said. "And, what about security?"

"We'll just have to keep an eye on him, and once we've gone down, he probably won't notice."

"There's another probably," Michael quipped.

"Well, unless you got a better plan, I think it's worth a try," Tommy said emphatically and that seemed to seal the plan.

They checked their flashlights and waited until ten-thirty to go to the museum. They almost waited too long. When they got inside the museum Tommy's grandfather was already in the elevator and on his way down. They quickly looked around for the security guard. They spotted him near the little desk by the front entrance. He was busily talking to the young girl seated at the desk.

"We gotta hide. I don't want my grandfather to see us," Tommy said.

"Over there," Michael said. "We can hide behind that partition."

They quickly moved behind the partition and watched as the Professor walked by not more that five feet from them. Once the Professor went out the door they went to the elevator swiftly, opened the gates and got in. Tommy tapped in the code for WORM DOWN and the elevator went into motion. After a few moments, they were at the bottom with their flashlights on. Tommy tapped in the code for

SIDEWAYS and as before the wall moved, the cage roof disconnected and they moved down the tracks to the old oak door. They stood in the cage for a moment looking at the door wondering what they would find on the other side.

"What if someone calls the elevator while we're down here," Michael suddenly asked.

Tommy could tell that Michael had been doing some thinking about the last time they were down there. "That's not a problem," Tommy reassured him. "The elevators won't respond to a call as long as the gate is left open."

"Yeah? Okay," Michael said a little nervously. "Well then…open the gate."

Tommy did as Michael wanted and they exited the cage. Michael held his flashlight on the key hole and Tommy inserted it. He carefully tried to turn the key. Just like it had upstairs, the key turned and the smooth Worm designed mechanism unlocked. Tommy rotated the key and removed it. He then grabbed the door knob and opened the door. They both shined their flashlights into the room. From what they could see, it didn't look like a very big room. They both stepped inside.

After a moment, Tommy said, "Something's strange here. Turn your flashlight off for a minute."

"Are you kidding me?" Michael inquired? "You've got to be joking."

"No, I'm not. Turn it off," Tommy ordered as he turned his own flashlight off. Michael reluctantly turned his flashlight off as well. As the light dimmed from their flashlights, the room began to glow. It glowed brighter and brighter with a soft blue white kind of light until the room was fully lit. However, neither Michael nor Tommy could see any source for the light.

"Michael, stop," Tommy ordered as Michael was stepping backwards to take in the room. "Step toward me and turn around." Michael did as Tommy asked and they saw the mirror for the first time. Michael had almost backed into it. It hung in the middle of the room. It wasn't hanging from anything. It just floated in mid air unsupported. The boys gazed at it for a moment, then, in his usual charge-in way, Michael reached out and touched it. It burned his fingers, instantly

The Life and Times of Tommy Travail

raising blisters on his index and middle fingers. Michael's fingers were already sore from two days of picking epoxy off them and it hurt like the dickens. Michael hollered out and instinctively stuck his burn fingers in his mouth.

They stepped back and looked at the mirror. It was sort of an odd thing. It had a center mirror with two winged mirrors, one on each side. The winged mirrors were attached by sophisticated multi-hinged arms. Each mirror was surrounded by a complex lacework of ordinate silver. The silverwork around the center mirror was the most elaborate. The sliver on the top of the mirror shaped up into a starburst kind of arrow head. The bottom silverwork was similar, but appeared to shape more into a triangle.

"Well," Michael said, "what do you make of that?"

"This has to be the chamber and mirror my father refers to in his journal."

"Well I wouldn't touch it if I were you," Michael advised.

"Oh, don't worry, I don't intend to," Tommy answered, and then continued, "I think we've seen enough and time's getting late. We better get out of here." Michael agreed still licking his burnt fingers occasionally. Tommy took a moment to look around the room one more time. The soft blue light filling the room amazed and confused him. The light seemed to be everywhere, yet it didn't seem to be coming from anywhere. It was just there filling the room, a soft blue white light.

Tommy turned around and they left the room, relighting their flashlights and relocking the door on the way out. They made the trip back to the main floor without incident. When the elevator arrived back at the main floor, they looked around to see if anybody was watching them. No one was.

"Michael," Tommy said, "get out and wait for me here, there's something I have to do." Michael got out without protest, which made Tommy happy. Tommy tapped in the code for THREE and the elevator took him to the second mezzanine level. He got out and went to the Curator's Office. Miss Woodword was sitting at her desk working on some papers.

"Hi, Miss Woodword," he said when he entered the office. "I want to go into my Grandpa's office and leave him a note."

"Sure," she said without looking up.

David G. Groesbeck

Tommy walked past her desk and into his grandfather's office. Tommy's nerves were raw, not because of what he had just been through, but rather, because of what he was about to do. He was going to take the wand and journal from his grandfather's desk and leave with them. He raged with guilt. "It's not stealing," he kept telling himself, "These were my father's items, and I have a right to them." But, it did no good. He knew it wasn't right to take something from his grandfather's desk without permission. Yet, he had a right to them. They technically belonged to him.

Tommy went around the desk and pulled the chair back. He knelt down, crawled under the desk and opened the secret compartment. He was just about to take hold of the journal when Miss Woodword called out his name, "Tommy, Tommy are you still in here?" She had come into the office to put some papers on the Professor's desk.

Tommy backed up and then raised his head slightly above the desk top. All Miss Woodword could see was his eyes. "What are you doing under there," She asked Tommy.

He knew if she came around to his side of the desk, she would be able to see the open compartment. Thinking fast he said, "I dropped the pen and it went under the desk."

"Well find it and write your note, and, be quick about it young man," she said as she set the papers on the Professor's desk. She then turn around and left the office.

As soon as she left the room, Tommy grabbed the wand and journal. He pushed the compartment door closed and stood up. He took the wand and, although he hated the way it felt, he put the wand inside the side of his waistband. He slipped the journal in next to the wand and pulled his sweater over them. He pulled the chair back to the desk, found a pen on the desk and grabbed the notepad. His emotions were ragged and he was full of guilt. He wrote the only thing that would come to his mind, "Dear Grandpa, I just wanted say I love you. Love, Tommy."

Tommy left the office, and as he passed Miss Woodword, once again seated at her desk, he said, "Tell Grandpa I'll see him tonight for dinner." He left the Curator's Office and headed to the elevator, the one he didn't like. After using the elevator over the past couple of days and seeing what it did, he was no longer afraid to use it. He rode the elevator back down to the main floor where Michael was dutifully waiting for him.

"So," Michael started as soon as Tommy opened the elevator gate, "what was that all about?"

"I'll tell you when we get back to the cottage," Tommy replied, "but we need to get out of here… as quickly as we can." They rushed back to the cottage, trying to be as inconspicuous as possible.

Once they got back to the cottage, and Tommy was sure that his grandfather was not home, he pulled up his sweater and pulled the wand and the journal out.

"Holy cow!" Michael exclaimed upon seeing what Tommy had. "You took them. Now, what you gonna do?"

"I don't know. But, I didn't want you to be part of me taking them. That's why I had you wait on the main floor."

"I would have gone with you," Michael said loyally.

"I know," Tommy responded, "and I appreciate it. But, you couldn't be part of that."

"So, what now?" Michael inquired. "And, what about that mirror thing?"

"I really don't know," Tommy answered. "I believe I need some time to think about all of this. Maybe it's best that we split up for now and think about it this evening. Then we can talk tomorrow."

"Yeah, I suppose you're right," Michael said reluctantly. "I guess I'll go back to the dorm and I'll call you in the morning."

Chapter Six

An Act of Defiance

Michael left the cottage and headed back to his dorm. Tommy made himself a cup of tea, took the wand and journal, and sat on the sofa. Mister Buttercup jumped up on the sofa and curled up next to him. Tommy just sat there for a few minutes and sipped his tea. It was as if he was in shock. He was numb. What did it all mean? Eventually, he picked up the journal and examined it. He could now see that the journal had been recovered. On the inside of the back cover, there were seams that joined the old and new covers. Someone had cut one of the seams to form a pocket between the inside and outside covers. He checked the pocket to see if anything was in it, but it was empty. Tommy figured that it probably had held his mother's note.

Tommy turned back to the first page of the journal and looked at his father's notations. He set the journal down and took out the copy he had made of his father's notes. He unfolded the notepaper and reexamined it. The notepaper indicated that his father's notations had ended on page three. He still could not remember how far he had gotten in the journal before he had fallen asleep. He opened the journal and turned to page three. There was his father's notation in the left margin, "Worm never found the wand, must have driven him crazy." Tommy turned the page. There was another notation there in the right margin of page four. It was a drawing of three somewhat pointed ovals. Under the center oval were three small vertical lines. A line, with an arrowhead on it, pointed to the oval on the left side.

The Life and Times of Tommy Travail

There were two vertical lines under it. Another line with an arrowhead on it, pointed to the oval on the right. This oval had three of the small vertical lines under it. Finally, another line with an arrowhead on it pointed back to the center oval. At the end of the arrowhead was one small vertical line. Written underneath the whole thing was his father notation, "This will take me Home. Finally, Home."

Tommy studied the sketch for quite a while. After some thought, he was sure the three ovals represented the mirror. He wasn't sure, but he thought that the vertical lines had something to do with the wand; wand stokes, more than likely. He committed the sketch to memory. The mirror and wand had taken his father home. Home to see Tommy's grandmother, and Tommy's mother had gone with him. The questions began to swirl in his head. Where was his father's home and why couldn't he travel there by a regular means of transportation? Could they still be alive? Maybe they just can't find a way to come back. Did his grandfather know for sure that they were dead? He found himself swimming in questions and emotions.

Tommy sat there for quite awhile. Mister Buttercup stood up and then stepped onto Tommy's lap. He stuck his nose right up to Tommy's face and purred. Tommy reached up with both hands and vigorously scratched him behind his ears. "I'm confused Mister Buttercup," he said. "I don't know what to do." Mister Buttercup pushed his face closer to Tommy's face. "What's a matter boy, you want to go out or something. Are you getting hungry?" With that, he looked at the grandfather clock in the corner. It was getting near time for his grandfather to come home. He set Mister Buttercup aside and grabbed the journal and wand. He took them into his bedroom and put them under his mattress. He went into the kitchen and filled Mister Buttercup's dish with Giorgio's Tiger Food, Tuna and Liver flavor. He retrieved his tea cup from the living room, took it into the kitchen and rinsed it out. He thought his grandfather would have been home by then. He was late. Tommy sat down and waited for his grandfather to arrive. The minutes dragged on. Finally, there was a click of the door and his grandfather stepped in carrying a pizza box and two bottles of drink. He had a huge jug of "Liquid Lime" for Tommy, and a smaller, "Fruity-All Fruit-Fruit Drink," Super Berry-Berry, flavor for himself. His grandfather set the box on the table and opened it, exposing a large pepperoni and mushroom pizza.

"That's artificially flavored, you know," Tommy said pointing at his grandfather's drink.

"Yes, I know, but it was the only non-carbonated drink they had." Tommy's grandfather didn't care for carbonated drinks very much. As Tommy got two dishes with silverware and set them on the table, his grandfather continued, "I got your note this afternoon and; look at me," Tommy did, "and I want you to know that I love you too. I want you to understand that I really do love you, Tommy. I really do." Tommy looked at his grandfather and forced a smile.

They sat down and helped themselves to the pizza. They both had eaten a couple of pieces each. "Tommy," his grandfather said in a soft reassuring voice. "Some things were taken from my desk today and I believe you have them. Do you know what I'm talking about?"

Tommy went flush. He had been caught, caught, already. Tommy really wanted to lie and deny any knowledge of what he was talking about, but he forced out a, "Yes, yes I do."

"I want you to return them to me," his grandfather said softly.

"I… I can't, Grandpa. They're my father's and I have a right to them," Tommy replied.

"Indeed, and you shall have them, but not until you're older."

"I'm old enough now," Tommy protested.

"You don't understand, son, they are dangerous, very dangerous and you must give them back."

"You don't know what I'm going through," Tommy said. "You didn't lose your parents."

"Oh Tommy," his grandfather responded. "But I did lose a daughter and an outstanding son-in-law."

Tommy hadn't thought about that. His grandfather was hurting too. Even thought the conversation was getting intense, they both picked at their pizza. It was more of a way of contemplating, than it was eating.

"Tommy," his grandfather continued, "you must give those things back."

"I can't," Tommy said. "I want to hang on to them for a while."

"Listen to me," his grandfather said in a slightly sterner voice. "Those things are dangerous. They may even be the things that killed your mother and father." Somehow his grandfather knew that he had just made a mistake, but before he could try to cover it up, Tommy interrupted.

"Do you know that my mother and father are actually dead? Do you know for sure?"

"Tommy," his grandfather said pleadingly.

"Do you?" Tommy cut him off. "Do you know whether or not my parents are actually dead?"

"Uh," his grandfather hesitated. "No. No I don't. But I will tell you, that if they were still alive, they would have returned by now. Nothing, nothing could keep them away from you."

"So," Tommy said, "they could still be alive. You don't know for sure. So they could still be alive," Tommy repeated. "Why haven't you gone looking for them? Why? Why aren't you trying to find them," Tommy asked with his voice getting louder.

"Tommy," his grandfather said in a very soft voice. "I haven't gone after them because… because I have you. I have you to love and to care for."

Tommy went momentarily numb. Of course, his grandfather couldn't be just taking off into the dangerous unknown. And it is my fault that he can't go after them," Tommy thought.

"If you can't go look for them, I will," Tommy suddenly said. "I will go find my parents and if they're still alive, I'll help them come back."

"I suspect you will," his grandfather said to Tommy's surprise, "but not until you are older."

"No," Tommy exclaimed. "I need to go now. They may need help and, if we wait, it might be too late. Show me how to work that wand thing," he said. He then realized it might be best to let his grandfather know just how much he knew. "How does it work? Do you wave it around and say some magic words or something?"

"Tommy," his grandfather said in soft tones. "I think that we have said enough on this topic for tonight. I want you to give me the wand and the journal. You will get them back when you're older. But, for now, I want you to give them back to me, do you understand?"

David G. Groesbeck

"Yes," Tommy replied. "I understand, but I won't give them back. I've hidden them and I've hidden them where you'll never find them," But, Tommy knew that if his grandfather did start to search for them, under his mattress is probably the first place he would look.

"Tommy," his grandfather said in a grave tone of voice. "You leave me no other choice. I will have to ground you until those things are returned. You will have to stay here in the cottage and you won't be able to leave without permission. Do you understand?"

"Yes," Tommy answered with a bit of defiance.

Tommy got up from the table, went to his bedroom, closed the door with a bit more force than was necessary, and threw himself onto his bed.

Tommy lay in bed all night thinking about everything; what his grandfather had told him, the mirror, the wand, and his parents. By morning, he had the makings of a plan. Things were cool between him and his grandfather in the morning, and not much was said.

"Remember," his grandfather said as he was about to leave through the back door, "You are not to leave the cottage and you will remain grounded until you return your father's things," and he left.

Tommy sat at the kitchen table for a while and then the phone rang. Tommy answered it and it was Michael.

"Meet you at the cafeteria in ten," Michael said.

"Can't," Tommy replied, "been grounded."

"What!" Michael exclaimed, "You got caught, didn't you? You got caught."

"Yeah, I'm afraid so," Tommy answered.

"So, what happened?"

"Come on over and I'll tell you. Grandpa said I couldn't leave the cottage, but he didn't say I couldn't have company."

"Okay," Michael said. "See you in about fifteen."

They said good-bye and hung up. While he waited for Michael, Tommy started putting his plan together. When Michael arrived, Tommy told him everything that had happened the night before.

"So what are you going to do now," Michael inquired after hearing the story. "Are you gonna give the stuff back?"

"No," Tommy answered quickly, "I'm going to try and make it work."

"What, the wand?" Michael interrupted.

"No," Tommy replied. "I'm going to try and make the whole thing work, the wand, the mirror, the whole thing. I'm going to try to go to wherever it is that my parents went. And I'm going to need your help."

"You bet," Michael said positively. "Two ordinary guys and friends for life, right!"

"Right," Tommy said.

"So, how you going to do it?" Michael asked.

"I'm going to take a lesson from you. I'm going to charge right in. I'm just going to go right over there and get in the elevator and take it down to the room."

"You'll get caught before you can do it."

"I don't think so," Tommy said. "I want you to go over to the museum and watch for my grandfather to leave. He's bound to go somewhere today. When he does, I'll make my move. I don't think he'll expect me to do something so soon after last night. He doesn't know how much I know and he'll think that it'll take me some time to piece things together. The problem is… that he might not go anywhere and you'll have to stay there all day."

"Hey, friends for life. I'll do it. I'll do it for however long it takes, days, if necessary," Michael said confidently.

"Okay," Tommy said. "When you see my grandfather leave, you come get me. I'll give you my museum keys so you can get in and out the back door, but you have to be careful. You don't want anybody to see you using that door if you can help it. When you come and get me, I'll make my attempt and you can go back to the dorm."

"Hey, wait a minute, I'm going with you," Michael said with protest in his voice.

"Oh Michael," Tommy said, "I don't think you want to do that. It could be dangerous. We could even be killed. And, if it doesn't work, we'll probably get caught, and then you'd be in a world of trouble. But… if I try it alone and it doesn't work, I'll give the wand and the journal back to my grandfather. I don't think I would be in too much trouble, if I gave the stuff back."

"I don't care. I'm going with you. There isn't anything here for me. And... you might need some protection yourself, and I'm the guy," Michael said boastfully.

"Can I talk you out of it?" Tommy asked rather flatly.

"Nope." And, that was it. They had been friends long enough not to argue needlessly. They, just somewhere along the line, agreed to ask questions like this straight up, with a straight answer and that would be it. This was one of those occasions.

"Okay that changes things a bit. I was planning on having a big breakfast while you went to the museum. I don't know how long it might be before we get to eat again. So now you'll have to eat too; that is if you want to, but I think it would be a good idea."

"Okay," said Michael, "what are we having?"

The boys went to the refrigerator and took out what they could find. Tommy made them some instant oatmeal and toast. They ate some left over hard boiled eggs and finished off the pizza that was left over from the night before. Michael had two cups of coffee and Tommy had three cups of tea.

"Okay," Tommy said when they had finished, "it's time for you to go on Grandpa- watch. Be careful. Try not to get noticed. And, if my grandpa leaves, come and get me as soon as he is out of the building, unless he's coming here of course."

"Of course," Michael repeated as he got up from the table. He hadn't realized it before he stood up, but he had eaten so much he could hardly move. "Oh boy," he said, "this might be harder than I expected," then he rubbed his stomach with both hands and smiled.

Tommy laughed. Michael went to the door and opened it. Mister Buttercup strode across the kitchen and headed towards the door. "Don't let him out," Tommy called to Michael. But before Michael could stop him, Mister Buttercup slipped out the door and rounded the corner of the cottage. Tommy was disappointed. Mister Buttercup had been his companion, and a sort of confidant, for quite a while. He had wanted to spend some time with him to say good-bye and now he didn't know if he was going to get the chance.

Michael turned around at the door to face Tommy. "I hope I'll be back soon," he said, and then turned back around and stepped out.

The Life and Times of Tommy Travail

With Michael gone, Tommy knew he had one more thing to do. He had to write his grandfather a note. He went into his bedroom to get a notebook out of his back-pack. But first, he checked under the mattress to see that the wand and journal were still there, and they were. He found his back-pack and, for a moment, thought of taking it with him. However, security didn't like back-packs in the museum. They weren't banned or anything, but it was just too easy to walk out of the museum with something stashed into a back-pack. So, they always draw a little extra attention, the very kind of attention he was trying to avoid. Ultimately, he decided not to take it with him. He opened the back-pack, took out his notebook, and returned to the kitchen.

He pushed the dirty dishes aside and sat down at the table. He opened the notebook and stared at the blank page for a few moments. Emotions started to well up in him as he wrote, "Dear Grandpa," He began to wonder if this is how his mother felt the day she sat down to write the pink note to his grandfather. Tears started to fill his eyes. He thought about how hurt his grandfather must have been when he read her letter, and he worried about how this letter was going to hurt him all over again. Before he could catch them, a few tears escaped his eyes and dripped onto the notepaper. "I'm sorry Grandpa," he wrote fighting his emotions back, "but I must find out what happened to my parents. I'm sorry, but I have to go, I have to try, please understand. I will try to let you know if everything is okay. I love you very much. Love, Tommy." A few more tears fell from his eyes onto the notepaper. Tommy sat back in his chair and wiped the tears off his cheeks.

He sat there for awhile trying to get his emotions back under control. After several minutes, he got up, went to the back door, and called Mister Buttercup a couple of times, but there was no sign of him. He cleared his and Michael's dirty dishes from the table, rinsed them off, and put them in the dishwasher. He tore the note to his grandfather from the notebook and placed it in the center of the table. He took the notebook back into his bedroom. As he was placing it into his back-pack, he remembered the medallion that was in the box he kept in the closet. He thought that it might be a good thing to take along with him, so he got it out of the box. He really didn't like the way it felt, but he slipped the necklace over his head anyway and let it drop around his neck. He then tucked the medallion under his sweater. He went back into the kitchen and called Mister Buttercup a couple of more times, but still no sign of him.

"Well," he thought. "Nothing left to do but wait." He went into the living room and sat on the sofa. He sat there for only a minute or two when he had to get up. He was getting nervous and he began pacing around the cottage. Doubts about what he was planning to do began to creep into his mind. "If Michael doesn't come back soon," he thought, "I don't know if I can do it. Yes, I can. I must." He went into the kitchen and put a cup of water in the microwave to make some tea. He thought about Mister Buttercup and went to the door to call him again. Just as he got to the door, Michael opened it.

"Okay Tommy Boy," he said as he opened the door. "It's time to go. Your grandfather just left."

Tommy's legs went weak. "Alright," he said after a moment, "I'll get the wand and the journal and you get the flashlights." Tommy went to the bedroom and retrieved the wand and journal. "Are you ready to do it?" he asked Michael when he returned to the kitchen.

"Let's do it," was Michael's only response and they headed out the door.

Tommy hesitated as they approached the stone benches on the breezeway. He thought briefly about his mother and the stories she used to tell him. Then, he moved on to the museum door. Tommy opened the door and they went in. Both boys automatically looked around to spot the security guard and to see if anyone else might be watching. Nobody paid any attention to the boys. They moved swiftly across the museum to the elevator and got in. Michael took out his flashlight and turned it on. Tommy had been carrying the wand in one hand and the journal in the other. He put them in the same hand then tapped the code in. The elevator took them to the bottom. He tapped in the sideways code; the wall moved aside, the elevator's roof disconnected itself and they began to move. Tommy set the journal down and took out his flashlight, turned it on and put it in his other hand with the wand. He picked up the journal and, in a few minutes, the cage came to a stop in front of the oak door. They opened the cage and stepped out. Tommy set the journal down on a rock next to the door to remove the key from his pocket. He unlocked the door and he and Michael entered the room. They shut off their flashlights

The Life and Times of Tommy Travail

and the room began to brighten. The mirror hung in the center of the room motionless.

"Okay, now what?" asked Michael.

"I think I have to stand in front of the mirror and wave the wand. I think I have to wave it with the number of strokes and in the pattern that my father noted in his journal," Tommy responded and he moved towards the mirror. As he stood in front of the mirror, he studied his own reflection. Michael moved up along side of him. Mister Buttercup sauntered into the room and sat down behind them. Between the wand, the medallion and the room with its mirror, Tommy had that tingly fuzzy feeling all over his body. He raised the wand and stroked three times in front of the center mirror. The wand emitted the faint blue streaks. He turned to the mirror on the left and stroked twice, then turned to the right mirror and stroked three more times. Finally, he returned to the center mirror and stroked the wand once. Nothing happened.

The two boys looked at one another. "Are you sure you did it right?" Michael asked with a quiver in his voice."

"Yes," Tommy answered, "Three, two, three and then one. I'm sure I did it right."

"Try it again," Michael urged.

Tommy repeated the process and still nothing happened. "I don't know what to do," Tommy said. "Do you think we can get back out of here and not get caught?"

"I don't know," answered Michael. "But I guess we might as well try…Hey, wait a minute," he said after a pause. "Try tapping the mirror with the wand."

Tommy raised the wand and touched the center mirror with the tip of the wand. A fierce jolt of that fuzzy tingly feeling shot up his arm and his whole body shivered with it. He touched the mirror twice more. As the wand touched the mirror, it puckered the mirror slightly and the mirror rippled as if it were liquid. He moved to the left mirror and tapped it twice. This mirror reacted like the first, but the tingly jolts shooting up his arm were more intense, becoming painful. He turned to the right mirror and tapped it three times. The mirror reacted and the pain going up his arm became almost unbearable. Then, he tapped the center mirror one more time. The wand instantly became

David G. Groesbeck

too hot to hold and he let go of it. The wand held its position with its tip touching the mirror. Tommy's brain squished like it had when he had tried to read the strange letters in his father's journal, only it was about a thousand times more intense.

Tommy tried to turn towards Michael, but he couldn't move. The only sound he heard was a single "meow," then there was a great rushing of feelings all over his body. He peered down to his feet and they appeared to be moving away from him. His legs and body were stretching away like a rubber band. His feet were getting so far away that he lost sight of them. His body became string like. His brain seemed to expand then snap back and vibrate as if it was made of gelatin. It squished back and forth. Then everything went black and he lost consciousness.

Chapter Seven

Carla

The ruins of a great castle sat in the middle of the ever encroaching forest. It once had tall wide fortifying walls surrounding it that were made of stone and mortar. To give the guards that patrolled the surrounding grounds a level of protection, the walls had been capped with a wide recessed walkway. Most of the walls were gone now, only small sections of its crumbling remnants remained. In many places, the ever expanding forest had over come what once had been a formidable barrier. Pieces of the wall could be seen trailing off into the thick of the forest. The great castle was cradled in the center of the outer walls. It had been a megalithic structure with walls and spinnerets raising many stories high. There had been many rooms, chambers and large halls. A tremendous battle had taken place here. Although much of the first floor walls and foundation still stood, almost all of the taller walls had been destroyed. The few taller walls that had survived were those interior walls that had some sort of supporting structure from other interior walls. The entire interior had been blackened and distorted by intense fire and explosions. A large horseshoe staircase arose out of the rubble and stretched into the empty sky. Only one of the many spires and spinnerets still stood. All the exterior walls that did remain had black starbursts where they had been struck by enemy fire. In the front center of the structure that remained, was the great archway that once held a large pair of thick oaken wood doors. They had provided good protection from the unwelcome, yet would have been opened wide for friends and guests. The uncontrolled fires that ravaged the castle during the battle had consumed them, leaving the large open archway to stand alone.

A dirt road came out of the forest and meandered its way across an area that once had been inside the fortifying walls. It passed in front of the remains of the castle. A wide stone walkway ran from the burnt door arch of the castle to the dirt road where a large stone sign had been erected. Across the road, where a large area of the encroaching forest had been halted, stood hundreds of trees arranged in rows to make a vast orchard. On the walkway, halfway between the castle and the road, was a stone wall circle about a foot and a half high and about fifteen feet in diameter. It had once been a fountain and wading pool. A statue, that squirted a stream of water into the pool, once stood on the castle side of the pool. Only the bottom half of the statue now remained, the top half had been destroyed by weapons fire. There was a drain near the middle of the pool, but now it was just a round hole filled with dirt and rocks. In the center of the now dried pool, lay three curled up bodies, two boys and one cat.

Tommy and Michael lay on their sides facing one another. Tommy was the first to move. It started with waves of tremors that moved up and down his body. His arms and legs twitched with the tremors. His squishy brain began sending distressing and unsettling signals to his stomach. In an instant, nausea erupted in his belly. He wasn't quite able to move or open his eyes, but the burgeoning eruption in his digestive tract was having no difficulty in moving.

With one sudden gasp for air followed by a sudden release, "Uggh," Tommy said involuntary. "Uggh, Uggghhh," and out of his mouth gushed the most foul smelling chunks and bits of partially digested oatmeal and hard boiled eggs. As he was yet unable to lift his head, he splattered the floor of the empty wading pool, his face, his clothes and Michael. Finally being able to move a little, he rolled over and got on his knees. He was just beginning to open his eyes when he heard the eruption of Michael's now distressed digestive system and warm vomit splattered the ground and onto him. This set him off again and this time up come the pizza with bits and pieces of mushrooms and pepperoni. The pain was enormous and he felt very weak. "Why," he thought. "Why, just why, did I eat so much?" But, this was a good thing. Even though his brain continued to squish and vibrate, he was beginning to think. Michael had not yet been able to get to his knees when Tommy finally got his eyes to open fully. What he saw astonished him, confused him, and made him throw up more of the pizza.

Everything looked topsy-turvy. It was a bizarre sight; it was as if his eyes were in his head upside down. Faint blue gray; more gray than blue, streaks of light shot across his field of view. They went in every direction; up, down and across. They moved away from him and some came directly toward him. They zigged and zagged, making sharp angled turns. His brain seemed to expand as if it were going to explode, then, with extreme quickness it contracted with one big slosh. It was so intense that Tommy closed his eyes very tightly and clinched his teeth. He heard a pop at his jaw line just below his ears. He opened his eyes and his view had righted itself. The blue gray lines were still there, but they were fading quickly. He looked towards Michael. Michael had the same clinched teeth and tightly shut eyes as he had moments before. Then Michael's eyes popped open. Tommy could see that Michael and he had been having the same experiences.

The two of them just sat there staring at each other for several moments. The foul smelling vomit dripped from their clothes, hands, and faces. They were a mess, and, they were very happy to see one another. The boys weren't the only ones to having all this fun. Mister Buttercup lay on the floor of the dried pool just below their feet. He lay on his belly with his paws outstretched. He had his head down between his legs and his chin rested on the ground. In front of him was an expanding puddle of green ooze with grass, kitty fur, and Giorgio's Tiger Food, Tuna and Liver flavor mixed in. There was also something that looked like a piece of mouse tail.

Michael, while looking at Tommy, was the first to speak. "Just two ordinary guys," he said, "friends for life, right?" He then smiled broadly.

"Right," Tommy managed to get out, and he smiled too.

They gazed at their surroundings. They studied the remains of the great castle. They viewed the grassy areas and the forest. The colors were richer and brighter than they had ever seen. The greens were in rich emerald shades and the flowers that were scattered round the grassy areas and on the edges of the forest, seemed to sparkle with brilliance. The trees, and all growing plants for that matter, were slightly different in appearance. They seemed more uniform in structure. The tree trunks and branches were straighter, not that they were straight, just straighter than trees they were used to seeing. There was a better balance to the plants and trees, wherever a branch or leaf grew, a uniform branch or leaf grew on the opposite side. There seemed to be much less randomness in their growth patterns.

It seemed to be early morning. The light had that early morning look to it, but that wasn't all. There was an early morning cool dampness to the air, and what they could smell, above their own stink, had early morning freshness to it. The sky, however, was disturbing. Without being aware of what the other was doing, both boys found themselves staring at the sky. It was black. The blackest black they had ever seen. There was nothing there, just blackness. There was no sun in the sky. The slightly blue light just seemed to be emanating from everywhere and yet nowhere specific. It was very much like the light that lit the room below the museum.

"Where do you think we are?" inquired Michael.

"I don't know," answered Tommy. "You got any ideas?"

"It sure doesn't look like any place I know of," Michael responded. "Maybe we've gone ahead in time."

"Or, maybe we've gone back in time," Tommy added. "But, somehow, I don't think so. I think we've gone to some other place."

"Do you think we're dead?" Michael suddenly asked with a bit of panic in his voice.

"I don't think so," Tommy answered not too reassuringly.

"Look," Michael said suddenly, "There at the end of this walkway, by the road, it looks like a sign or something. Maybe it can tell us where we are."

The two boys tried to stand up and both almost fell back to the ground. Their legs were weak and didn't want to support their weight. It took them a moment to catch their balance. In all his confusion, Tommy had failed to notice him before and now saw Mister Buttercup for the first time.

The Life and Times of Tommy Travail

"Mister Buttercup," he said with excitement and joy, and then he said, "Oh, Mister Buttercup," with great sadness. "What have I done? What have I gotten you into?"

"Meeoow," Mister Buttercup answered as he crawled to Tommy's feet.

Tommy squatted down, and almost fell over in the process. He took Mister Buttercup's head in his hands and wiped his face and whiskers. Mister Buttercup began to purr. Tommy could tell that he was going to be okay. The whole experience didn't seem to have been any worse on him than it had on them.

"Let's go see what that sign says," Michael said.

The two boys, followed by Mister Buttercup, started working their way toward the dirt road. It was hard work to walk; their legs simply did not want to move. Eventually, they got to the sign and went around it to have a look. It was written with the same squirming letters that Tommy had seen in his father's journal, only they were much more active in the minds' eye. Within moments, both boys' nausea returned. Tommy puked up his last piece of pizza, which was soggy with his grandfather's finest tea. He looked at Michael then returned his attention to the sign. Michael was going through the motions of vomiting, but he must have already emptied his stomach because all that was coming out was an acidy drool.

Despite his nausea, Tommy stared at the writing on the sign. His brain squished and the moving letters began to form words, and after a few moments, he was able to read the sign. "Michael," he said. "Look at it. If you look at it long enough, you can start to read it."

"I don't think I can take any more of this," Michael said with desperation in his voice.

"Come on Michael. You can do it, I know you can," Tommy encouraged.

Michael turned his attention back to the sign and after a few moments, Tommy could see him squint his eyes and clench his teeth as he experienced another brain squish. Michael's eyes opened wide and Tommy knew he could read the sign as well. It said, "<u>The Old Castle</u> Destroyed by The Kindlewalkers in the year Andrew 9123 Lw."

"Well, that tells us exactly nothing," Michael exclaimed.

Suddenly a hooded black robed figure came running down the road in their direction. Tommy thought he saw the figure come out of the orchard across the road. The figure was hollering something, but they couldn't make it out. "Gubamon. Gubamon. Gubamon Yatcha Or, Gubamon Thow," the figure shouted, repeating the phrase over and over.

Tommy and Michael gritted their teeth and tightly closed their eyes and they felt the nausea return with the start of another brain squishing episode. The squish came and went and they were able to contain their nausea to a few choking gags. However, after the squish they were able to understand what the figure was saying, "Run. Run. Run for your lives and hide." The figure zoomed past them and Tommy noticed that the figure's feet were not touching the ground. The figure crossed the road and dashed into the forest. Then there was a great ground shaking rumble, "Thrump. Thrump. Thrump," and two great beasts emerged from the forest near the orchard. One was slightly ahead of the other and they were coming directly toward the boys. Mister Buttercup dashed behind the sign, and Tommy was surprised to see how fast he moved, given that Michael and he could hardly walk, let alone run. The beasts looked like wild boar, only they were as large as a rhinoceros, maybe larger. They had long crossed tucks that stuck out each side of their jaws and thick hairy manes. They were running at a gallop and, as they got closer, the boys could see riders on their backs. When they spotted the boys, they slowed down and approached at a walk. The rider on the first beast to arrive was a large man who was broad across the chest with a large round belly. His hands were large and his fore arms were as big around as Tommy's leg. He had long straggly hair and a bearded face. His skin looked tough and leathery. He wore a black leather vest with a red sash, black trousers and leather boots.

'Oh, oh my. What have we here?" the first rider said in a deep strong voice as he got close enough to see, and, smell, the boys. "Hey, Clifford," he said to the second rider, "Look what we have here." Then he laughed deeply, "Ha, ha, ha," and his belly shook.

The second rider nudged his beast forward slightly to get a better look at the boys, "What's that, Stan?" he said.

"I think we got two boys here that have gotten their first taste of the Queen's Tinkleberry wine. You gotta take it easy on that stuff," he said to the boys "It takes some getting used to." And, he laughed some more. The second rider upon seeing the boys joined in on the laughter.

"We got a report that someone was stealing from the Queen's orchard," the first one said. "You boys wouldn't know anything about that would you?"

"No sir," both boys answered simultaneously.

"Didn't think so," he remarked. "If you boys have been into the Tinkleberry wine, I don't think you'll be eating much for a while. I think it's that Carla Crosswell girl anyway," he said rhetorically. "I'm gonna catch that little witch one of these days and she's gonna spend a week in my jail, or even better, a week in the Queen's dungeon. Yeah, that oughta teach her a lesson, a week in the Queen's dungeon. You boys haven't seen her have you?"

"No sir," they both lied.

"Okay boys, if you see her, you tell her I'm gonna get her. And, you two take it easy on the Tinkleberry wine; you both look a little young." With that, both riders snapped their reigns and the great beasts took off in a trot.

Once the riders were down the road and out of sight, the black robed figure emerged from the forest and glided up to them, her feet not touching the ground until she came to a stop. She pulled her black hood back and revealed a stunningly pretty face. She had big round, richly deep blue eyes. She had straight black hair and it was cut straight around her head just below her ears in a short bob. "Yuck," she said as she saw and smelled the boys. She pulled out a wand from under her sleeve, held it horizontally in front of Tommy and moved it down from his head to toes. She then repeated the process in front of Michael. The boys looked at each other in amazement. They were clean, as clean as if they had just stepped out of the bathtub and dressed in their cleanest clothes. They no longer smelled and even seemed to have a fresh scent about them.

"There that's better," she said, her voice chirpy and cheerful, "I haven't seen you boys around here before. Where you boys from?"

"We're from the University Of Brookfield," Tommy responded without thinking.

"Universe City," she said curiously. "Nope, don't think I've ever heard of that. But, Brookfield, isn't that somewhere on the other side of the mountains? Yes, think it's on the other side of the mountains. So, what are your names? My name is Carla Crosswell and I'm special." Tommy and Michael looked at one another with that, "Oh boy, not another one" look.

"My name is Tommy Travail," Tommy said.

"And I'm Michael Woden," added Michael.

"It's a pleasure to meet you boys," Carla continued. "And, by the way, thanks for not telling the Queen's Policemen where I was hiding. You boys on your way for the testing? How old are you? I'm four thousand and seventy-one, and did I mention, I'm special. Anyway, you gonna be here long? How did…"

"Hold on Carla," Tommy said. "We're a bit confused and I think we got lost. Can you tell us where we are?'

"Why, you're at Old Castle, silly boy. It's kinda hard not to notice. And if you're confused, well, Tinkleberry wine will do that to you," Carla said with her voice getting a little sterner. "You boys should know better than that. How much of that stuff did you guys drink anyway? You were quite a mess, you know. I don't think you're gonna be in too much of a hurry to do that again. If it…"

"Carla," Tommy said interrupting her again. "Don't you ever take a breath? Wait, no, don't answer that." Tommy didn't want to get her started again. "Like I said, we're a little lost. Can you tell us where we are, I mean, what's the name of this place?"

"Like I said," she began, "Old Castle, and that down the road, well you can't really see it from here, but anyway, that's Old Castle Village. That's where I'm from. Well, I really don't live in the village. I live just outside of town, but that's my village. And I'm special; I did mention that, didn't I? Yes, I think I did. Well, I'm leaving for New Castle tomorrow, for the testing, you know. Are…"

This time Michael interrupted her, "Slow down you're making my head spin."

"It's the Tinkleberry wine," she said. "I told you…

The Life and Times of Tommy Travail

"Wait," Tommy said emphatically. "Let's just do this one question and, one answer at a time."

"Okay," Carla agreed impatiently. She rose up, her feet leaving the ground, and then she settled back down with her feet returning to the ground.

"So this is Old Castle and Old Castle Village," Tommy continued, "but what do you call this place; in a larger sense, I mean?"

Carla thought for the briefest of moments and said, "Home."

"I mean," Tommy tried to clarify. "What's the name of your country?"

"Well," Carla explained, "we are in the Realm of the Queen. Surely, you know you're in the Realm of the Queen, you know, formerly Realm of the King, but it's been the Realm of the Queen for quite a while now. I know that there are an endless number of Realms in our Plane, but come on, not to know you're in the Realm of the Queen, really! You guys are confused. I'm telling you, it's the Tinkleberry wine."

"Realm of the Queen? Realms of the Plane? What do you call this Plane," Tommy questioned.

"I told you, silly boy, Home," Carla said impatiently as she crossed her arms, pursed her lips together and once again rose up off the ground and back down.

"How old did you say you were?" Michael suddenly interjected.

"Four thousand and seventy-one light waves. How old are you?"

"Were both twelve," Michael responded.

"Twelve," Carla said and then started to laugh. "How can you be only twelve light waves old? That would mean that you were born a little more than a week ago."

"I think I get it," Tommy said doing some quick math in his head. "You keep time in days. One light wave equals one day."

"One day and one night," Carla interjected. "I'm four thousand and seventy-one, so how old are you guys really?

Tommy did some more quick math and said, "I'm four thousand, five hundred and ninety-three, and Michael is four thousand, four hundred and thirteen."

"So how old does that make her," Michael asked Tommy under his breath. Michael was not as quick as Tommy in math.

85

"A little more than eleven," Tommy answered Michael in a whisper. He then turned his attention to the Old Castle sign and asked Carla, "So tell me how you would read this date?"

"That's, Andrew, Ninety-one twenty-three. Andrew was King then and it was nine thousand, one hundred and twenty-third light wave of his reign," Carla answered, and then added, "It was also the last day of his reign."

"So what is the date now," Michael asked.

"It's Lucinda Fifty-six Fifty nine," Carla answered.

"Did Lucinda come right after Andrew," Tommy asked.

"Oh my, no. There were lots of other Kings and Queens between the two of them. Before Queen Lucinda, was King Richard, who was Queen Lucinda's husband, he died. And before him, was King Anthony. And, before…"

"Okay, okay. We get the point," Tommy said cutting Carla off.

"Hey, just because you're older than me, it doesn't mean you can boss me around," Carla said a bit angrily, as she did another one of those little floating up and down things. "I did tell you I was special, didn't I? I'm sure I did," she added.

Tommy and Michael looked at one another. Since they had been through this kind of thing many times before back at school, without talking, it was decided that Michael would ask the question.

"Okay," Michael began. "What makes you so special?"

"I popped early," Carla said very quickly. To Carla, it seemed that she had been waiting forever for one of them to ask that question. "Magically that is. I popped over a thousand light waves ago. I am way ahead of other kids my age. I mean, everybody will eventually catch up, but for now, I can do a lot of the stuff the other kids can't. Have you guys popped yet? Not everybody pops, you know, and if you guys haven't popped by now, I'd be getting worried, if I were you. So, have you guys popped and how long ago was it, if you did?"

Michael and Tommy looked at each other, but neither of them knew how to answer. After a considerable pause, Tommy finally said, "I don't know. How can you tell?"

"That's easy," Carla said confidently. "Here Tommy, take my wand and point it at something. If nothing happens, you haven't popped."

Tommy took the wand. The blue gray lines, the ones he saw when he first opened his eyes, again appeared for a very brief moment. Before Tommy could take aim at anything specific, a massive fire bolt erupted from the end of the wand and shot across the road to the orchard. It struck one of the fruit trees and sent it crashing to the ground. Tommy immediately tossed the wand back to Carla. The tip of her wand had been blackened by the discharge.

"Wow," Carla exclaimed. "I'd say you popped alright. But, we had better get out of here. When the Queen's Policeman sees that tree, he's going to be furious. He'll have a lot of explaining to do and a ton of paperwork. He's gonna be mad."

"Can't you use some magic to repair it," Michael inquired.

"Repair it, yes. Make it live again, no. The first law of magic says that magic can not create life or anything that was ever alive. You can sometimes repair living things if the injury is not too severe. And, a trained and practiced medical magician can do much more than the average witch or wizard. You can make facsimiles or artificial repairs, but you can't make it live, and I'd say that tree's a goner. So we had better get moving."

The three of them started walking down the roadway. Tommy suddenly stopped, turned to Carla and said, "Give it to Michael."

"What?" Carla inquired.

"Give Michael the wand. We might as well see if he has popped. But, when you take it Michael, make sure it's pointed at something safe, like that section of the old wall."

Carla handed the wand to Michael, keeping it pointed at the section of the old wall. As quickly as it had happened with Tommy, a fire bolt erupted from the tip of the wand. It struck the wall shattering a corner and sending pieces flying everywhere. It wasn't quite as powerful as the one Tommy had created, but it was very powerful.

"My," Carla declared. "You guys are pretty strong for two guys who didn't know if they had popped or not. That's pretty curious, yes, pretty curious."

Tommy suddenly remembered Mister Buttercup and called to him. Mister Buttercup didn't answer and, since they hadn't gone very far, Tommy went back to the sign to look for him, but he was nowhere in

David G. Groesbeck

sight. Tommy called for him several more times, but there was no sign of him.

"Come on," Carla said. "We better be getting out of here."

Tommy hated to leave Mister Buttercup behind, but he didn't feel he had much choice. He hoped he would be able to return later to look for him. As they started to walk down the roadway again, Carla advised them, that if the Policeman returned, they should all head into the forest and hide.

Chapter Eight

The Road To Cantwell

"So what are you guys doing here anyway," Carla asked. "Are you on your way for the testing? Although, I don't know how you could be doing that, I mean, given that you didn't even know you had popped and all."

"We're looking for my father and mother," Tommy answered. "They've gone missing and we're trying to find them."

"Oh my, that's awful. Well then you should see my father. He's the Wizard Master of Old Castle. He might be able to help you. You wanna come to my house and meet him?"

Tommy and Michael looked at one another and Tommy said, "Might as well, it can't hurt." The three of them then set off under Carla's direction. "Say, Carla," Tommy continued, "what's this testing all about? You say you're going tomorrow?"

"Yes," Carla said proudly. "It's for the Queen's Academy. Once a year they hold a testing at New Castle for all the kids who have popped and completed their basic educations. They only accept the best, and if you get even one poor on a test, your chances of getting into the Academy are pretty slim. But, if you are accepted, well then you can expect a grand life. After your third year, everyone is separated into either the Political division or the Military division. And, after two more years, you then graduate. If you graduate from the Political School, you become a Witch or Wizard of the Realm. You'll become an Ambassador of the Queen and may travel throughout the different Realms of the Plane as her representative. If you graduate from the Military School, you become an Officer in the Queen's Army. And, one graduate from the Military School each year is selected to join the Queen's Guard. That's a real high honor."

"What do they test you on?" asked Michael, "Magic stuff?"

"Oh, no," Carla said. "They test you on your basic education. You know, the natural sciences and math, and language skills, of course. You know, all the basic stuff. If you get in, they teach you the magic… and loads of other stuff too."

"What happens if you don't ever pop," Tommy inquired.

"Well, you just go to work in one of the non-magical jobs. The Queen sees to it that everyone has a job, whether magical or non-magical. She really is grand you know. She takes care of everybody and protects all of us."

"Is the Queen at New Castle," Michael asked.

"Oh no," Carla answered. "She's at Newest Castle. Many years ago, when they finished Newest Castle, the Royal Family moved there, and then they moved the Academy into New Castle. It's really great. The whole castle is now the Academy. There are dormitories, class rooms, large conference halls and laboratories. My dad graduated from the Political School and he says he had some of the best times of his life there. You guys want to go to the testing with me tomorrow? How's your basic education? Your language skills seem plenty good enough."

"What do you think Michael?" Tommy asked. "Shall we give it a try?"

"Well, it might be fun, and since we have to start looking for your parents somewhere, it might as well as be there as anywhere."

"Okay!" Carla exclaimed excitedly. "We'll all leave tomorrow for New Castle and the testing."

The light had been getting steadily brighter. It looked and felt like it must be midday, but still no sun in the black sky. They had walked a ways and the road was now taking them out of the forest area. Houses were beginning to appear. The houses were odd in appearance. Some were neatly built, almost too perfect looking, and others were a hodge-podge of this and that without any clear architectural plan. Carla explained that the houses were reflective of the skills of the witch or wizard that built them. Carla pointed out her house as they got near it. Her house was a little bigger than the other houses and was one of those that were exquisitely built. It looked a bit like a Victorian house, in that it had multi floors and a couple of spires. It was made of stone and, unlike many of the other houses that had a plastic look, Carla's house looked solid and majestic.

Carla invited them in when they got to the house. After she saw to their comfort, she went to find her father. While she was gone, Michael and Tommy took the opportunity to talk some about their experiences. There was so much to discuss. They soon realized they were going to have to get some time alone so they could try to make some sense of it all. Carla returned with her father and introduced him to the boys. He was a stately looking man. He had dark black hair, except for a patch of gray near his right temple, above his ear. He had the same richly deep blue eyes as Carla and a soft friendly voice. Tommy thought he looked young for a Master Wizard, although Tommy had no idea how long it took to become a Master Wizard. Carla explained to her father that Tommy was looking for his parents, and that they had become confused and lost. She didn't say anything about Tinkleberry wine and the boys were happy for it. Carla's Father, Master Wizard Abernathy Crosswell, said that he had never heard anything about a Sara or Steven Travail, but he said he would make some inquires that afternoon. Carla told her father that Michael and Tommy were going to go with her to New Castle the next day for testing. She told him that they needed a place to stay for the night and asked if they could stay there as her guests. Her father said that it would be okay and that the boys could share the guest room. He then said he was going to return to work; that he'd make some inquiries about Tommy's parents, and he would see them at dinner time.

Tommy and Michael told Carla that they were really exhausted and asked her if they could rest for a while. Carla took them to the guest room and showed them the bathroom. She told them to make themselves at home and to freshen up if they wished. She then left them alone. The boys discussed the details of the day at great length until near dinner time. Michael was thoroughly enjoying himself, all except the puking part of course. Michael reminded Tommy several times that it was Tommy's idea to eat a big meal before they left. Tommy reluctantly admitted that was a mistake, several times. Something about that sign at the Old Castle had been bugging Tommy almost all day. It finally dawned on him. The letters on the sign had originally been squirming about like the letters in his father's journal. But his fathers journal; how could he have been so stupid, he had set it down to unlock the door to the room with the mirror and forgot to pick it back up. He left it behind. Now that he might be able to read it, he didn't have it. Tommy was extremely disappointed. The journal may well have contained clues as to where his father had come from and where he might have gone. Tommy then remembered the medallion and pulled it out from under his sweater. Sure enough, he could now read the writing around its edges. It said, "The King's Noble Table +++ Order of Merit." And, there was a date, "Richard 10259Lw." He noticed that it no longer gave him that fuzzy, tingly feeling when he touched it, although it still felt warm to the touch. Just as he tucked the medallion back under his sweater, Carla knocked at the door.

"It's almost dinner time," she said through the door. "Are you boys coming to dinner or has the Tinkleberry wine still got you."

Tommy immediately opened the door. "Yes, we're coming to dinner," he said, "and please cool it on the Tinkleberry wine stuff. It's embarrassing."

"Well you should be embarrassed," she said in her most judgmental voice. "Come on, let's go eat and you can meet my mom."

Carla's mother, Lady Witch Leila Crosswell, was a neat aristocratic looking woman. She, like Carla's father, had also attended the Academy and the Political School. The Academy is where Carla's parents had met. Lady Crosswell had been out shopping earlier when the boys had arrived and was pleased to meet them now. Carla's father had returned home from work and the five of them sat down to a delicious meal. The boys weren't always sure what they were eating, but they were very hungry and enjoyed everything. During dinner, Carla explained that the boys had only recently popped and that they hadn't had any training. She asked her parents if she could give the boys a couple of her baby wands to learn with, and her parents said okay.

After dinner, Carla gave Tommy and Michael each a small wand. She instructed them to put the wands in their pockets and not to mess with them. She said she would teach them some stuff on their way to New Castle the next day. Master Wizard Abernathy told Tommy that he wasn't able find out anything about his parents, but that he would continue to make inquires. He said he would let Carla know if he discovered anything and she could pass it along to him. Tommy showed Carla's father his medallion. Although he said he had never seen anything like it, he guessed it was an award that the King had given for some kind of achievement. He said it might be a sporting medal of some kind. They spent the rest of the evening talking about what they could expect at the testing. Lady Witch Leila gave them some advice on how to take the tests and what kinds of questions they may be asked. After some time, Carla's mother ordered everybody off to bed, as it was getting late.

The next morning the boys awoke to Carla banging on their door and ordering them to get up. She said that it was getting late and, if they were to have any breakfast before they left, they had to get moving. The boys washed up and got dressed quickly. They went downstairs and had breakfast with Carla and her parents. Michael inquired as to how far they would have to travel. Carla told them that it would take only a few hours if she could teach them to ride the waves. She explained that riding the waves was what she was doing when they first saw her. She didn't mention that she was running from the Queen's Policemen. Her parents wouldn't have taken too kindly to that. She said that, if they had the magic for it, wave riding could be the first step in learning to fly. But, she said that only a few witches and wizards have the magic for flying. However, if it turned out that they did have the magic for it, the Academy would teach them how to fly.

When they finished their breakfast, Carla and her parents said their good-byes. Carla's mother told them to have a safe journey and wished her and the boys good luck on their tests. Carla told the boys that it was a very good thing when a Lady Witch wished someone good luck. Carla and the boys left the house by the side door. The wonderful meal the night before followed by a good night's rest and a fulfilling morning breakfast had reinvigorated the boys. They felt reenergized and were anxious to get going. They stepped out the door onto the porch and, to everyone's astonishment, there sat Mister Buttercup.

"Mister Buttercup!" Tommy exclaimed with excitement. "Where have you been and how'd you ever find us?"

"Meow, meow," was Mister Buttercup's only reply, except for maybe a little soft purring.

"Well I'm glad to see you," Tommy said as he bent down to pet him. He noticed two bowls next to Mister Buttercup. One bowl had a little of what looked like leftovers from the night before and the other was half full of milk. Tommy guessed that Carla's mother must have put them out. "I'm glad you've eaten big boy because we've got quite an adventure ahead of us today." The four of them set off.

Carla was wearing her black robe, but she had the hood pulled back. The early morning light made her jet black hair glisten. "I want to go through Old Castle Village on our way," she said. "I want to pick us up some supplies."

"What kind of supplies?" Michael inquired, "We don't have any money." Tommy thought about the Euro he still had folded up in his pocket, but he didn't figure that it would spend very well here.

"Oh, you'll see when we get there," Carla answered. "And, I think I can make the money we'll need."

The three of them, with Mister Buttercup following behind, entered the Village limits. The main street was lined with buildings of various shapes and sizes. Business signs of all sorts hung from store fronts and many had signs in their windows as well. The Village was very busy, even though it was still quite early in the morning. People were busy going from shop to shop. There were carts and wagons from which people were selling their wares. There were fruits and vegetables. One wagon was overflowing with all sorts of pots, pans and kettles. There were many different shapes and sizes that hung from every possible location around the wagon. The wagon had a sign on it that said, "Witch Ware -- Crafted from the finest metals ever brewed in a caldron."

"There's the first shop I'd like to stop at," Carla said pointing toward a yellow building with black and white trim around the windows. It had a sign above the door that said, "Daffy Taffy's Treats for All Occasions."

They entered the shop and candy was everywhere including chocolates in a variety of sizes and configurations. There were white chocolates, milk chocolates and dark chocolates. There was a whole row filled with chewy candies. There were boxes of hard candies, gum balls and jaw breakers. The back wall was completely lined with open boxes of every imaginable kind of sucker. There were giant suckers, small suckers, goo- filled suckers and suckers that fizzed when they were licked. The boys were amazed. Carla went around the shop gathering up a little of this and a little of that. She took the items she had picked up to the counter and set them down. A smiling clerk greeted Carla. He obviously knew her and Tommy could tell she had spent quite a bit of time in this shop.

The clerk told Carla that the items would cost one cube of copper. Carla pulled out her wand and mustered as much energy as she could. She pointed the wand at the counter. Green light emitted from the tip of her wand and formed a perfectly shaped cube of copper. The clerk took the copper cube. Carla gathered up her items and placed them in a small leather bag she had under her robe.

"Wow," Michael exclaimed. "You can make money?"

"I can make copper. It's the easiest for me. It takes a lot of energy to make metals and the harder it is to make a metal, the more valuable it is. It's different for different people. A metal that is hard for me to make, might be easier for someone else. However, there are some metals that are very hard to make, even for the most powerful witches and wizards. They, of course, are very valuable. Okay," she continued, "there's one more place I want to go. Come on."

They left the shop. The village was getting even busier. "Now that you both have popped," Carla said, "you should have robes. We can't have you guys going around naked."

"We're not naked," Michael protested.

"If you've popped, you are supposed to be wearing robes, and, we can't have you journeying all the way to New Castle looking like that. Only kids who have popped can go to the testing, remember? There's a used robe shop at the end of the street, maybe we can find something for you guys there."

Tommy hadn't really been paying attention, but now that Carla mentioned robes, he noticed that almost everyone was wearing a robe. There were blue ones, green ones and red robes. Some had gold trim and sashes. There were black robes and some were in shockingly bright colors of yellow or pink. Some people were wearing robes with hoods and some were wearing robes without hoods. But not everyone was wearing a robe; a few were wearing clothes that were much more familiar to him. The man that was selling the goods from the Witch Ware Wagon was not wearing a robe. He had on a checkered shirt and a light pinstriped pair of trousers with pleats on the front. He had a pair of bright red suspenders holding up his trousers and a green derby styled hat. "These must be people who simply never popped," Tommy thought, "yet, they seemed to be as happy as everyone else."

"I want to get one of those emerald green robes," Michael said.

"You can't," Carla said. "Girls wear black robes and boys wear blue robes. Only adults can choose what color they want to wear. Some officials have special colors and only the royal family can wear purple."

"Well, blue it is then," Michael quipped.

They arrived at the used robe shop. "Hello there Carla," the elderly lady said when she saw Carla enter the shop. There were numerous racks of robes in various sizes and colors. Tommy and Michael were both surprised; the elderly lady shop keeper was not wearing a robe.

"Hello, Misses Handover," Carla responded. "I've got two boys here that need robes."

"Oh, yes," Mrs. Handover said. "Looks like a fourteen for the tall one and a twelve for the shorter one. What I have is over this way." Mrs. Handover walked over to two circular racks and took a robe from one of the racks."

"They need to have hoods," Carla added. "We gotta have hoods, right boys?"

"Uh, yeah, I guess," Tommy said.

"I definitely want a hood," Michael said with certainty.

"Oh," Mrs. Handover said as she replaced the robe. "Here's a nice one in a fourteen. Try it on lad," she said handing it to Michael. "Oh, yes, yes here's a real nice one in a twelve. It's a 'Lawrence LaLoose,' one of the best robes made, you know." She handed it to Tommy and he tried it on. "I'd say they're a pretty good fit; yes, a nice fit indeed."

Michael and Tommy looked at each other and they had to admit that they looked pretty sharp. "How much are they," Carla asked.

"For you my dear, one drop of gold for the both of them," Mrs. Handover replied pleasantly.

"Oh," Carla said with clear disappointment in her voice. "I don't have any gold and I can't make it."

"Oh dear," said Mrs. Handover. "Let's see, I could let you have them for two drops of silver."

Carla motioned for Michael and Tommy to come closer to her. When they got next to her, she said, "I might be able to make two drops of silver, but if I do it will leave me a little magically weak and I won't be able to ride the wave for a while. That will make our journey to New Castle take longer."

"Will we still get there in time to register for the testing?" Michael inquired.

"Oh, I don't think that would be a problem," Carla answered. "We should have plenty of time. Registration takes place all day long today."

"Well," Tommy said, "Michael and I don't know how to ride the wave yet anyway. Maybe you can recover your energy while we're learning, but it's up to you."

"It's okay with me," stated Carla. "But to tell you the truth, I don't know if I can even make silver. I might expend all that energy and we still won't be able to buy them."

"I think it's worth the try, if you're willing Carla," Tommy said.

"Yeah, I agree," said Michael. "If you're willing to try, that is."

Carla agreed and went to the counter. She pulled out her wand and concentrated. Then, gritting her teeth and squinting her eyes, she lowered the tip of her wand towards the counter top. A white light glowed from the tip of her wand and a drop of sliver appeared on the counter. Only it really wasn't a drop, so much as it was a splat of silver. Carla concentrated again and produced a second splat of silver. Mrs. Handover looked at the results of Carla's efforts and smiled.

"Not the prettiest drops of silver I've ever seen, but I'm sure it will do," Mrs. Handover said. "Is there anything else I can get for you kids?"

Carla took a deep breath, "Phew, I don't think we can afford anything else. Thank you very much Mrs. Handover."

They left the store and the boys thanked Carla over and over again. All the while, Mister Buttercup followed behind. They followed the roadway out of the village and started their journey to New Castle.

They had been walking for a while, but Carla hadn't said anything since they left the robe shop and that was an amazing thing on its own. "I was thinking," she finally said, "and, I don't want you to take offense to this, but, the Realm you call Home must be awfully backwards because you guys don't know very much about magic. Don't they teach kids about magic before they pop? I think all kids should be taught about magic, whether they've popped or not. You just never know when a kid is going to pop. So anyway, I'm going to assume that you guys don't know anything. Magic is the controlling and directing of all the forces that surround us. You imagine them, you shape them and you direct them. You can do this in as many ways as you can create. You can learn to direct them with words. You can direct them through the mixing of ingredients and you can direct them with a wand; some things work and some things don't. Some people can do things and others can't. Some people have more power than others do and some people can create ways to enhance their own power. The wand is one of the most common ways people do magic. The construction of the wand makes it a focusing device. Even people who are magically weak, can to do some magic with a good wand. The really powerful can shape and control magical energy with their bare hands, and the most powerful can do it with just their minds. It's said that they can actually see the forces of magic."

They were approaching a bridge with a small stream passing underneath it. Carla indicated that it might be a good place to stop and take a break. They left the roadway and walked down to the stream. Tommy and Carla sat down and Michael went over to the stream and splashed some of the cool water on his face. Mister Buttercup went to the stream and took a drink. They rested a bit and when they got up to leave Carla asked Tommy and Michael to come closer to her.

"I'm going to show you a basic magic move," she said. "Take out your wands and hold them out in front of you." Then without her wand in her hand she said, "When I say begin, I want you to close your eyes and imagine that you are pulling in the forces of magic into your body the way you might take a breath. When you have imagined that you have drawn the force in, open your eyes and make a circle with your wand like this," she made a circular motion with her empty hand, "then point it to the ground and think release and let go of the energy. Okay? Ready, begin."

The boys did as they were instructed. First, they closed their eyes for a few moments, and then they opened their eyes, circled their wands and pointed them to the ground. The force Michael released was like being hit with a strong wind and caused him to lean way back, but the force Tommy released was like being hit with the force of a powerful ocean wave. It instantly knocked him flat on his butt. Carla laughed.

"Michael that was excellent," she said. "But Tommy, after what I saw yesterday with the tree, and what I'm seeing now, you're going to have to learn to be gentle of mind and wand. When you imagine you're gathering the magic, do it softly. Now, that's what is called a Pushback. Some people call it a stop, but it's properly called a Pushback. Being you released it at the ground, it pushed you back, but if you had pointed it at someone or something else, it would have pushed them back. Just remember, Tommy, gently and softly. Okay, it's time we got going. Would anybody like a 'Chewy Chew Chews?'"

Both the boys said yes. Carla took out the bag from under her robe, gave them a couple of pieces and took a couple for herself. They popped them into their mouths and they were deliciously sweet and chewy. They walked up to the roadway and continued their journey. Carla was silent again for a while. The countryside had turned slightly hilly. There were clusters of trees here and there with a lot of open grass land in between. They were approaching a place were a large tree was growing alongside the road. Carla had been feeling the return of her energies quicker than she expected. It may have been a combination of the rest they took along the stream and the 'Chewy Chew Chews," or, it might have been because she was getting older, and she was getting older, light wave by passing light wave.

"Let's stop here," Carla said as they got to the tree. "Now, I want to show you how to do this." Carla rose up off the ground and wiggled her toes, then set back down on the ground. "This is quite a bit harder than the Pushback, but I'm sure you two can do it. There are two ways to do it. The best way is to release the magic through your feet, but that is the hardest to master. There are many balancing problems involved. The second way is to release the magic from under your arms. You want the push to go downward from your arm pits. It will give you the feeling of being picked up by your shoulders. There are a lot less balancing problems with this method. However, if you master the foot method, you can glide and turn much better. You have much more control. So, let's try that method first and see how you do. Now remember, Tommy, gently and softly."

Carla instructed the boys how to gather the magic and how it should be directed. When they first attempted it, they both did indeed rise off the ground, but for them it was like standing on a small pedestal and they couldn't keep their balance. They both fell over landing on the ground with a bit of a thud. They made several attempts at this and each time they failed with a tumble to the ground.

"I told you," Carla said. "It's not easy and takes some practice. We don't have time to practice now and you can do that later anyway. So, let's try the other method." Carla gave them instructions, and on their first try, they were able to float in the air. "I told you this method was easier. Now, while your still floating, lean forward and imagine the magical force as a wave behind you, gently pushing you forward. Do it very easy at first until you can learn how to control the amount and speed of your movement. Don't try to move more than a few feet and straighten up to stop."

The boys did as she instructed and they were both able to move a little ways. Carla congratulated them both. They practiced this for a short bit until Carla was confident of their ability to control their movement.

"Okay," she said. "Now we can make some real time. There's one other thing. If you should lose control, or if you find yourself going too fast and have to stop quickly, the Pushback can be used as an emergency brake, so you should always have your wand in your hand when you're riding the wave. Just aim your wand at the ground slightly ahead of yourself and do a Pushback if you have to stop quickly. And Tommy, remember, do everything gently or you might find yourself flat on the ground. When you get better, you'll learn many ways to stop and control your motion, especially when you learn the foot method. Come sit down for a minute," she said as she sat down and patted the ground next to her. The boys did as she asked.

Carla took out her little bag and took out some chocolates. They each had several pieces. Carla said that the chocolates would fortify and replenish them. While they ate their chocolates, she told them, that if all goes well, their next stop would be at a small village just outside of New Castle called Cantwell. She told them that it was the place were the Academy kids go when they have a break from school. New Castle Town itself was where many of the professors and administrative staff of the Academy lived; correspondingly, they had a lot of rules and regulations. Plus, in New Castle Town, there was always a chance that a professor or staff person might see you misbehaving, if you should be misbehaving that is. She said that they would probably meet up with a number of other kids in Cantwell who were also going to New Castle for testing.

"How do you know all this stuff?" Tommy asked Carla.

"From my parents," she replied. "They've been telling me stories all my life about their times at the Academy. I'll bet I heard some of them a thousand times, well maybe not a thousand times, but enough times that I remember all the details of their adventures. Well, okay, if you two guys are ready, let's give it a try."

They stood up and all three rose off the ground. They leaned a little forward and they were off. Tommy and Michael took to wave riding very quickly. It wasn't long and they were having mini races. They zoomed back and forth. They were having a great time. There were a few spills along the way and both Tommy and Michael had a few skinned marks and bruises. Carla thought they were being reckless and, at times, she knew that they were going far too fast, but she couldn't stop them. Tommy tried to think of the last time he had so much fun, but he couldn't think of any time in which he had *this* much fun. It was a blast. Tommy kept an eye on Mister Buttercup, but no matter how fast they went, he seemed to be able to keep up, and he didn't seem to be getting tired either.

Chapter Nine

The New Castle and Registration

It wasn't too long and the kids were on the outskirts of Cantwell. Carla began slowing down. She came to a stop and settled back to the ground. The boys did as she did. "We'll walk from here," she said. "It's considered bad manners to wave ride in town. And, because so many people could get hurt, some towns have rules against it. In town there is a soda shop called, 'The Deep Well of Cantwell' and they serve the best all natural Roddenberry root, root beer. It's yummy and if you drink enough of it, or fast enough, it'll make your nose feel fuzzy."

They walked into town. It was much like Old Castle Town, but it was more entertaining and youth oriented. There were game rooms and theaters; restaurants and bars; and, there was a whole street lined with shops for students. There were robe shops, clothes shops, and books shops, shops for magical supplies and shops that carried all sorts of general merchandise that a student might need. The streets were crowded. There were many young people in their blue and black robes coming and going. There were so many conversations going on that the town had kind of a buzz about it.

About a third of the way into town they saw The Deep Well sign. They headed for the soda shop and went in. They spotted an empty table and took a seat. Tommy looked around the shop and it was filled with young boys and girls. The only exception was a shabby older man who was sitting in a far corner. He was sitting with a young man in a blue robe. The young man had his hood pulled up so Tommy could

The Life and Times of Tommy Travail

only see part of his face. Another young man in a blue robe came over to their table and asked if he could take their order. "I've waited almost my whole life for this," Carla exclaimed and she ordered three Roddenberry root, root beers. While the young man was getting their drinks, Carla pulled out her wand and made three perfectly shaped cubes of copper. "That oughta do it," she said.

In a few moments, the young man returned with their drinks. He took one of the copper cubes, smiled and left. Michael and Tommy were having the time of their lives. The wave riding had them all hyped up and the atmosphere of the town and the soda shop was exhilarating. "Just two ordinary guys and friends for life, right," Michael suddenly declared.

Tommy, who happened to be looking at Carla when Michael said that, saw her face saddened slightly and her eyes drooped. "No," Tommy said. And, Michael frowned. "No," Tommy repeated looking at Carla. "Just two ordinary guys, and one *special* girl, friends for life. Right?...Right," he repeated looking directly at Carla.

When she realized what he had said, a broad smile spread across her face and her beautiful eyes brightened. "Right," she said enthusiastically.

"Right," Michael joined in.

They picked up their mugs of Roddenberry root, root beer, clinked them together and took big, deep drinks.

Two young girls came into the shop and spotted Carla. "Hey, Carla," one of them called and they came over to the table. The two girls looked very similar, but were slightly different. They both had long bright red hair that hung down their backs in curls and deep emerald green eyes. They had freckles, and both girls had a dimple. However, one had a dimple in her right cheek and the other had a dimple in her left cheek.

Carla introduced the new arrivals to the boys. She said they were Kristy and Misty Firefist and that the two were cousins. Their fathers were brothers, and, as it happens sometimes, Kristy's father was a wizard, but Misty's father was non-magical. Carla said that Kristy lived in New Castle Town where her father owned a magic mirror store, and that Misty lived with her parents on a farm near Old Castle.

"Would you ladies like to have a seat?" Tommy invited. The girls accepted and sat down. Michael motioned to the young waiter and, in moments, the girls had ice cold mugs of Roddenberry root, root beers.

"Have you registered yet," Kristy asked.

"No," Carla answered. "We haven't been up there yet. Have you registered?"

"I'm staying at Kristy's house for the testing," Misty said, "and we registered this morning. Testing starts early tomorrow morning. If you guys are staying in the dorms, you better get up there and register before all the good beds are taken."

"We are planning on staying in the dorms," Carla said, "but we've got one more thing to do after we finish our root beer, then we'll be going up there to register." The five of them got to know one another while they drank their root beer. They reassured each other that they were all going to be selected and nervously joked about the difficulty of the upcoming tests. They were having a good time. "When we leave," Carla said as she looked at her near empty glass, "we'll go out the back door. I want to see the well before we leave town." Carla pointed to the rear exit. "We should get going soon, so let's drink up." They finished their drinks, said good-bye to Kristy and Misty, and excused themselves.

They went out the back door onto a large porch. There were several tables with chairs around them. Some of the tables had umbrellas covering them. Somewhere along the way, they had lost Mister Buttercup, but when they stepped out onto the porch, he was sitting on one of the chairs waiting for them.

"Hey, Mister Buttercup," Tommy said as he walked over to him. "How'd you know we'd come out the back door?" Tommy bent down and scratched him behind his ears. "Wow," Tommy exclaimed as he noticed what lay beyond the porch. In front of them was a large park filled with decorative trees and flower gardens. Pathways crisscrossed one another as they meandered through the flower gardens. There were thousands of flowers with many of them in bloom. The variety of shapes, sizes and brilliant colors was breathtaking. The park was square in shape and was bordered on all four sides by the back of the store buildings that lined the streets. Most of the stores were more decorated on the park side than they had been on the street side. Many of the stores had porches or verandas. Even the store signs were more elaborate and done in a more artistic way.

The well was in the center of the park. It was circular and had a walkway that went all the way around it. Perpendicular to the buildings, wide walkways extended out from the well on four sides. Where the walkways met the buildings, there were gaps so the walkways could extend out to the streets. The four of them, including Mister Buttercup, left the porch. "This is where my father courted my mother," Carla said. "Isn't it romantic?"

"I don't know about romantic," Michael replied. "But, it is beautiful."

They cut over to one of the main walkways. It was an impressive view as they walked toward the well. The walkway, lined with flowers and decorative trees, seemed to frame the approach to the well. The well stood at the end of the walkway. It was circular and about twenty-five feet in diameter and it had a raised brick wall around two-thirds of it, two and a half feet high. The remaining third had a wall that started at two and half feet and rose to a height of twelve feet at its apex before descending back to the two and a half level. It formed a cove reminiscent of a clam shell. In the center of the clam shell there was a larger than life marble statue of an attractive, but unusual looking woman. She had dragonfly like wings that were folded back slightly. The wing tips were attached to the wall, which suspended the statue out over the edge of the well. The woman had her arms stretched out from her sides and slightly in front of her at waist height. She had the palms of her hands turned slightly upward. It gave her the appearance of embracing the circular well before her. Her head was disproportionally taller than it was wide. This gave her a thin oval shaped face. She had thin lips and a smooth delicate nose. Her ears held tight to the side of her head and she didn't have any hair. Her eyes were round and large. And, there was a tear just forming in the corner of each eye. In the brick wall behind her were three large marble inserts, one was off to her left and one was off to her right. The third one was above her head. Each marble slab was engraved with a starburst.

Directly across from the statue on the opposite side of the well, a pulpit extended out some five or six feet over the well's edge. It was about four feet wide and was rounded at the end. The brick wall that encircled the well followed the contour of the pulpit out over the well. A gate closed off the area of the pulpit. A black wrought iron fence had been erected some two feet away from the well's edge and it went all the way around the well. Three foot tall iron posts were place at regular intervals around the well. On top of each post was a bronze table with an inscription.

When they got to the wrought iron fence, Tommy could see that each brick making up the well was embossed with a coat of arms similar to the one on his medallion. Michael went over to one of the posts with the bronze tablets and read the inscription. It had a large 'skull and crossbones' and had danger written in large capital letters. It said, "Stay away from the well's edge. Entering or falling into the well will certainly be fatal." Someone had etched the word "almost" between the words "will" and "certainly."

Michael turned his head slightly to read the word almost when a deep voice came from behind him. No one had noticed him until he spoke. He was a large man with a well rounded belly. His hair was a bit scruffy and he had a full-face, black beard. He was wearing a buckskin-like shirt and work trousers. He had a sword in its sheath across his back. The handle could be seen above his left shoulder. The sword and sheath were held in place by a strap that went over his shoulder and across his chest. "Don't you laddies be gettin' too close," the big man said. "Everybody that's ever gone into that well has died, except one that is. Yep. They all died, except for old Jack Rockslide. Oh, oh," he said with a bit of a surprised expression on his face. "Let me introduce myself, name's William Jingleshangles, and who might you three be?" They all introduced themselves and Tommy introduced Mister Buttercup, which made the man chuckle.

"I've lived around here pretty much my whole life," he continued. "Know all the stories, I do. Like that of old Jack Rockslide. We call him Crazy Jack nowadays. Jack was a miner in the mountains outside of Old Castle. He's a non-magical just like me, but he's a short little fellow; being little makes it easier to crawl around in the mines, you see. Anyway, Jack got the bright idea one day that he could descend into the well. Now why might he want to do that, you ask. You see, this well was originally built by King Oleander to supply water for the construction of the New Castle. The village of Cantwell was created for the people who worked on the castle. By the time the castle was finished, the well was no longer needed for water. A young wizard named, Oliver Partsman, successfully enchanted the 'Forever Water-Water Device'. They're everywhere now. They're in all the homes and buildings. The park even has several of them to serve as drinking fountains. Partsman went on later in life to assist the King in organizing the first Ministry of All Things Magic. Anyway, when the castle was finished, King Oleander built the park and the well as you see it today, all except the wrought iron fence work. The town's folk put up the fence after a number of people either fell or jumped into the well. And, like I said, none of them ever came back, except Crazy Jack. Anyway, King Oleander dedicated the well to his lost love, a Telesthesian named, Damiana."

"So, what ever possessed Crazy Jack to go into the well?" Carla asked a little impatiently.

"I was just gettin' to that," Jingleshangles replied. "On the day King Oleander dedicated the well; he stood out on the pulpit, faced the crowd and made a Pronouncement. He said that everyone who worked on the construction of the well, both at the original digging and the rebuilding, shall add the suffix of "well" to the end of their family name. Following his Pronouncement, he turned to the well and said an incantation. He announced that he had enchanted the well and proclaimed that Damiana would grant a wish to anyone who tossed a piece of precious metal into the well. The King then tossed a large cube of gold into the well and whispered a wish. After he made his wish, he placed a curse on the well to protect its depths from invaders and thieves. Ever since then, strange sounds sometimes come from the well. The townsfolk say it's the spirits of King Oleander's curse. King Oleander returned to the well every year, tossed in a cube of gold and made a wish. This started a tradition that has continued with all the Monarchs right up to the present day, once a year the reigning Monarch takes a journey to the well and makes a wish. For generations, people have been tossing bits and pieces of precious metals into the well while making wishes. Old Crazy Jack, being a miner you see, figured he could go down into the well and gather up some of the treasure that must have accumulated at the bottom. Jack bought himself an invisible rope from a curiosity shop in New Castle called, Things Mostly Curious."

"Hey," Carla said. "I know that shop. Mister Keepers has all kinds of weird stuff in that shop." Carla was clearly getting impatient. This was probably the first time she ever met anyone who could talk as much as she could.

"Never been there myself," Jingleshangles continued, "but I've heard that. So anyway, one night with his tools and things strapped to his back, Crazy Jack tossed the invisible rope over the edge of the well and secured it to the wrought iron fence. He then lowered himself into the well. He was down there for ten days before he was able to find his rope and crawl back to the top. When he came out, his hair had turned white and his eyes were distant and glassy. He kept mumbling about demons and sole eaters. He was nuttier than an Allnut nut tree. He went back to the mountains where people say he lives in a cave and spends his days fighting invisible demons."

Carla had taken out her wand and made three perfectly formed cubes of copper. "This is why I wanted to see the well," Carla said. "My parents told me that it is a wishing well and I thought that we might all make a wish. What do you say that we wish for all three of us to get into the Academy?"

"Sure," Tommy said.

"It sounds good to me," Michael confirmed.

Carla gave them each a cube of copper and picked up one for herself. "Okay," she directed, "make your wish and toss it in." The three of them whispered their wish and tossed the cubes of copper into the well.

Jingleshangles laughed. "I hope you all do well on your tests tomorrow. I might enjoy having you three around these parts for a while."

"We should get going," Carla said. "It's getting late."

"Just one more thing, Mister Jingleshangles," Tommy said. Carla pursed her lips and put one hand on her hip. "What can you tell me about the coat of arms embossed on the bricks?"

"Oh, yes," Jingleshangles said. "They're based on King Oleander's own coat of arms, but each one is slightly different. They say there are no two alike. The King said that they represent his belief that we are all of Royal Blood, just slightly different from one another. The story of King Oleander's life is a great tale. You see…"

"I think you'll have to tell us that story next time," Carla interrupted. "We really must go."

"Oh, okay," the big man said. "Off with ya and good luck on those tests tomorrow."

"It was a pleasure to meet you, Mister Jingleshangles," Tommy said.

"Just call me Willy, all my friends do," Jingleshangles encouraged.

"Okay Willy," Michael said, "till next we meet."

The three of them, Mister Buttercup had disappeared again, turned and took the wide walkway out to the street. They followed the street out of town and began a wave ride to New Castle. They could see the outline of the New Castle almost right away. The closer they got the more details they could make out. They came to a stop at a spot near the castle where the roadway split. The road to the left wound its way towards the castle. It was lined with trees and there were large areas with lawns and flower gardens. The road ended at a large archway that led to the castle's inner courtyard. The second road went to the right and led into New Castle Town. Some of the buildings and roof tops of the town were visible from there. They could see yet another roadway that went from the large archway of the castle directly into New Castle Town.

The castle was very large with many towers and spinnerets. Its exterior walls were made of white, finished stone. The large stone archway was the central entrance. Huge wooden doors once filled the archway to protect against enemy, but they were gone now. This castle was noticeably different from that of Old Castle. Old Castle was built with the outer fortifying walls enclosing the interior grounds and it had a centralized castle structure. This would have provided a place were villagers could go for protection. Orchards and gardens could be planted inside of the fortifying walls, and farm animals could be raised. The King as well as the villagers would have been able to fight off an invading enemy for a considerable time. The New Castle, on the other hand, provided no protection for the villagers. It was designed for the sole protection of the King. There are no large protected open areas, so it was not possible to raise crops or cattle. Under siege, the defense of the castle could only last as long as the stored food and goods lasted. The Old Castle had been built to defend the Kingdom, whereas, the New Castle was built as a grand, and highly defendable, residence for the King and his Court.

"We better walk from here," Carla said. "I don't know the rules."

They began the walk to the castle. As they got closer, they could see people scattered about the outer courtyard and near the large archway. The whole sight was breath taking. The lawns and gardens were beautiful and fragrant, as wonderful aromas came from the many different kinds of flowers. The huge castle structure stood mightily in the center of all the beauty. It was awesome. As a castle, it was extraordinary, but as the three of them began to realize, it was also the Academy and that was very exciting. All three of them suddenly stopped at the same time. With luck, and good test results, they would be living and studying there. They were speechless for a few moments as they tried to absorb it all. Then together, they marched the rest of the way up to the archway. They stopped to talk to the first group of kids they came upon.

There were two boys and a girl. The girl introduced herself as Debbie Vantalkin and the two boys as, Jeremiah Jetfoot and Ronald Lockhard. Debbie had shoulder length brown hair and golden brown eyes. She had lovely long eyelashes and a bright smile. Jeremiah was a short, but stocky built boy who was broad across the chest. He had well toned muscles and strong looking arms and hands. He had longish brown hair and his smile revealed a missing front tooth. Ronald was a dark complexioned lad of medium height and weight. He had dark curly hair and dark brown eyes. He had a well educated look about him.

"Everybody just calls me Jay-Jay," Jeremiah said as they all shook hands. "You come for the testing, eh?" You all better have your wits about you, there's some real sharpies here and they're only going to take the top thirty."

"We'll give it our best," Michael said. "Have you guys registered yet?"

"Yes," Ronald answered. "We just finished. It only takes a couple of minutes once you get to the desk, but we had to wait in line for a bit."

"What do we have to do?" asked Carla.

"Just go through the archway there to the inner courtyard," Debbie said. "There are a couple of lines formed up. Just get in either line, and when you get to the desk, they'll take your name and sign you up. They'll also assign you to a dormitory if you're going to stay here tonight. They'll give you your test schedule too."

With that, they wished each other good luck, and Carla and the two boys headed for the archway. Once they reached the inner courtyard, they saw the lines and got in the shorter of the two. Tommy was ahead of Michael and Carla in line when he noticed Debbie standing in line in front of him.

"Hi, Debbie," he said wondering how she got from outside and into the line ahead of them.

The girl turned around expecting to see someone she knew, but she didn't know Tommy. "Uh, hi," she said hesitantly.

"Say, how'd you get in here so fast?" Tommy asked somewhat confused.

The girl's face broke in a bright smile and she giggled. "Oh, I'm the twin. I'll bet you met my twin sister outside. Hi," she repeated, "I'm Debbie Kay; you probably met my sister Debbie Kaye outside."

"Wait a minute," Tommy said. "You're twins and you're both named Debbie Kay?"

"No," she said, "I'm Debbie Kay and my sister is Debbie Kaye."

If there was a difference, Tommy sure couldn't tell, but obviously, to Debbie Kay there was a difference. "Debbie Kay and Debbie Kay," Tommy questioned.

"Sort of," she said. "I'm Debbie Kay with no 'e' and my sister is Debbie Kaye with an 'e'."

Tommy thought he understood what she was saying. He smiled, put out his hand and said, "I'm Tommy Travail and it's a pleasure to meet you Debbie Kay with no 'e'."

Debbie Kay shook his hand and said, "Well it's a pleasure to meet you too, Tommy Travail." She smiled and by that time, it was her turn at the desk.

Tommy was concerned about the registration, but it went well. The young man at the desk, who looked as though he was a senior student, took Tommy's name, wrote it down and assigned him a dorm room and bed number. There was a buffet table set up in the courtyard for the prospective students and it was filled with many different kinds of food. When the three of them finished with registration, they helped themselves to a hearty meal. They studied their test schedules, and, to their delight, they all had the same schedule. They were going to have to start very early the next morning. They needed to be fresh for the tests, so they decided to find their dorms and turn in for the night. They left the courtyard, entered the castle through the main entrance and stepped into the Grand Foyer. It was a magnificent large circular room. The Grand Foyer was actually the bottom level of the tallest tower in the castle. On each side of the entrance was a wide staircase that curved around the room winding upward to the next level. At the next level was a large landing area with a balcony that extended out slightly toward the center of the tower structure. Opposite the balcony, a double wide staircase extended straight out and up. Tommy looked up and, just about as far as he could see, there were curving staircases. But given the angles involved, he couldn't see how they were connected nor could he see if there were other adjoining staircases. The walls along the staircases were lined with paintings of different Kings and Queens and other Royal Family members. A set of double doors were located under each staircase.

In the center of the Grand Foyer was a fountain. In the middle of the fountain was a large statue of a beautiful young woman wearing a crown. The artistic style of the statue didn't quite seem to go with the architectural style of the rest of the fountain. It looked as if the current statue may have replaced a previous statue or sculpture. They went together well, but there was a slight style difference and the statue had a fresher looking cut to it. The circular wall making up the fountain was capped with a wide flat stone that made a bench all the way around the fountain. Above the fountain and slightly above the second level, a chandelier hung from a cable. The cable stretched up as far as there were levels and there was a chandelier attached every couple of levels.

Directly across from the main entrance were two sets of double doors that led into the Main Hall. The two sets of doors were separated from each other by several feet. On the wall between them was a large framed and glass covered diagram of the Castle. It was done in four different views. There was a floor plan view, an aerial view, an exploded view and an inside out view. Above the frame it said, "CASTLE DIRECTORY".

"I think that will show us where we need to go," Carla said pointing to the Directory, and the three of them headed in that direction. "This is Queen Lucinda," she added as they passed the fountain and statue.

"Wow," Michael said. "She's pretty young."

"Oh," Carla said with a chuckle. "She's much older than that. She wasn't even really Queen when she was that young. When she was that young, her husband, King Richard, was still alive. I think it's got more to do with Her Royal Vanity than anything else."

They got to the Castle Directory and examined it. Across the top, it said, "NEW CASTLE," and, a line just below it said, "Lucinda 5660 Lw 06:41 day."

"Look," Carla said, "it gives the date and time."

Michael looked at his watch and reset it. "I don't think this things working right anymore," he said. "It keeps losing time."

They examined the floor plan view of the Directory. When they found the Grand Foyer and the spot where they were standing, they saw three little figures. As they looked further, they could see that the doors under the staircases led into rooms labeled temporary dormitories, with the girls' dorm being through the door to the right, and the boys' through the door to the left. Carla and the two boys said good night to each other and headed for their respective dormitories. As they moved, so did the little figures on Castle Directory. The little figures traced their steps until they past through the doors into their dormitories, then they disappeared.

Chapter Ten

Historical Problems

Newest Castle and Newest Castle City were vastly different from Old Castle and New Castle. Newest Castle City was a city. It was not the kind of city that Tommy or Michael would have been familiar with, but it was a city none the less. It was a planned city in what is known as the 'Water Drop Design'. From above, the city looked like the surface of water when it is struck with a single drop of water. In the center of the city was the circular castle complex. The complex was about a half mile in diameter with a roadway going all the way around it. Fifty additional roadways went in concentric rings around the city. The first road around the castle complex was lined with expensive retail shops, selling everything from the largest and most expensive gemstones to shops that carried the finest wands ever made. The second road out from the complex was called ambassadors row and was lined on one side with the foreign embassies from many of the known Realms. The other side of the road was the first row of very fancy and elegant houses. The houses and shops became smaller and of less quality the further the encircling roadway was from the central castle complex. The outer most roadway was exclusively for manufacturing.

There really wasn't a castle in the castle complex. The castle complex was comprised of many buildings of differing sizes and shapes. In the very center of it all was the largest structure. It was the closest thing to a castle in the complex. It rose stories above all the other buildings and it was designed to resemble the first rebounding splash in the 'Water Drop Design'. It looked similar to an upside down teardrop. This was the Queen's Palace. The whole complex was guarded by the Queen's Guard. But, unlike Old Castle and New Castle that were built with defense in mind, the Palace at Newest Castle could only put up minimal resistance to an invading enemy. Below the Palace was the thing that all three castles had in common, like Old Castle and New Castle, the Palace had a dungeon below it.

The Queen was beloved by most of the people of the Realm. Her husband, King Richard, had been the most popular King in the history of the Realm. All the people mourned with Queen Lucinda when he suddenly died, and their hearts went out to her when her son went mad shortly thereafter. It was kept very quiet within the Royal Court, but it is generally accepted that the Queen's son took his own life.

The Queen did have one enemy though, a very powerful enemy. A witch with extraordinary power had established herself in the mountains south of Old Castle and her only desire in life was to destroy the Queen. With intense passion, she dreamed of the day that she would strip the Queen of her disguises and burn her to a pile of ash. Her hatred of the Queen drove her to endure many hardships, but as she endured, she got stronger. She was able to gather supporters and protectors who helped her stay ahead of the Queen's forces. She knew that eventually she would get her chance with the Queen, and when she did, she would rain down on her with all the power she had and take her apart bit by bit.

While Michael, Tommy and Carla were bedding down for the night at the Academy, the Queen was meeting with her most trusted advisor, Victor Mordian, at her Palace. "The Ministry of All Things Magic recorded the disturbance in the magic flow yesterday morning," Advisor Mordian was explaining, "in the region of Old Castle. We dispatched two of our best agents to the area."

"And," the Queen interjected, "what have they discovered?"

"After making several inquires, all they found was a shattered and fallen fruit tree on the edge of your Majesty's orchard. It appears to have been hit by lightning, and that may have been the cause of the disturbance. Your Majesty's policemen reported two drunken boys and a young witch in the area at the time. We've been told that they have gone to the Academy for testing tomorrow and our agents are on their way there to question them. But so far, it doesn't look like that evil Witch had anything to do with it."

"That Witch," the Queen said bitterly, "her and her cauldron of black magic. When I get her, she'll spend the rest of her life in my dungeon. You're sure this isn't her work? You're sure it's not some new magic she's working on?"

"We will continue to investigate it, your Highness. But, it does look more like it had a natural cause," the Advisor replied reassuringly.

"I'm not so sure," the Queen said. "Something in the magic feels amiss. I want a full report on these children after they're questioned. They may need our protection if the Black Witch has tried to work her magic on them."

"Yes ma'am," the Advisor acknowledged. "They'll be questioned first thing in the morning and you will get the report immediately."

*

At the Academy, Carla and the boys were beginning to settle into their dormitories. Tommy and Michael's dormitory had fifty beds lined into rows. Tommy's bed assignment was twenty-six and Michael's was thirty-nine. The boys found their beds and got comfortable. Tommy lay back on his bed and began to think and make plans. After a while, he fell asleep, still fully dressed. Tommy slept well until he was awakened by sharp burning sensation on his chest. The earliest of morning light was beginning to shine through the windows and all the other boys were still asleep. He grabbed his chest and felt the medallion under his robe and sweater. He reached in and pulled it out. The back side of the medallion was glowing; Tommy turned it over and saw squiggly letters starting to form. He read the words as they formed. There were two separate messages. After reading what they said, he let the medallion fall back to his chest. He should have held on to the medallion for a moment longer because a third message appeared, but Tommy would never see it. He sat there for a moment unable to move. He then gathered himself together and went to find Michael.

"Come on, Michael," he said quietly. "You've got to wake up." He had to shake him a couple of times, but Michael opened his eyes and asked, "What's up? Is it time to get up already?"

"Yes," Tommy responded. "We gotta talk. Come on get up."

Michael sat up on his bed, "What's going on? Did you come up with a plan?" he asked in a haze, as he still wasn't fully awake.

"Yes," Tommy answered. "Sort of, more like the beginning of a plan, but we have to talk."

Michael got up. The two of them went into the bathroom, washed their faces with cold water, and freshened up as best as they could. They left the bathroom and crossed the Dormitory. Tommy opened the Dormitory door and stepped into the Grand Foyer. Partway across the foyer, in the entranceway to the Main Hall, was a man in a dingy gray cloak with a hood. He handed something to an older boy who was wearing a red robe and standing just inside the Main Hall. When they saw Tommy, the older boy stepped back behind the doorway and the gray cloaked man pulled his hood up to cover his face. The man with the gray cloak didn't appear to be wearing a wizard's robe. Tommy, with Michael following behind, went in the opposite direction and headed for the main entrance. The boys went out the door to the inner courtyard. They walked over to a far corner of the courtyard and Tommy began, "In the bigger picture we have to find my parents and a way back to our world."

"Wait a minute," Michael interrupted. "I've been thinking about it and I'm not going back. I don't have any reason to go back. I'm planning on staying right here."

Tommy frowned, and then said, "Whether you go back or not, we still need to find the way to our world. We need to know how to go back for our own safety."

"Safety?" questioned Michael. "I haven't seen anything dangerous here."

"I have something to tell you, but hear me out first. Like I said, finding my parents and a way home is what we need to do in time, but we also need to make some more immediate plans. First, we must pass these tests today. It will give us a place to live and we can do our research from here. Secondly, if we do pass our tests, than I think we should tell Carla."

"Tell her what," inquired Michael.

"Everything," Tommy answered. "First we swear her to secrecy, and then we tell her where we come from and how we got here. We tell her everything."

"Why would we want to do that?"

"Because," Tommy continued, "we don't know enough about this place and we're going to raise suspicions sooner or later. She can be, as she already has been, a great help for our survival here. And, I believe we can trust her. But, we'll only tell her if we pass the tests and get into the Academy."

"Agreed," said Michael with a level of uncertainty.

Tommy started, and then hesitated as the man in the dingy gray cloak came out the main entrance, strode across the courtyard and went out the big archway. Once he was out of sight, Tommy started again, "Now I have to tell you the worrisome part." Tommy took his time and told Michael how the medallion had awakened him. He told him how it glowed and how the message had formed on the back of it.

"What did it say," Michael asked impatiently.

"There were two messages. The first one said, 'You may be in mortal danger', and the second one said, 'The Black Witch knows you're here'."

"What the heck does that mean," asked Michael fearfully.

"I don't know," answered Tommy, "but, I don't think we should draw any attention to ourselves. We need to appear as just two ordinary guys that have come for the testing."

"Well that shouldn't be too hard," Michael quipped and then smiled.

"Our schedules call for us to have breakfast in the Main Hall this morning," Tommy said, "We've been out here for quite a while, maybe we should head back in."

They went back across the courtyard and reentered the Grand Foyer. They ran right into Carla.

"Where have you two been?" Carla questioned. "I've been looking for you everywhere. Everyone is starting to arrive for breakfast. Let's go and find a seat."

They entered the Main Hall from the Grand Foyer. It was a very large oval room. It comfortably held all of the students and test takers. It had a raised platform with a single long table with chairs that extended halfway around the outer walls on one end. Along the straight outer walls, temporary tables and chairs had been set up for those who had come to take the test. Filling the center of the room were the tables and chairs for the students who were already attending the school. Although the room was filling rapidly, one set of tables in the center area remained empty. The three of them found one of the outer tables where they could sit next to each other, and sat down. Most of the seats on the raised platform were filled with Professors wearing red robes. In the center of that table sat an elderly gray haired woman wearing a white sash over her red robe and a pointed black hat. She stood up and the room fell silent, except for a few murmurings coming for the test takers tables. They apparently didn't know better, but they too soon quieted.

"I would like to welcome all of the prospective students that have come here today for the testing," the gray haired woman said. She was tall and firmly built. She stood quite erect and proper as she spoke. "For those of you who are here to take the test, let me introduce myself, I am Griselda Grandforth, the Head Witch and Mistress of the Queen's Academy."

The room erupted in applause as all of the students stood up clapping their hands. There were three groups of students in the hall. There were the under study students and two groups of senior students, those in the Political School and those in the Military School.

"Please. Please take your seats," the Head Mistress said and motioned with her hands for the students to sit back down. "This is always an exciting day at the Academy and I am pleased to see so many prospective students here today. The tests will begin immediately after breakfast. I trust that you all have your schedules showing the locations and times of your tests. Make sure you consult the Castle Directories to locate the classrooms and other parts of the Castle. Remember, they change as the Castle changes. They are located in all the dormitories and throughout the Castle. They will always show you where you are and how to get to the Grand Foyer staircases. If you have any questions, ask one of the Prefects." She motioned with her hand and several students around the room stood up. They were all wearing red robes, girls and boys alike. She motioned again with her hand and they all sat back down. "Please don't bother the Professors with your questions," she continued. "The Prefects can help you with any problem. All of you will return here for lunch. The test results will be made available in the courtyard this afternoon along with the list of selected students who will become this year's class. All of you who are lucky enough to be selected will meet back here for our evening meal. I want to wish you all good luck and I hope to see you this evening." As everyone's attention was focused on the Head Mistress, no one noticed the two men in dark robes and cloaks that appeared in one of the doorways from the Grand Foyer, no one except the Head Mistress that is. "There is one other thing. Would Miss Carla Crosswell, Mister Tommy Travail and Mister Michael Woden please stand up?"

The three froze for a moment, and then reluctantly, they stood up. "So much for going unnoticed," Michael thought. Every pair of eyes in the entire hall was now looking at them, including the Professors. One of the cloaked men walked over to them.

"Who's who here?" the man asked when he got next to them. Tommy, Michael and Carla identified themselves. "Might as well start with you," he said pointing to Tommy. Tommy almost passed out. The man took Tommy by the arm and escorted him to the Grand Foyer. In the Foyer, a small table had been set up. It had two chairs on one side and a single chair on the other side. The man directed Tommy to sit in the single chair. He then went around the table and sat down across from Tommy. The second man joined them, but he remained standing. Tommy's heart was pounding so hard that he could hardly catch his breath. The seated man talked first. He asked Tommy about the morning two days ago at Old Castle. He asked him if he had seen or heard anything unusual that morning. Tommy thought fast and told the man that he really couldn't remember much of that morning. He told the man that he and his friend were coming here for the testing when they bought a bottle of Tinkleberry wine from a street vendor. After that, he didn't remember too much until they got to Carla's house. The man laughed slightly, and then asked him if he knew anything about a shattered and broken fruit tree. Tommy told him that he didn't recall seeing it, not that he could remember anyway.

"I don't think he knows anything," the standing man said to the seated one. "Okay," he said to Tommy, "you can return to your breakfast and send out the other boy."

Tommy got up and headed back to the Main Hall. "They sure take damaging their fruit trees seriously around here," he thought.

When he entered the Main hall, all the tables were filled with food and everyone seemed to be having a good time, all except Michael and Carla of course. Michael was stuffing his face with everything he could get his hands on. He seriously thought that this might be his last meal.

"They want to see you next," Tommy said as he approached Michael. Then he added under his breath, "Coming here for the test… vendor, Tinkleberry wine, don't remember anything until Carla's house. Play dumb." Tommy sat down and Michael got up and went to the Foyer.

"What's it all about," Carla asked anxiously.

"I'm not sure, but I think they're looking for the person who destroyed the fruit tree at Old Castle," Tommy answered. "I told them I didn't see or notice anything until I got to your house. I told them it was the Tinkleberry wine." Carla laughed a little as she remembered how the boys looked when she first saw them. "I don't think we should tell them anything, if we can avoid it."

"I agree," said Carla. "Don't worry, I can handle this."

Michael returned with a smile of relief on his face, "It went okay. They want you now, Carla."

"Is she going to be cool?" Michael asked as soon as Carla was gone.

"I have no doubt," Tommy responded. The two boys turned their attention to the food and ate well while Carla was gone.

Carla exited the Main Hall into the Foyer and saw the two men at the table. In her sort of bouncy way, she pranced up to the table and sat down.

One man was still seated and the other remained standing. "We're here to ask you about the morning two days ago at the Old Castle," the seated man informed her.

"Oh yes," Carla started. "That was a beautiful morning. I decided to take a wave ride that morning. I'm special, you know. I popped early so I've been wave riding for ages. Anyway, as I was saying, that stretch of road by the Old Castle and the Queen's Orchard is so nice in the morning, I can't resist taking a ride down there whenever I can. So I was just cruising along when I come across the boys. They had just had a night with the Tinkleberry wine. That stuff's really not very good for you, you know. They looked a sight and were a little confused, so, with great effort on my part, I helped them to get to my house in Old Castle Village. My father, he's the Master Wizard of the Village, you know."

"Yes," said the man that was standing. "We talked with him."

"Well, like I was saying," Carla went on without hesitating. "I got the boys to my house and they were coming here for the testing, so my father invited them to spend the night as our guests as I was coming here myself the next day. Then the next morning…"

"Wait," interrupted the seated man. "That morning at Old Castle, did you see or hear anything unusual?" Did you notice a damaged tree in the Queen's Orchard?"

"Nope, can't say I did," Carla answered. "Like I told you, I had my hands full with those two boys. I wouldn't drink that Tinkleberry wine, if I were you. So anyway, the next morning we …"

"I think we've heard enough," said the standing man. "You can go back to your breakfast and your friends."

Carla stood up and kind of skipped her way back to the Main Hall. As she did, she heard one man tell the other, "I told you this would be a waste of time."

She returned to the Main Hall and promptly said, "Not a problem," before either of the boys could ask. She was just beaming. Carla had just enough time for some tea and toast before they had to leave for the first test. They checked their schedules. There were seven tests. Each test was limited to thirty minutes with a five minute break between to change classrooms. The tests would take four hours. There would be tables set up between classrooms with snacks and drinks for the kids as they changed classrooms. Their first test was 'Diction and Communication Skills' with Professor Colette Clearvoice testing. Carla finished her toast and the three of them departed for their first test. After consulting one of the Castle Directories, they found their first classroom and took a seat.

Professor Clearvoice introduced herself once everyone was seated. She then started passing out test papers. "This test," she began, "is a timed test. It is expected that you will *not* be able to complete it. Complete as much as you can. It is more important to answer the questions correctly, than it is to answer all the questions. If anyone doesn't have a pencil, or if you break your pencil during the test, I have extra pencils at my desk." The prospective students were going to hear those instructions six more times before they finished the testing that morning. Tommy and Michael went to the desk and they each took a pencil. Once they returned to their seats, the Professor said, "If everyone is ready," she paused for a moment, and then continued, "you may begin."

Thirty minutes later, Carla, Tommy and Michael emerged from the classroom. Michael and Carla were smiling, but Tommy was frowning. "What's the matter Tommy Boy," Michael said. "I thought that was pretty easy."

"So did I," Tommy said. "It's the *next* test that I'm worried about. It's 'Home History- Truth and Lies' with Professor Landon Pastorie testing. It's a history test."

"So," Michael questioned.

Tommy tried to indicate that he didn't want to say too much in front of Carla. "Its history, you either know it, or *you don't know it*."

Michael's eyes widened a bit and then he frowned a bit. Tommy could see that Michael understood. History is a collection of facts about the past. Since they knew almost nothing about the past of this place, it was going to be very difficult for them to pass this test.

"Guess," Michael said pointedly. "Just use your best judgment and guess. It's the only thing we can do."

"I *guess* you're right," Tommy replied and then chuckled at his own joke.

Thirty minutes later they were leaving the classroom and the boys were sweating. They had done their best, but neither of the boys felt there was much of a chance of passing. Carla, however, was smiling.

The next test was, 'Basic Strategy and Tactics for the Military and Political Arenas' with Professor Ambrost Krusher testing. The three of them stopped at one of the snack tables and took a snack pack and a drink with them to the next classroom. On their way, they ran into the Vantalkin twins. The twins, like everybody else, except Carla that is, didn't want to talk about their performance. Tommy and Michael expected to do well on the Strategy and Tactics test and when it was finished, they were both smiling.

The fourth test was 'Practical Magic' with Professor Catherine Lightwood testing. "Say Carla," Tommy asked as they approached the next classroom, "do you think we know enough about magic to get through this next test?"

"I imagine so," Carla responded. "I wouldn't expect a high mark, but you should do okay. If they have a bonus essay question, do it on wave riding. You'll probably be able to pick up a couple of extra points there." Bonus questions had been on all the tests so far. They took the test and, indeed, there was a bonus essay question. Both boys did as Carla had suggested. When the test was over, they both felt as though they had passed.

The fifth test, 'Social Skills in a Polite Society,' with Professor Gertrude Grumble testing, was fairly easy. Everyone was feeling good and they only had two more tests to go. The boys didn't foresee any real problems with the last two tests: 'The Natural and Theoretical Sciences' with Professor Cecil Welkin testing, and, 'Numbers and Abstractions' with Professor Albert Boardman testing. They were very good in these subjects. Although they knew the tests would be difficult, they were sure they would do well.

Carla had been exuberant all day. She felt she was doing well on every test and, in her own sweet and unique way, she had been showing it. After the last two tests, Tommy and Michael were feeling the same way. They felt that they had done superbly on the science and math tests, and, what was even more uplifting was the fact that they were finished.

"I'm starved," said Michael as they left the last classroom. "How long 'till lunch?"

"We've got fifteen minutes to go back to our dormitories and freshen up before we have to return to the Main Hall," Carla answered. "I'll see you guys there," and in her bouncy way, she left.

Chapter Eleven

Results and Consequences

Michael and Tommy went back to their dorm. Both boys took the opportunity to wash up with some cool water. It helped to rejuvenate them. Afterward, on the way to the Main Hall, they discussed the tests. They both felt that they did well on everything, but the history test. The History test involved so much guess work that there was no way to know how they had done. Carla was waiting for them at the entrance to the Main Hall. They went in and the outer tables that seated the test takers were buzzing with chatter. Throughout the testing, everybody had been reluctant to talk, but now there was an explosion of conversations. It was as if everybody was talking to everybody else at the same time. The excitement in the air was stimulating and with Carla leading the way, they were soon caught up in it. Everyone wanted to know how everyone else did. They were all calculating their chance of being selected.

The Professors were not present; presumably, they were scoring the tests. The Head Mistress came in and took her position at the main table. The commotion began to settle. She raised her hand and the room fell silent. "I have very exciting news," she began. "The Queen has decided that she will make this year's selections. Being selected by the Queen is quite an honor, one that you can carry with you throughout your time here at the Academy. I will expect great things from each one of you. As exciting as this is, it does change the plan for this afternoon. We will not be able to post the test scores and the

David G. Groesbeck

selections at the same time. Instead, we will post the test results just as soon as they become available and we'll immediately send a copy of them to the Queen. Once she makes her selections, she will notify the Academy and we will post them. I can't tell you how long you may have to wait, so be patient. We will do our best to get the selection lists out to the courtyard as quickly as we can. For now, enjoy your meal, and once again, good luck to you all." With that, she sat down and food began to appear on the tables.

The boys thought that this might be their last free meal, so they ate well. They were almost the last ones to leave the Main Hall. Tommy had been watching the temporary tables. Once a table was vacated, the remaining food and dirty dishes disappeared. The table then folded itself up and blended into the wall. Tommy looked at Michael and saw that Michael had been watching the tables as well. They looked at each other and just sort of shook their heads. Carla and the boys left the Main Hall and went out to the courtyard. They found an uncrowded corner by a flower garden and sat down. Tommy asked Carla if she knew how the tests were graded. She told them there were four possible grades. The highest grade was 'Of Queen's Notice'. She told them that to get an OQN they had to get all the answers correct, plus they had to get full credit for all bonus questions. The second highest grade was 'Superior', followed by 'Acceptable' and then the lowest grade was 'Poor'. She told them that a Poor would probably exclude anybody from entrance to the Academy.

They hadn't been waiting long when a bell rang out with a single chime. It was the notice that the scores were going to be released. And released they were; a window opened above the courtyard and a stream of paper spewed out, one sheet after another. In moments, they were floating to all areas of the courtyard. Everyone was scrambling to get a hold of one. One landed right at Carla's feet and she picked it up. She looked at it and a broad smiled spread across her face. One floated near Tommy and he grabbed it. Carla's smiling face turned sad and tears started to form in her eyes. Tommy looked at his sheet and Michael took Carla's sheet from her hand. Almost instantly, frowns appeared on their faces. Michael and Tommy both got Poor on their history test. They had not done a very good job of guessing. Carla grabbed another sheet as it floated by.

They all studied their sheet for a while. Two things became apparent right away. One was that Carla and another girl, Abigale Antwerp, were tied for the highest score. They both received six OQN's and a Superior in 'Strategy and Tactics'. The second apparent thing was that Tommy and Michael had the lowest score. Although Tommy got OQN's in 'math' and 'science', and Michael got OQN's in 'science' and 'strategy and tactics', they were the only one's to have received a Poor.

"Well, now what," Michael said with great disappointment.

"I don't know," Tommy replied. "We might as well get ready to hit the road. There's no reason for us to hang around here any longer."

"Oh please don't go yet," Carla begged as she wiped the tears from her cheeks. "Please don't go until the selections come. I can't bear the idea of us splitting up. I'm going to miss you guys so much. Please wait with me. We can use the time to talk about your options. You know you can take the test twice, so next year you could try again. And, maybe I can teach you some magic that will help you on your journey."

"The truth is," Tommy began. "We don't want to leave you either, Carla." Tommy looked at Michael, and he nodded in agreement. "So, we'll wait with you." The extra score sheets that hit the ground began disappearing.

"Let's go outside the archway where we can have some privacy," Carla suggested as she got up. The boys followed her out of the courtyard to the outside lawns. They found a nice place under a tree and sat down.

"Okay," she said. "Take out your wands and I'll try to teach you how to make a metal." They took out their wands. "Let's try to make copper. Most people find it the easiest. When I tell you, point your wands at the ground and close your eyes. Try to imagine the metal. Imagine the way it looks and the way it feels. Imagine it has a scent. Now, imagine that you are forming the metal in the palm of your wand hand. See it taking shape. See the color. Once you can see and feel it in your hand, imagine you are squeezing it from your hand into your wand. Will it into the wand. Then energize it and push it out the end of the wand. Okay, give it a try."

They did as she instructed. After a few minutes, Michael had a few spits of energy come from the end of his wand, but nothing formed. Tommy wasn't having any luck either. Nothing was happening at all. He felt that he was probably too distracted with their failure on the tests and difficulties that they were now going to have to face. He really couldn't get his mind to focus on copper, and he knew that was part of the problem. A thought occurred to him and he reached under his sweater and put his hand around the medallion. He instantly felt a surge go through his body. He squeezed the medallion and felt its warmth. He imagined the shining gold finish. With a massive build up of magical energy, he directed his wand toward the ground. Light and energy came from the wand and a large pool of gold formed.

"Wow," Carla declared. "That's not copper. That's gold, and enough of it to buy supplies for a hundred light waves, or more."

The expenditure of magic energy left Tommy feeling weak, not physically weak; it was more like feeling weak of spirit or soul. He just felt drained.

"Do it again," Carla said excitedly.

"I can't," Tommy replied. "I feel like the life has been pulled out of me."

"Oh yes," Carla said understandingly. "It'll take a while, but you'll recover." She reached into her little bag, pulled out some Chewy Chew Chews, and gave them to him. "Munch on these. They'll help."

Michael's eyes were wide and his mouth was open. "Well, that'll solve one of our problems," he said as he picked up the chunk of now solid, but still warm, gold.

The three of them just sat there for some time while Tommy recovered and Michael played with the hunk of gold. Carla took out her bag and pulled a mirror out of it. She tapped the mirror a couple of times with her wand, then using her wand to write with she started a message to her father

"What's that," Michael inquired.

"It's a message mirror," Carla answered. "I'm going to write my dad and…" The bell rang one time interrupting her. "Well, I guess this is it," she said as she stood up. Tommy and Michael didn't move. "Are you guys coming?'

"No," Tommy responded. "You go ahead and we'll wait here."

The Life and Times of Tommy Travail

They were not too far from the big arch and Carla headed for it and the courtyard. When she got there, it was bedlam. Two very powerful emotions were erupting everywhere. There was great joy and great sadness. Some kids were shouting and whistling, while others were frowning, some were even crying. Carla grabbed one of the papers as it flew by. She studied it for a few minutes, then turned around and headed back out the big arch.

Tommy saw Carla coming back. As she came toward him, she was smiling and doing that half bouncy, half skip thing she did. For a moment, Tommy resented her happiness. Then, he realized that she had a right to be happy. She had done exceptionally well on her tests and now she was about to begin her lifelong dream of following in her parents footsteps. "Good for her," he thought as she got near him and Michael.

"Here," she said when she got within arms length. "You wanna look at this?"

"Not really," Tommy replied with discouragement in his voice.

"Well, don't you at least want to see who made it?" she asked.

"I guess," replied Tommy as Michael moved closer so that they could both see the single sheet of paper.

The names were in alphabetical order. At the top of the list was, Antwerp, Abigale. Tommy scanned down the page and saw, Crosswell, Carla and, further; Firefist, Kristy followed by Firefist, Misty. Then there was Jetfoot, Jeremiah and Lockhard, Ronald. Tommy scanned further down the page and froze. There it was, as impossible as it could be, Travail, Tommy. His eyes jumped down the page, past the Vantalkin twins and, sure enough, it was there too; Woden, Michael. Michael and Tommy looked at one another with confused looks on their faces, then, they both looked at Carla with inquisitive looks.

Carla shrugged her shoulders and said, "Don't ask me." And then a big smile spread across her face and she started to laugh. The boys joined in. Carla fell to the ground with laughter and excitement. The three of them rolled around, laughing and shouting. Tommy's and Michael's wands lay on the ground along with the chunk of gold. Mister Buttercup strode up and sat down next to them.

"What do you think happened?" Tommy asked as he tried to control himself.

"I don't know," Carla answered. "Maybe you did so well on one of your other tests that the Academy was willing to over look the History thing. You both got a couple of OQN's."

"But," Tommy said, "It wasn't the Academy that made the selections, it was the Queen."

"Oh, but I'm sure they probably advised her. Don't you think?" Carla suggested.

"Could be," Michael said. "But all I know is that, I'm happy."

Tommy and Michael noticed three kids standing just outside the arch. There was a tall boy. He had on a red robe with gold piping on the cuffs. He looked old enough to be called a young man. He had short cropped light brown hair. His nose was narrow with a sharp ridge and a little longer than normal. His sharp gray eyes were narrow and he had a firm ridged jaw line. Next to him stood an older girl; and next to her, was a younger girl. The younger girl looked very sad and it appeared that she had been crying. The older girl was pointing at them. They started walking toward them. As they got closer, Tommy recognized the older boy as the one he saw that morning with the gray cloaked man. When they were about halfway to them, the older boy said, "Travail, Woden." Carla instinctively slipped the chunk of gold under her robe. Then, when they got within a few feet, he said it again, "Travail, Woden."

"Yeah," Tommy said.

The boy reached under his sleeve and pulled out his wand. With a brief flick of his wrist, Tommy and Michael were snapped upright into a standing position. "When your name is called by anyone wearing a red robe, you will automatically stand up, without hesitation. Do I make myself clear?" Both boys said yes with quite a bit of shock in their voices. "And, you will address every superior by title, or with a sir or ma'am. Have you got that?"

"Yes, sir," responded both boys.

"Now tell me," the tall boy went on. "Just what makes you two so special?"

"Uh," Tommy said as he and Michael looked at each other. "We're not special. We're just two ordinary guys."

"Well is that so," the boy said rhetorically. "My name is Reginald Whitelace. See the girl next to me? This is my girlfriend, Eva Hasselback, and that girl standing next to her is her younger sister Melody. As you can see Melody is very unhappy, which makes Eva unhappy. And, when Eva's unhappy, I'm unhappy. Do you know why Melody is so unhappy?"

"No, uh, sir," Tommy stuttered.

"Well I'll tell you why she is so unhappy. You see, she got better scores than you did and she should have been accepted to the Academy, but for some reason, you two with your dismal scores were selected and she was bumped. So, I ask you again, what makes you so special?"

"Nothing," Tommy started. "We're just a couple of ordinary guys that came for the testing, uh, sir."

"Well for some reason, you two are on this year's list and Melody is not. And, I'm going to find out why."

"Oh look, Reggie," Eva said as she spotted the boys wands. "They're using baby wands. Now isn't that cute." Reginald laughed slightly. Eva giggled. Melody however, continued to pout.

"I don't know what you two are about," Reginald continued, "but, I don't think I like it, so, I'm going to be watching you two, and you better be following the rules. Let me put it this way, just so there can be no misunderstanding: if, by chance, either of you, or maybe even both of you, were to be expelled; well, then little Melody here, she just might get called back to this year's class. Am I making myself perfectly clear?"

"Yes, sir," both boys responded.

Reginald took a slow look at each boy from head to toe, then turned to Eva and said, "I don't think it will be too long before these losers are out of here; one way or another. Come on, let's go." The three of them turned around and headed back toward the courtyard.

"Wow," Tommy said, "that wasn't too cool. Who does that guy think he is anyway?"

"He's a Prefect," Carla said. "My dad told me to be on my best behavior around the Prefects. He said the Military School Prefects are the worst and the more senior they are, the worse they get. Did you see those two gold pins on his collars?"

"Yeah," answered Tommy.

"Well," Carla continued. "The one on his right collar is for the Military School, and the one on his left collar, the one with the two bars, that indicates this is his second year; in other words, the worst of the worst."

"We sure are keeping a low profile," Michael popped in sarcastically.

"Ah, forget him," Tommy said. "We're in and that's all that matters right now." All three of them smiled and Mister Buttercup chimed in with a meow. "Now that we are in," Tommy continued, "there is something important that we have to do." Tommy looked at Michael and Michael nodded. "Carla," he started. "We need your help, but first we have to tell you something and you have to promise to keep it a secret. Can you promise to keep our secret?"

"Hey, of course," Carla responded. "Just two ordinary guys and one special girl, friends for life, right?"

"Right," Tommy and Michael responded simultaneously.

"This is serious, though," Tommy continued. "This really must be kept secret."

"You have my word," Carla pledged.

"This is going to sound fantastic, but we're not from here," Tommy began.

"Ah, no kidding," Carla interrupted. "You're from somewhere around Brookfield."

"That's not quite what I meant," Tommy continued. "We're not from this place you call Home. We're from a different kind of place. We call it Earth. That's our home." In a very general way, he told her a little bit about his world. He told her it was a non-magical place, or at least he had always thought of it as a non-magical place until they discovered the wand and the mirror.

Carla had been listening intensely with a wide eyed expression on her face until Tommy mentioned the wand and the mirror, and then she frowned slightly. When Tommy told her that he and Michael had used the wand and mirror to transport here, she really frowned. "Why would you guys do this to me?" she suddenly asked. "I thought we were friends and could trust one another. Why would you pull this kind of joke on me?"

"This isn't a joke," Tommy pleaded.

"Of course it is. It's the Foundation Legend," Carla said firmly. "Didn't you think I'd recognize it? You're making up a story around the Foundation Legend and trying to get me to believe it."

"Honest Carla," Tommy said softly. "It is the truth… but maybe you should tell us about this Foundation Legend."

"If this is a joke," Carla started, "I'm really gonna be mad."

"Honest," Michael tried to reassure her. "We wouldn't try to make fun of you. Please, tell us about the Foundation Legend."

"Well," she started again. "Every kid knows about the Foundation Legend, even before they start school. It's the story of Erlin, the first one of our kind to arrive here. Some of it might be true, but most of it is considered myth. Erlin was a wizard in another dimension. We call it the Other Place. He and a witch named Griselda built two mirrors. They cast great magic onto the mirrors and Erlin used one mirror to transport himself here. He brought the second mirror with him to use for his return to the Other Place. When he arrived here, this land was occupied by the Kindlewalkers."

"Aren't they the ones that destroyed Old Castle?" asked Tommy.

"Yes," Carla answered. "The Kindlewalkers were fire throwers. They welcomed Erlin when he arrived and provided him with food and shelter. Erlin lived with them for some time before returning to the Other Place. When he came back here, he had Griselda with him. In time, many more people came from the Other Place. A few who came found that they had no magic abilities at all. But, for some reason, most of those who came here from the Other Place had an extraordinary ability to control the magic. Many of them became great Wizards and Witches. They found that when they returned to the Other Place, their magic went with them. The Legend says that many witches and wizards regularly traveled between Home and the Other Place. In time, Erlin and Griselda built the village and the castle at Old Castle. This all made the Kindlewalkers very nervous and occasionally hostilities would break out between the two peoples. Eventually Erlin and Griselda died. Several generations came and went, and then, a great war erupted in the Other Place between the magical and the non-magical people. Numerous witches and wizards were killed. Many of those who escaped death, returned here. The legend says the King at the time destroyed Erlin's Mirror to stop the war from spreading here. The sudden growth of our people here created a situation that was unacceptable to the Kindlewalkers. A long and bloody war erupted. We eventually won the war, but not through military might. The war was won through political diplomacy. From then on, the Royal Court of every Monarch has been equally divided between the Political section and the Military section."

Carla paused to gather her thoughts. "So," she said after a few moments, "that's the Foundation Legend. Some of the Legend we believe to be true, but a fair amount of it is myth. Since Home is infinite in size, most people believe that Erlin and Griselda simply came from one of the more distant regions of Home."

"Carla," Tommy said, "I don't know how much of the Foundation Legend is true, but we really did find one of Erlin's mirrors, and we really did use it to come here. I can't tell you that we come from the Other Place, but from what you just told us, I think we did. My father was from here and traveled to my world. He met my mom there and I was born there. Michael and his family are from there. That's why we need your help. We don't know anything about this place."

"Well," Carla said slowly. "That's pretty unbelievable. I'm going to have to think about this for a bit. But first, I want to finish my letter to my dad. And, it's almost time for us to go to dinner, so when I finish, we can go get something to eat. That'll give me some time to think about all of this." The boys said okay and Carla picked up her message mirror and cleared the message she started earlier.

"Dear Father," She wrote. "I got six OQN's and a Superior in 'Strategy and Tactics', one more OQN than you and Mom got. Tied for the highest score. I'm in. Send my trunk and things. Michael and Tommy got in too. Tell you more later. Love, Carla." She tapped the mirror with her wand; the message blinked once, and then disappeared.

"Okay, I'm ready to go," Carla said as she picked up Tommy's pool of gold and put it in the bag she kept under her robe. "I'll keep this for you until you have someplace to put it," she said, and Tommy agreed. They got up, went through the courtyard to the main entrance, and entered Grand Foyer.

Chapter Twelve

Rules and Code of Conduct

Carla and the boys crossed the Grand Foyer and entered the Main Hall. The temporary tables and chairs were gone. The table in the center of the room that had been vacant all day, now had a stack of papers at each place setting along with a name tag. The table was long and had fifteen chairs on each side. Michael and Tommy had no difficulty finding their name tags. They were the first seats on each side of the table as they approached it. They began looking for Carla's name tag. The boys went down one side of the table and Carla went down the other. It wasn't until they got all the way to the other end of the table, the end closest to the raised area where the Professors sat, that they found Carla's name tag. Directly across from her seat was Abigale Antwerp's name tag. There was a pretty girl sitting in the seat. She had long blond hair with just the slightest curl to it. She had bright blue eyes, but they were somewhat hidden by the glasses she wore. She had a cute small nose and smooth lips. She smiled as they approached. They all introduced themselves, then Michael and Tommy excused themselves so that they could return to their own seats.

The room filled in no time at all. Jeremiah Jetfoot, 'Jay-Jay', sat next to Michael and Debbie Kay Vantalkin sat next to Tommy. There was quite a rumble of conversations going on around the room, but the moment the Head Mistress stood up, the room fell silent. "I would like to congratulate our successful candidates and welcome you as this year's new class. You will find a stack of papers in front of you that contains a number of very important items. The first thing you will see is the Academy's 'Rules and Code of Conduct Manual'. Read this manual and commit it to memory. The Prefects will test you on it. Next, you will find your schedule of classes. In general, you will all attend classes together for your first three school years. Some exceptions will be made for students who are ready for more advanced training. They may be permitted to attend some classes with a more advanced year," She said this while she was looking directly at Carla and Abigale. "But," she continued, "for the most part, you'll attend classes together. You will also be sharing the same dormitory. There are five dormitories all together and you will be staying in Crow's Nest. This will be your dormitory for the next three years, then, of course, you'll be moving into the Political or Military dormitory. If you have left anything in the temporary dormitories, please remove it as soon as you've finished your meal. The rooms will be changing tonight."

The Head Mistress paused and then continued. "You will be on 'Academy Time' while you are here. That is, each light wave is divided into twenty-six hours, and each hour is divided into sixty-five minutes. There are thirteen 'day' hours and thirteen 'night' hours. Thirteen o'clock 'day' is when the light wave is at its brightest and thirteen o'clock 'night' is when the light wave is at its darkest... Just as a side note, you may have noticed that 'Academy Time' seems to be catching on around the Realm."

"So much for my watch," Michael whispered to Tommy.

"The Academy week is six light waves long," the Head Mistress continued. "You will attend classes for five days and then have one day without classes. You will attend five semesters per school year of ten weeks each. Between each semester, you will have a two week break, except at the end of the fifth semester, when you will have a four week break between class years. Tomorrow is a no class day. We do this so that you might go into New Castle Town or Cantwell and get the supplies, books and the other items you will need. You'll find a list of those things attached to your class schedules. Enjoy your day in town as the following day you'll begin classes. And, with the amount of homework you will have to do on future no class days, it may be a while before you get a chance to go back into town."

The Life and Times of Tommy Travail

The Head Mistress took a deep breath. Looking directly at Tommy and Michael she began, "Today you have proven, by your excellent scores, that you have completed your basic educations. As you know we don't teach the fundaments here at the Queen's Academy, we teach <u>magic</u>!" She waved her hand out across her body and thousands of multicolored butterflies spewed forth. Their brilliant colors glowed brightly and they soon filled the room. They fluttered about to the 'oohs and aahs' of the students. One by one, they flicked and disappeared. "As for now," she said with a smile, "eat and enjoy yourselves. Classes begin the day after tomorrow."

The room erupted in applause and the Head Mistress sat down. The applause died down and food began appearing on the tables along with plates and silverware. If the new students didn't move their stack of papers quickly enough, their plates appeared on top of their papers. The Head Mistress then stood back up and said, "Mister Travail and Mister Woden." She then paused. The boys were so stunned by their names being called for a second time in front of the entire class body that they didn't move.

Reginald Whitelace stood up and looked directly at the boys. His piercing gray eyes glared at them. "Travail and Woden," he said very firmly, "what did I tell you about standing when your name is called? You will both stand up immediately."

Tommy and Michael shot to their feet. "I would like the two of you come up and see me," the Head Mistress directed. Whitelace sat down. The two boys walked the length of their table. Carla gave them an inquisitive look when they got to the end of the table. Tommy just shrugged his shoulders. They approached the Head Mistress. "I don't know why the Queen selected you two," she began. She spoke softly so the other students wouldn't hear, however, the authority of her voice remained firm. "We have never had a student here before that scored less than a Superior on any test, and now I have *two* who only managed a poor on their History tests… and we can't have that! So, I've talked to Professor Pastorie and he agreed to hold a remedial class just for the two of you. When he's satisfied with your progress, he will give you the History test again. The scores you earn on the second test will become your test scores of record. I will expect at least a Superior out of each of you. Since the Professor will also be teaching your 'Historical Magic' class, you can see him then and set up the schedule for your remedial History classes. Understand?"

"Yes ma'am," Tommy said.

"Yes ma'am," Michael repeated.

"Okay," the Head Mistress said. "You may return to your seats. And, remember what I said, no less than a Superior." Both boys nodded and started back to their seats.

Carla gave Tommy that same inquisitive look as he approached her. "Everything's okay," he reassured her as he passed by. "We just have to take an extra class. Tell ya later."

Michael and Tommy returned to their seats. Everyone was eating, joking and, basically, having a good time. "What was that all about," Jay-Jay asked as they sat down.

"Oh just some extra class work we're going to have to do," Michael answered. "It's no big deal."

Tommy turned to Debbie Kay Vantalkin and asked her where her twin sister was. "Oh," she replied, "she's up there a ways. See her? She's about a quarter of the way from the front." She paused and then added, "You know, I'm the one with the good looks and she's the one with the brains."

Tommy looked at her with an odd expression on his face, and then, realizing that she was having a bit of fun with him, he began to smile and then laughed. They both laughed. Tommy began filling his plate. "Do you think that we'll have to sit in these same seats all the time," he asked as sort of a general question to anyone who was listening.

"Don't think so," Jay-Jay said. "Don't remember my brother ever saying anything about assigned seats."

"We better not," Debbie Kay cut in. "I want to sit with my sister."

"Like I said," Jay-Jay repeated. "I don't think so. I think it's just for this orientation."

They got to know one another a little better as they ate. The boys learned that Jay-Jay had an older brother who graduated from the Military Section the previous year and that both of Debbie Kay's parents had graduated from the Political Section. Tommy and Michael were just about finished when Carla came up and tapped Tommy on the shoulder.

"Are you guys about done," she asked when he turned around.

"Just finishing," Tommy answered. "You're ready to go, I take it."

"Yeah," she replied. "We should go. We've got a lot to talk about."

The boys took their final bites and excused themselves and, following Carla, they left the Main Hall. Carla suggested that they find their dormitory, so they consulted the Castle Directory in the Grand Foyer. Three little figures appeared on the Directory. "The Castle is enchanted," Carla said. "Abigale told me. She said it changes to fit the Academy's needs. See, the temporary classrooms where we took our tests today are gone." The boys looked at the floor plan, and sure enough, the temporary classrooms were no longer appearing anywhere. It took them a while to find the Crow's Nest dormitory, but when they found it, they understood the name. It was located on the top two floors of one of the corner towers. It wasn't the tallest tower, the Grand Foyer tower was the tallest, but it was the largest in circumference.

"How do we get there?" Michael asked.

"Heck if I know," Tommy responded. The three of them puzzled over the directory for a few minutes. A fourth little figure appeared on the directory.

"Trying to find our dormitory?," said a voice from behind them. They turned around and it was Abigale.

"No," Carla answered. "We've found the dormitory alright, but we can't quite figure out how to get there." Carla pointed toward Crow's Nest.

"Oh," Abigale said. "Let me show you. A Prefect showed me earlier today. All you have to do is touch the place you want to go to." More little figures were appearing on the Directory. Abigale touched the Crow's Nest with the tip of her finger. Suddenly thin blue lines appeared across all four diagrams. Little white flashing triangles appeared every so often along the lines. "See," she said. "All you need to do is follow the line. The little triangles indicate the locations of other Castle Directories. If you can't remember the whole route, you can just go from Directory to Directory."

"That's pretty cool," Tommy said.

"Yeah," Michael agreed.

"Shall we go," Abigale asked.

"I think we're going to have to study this a bit," Tommy said.

"No," Abigale said confidently, "I got it."

"Are you sure?" asked Carla.

"Yep," Abigale responded. "Guaranteed."

They turned around and saw that a number of their classmates had joined them at the Directory. "Oh," Abigale said in surprise as she saw the other students. She paused for the briefest of moments and then said, "If everyone's looking for the Crow's Nest, I'll lead the way, if you want." There was a general agreement and they all set off with Abigale in the lead.

They went up stairs, down hallways, back down some stairs and around what seemed like endless corners. Tommy made them stop twice at Directories to make sure they were on track, and each time Abigale was dead on. Finally, after going up a series of circular staircases, they arrived at the door to their dormitory. They all stopped and stared. The massive wooden door was covered with door knobs. There were big ones and small ones. Some were round and some were levers. Some were made of crystal and some were made from precious metals. Abigale tried one of the door knobs and nothing happened. She tried several others, and the door still did not open. Sometimes when she turned a knob, one, two or more other knobs turned.

"Let me have a go at that," said a voice from the group. "I'm pretty good with mechanical things. And, I know a charm that will open some locked doors." It was Ronald Lockhard. He stepped forward and took out his wand. While pointing it at the door and making a circle he said, "Turning tumblers, tumble and turn." There was a resounding "BOINK" sound and nothing happened. "Oh well," Ronald said, "it doesn't work all the time." He studied the door knobs for a few minutes and then tried several of them without luck.

"Castle," Abigale suddenly said with quite a bit of authority. "This is Abigale Antwerp and the Queen's Class." Clearly, Abigale had been thinking about a class name, and she was right, they were the Queen's Class. "Show us how to open the door," she ordered.

In a random fashion, the doorknobs began to flash on and off with a blue glow. As one went out, another one lit up, and then went out. It gave the appearance that the light was moving about the door. Finally, one doorknob lit up and stayed lit. However, the flashing

The Life and Times of Tommy Travail

continued until eventually a second knob lit and stayed lit, and then the flashing stopped. The two knobs continued to glow and a small curved arrow now appeared above each knob, one curved to the left and the other turned to the right.

"Can everyone see which doorknobs are lit and the direction the arrows are pointing?" Abigale asked. There was some shuffling about, but it seemed that everyone had a chance to see which two were glowing. Abigale then grabbed and turned both doorknobs simultaneously. She turned the knob in her left hand to the left and the one in her right hand to the right. Every door knob on the door turned, some turned clockwise and some turned counter clockwise. There was a loud, massive "CLUNK" and the door popped open. A cheer went up from the group.

"Ya hoo," said a voice from the back. "It's about time."

"Nice thinking Abigale," said another voice.

Carla patted Abigale on the back and said, "Lead the way. You're doing pretty good so far." Everyone who heard Carla's comment smiled. Although they didn't know it at the time, finding their way to their dormitory and discovering how to get in had been their first test as Academy students, and they all passed.

Abigale led the way and they all entered the room. It was the Community Room. There were four black leather sofas and several over-stuffed black leather chairs. Some of the chairs swiveled and rocked while others reclined. On one side of the room was a large fireplace that took up nearly half the length of the wall. The doorway they had just come in was also in this wall, slightly to the left of the fireplace. The door closed when the last student entered. There was a Castle Directory on this side of the door and only one doorknob. The wall opposite the fireplace was curved and lined with windows. In the corners to the right and left of the fireplace were spiral stairways that went up to the next level. The remaining two walls had doorways with open doors. From what they could see of the rooms beyond, they looked like study rooms. There were tables and bookshelves along the walls full of books. A knock came to the massive entrance door and one of the students opened it. Another group of students was standing outside. As they came in, the boy who opened the door showed the new group which doorknobs to use and which direction to turn them.

Carla did a quick head count and it appeared that the entire class had arrived. Tommy turned his attention back to the Community Room and to his surprise, in the middle of the largest sofa, in the middle of the room, lay Mister Buttercup. He was curled up and apparently sleeping. With all the commotion in the room, he hadn't moved.

"Mister Buttercup," Tommy exclaimed as he walked over to him. Hearing his name, Mister Buttercup raised his head. "I don't know how you always seem to know where I'm going and, I certainly don't know how you get into these places." Tommy bent down and scratched him behind his ears. "You know, you're the most amazing cat ever," he added. Tommy then introduced Mister Buttercup to everybody. Some students came over and petted him. Mister Buttercup purred.

Carla suddenly spoke up, "It says in our Rules and Code of Conduct Manual that each year we're supposed to elect a Dormitory Leader, so I nominate Abigale." There seemed to be general agreement. "Is there anyone opposed," she asked. No one said anything. "Then it's agreed, Abigale is our Dormitory leader." Unwittingly, they had all just passed their second test as Academy students.

Some students went over to Abigale to shake her hand and there was a general rumble of congratulatory remarks sent her way. After she received her congratulations, Abigale did her first official act as Dormitory Leader. She walked over to the Castle Directory on the back of the entrance door. She studied it for a couple of minutes and then said as she pointed to her right, "Girls' bedroom and bathrooms, the stairway to the right," then pointing to her left, she said, "boys' to the left."

The group began dividing as the girls headed for the girls' stairway and the boys headed toward the other one. Carla did another fast head count and for the first time she realized that the class was equally divided between boys and girls. There were fifteen of each. "Meet you guys back down here in fifteen minutes," Carla said to Tommy and Michael before she started for the girls' stairway.

Tommy and Michael went up the spiral stairway. When they got to the second floor, they found themselves in a large room with fifteen beds lining the walls. Two walls had doorways that led to adjoining bathrooms. Next to each bed, there was a nightstand with a lamp upon it. Some of the beds also had a window next to it. The footboard of each bed had a rustic looking name plate with each student's name on it. They looked like they had always been there, even though they couldn't have been. Tommy spotted his name on one of the beds and Michael's was right next to it. There was a window between the beds and their night stands were on the opposite sides. Tommy pointed to Michael's name plate and Michael acknowledged him. They both sat on their beds and bounced a little as if to test it for comfort.

"Not bad, eh?" Michael said to Tommy.

"Nope," Tommy replied. "Not too bad at all." They both smiled with broad smiles.

They put their papers in their nightstands. After a few minutes of taking in their new home, they decided to head back downstairs. Michael suggested that they take their rules manuals along. Tommy thought that was a good idea, so they tucked their manuals inside their belts and went down the stairs. Surprisingly, Carla was waiting for them. She suggested they go into one of the study rooms. They did so and Carla closed the door behind them. They sat down at one of the tables.

"So what do you think?" Tommy asked Carla.

"I think it's fabulous," she responded.

"So do I," Michael added.

"And," Tommy went on, "now that you've had some time to think about it, what do you think of our story?"

"Oh," Carla started, "I think it's obvious. You must be telling the truth."

"And why is that?" Tommy asked.

"Well, you two don't seem to know some of the things you should know, I mean like not knowing about magic and all. You know, the ill effects of the Tinkleberry wine lasts only so long. And, because you guys pretty much flunked your History test. I don't think you would have done so badly if you had known the legend of Erlin and Griselda. If you knew their legend well enough to be making up a story about it, I don't think either of you would have gotten a 'Poor' on the test. You might not have gotten a Superior, but I don't think you would have gotten a 'Poor' either. So, it's obvious, you must be telling the truth."

"Hey," Michael said, "you've convinced me." They all laughed.

"So will you promise to keep our secret and help us?" Tommy asked.

"Of course and I've come up with a plan," Carla said. "But first, I have to tell you what I learned about Reginald Whitelace. He's bad news. Stay away from him. Abigale told me he's Head Boy. Remember the gold piping on the cuffs of his robe; she said that's the sign of Head Boy. Abigale said he and another boy, Gottfried Titlemost, are running neck and neck to be this year's selection for the Queen's Guard. Each one is trying to outdo the other for recognition. This means that they'll be looking to write up anybody, even for the slightest violation, so we must memorize our Rules and Code of Conduct Manual. We need to push everyone to memorize it as quickly as possible. Since there's so much I have to teach you, I'm going to teach you a little bit of magic my mother taught me, but you'll need your manuals."

"We're a bit ahead of you there, Carla," Michael said and the two boys pulled their manuals out from under their robes.

"Wow," Carla exclaimed. "I'm impressed. So great, let me show you this. Pull out your wands. Now find the list of 'The Rules Most Important', I think it's on page five."

"How do you know what's in the manual," Tommy asked as he thumbed through his manual.

"Silly boy," Carla replied with a smile. "I read it at dinner." She then continued, "Have you found it?" Both boys nodded. "Take your wands and turn it sideways like this." She turned her own wand sideways to show them. "Hold it against the top of the page and close your eyes. Now think of chicken legs, a bat's snout, a crawdad claw and two sprigs of peppermint."

"What!" Tommy exclaimed. He could hardly believe his ears.

"Listen," Carla said firmly. "You got to get this right. Close your eyes and imagine," she then spoke slowly, "chicken legs, a bat's snout, a crawdad claw and two sprigs of peppermint. Got that?" Both boys nodded hesitantly. "Okay, with your eyes still closed and those items pictured in your mind, slowly and gently slide your wand towards the bottom of the page. When you reach the bottom of the page, open your eyes and carefully take proper hold of your wand. Once you're gripping it properly, touch your temple lightly with the tip. The boys did as she instructed. When they touched their temples with the tips of their wands, the memory of that page appeared in their minds.

"Say what!" Michael said excitedly. "I'll never have to study again."

Carla laughed and said, "It won't last. You have to refresh it frequently with another touch to the temple and, if you use your wand for any other purpose, it all disappears, from your wand and your mind. It's my mom's own secret recipe; she calls it 'Duplicato'. Since it's one of her secret recipes, I can't really share it with the others, but we need it to shore up our memories until we have fully memorized the manual. It'll give us some of the extra time we need for all the other stuff I have to teach you."

"This is going to help a lot," Tommy said.

"Yes it will," replied Carla. "Since it's one of my mom's secret recipes, I debated whether or not I should even teach it to you. But, I decided that if my mom knew the circumstances, she would approve. What, may I ask, did the Head Mistress talk to you about at dinner?"

"She said she talked to Professor Pastorie and they have arranged for him to teach us a remedial History class," Tommy answered.

"Outstanding," Carla said. "I was hoping it was something like that. Since Professor Pastorie is going to be teaching you History, I won't have to. We can go on to other things. Tomorrow we're going to Cantwell. I'll teach you as much as I can on the way there and back. I can also try to teach you some things while we shop."

"Sounds great to me," Michael confirmed and Tommy nodded.

"It's getting late and I think we should head off to our bedrooms," Carla said, "but I think we should study our manuals a little before we go to sleep." The boys agreed. They said good night to each other and returned to their bedrooms.

When Tommy reached his bed, he stepped over and looked out the window. He could see most of the inner courtyard and quite a ways out beyond the big arch. Although it was getting dark, he saw a figure in a red robe exit out the big arch. Tommy couldn't see who it was, but he thought he saw a glimmer of gold on one of the figure's sleeves. Tommy was finding the perpetually black sky unsettling. He missed the sun during the day and the moon and stars at night. Michael was lying on his bed studying his manual, so Tommy did the same. They both fell asleep.

The next morning, Tommy was awakened by his bed shaking. It shook for a couple of moments and then stopped. Then it shook again. He opened his eyes and all the beds were doing the same thing. As the kids got out of their beds, they stopped shaking. Tommy got up and saw that Michael was standing next to his bed. "That's some alarm clock," he said to Michael.

"Yeah," Michael responded. "If that happens every morning, it'll be pretty hard to over sleep."

They headed for the bathrooms. They showered and freshened up. Tommy told Michael to remind him to ask Carla to do that clothes cleaning thing again. Their clothes were getting a little gamey, as they had slept in them for two nights. They went through their paperwork and pulled out the page that contained the list of items they needed to buy. They took a quick look at the items on the list before folding them up and putting them in their pockets. They dressed and went down stairs. Carla was waiting for them. Tommy asked Carla to do the clothes cleaning thing.

"Put that on the list of things I need to teach you," Carla said as she passed her wand over each of them. "I'm not going to be doing your laundry." They consulted the Castle Directory and headed for the Main Hall and breakfast.

Chapter Thirteen

Return to Cantwell

Carla talked in an instructive manner all the way to the Main Hall. When they got to the Main Hall, they found out that there was no assigned seating. They found three seats together and sat down. Carla continued her instruction in softer tones through most of their breakfast. The boys didn't think they could like Carla more than they already did, but the more she talked and the harder she tried to teach them, the more they liked and appreciated her. She was earning their respect, not only through the commitment she was showing, but also because of her vast wealth of knowledge. They were impressed with her organization and her sincere understanding of their predicament. They found they were rapidly learning many of the everyday things that they needed to know in order to survive without being discovered.

They finished breakfast and went out through the courtyard and the big arch. Although the boys already knew it, Carla could talk. She barely skipped a beat. They did a soft wave ride to Cantwell and Carla instructed them all the way. When they got within the town limits, they ended their wave ride and Carla ended her instruction. "We need to go to the bank and deposit your pool of gold," she told Tommy. "That way we can get some spending drops."

Carla had seen the 'Queen's Bank' on their previous trip through Cantwell and she led them right to it. The bank had several wide steps that went up to a large set of doors. They went up the steps and entered the bank. It was a very large room with almost nothing in it.

There were two overstuffed chairs along the wall to their right and two more along the wall to the left. In the center of each wall was a large portrait of the Queen. Her portraits were bordered on both sides by smaller paintings of older distinguished looking wizards. The entire main floor area was empty except, in the very center of the room, there was a small cage like structure. There was just enough room for one person to be seated comfortably. The cage had a narrow counter that went all the way around it with seven evenly spaced teller windows. Each teller window had bars in front and a sign above it. The seven different teller signs were; DEPOSITS, WITHDRAWALS, NEW ACCOUNTS, INTEREST AND BALANCE INFORMATION, GENERAL INFORMATION, CLOSING ACCOUNTS and PAYMENTS.

Tommy walked over to the teller window labeled GENERAL INFORMATION. There was a very old wizard seated inside the cage like structure. When Tommy approached the window, the old wizard looked up and asked very slowly, "Can I help you?"

"Yes," Tommy said, "I'd like to open an account."

"Very good," the old wizard said and he pointed to his right, "You'll have to go to NEW ACCOUNTS. It's around the corner."

Tommy walked around the small cage, past INTREST AND BALANCE INFORMATION to the window labeled NEW ACCOUNTS. When he reached the window, the old wizard swiveled in his chair and asked Tommy very slowly, "Can I help you?"

"Yes," Tommy repeated, "Like I just said, I'd like to open an account."

"And what is your name," the old wizard slowly asked.

"Tommy Travail," Tommy answered.

The old wizard wrote on a piece of paper. After a moment, he reached under his counter and pulled up a card. He handed it to Tommy. Tommy could hardly believe it, but the card had his name and picture on it. "This is your account card," the old wizard said. "Keep it safe."

Carla handed Tommy his pool of gold and he set it on the counter. "I'd like to deposit this," he said.

"Very good," the old wizard said and pointed to his right once again "You'll have to go to DEPOSITS. It's around the corner."

Tommy walked further around the small cage, past WITHDRAWALS to the window labeled DEPOSITS. When he reached the window, the old wizard swiveled in his chair and asked Tommy very slowly once again, "Can I help you?"

"Uh, yes," Tommy repeated impatiently. "I'd like to deposit this." He once again set the pool of gold on the counter.

The old wizard took the pool of gold and set it on the counter to his left. "That's two hundred and seventy-one drops. Do you have an account card?"

Tommy made a funny face and gave the card back to the old wizard. He then turned and asked Carla, "How much do you think we'll need?"

"Ten drops ought to be enough," she answered.

The old wizard gave Tommy his account card back and said, "You have two hundred and seventy one drops of gold now on deposit."

"I'd like to make a withdrawal?" Tommy said to the old wizard.

"Very good," the old wizard said and pointed to his left this time. "You'll have to go to WITHDRAWALS. It's around the corner."

Tommy stepped back around the cage to the window labeled WITHDRAWLS. When he reached the window, the old wizard swiveled in his chair and asked yet again, "Can I help you?"

"Yes," Tommy said gritting his teeth. "I'd like to make a withdrawal."

"And how much would you like to withdrawal," the old wizard inquired.

"I'd like to withdraw thirty drops of gold," Tommy responded still gritting his teeth.

"Do you have an account card?" the old wizard asked again.

"Yes," Tommy said as he gave his card to the old wizard. Tommy's voice was getting a little louder as his patience was getting thinner.

The old wizard opened a drawer below the counter and took out several drops of gold. He counted out thirty and put them on the counter in front of Tommy along with his account card. "If you want to know your account balance," the old wizard said. "You'll have to go to INTEREST AND BALANCE INFORMATION…"

"I know," Tommy said. "It's just around the corner, right?" Tommy picked up his card and scraped the drops of gold into his hand. Tommy was so happy to have this little ordeal over with, that he genuinely thanked the old wizard. The old wizard smiled and gave him a wink. Suddenly, Tommy realized he had been had, and that brought a smile to his face. He put his card in his pocket, counted out ten drops of gold and gave them to Michael. He counted out another ten and gave them to Carla.

"I meant," Carla started, "that we'd need about ten drops of gold in total for all of us."

"I know what you meant," Tommy replied, "but I think we should have a little extra spending money in our pockets, plus you'll need an extra drop for the well. I don't know about you two, but I want to make another wish."

Michael and Carla thanked Tommy and they left the bank. "The first thing we need to do," Carla began, "is to buy you guys new wands. Those baby wands will only get you so far. You'll soon be needing a good intermediate wand. But, whatever you do, don't buy a professional wand. Professional wands do a lot more than intermediate wands, and they feel really good in your hand. But, at your skill level, you wouldn't be able to control one, and that could be bad for everybody around you. You need to be a very skilled witch or wizard to correctly use a professional wand. They require sophisticated magic."

They went past 'Hector's Hexes' and entered 'Wanda's Wonderful Wands'. After testing several wands, the boys each found one they liked. In the process of making their choices, they couldn't resist trying a couple of professional wands. They found that Carla was right. The professional wands really did feel good to hold on to, but it instantly made them nervous. It was like holding on to a stick of dynamite and not knowing for sure whether the fuse had been lit or not. The boys paid for their wands and the three of them left the shop.

"Next," Carla said, "we need to get you guys a couple of trunks to store your stuff in back at the Crow's Nest. I'd recommend that you get an all-stuffing, self-locating trunk. That's what I got. They never get full and they will travel to any location you designate on their own. They'll follow us around while we shop. When we're done shopping, you'll be able to direct them to go to Crow's Nest. By the time we get back, they'll be there waiting for you. I'd also recommend that you get a bag like I have to wear under your robes. It's quite handy. It's also an all-stuffer, a weightless all-stuffer. No matter how much you put in the bag, it never gets any heavier than its empty weight. You have to be careful though, if you put a lot of stuff in the bag it gets really difficult to find things."

"I definitely need one of those trunks, but I don't think I'm about to start carrying a purse," Michael declared.

"I think there might be some real advantages to having a bag like that," Tommy responded, "and you do keep it under your robes, so nobody sees it."

"I really do think it's a good idea to get one," Carla said reassuringly. "Besides, everybody wears one."

"Really," Michael questioned, "even the boys?"

"Yes, of course," Carla answered. "Some of the non-magicals don't carry bags, but all the witches and wizards do."

They located the outlet store for the 'Closed Lid Trunk and Baggage Factory' and went in. Carla showed the boys a bag that was just like hers. Although Michael was still a little reluctant, he and Tommy both decided to buy one. Next, they looked at trunks. Tommy decided to buy a 'Sebastian Hump-Top Mark 3' that he really liked. It had brass hinges and corners along with a brass locking mechanism. Michael decided to get one just like it, but he couldn't find one in that model that would unlock for him. The lock had to be opened with the tip of a wand. If the trunk didn't like your magic, it wouldn't unlock. Michael had to settle for a 'Cabot Flat-Top Model 6', but even though it unlocked for Michael, it still snapped its lid at him a couple of times. A fifteen minute training session went along with every trunk. It was called, "The care, cleaning and training of your new trunk and/or baggage product." The biggest part was the training part. The store clerk instructed them on, 'Getting to know your trunk' and 'Letting your trunk get to know the real you'. There were also parts on, 'Giving travel instructions', and 'When discipline becomes necessary'. By the end of the training session, the boys were controlling their trunks reasonably well; however, Michael's continued to snap at him occasionally. By the time they paid, their trunks were following them around like a couple of puppies.

The three of them stopped at several other shops. Tommy and Michael bought themselves an extra pair of trousers and a couple of new shirts; however, they decided not to replace the robes that Carla had bought. They went to several book stores. They got all the books they needed for their regular classes, but had difficulty finding "Underlying History" by Cecil Fibb. Professor Pastorie had added the book to their list for the remedial History class. They finally found two used copies in 'The Last Word', a small back-alley used book shop. At a school supply store, they each bought a supply of paper, pens and pencils. They also bought small back-packs and school grade caldrons at the same store. The back-packs weren't all-stuffers, but they were self-organizing. Once the pack-back gets to know its owner, the next item the owner needs will be at the top, or very near the top. After the school supply store, they stopped at a candy shop. They each bought a bag of chocolates and Chewy Chew Chews. Next to the candy shop was 'Polly's Potion Shop' were they would get the last item on their list. Once they got to Polly's, they each bought a 'First Year Student Pack' of potion ingredients. The shopkeeper told them that it contained all the ingredients they would need as first year students in a sufficient quantity to last for a semester.

It was a little past midday when they finished their shopping. Carla suggested that they lock up their trunks and send them to Crow's Nest. She put her packages in Tommy's trunk. The boys followed the instructions they got at the trunk store and Tommy's trunk vanished. Michael's trunk hassled with him for a bit, but after a little extra encouragement on Michael's part, it too vanished.

"Let's go to the Deep Well soda shop and get some lunch," Carla suggested.

"I'm starved," was Michael's only response.

"Me too," added Tommy.

On their way to the soda shop they passed by a game room. "I'd like to take a peek in there and see what kind of games they got," Michael said. They agreed to stop, but for only a few minutes. They went inside. There were quite a few kids playing several different kinds of table games. One game that caught Michael's eye right away was a billiards-like game that was played on a square table. The table had eight pockets, one in each of the four corners and one pocket halfway between each corner. The game started with thirteen balls grouped together in a circle in the center of the table. There were twelve green balls and one yellow ball that was placed in the center of the group. There was one additional black ball that was used as a cue ball. The players used their wands with small spits of magical energy to strike the cue ball. The object was to bank either the cue ball or the object ball off a rail and pocket the object ball without letting the black cue ball come into contact with the yellow ball. If the cue ball struck the yellow ball at any point, it was a scratch and the opponent player could place the cue ball anywhere on the table for the next shot. After all the green balls are pocketed, the player who pockets the yellow ball wins the game.

There was a group of guys standing next to Michael who were also watching the game. "What's the name of that game?" he asked one of them.

"It's called Stinger," the boy said.

"Come on, Michael," Tommy said, "I want to get something to eat."

"I want to learn how to do that," Michael said to Carla, ignoring Tommy. "Can you teach me how to shoot that little bit of energy with my wand without me blowing up the table?"

"Put it on the list," Carla said jokingly. "Seriously though, remind me sometime when we have a few extra minutes and I'll teach you. It's really an easy one and doesn't take very much magic."

Tommy took hold of Michael's arm and gently escorted him out of the game room. They went a short ways down the street and arrived at The Deep Well. They went inside and there weren't as many kids in there as they had expected. They had been running into fellow students all day and figured they would see some of them there. They decided to eat their lunch on the back porch, so they ordered burgers and fries with tall glasses of Roddenberry root root beer at the counter and went outside to wait for their meal.

"I wonder where everybody is," Tommy said as they approached a table.

"I think we just missed everybody," Carla said. "It's quite a bit past lunch time now."

Someone had left a newspaper on the table. Carla pulled it in front of her as they sat down and started to read it. It was that day's issue of the Newest Castle News. Carla scanned the front page and then picked it up and opened it to the second page. When she did that, Tommy saw the front page. In the lower left hand corner was a picture of a scruffy looking man. The head line of the article next to the picture said, "It Never Happened."

"Hold on," Tommy said. "I've seen that guy before."

"What's that?" Carla asked.

"That guy on the front page," he replied. "I've seen him before. What does the article say?"

Carla turned the paper back to the front page and found the picture and accompanying article. Carla read, "We reported in yesterday's paper that the Ministry of All Things Magic said that there had been a break in at the Ministry the previous night. We reported that a Ministry spokesman had told reporters that agents, probably working for the Black Witch, broke in and stole some ancient scrolls relating to the Tears of Damiana. A spokesman for the Queen said today that it didn't happen. He said that it was simply a misunderstanding. However, he said that the Queen's guard is seeking known thief and hooligan, Barnabas Skeezicks, for questioning in relation to the incident that didn't take place."

"I can't believe it," Tommy said excitedly. "He's working for the Black Witch and I've seen him twice. The first time I saw him was here inside The Deep Well and the second time I saw him was yesterday morning in the Grand Foyer at the castle. He gave something to Reginald Whitelace. You remember Michael. It was when we went out to the courtyard yesterday morning."

"I remember," said Michael, "but I can't say I saw him well enough to recognize him, he had his hood up."

"But he didn't when I saw him with Whitelace." He pulled his hood up when he saw me, and Whitelace stepped back into the Main Hall. Let me ask you a question, Carla. How unusual would it be for the Head Boy to wear a blue robe instead of his official red one?"

"That would be really unusual," Carla answered. "About the only reason he would do that is if he was trying not to be recognized."

"That's what I thought," Tommy said. "I'm sure it was Whitelace that I saw, right inside there at that corner table. He was sitting talking to this Barnabas character. He was wearing a blue robe, but I'm sure it was Whitelace now that I think about it. That means that Whitelace may be in league with the Black Witch and, what's worse, he could be the one who gets selected for the Queen's Guard."

"I wouldn't be messing with Whitelace if I were you," Carla advised. "I told you he's trouble."

"Maybe we should report this to the Head Mistress," Michael suggested.

"I don't think so," Tommy responded, "for two reasons. One, if we're wrong and he was doing something perfectly innocent, say for the Head Mistress or one of his Professors, we'd be in a world of trouble with him. He'd never leave us alone. And, two, if he is in league with the Black Witch, who else might be involved, a Professor, or even the Head Mistress, maybe all of them for all we know. We need more information, and what's this about Damiana's Tears?"

"It's part of the legend of King Oleander," Carla answered. "It has to do with the more mythical part of the legend, when he was a young Prince. That's when he knew Damiana." Just then, Willy Jingleshangles came out the back door of The Deep Well. "Here comes Willy," she said "Let's ask him. I'll bet he knows every detail about the legend."

"Hey Willy," Tommy called out. Willy smiled and came their way.

"Say how's it goin' lads?" Willy said greeting them. "How'd you do on your test?"

"We all made it in," Tommy said.

"I'm glad to hear that," Willy replied.

"Say, Willy, have you got time to tell us the legend of King Oleander?" Tommy asked.

"Sorry, lads," he answered. "I'm on an emergency run. Witch Wooly from the creature shop sent me a message asking for my help. It seems that a bunch of Squirmies that she was keeping as food for the baby Dragonsours have escaped and are running amok in her shop. She asked if I'd come and help her catch them before they destroy her shop. Sorry, but I've gotta go. Maybe next time." He waved bye and headed across the park in the direction of the creature shop.

"Ah, too bad," Tommy said. "Oh well, we can look it up in our History books when we get back to Crow's Nest, unless you got more Carla."

"Yeah, but..." The young waiter came through the door carrying their lunch orders.

"Great," Michael said. "I'm starved."

"Yeah," Tommy said as he eyed his burger, "and if you'd had your way, we'd still be in that game room."

"Would not," Michael replied.

"Would too," Tommy said then took a big bite of his burger. Carla picked at her food in a very lady like way, but the boys dug in and stuffed themselves. Michael took a big gulp of root beer and then belched loudly. Tommy laughed, but Carla gave him a very stern look.

"Oh," Michael said apologetically, "I'm sorry. That just sort of slipped out."

"Did not," Tommy asserted.

"Did too," Michael responded.

Carla just watched the two of them, shook her head slightly and smiled, then started thinking. These were her friends. She never had any real close friends. Other kids, and their parents, felt uncomfortable around her because she popped so early. Then, these two guys came out of nowhere. This thought made her chuckle to herself, as it now appears they may indeed have come out of nowhere, in a manner of speaking. They have freely offered her their friendship and have openly accepted her without reservation. She was enjoying herself and she was happy.

"Say Carla," Michael suddenly asked, "didn't you want to be Dormitory Leader? You're every bit as smart and clever as Abigale Antwerp."

"Of course I did," Carla answered. "I've dreamed about that for a long time."

"Then how come you nominated Abigale," Michael asked.

"Well," she began, "by that time, I realized you guys must be telling the truth, and, well, you asked for my help. So, I figured that I'd be too busy keeping you guys out of trouble to fulfill the duties of Dormitory Leader."

"Oh, Carla," Michael said. "We didn't want you to do that. I mean, yeah, we asked for your help and all, but, we never meant for you to give up the stuff that's important to you, did we Tommy?"

"No," Tommy answered. "We didn't Carla. We may have been a little short sighted in our own desperation, but we didn't think…"

"Are we friends," Carla cut in.

"The best," Tommy replied.

"Then nothing more need be said," Carla said with finality, "But next year, Abigale better watch out." She smiled and the boys returned her smile.

They finished eating. Tommy folded up the newspaper and slipped it under his belt. "Let's go to the well," Tommy said. "I think it's time to make a wish." They all got up and started across the park. On and off through the day, Tommy had thought about making this wish. He thought about what he wanted most of all. He wanted to know where his parents were and if they were all right. But, that seemed like two wishes to him, so he had been trying to think of a way to word his wish so that both questions might be answered. They reached one of the main walkways and approached the well. Tommy studied the well for a while. Carla and Michael got out a drop of gold. Michael went first. He whispered his wish softly and tossed the drop into the well. Carla thought for a moment, then whispered her wish and tossed her drop into the well. Tommy took out a drop of gold and whispered, "I wish to know the fate of my parents," and then tossed his drop into the well.

"What you say we find a quiet place and I'll teach you guys some magic," Carla suggested. "We don't have to return to the castle for quite a while."

"Sounds good to me," answered Tommy.

"Fine by me," Michael agreed.

They found a secluded spot not too far down one of the paths that still afforded a view of the well. "Could you teach me how to make a shot in that Stinger game," Michael asked Carla.

"Sure," she said. "Both of you, watch me. Put your lips together softly and push out a short puff of air like this, PUH. Now you try it." They did, and when Carla was satisfied that they got the gist of it, she continued, "Okay," Carla walked over to a near by crab apple tree and picked up a hand full of apples that had fallen to the ground. She set them on the ground a couple of feet in front of the boys. Now, aim your wand at one of the apples. Focus the magic into your wrist. Give it the same little kind of push. Release the magic through your hand and out your wand, but remember two things, you're now using intermediate wands, and, this is a gentle piece of magic.

Michael went first. He did as she instructed and blew a hole through the apple. Tommy laughed. Carla, however, told Michael he did really well. She explained that a Stinger ball is much heavier, and of course, much harder. She said that if the apple had been a Stinger ball, it would have been just right for a shot all the way across the table. Tommy went next. He followed her instructions and blew the apple to smithereens. Little bits of crab apple flew everywhere. Michael broke out in wild laughter and Carla giggled. With Carla's continued supervision, they practiced. Carla gathered and set up apples while Michael and Tommy took turns. After a while, they got reasonably good. They got where they could hit an apple soft enough to roll it, or strong enough to neatly pierce a fine hole through it.

"Okay," Carla said, "that's enough of that. Here's another easy one. You'll never be in the dark if you learn this trick. You can make your wand tip glow like a little spot light. To do this, just hold your wand upright, close your eyes and imagine what it's going to be like when you open them and the light first strikes your eyes. Then, open your eyes, let that first light come into your eyes and travel down your arm to the tip of your wand. It should start glowing, once it does, you can control the light intensity just by willing it to be brighter or dimmer. With a little practice, you should be able to turn the light on and off with just a thought." The boys followed her instructions and quickly learned this little bit of magic.

Carla next suggested that they work on their balance for the foot method of wave riding. Even though there were "No Wave Riding" notices posted around the park, Carla thought it would be okay if they just practiced their balance. She said if they could learn to keep their balance a little, then they might be able to practice the foot method of wave riding on their way back to the castle. One at a time, either Michael or Tommy would lift off the ground while the other one and Carla held on to him. After more than an hour, they were both lifting off the ground and keeping their balance without assistance. They were still shaky, but they were doing it. Both boys were magically drained, so Carla suggested they have some Chewy Chew Chews and rest for a while. They did as she suggested.

"After a while, Carla said, "There's one more thing I like to show you before we head back to the castle. It's the Clean and Press. That's

The Life and Times of Tommy Travail

the magic I used to clean you guys up." Carla showed them how to hold their wands and how to generate the correct magic. Carla laughed after their first try. The boys looked much more disheveled after their attempt than they had before the attempt. The boys didn't necessarily see the humor in their appearance, but they also laughed because Carla found humor in it. They made several 'Clean and Press' passes across themselves and each other. They got better with each successive attempt.

Once Carla was satisfied, she stopped them. "Okay," she said. "I think it's time we head back to the castle. You guys up to practicing the foot method?"

Tommy looked at Michael and he nodded back. "I think we could do that," Tommy said.

"We can't start wave riding until we get outside of the town limits," Carla said, "so that'll give you a little more time to recover your magic." The three of them took the path back to the well. Tommy took one last look at the well as they decided which of the main walkways would lead most directly to the castle roadway. They made their choice and headed out of the park. Carla figured the boys had learned enough for one day, so she didn't say anything until they got to the castle roadway.

There were other kids on the roadway going back to the castle; many of them were carrying bags and packages. Most of the kids were wave riding, but some were walking. "Okay," Carla said. "If you're ready, let's go, but be careful. The other kids will be watching. Don't try anything fancy; you might wind up embarrassing yourself."

The three of them popped up using the foot method and pushed off. Tommy and Michael found it much easier to keep their balance once they were moving. They cruised along steadily. Their skill and confidence built. As they neared the castle, Michael and Tommy couldn't resist having one race. Tommy jumped the start and took the lead. Michael gave several hard pushes and started to catch Tommy. Tommy pushed harder and kept the lead. They were going faster and faster. Michael hit a dip in the road that he didn't see and started to lose his balance. He rose up on just his left foot, when he tried to force his weight back onto his right foot, he over corrected and fell. He tumbled for thirty feet before he came to a stop right next to Jeremiah

Jetfoot. A number of kids saw Michael fall and they all gathered around to see if he was all right. Michael stood up slowly and checked to see that everything still worked. He assured everybody that he was okay. However, he had a cut on his chin that was bleeding slightly and a good size bump growing on his forehead.

"Wow," said Jay-Jay. "That was one of the best falls I ever saw. You keep that up and you'll be needing some dental work just like me." He then grinned revealing his missing tooth. Michael smiled and automatically ran his index finger across his teeth to make sure they were all there.

Carla arrived with a handkerchief in her hand. She wiped the blood from Michael's chin and examined the cut. "Not too bad," she said. "Take this hanky and press on that cut until it stops bleeding." After looking at the ever growing knot on his forehead, she took another handkerchief from her bag, pulled out her wand and made two ice cubes in the middle of the hanky. "Here," she said to Michael, "put this on that bump, it'll help with the swelling." Carla's magical ability to make ice cubes impressed everyone. The other kids resumed their trip to the castle once they were sure that Michael was all right.

Tommy, Michael and Carla walked the rest of the way. "What did I tell the two of you," Carla admonished once the other kids were out of hearing range. "Didn't I say no fancy stuff? I don't know what I'm going to do with the two of you. You guys get into more trouble than a bin full of Snuffle Wompers."

"If I hadn't fallen, I'd have won," Michael said ignoring Carla's criticism.

"Would not," Tommy responded.

"Would too," Michael answered back. "Besides, if you hadn't cheated and jumped the start, I know I would have won."

"I didn't cheat," Tommy declared.

"Did too," Michael replied. The two of them debated the issues the rest of the way back to the castle. Carla just listened and shook her head.

Chapter Fourteen

Whitelace's Mission

They went straight to the Crow's Nest once they arrived back at the Castle. Carla wanted Michael to go to the Infirmary to be checked out, but Michael insisted he was all right. When the boys got back to their bedroom, their trunks were there at the foot of their beds. Michael went to the bathroom while Tommy removed Carla's things from his trunk and took them down to her. Michael examined himself in the bathroom mirror. The ice Carla gave him helped, but he still had a good size knot on his forehead and it was turning black and blue. The cut on his chin was small and had stopped bleeding. He hadn't told anyone, but he had landed hard on his right shoulder. He removed his robes and took off his shirt. He had a large bruise covering his upper arm and part of his shoulder. He touched it and winced with pain. He gently swung his arm up and around. It hurt, but he was sure that nothing was broken. He washed his face and put his shirt and robes back on before returning to the bedroom.

Tommy was sitting on his bed thumbing through his History book when Michael came back from the bathroom. "Everything still in working order?" Tommy asked Michael as he approached.

"Pretty much so," Michael replied, "but I've got a whopper of a bruise on my shoulder and it hurts like the dickens."

"You sure it's gonna be all right?" Tommy inquired.

"Yeah," Michael answered. "It's just going to be sore for a while."

Ronald Lockhart reached the top step into the bedroom area. "Hey, you guys," he said to Tommy and Michael, "Carla's waiting downstairs for you two. Say, Michael, I heard you took a pretty cool fall on the way back to the castle. Wow. That's a beauty," he added once he saw Michael's face. "You alright?"

"Yeah," Michael answered, "but I'm gonna be sore for a while."

"I heard you were setting some kind of speed record when you fell. They say you tumbled for over a hundred feet. Must have been spectacular," Ronald said admiringly.

Michael smiled with pride. Tommy put his History book away and asked Ronald if he was going to the evening meal. Ronald said he was, but he wanted to freshen up a bit before he went. Tommy and Michael said they'd see him later and went downstairs. Carla was sitting on one of the sofas with Mister Buttercup in her lap.

"Took you guys long enough," she said. She moved Mister Buttercup off her lap and stood up. "Everyone's talking about your fall," she said to Michael, "seems like you're building a reputation."

"Yep," Tommy said grinning. "His reputation precedes him, head first followed immediately by his butt and other body parts." Michael and Carla laughed.

"Aw, it was nothing," Michael added, still laughing. "Wait till you see my next trick."

Carla frowned and Michael put his right arm around her shoulders. He winced slightly with pain and said, "I'll be more careful next time."

"Next time," Carla exclaimed. Michael squeezed her shoulders a little tighter and smiled at her. She realized he was teasing her and smiled. Then, almost immediately, she got a serious expression on her face, "You really do have to be careful, you know."

They headed out the door and went to the Main Hall. When they arrived, the fourth and fifth year Military tables were full. There were some empty seats at the fourth and fifth year Political tables, and the second and third year tables had a few more empty seats. Although most of the first year students were seated at their table, there were more empty seats at their table than at any other. Most of the Professors were seated at their table; however, the Head Mistress was not there. The food was already on the table and everyone had started eating. When Michael entered the room, everyone at the first year table stopped eating and looked at him. Many kids at the other tables also stopped eating and watched Michael as he entered. Many of the girls had looks of concern on their faces. Most of the boys, however, looked at Michael with a bit of envy and admiration; a few even gave Michael a thumbs-up.

Michael's injuries didn't seem to hurt as much as they had a while earlier. They found seats together and everyone watched Michael until he sat down. A moment after he sat down, a butterfly like thing fluttered into the room through the doorway. It fluttered around for a couple of moments, and then landed right in front of Michael. It was a small piece of paper that had been folded to make wings. When it landed, it unfolded itself. It was a note addressed to Michael Woden from the Head Mistress. It instructed Michael to report to the Infirmary as soon as he finished his meal.

"See," Carla said as she read the note. "The Head Mistress even knows about you're foolishness." The pride Michael had been feeling began to fade. Carla must have seen it in his face, because she didn't say any more.

They all had a good meal and left the Main Hall. They checked the Castle Directory in the Grand Foyer and made their way to the Infirmary. There were several other kids there when they arrived; most of them were first years. All the sweets and goodies, topped off with plenty of Roddenberry root root beer, had left them with stomach aches. Misty Firefist was seated on the edge of one of the beds. She was being tended to by the Head Physician, Medical Wizard Cornelius Healsau. The Physician looked up when they stepped into the room.

"Ah, Mister Woden," the Physician said. "The Head Mistress said you'd be stopping by. Here, have a seat on this bed." He pointed to the bed opposite to Misty. Turning his attention back to Misty he said, "There, that ought to take care of it. Just sit here and rest for a few minutes and you should be okay."

Michael sat down on the bed and smiled at Misty. She smiled back, but her face turned to one of concern when she got a good look a Michael's face. "It's not really too bad," Michael said to her.

"I'll be the judge of that," Physician Healsau said as he turned around to face Michael. "The Head Mistress informs me you took a pretty good spill today. She said that she was told that you tumbled over a hundred and fifty feet."

"It wasn't quite that far," Michael replied.

The Physician examined the bump on Michael's forehead and cut on his chin. "Is there anything else," he asked.

Michael slipped his robes off and pulled the short sleeve of his shirt up over his right shoulder. Carla scowled when she saw his shoulder, and Misty fainted when she saw it. Physician Healsau turned his attention back to Misty and revived her. He told her to close her eyes and lay on the bed for a bit. He turned back around to Michael. He pushed on Michael's bruised shoulder with his index finger.

"Ow!" Michael shouted.

"Does that hurt?" the physician asked.

"Well, like yes," Michael said in an obvious tone.

"Any restriction of movement?" he asked.

"No, not really," Michael answered.

No one had noticed, but the Head Mistress had entered the room. "How is he?" she asked. Her voice startled everyone except Physician Healsau.

"He'll be just fine," the physician answered.

The Head Mistress stepped in front of Michael and examined him. "Looks like you had a good fall, Mister Woden."

"Yes ma'am," Michael answered.

"You're going to have to learn some caution young man," she said. There was a stern firmness to her voice, but there was a tender warmth in her eyes.

"Yes ma'am," Michael answered again.

"Professor Krusher may want to talk to you tomorrow," the Head Mistress advised Michael. Then, speaking to Physician Healsau, she said, "Heal him up and let me know if there are any complications." She patted Michael's bruised shoulder. Michael instantly felt her magic and his shoulder felt a little better. She gave Michael a bit of a smile, turned and left the room.

Physician Healsau touched the knot on Michael's forehead with the tip of his wand and the swelling went down, but it remained black and

The Life and Times of Tommy Travail

blue. He then moved his wand along the cut on Michael's chin, as he did, the cut healed. The physician turned his wand sideways and run its side over Michael's shoulder several times. Bit by bit, almost all the pain left Michael's shoulder. However, like his forehead, it remained black and blue.

Physician Healsau told Michael he could put his robes back on. He then told him he could go unless there was something else. Michael shook his head no and stood up while he put his robes back on. The physician turned his attention back to Misty and helped her sit up on the bed.

"I'm all right," Misty said as she sat up.

"Let's see you stand," the physician directed. Misty slid off the bed and stood up. Her legs were a little wobbly, but she was okay. Physician Healsau nodded his approval and told her she could also go.

Misty, Carla and the boys left the Infirmary and headed toward the Crow's Nest. Carla still had a scowl on her face. "What's a matter?" Michael asked her.

"How come you didn't tell me about your shoulder?" she asked with a little anger in her voice.

"Well," Michael started, "At first, I didn't want to make you any angrier than you already were, and after I saw it in the mirror at the dormitory, I didn't want to worry you."

"You still should have told me," Carla scolded. "You could have been hurt worse than you thought. Plus, I wanted you to go to the Infirmary, didn't I, and I didn't even know about your shoulder."

"I'm sorry," Michael apologized. "You're right. I should have told you." Michael's apology seemed to satisfy Carla a bit.

The four of them arrived back at the Crow's Nest and headed for their bedrooms. Carla and the boys agreed to meet back in the Community Room with their schedule of classes and text books. In a few minutes, they were back in the Community Room with their arms full of books and papers. Since there were a number of their classmates already lounging in the Community Room, they decided to go into one of the study rooms. One study room had several kids in it preparing for their first day of classes, but the other study room was empty, so they went in. They set their books and papers on one of the tables and sat down.

Carla decided that they should review their class schedules. They had a total of seven classes. Four of the classes met for an hour and a half each on the first, third and fifth days of the school week, and three of the classes met for two hours each on the second and fourth days of the week. Tommy and Michael also had to fit their remedial History classes into their weekly schedule, but they wouldn't know when the classes would be held until they met with Professor Pastorie. On the first, third and fifth days of the week, their morning classes were with Professor Grumble for Political and Social Magic, followed by Professor Pastorie for Historical Magic. In the afternoon, they had Professor Krusher for Military Magic and Professor Clearvoice for Vocalized Magic. On the second and fourth days, their morning classes were with Professor Welkin for The Sciences of Magic and Professor Lightwood for Magical Skills. In the afternoon, they had Abstract Magic with Professor Boardman. They had to start school a half hour earlier on these days because they had two classes for two hours in the morning, but then they had short afternoons because they had only one class for two hours.

"This isn't half bad," Michael said after they had looked through their schedules. "Compared to Brookfield, we're gonna have lots of free time."

"I wouldn't count on it," Carla replied. "I think they have that extra time built in for homework and practice."

"Yeah, you're probably right," Michael agreed.

They organized their text books in the order of their classes. As they did, they took a little time to thumb through each book. By the time they had sorted all their books, they had a reasonably good idea of what they'd be learning in the coming year. When they finished with the books, Michael said that the day had caught up with him and that he was going to bed. Carla and Tommy wished him goodnight. Michael gathered up his things and left for the bedroom. Tommy reached for his History book, but Carla stopped him.

"I want to know more about you and Michael," she said, "How long have you known each other? Have you been friends for a long time?"

Tommy started to tell her how he and Michael met, but he hesitated. He wasn't sure how much he should tell her about Michael and Michael's parents without discussing it with him first. He suddenly realized that this was the first time that he and Carla were alone together. He wasn't sure why, but that realization made him feel slightly uncomfortable. He pushed the uncomfortable feeling aside and returned his thoughts to Michael and how much he should tell Carla. He remembered that he and Michael had agreed to tell Carla everything. And, since everything is everything, he decided to tell her everything.

He told Carla about the University of Brookfield, the Prep school and the museum. He told her about Michael's parents and how he and Michael had met. He also told her about his parents and his grandfather. Tommy admitted that he sometimes gets really depressed when he starts thinking about his parents, and that Michael sometimes erupts in a rage when he gets thinking about his parents. Even though he had already told her about the mirror, he told her about it again, but this time he told her how he and Michael discovered the wand and journal, which eventually led them to the mirror.

Carla listened as he talked. She asked a couple of questions here and there, but mostly she just listened. By the time Tommy had told her everything that he thought was important, it was late and it seemed that everyone else had gone to bed. Carla suggested that they had better turn in as well and Tommy agreed. She told him she would see him in the morning at breakfast. She said she wanted to do a couple of things before breakfast, so she said she would meet them in the Main Hall. She reminded him that he and Michael should do the Duplicato transfer on the school rules before they left the Crow's Nest in the morning. They said goodnight to each other and went up the stairs to their bedroom areas.

Everyone else was in bed by the time Tommy reached the bedroom. The only light came from the lamp on the nightstand next to his bed. He approached his bed and set his books on the nightstand. Michael was in bed and sound asleep. Mister Buttercup was sitting on the ledge of the window. Tommy walked over to Mister Buttercup, scratched him behind the ears and whispered, "I take it you've found the kitchen. I hope you're getting enough to eat." Mister Buttercup purred and Tommy took that to mean yes. Movement in the courtyard below the window caught Tommy's attention. He looked out the window and saw a figure leaving the courtyard through the big arch. Like the night before, he couldn't see quite well enough to say for sure, but he was fairly confident that it was Whitelace. Tommy slipped out of his outer clothing, grabbed his History book and got into bed. He intended to read some, but just about the time his head hit the pillow, he yawned, closed his eyes and fell asleep.

Tommy was awakened by the shaking of his bed. It seemed like he had just fallen asleep, but the morning light was shining through the window. He rubbed his eyes and saw Michael who was already fully dressed. Michael's forehead was still black and blue, and there was a little yellowing were his chin had been cut. Michael was standing at the foot of his bed trying to open his trunk. The lid opened slightly and snapped at him a couple of times before opening fully. Michael started muttering something to himself when he noticed Tommy rubbing his eyes.

"Time to get up, Tommy Boy," Michael said. "We got a big day ahead of us, and I can't wait to get started."

"You? You can't wait to start school," Tommy mumbled. "They'll never believe it when we get back home."

Michael's face hardened a bit, then he said, "I told you, I am not going back there, Home is now my home."

"How's your shoulder?" Tommy asked ignoring Michael's comment.

"It's okay," Michael answered. "It looks terrible, but it feels fine."

Tommy gave him a thumbs-up and got out of bed. He dressed and went to the bathroom. By the time he returned, Michael had already put his things in his back-pack and was ready to go.

"I'm going downstairs to wait for you and Carla," Michael said.

"No wait," Tommy responded. "Carla won't be down there. She said she had something to do this morning. She said she'd meet us in the Main Hall. Plus, we need to do the Duplicato charm before we go." Although Michael was eager to go, he agreed. They took their time and magically transferred the school rules into their minds. Once they completed the charm, Tommy put his books and papers in his back-pack and they went down to the Community Room. After checking the Castle Directory, they left the Crow's Next and headed for the Main Hall.

Tommy was telling Michael about his conversation with Carla and all the things he had told her as they went around a corner. Halfway down the following hallway was Reginald Whitelace. He was leaning against the wall with one of his friends at his side. Tommy and Michael hesitated for a moment. "Keep your head down and don't look at them," Tommy whispered. "Maybe they won't pay any attention to us."

"Fat chance," Michael whispered back.

They lowered their heads and proceeded quickly down the hallway. As they approached Whitelace and his pal, Whitelace let his wand slip from under his sleeve into his hand so that just the tip extended beyond his fingers. He gave it a quick little flick. He was aiming at Michael's feet, but the handle of his wand caught on his sleeve and the magic hit Tommy's feet. The toe of Tommy's right foot caught the heel of his left foot and he tumbled, face forward, to the stone floor of the walkway. A couple of his books and his class schedule popped out of his back-pack and slid across the floor. Although he was a bit shaken, he wasn't hurt. He rolled over and, as he looked toward Whitelace, he saw Whitelace's wand slip back up his sleeve.

"Travail," Whitelace said sharply.

Tommy quickly got to his feet. "Yes sir," he said as he brushed himself off.

"I see you're as clumsy as your buddy Woden here," Whitelace remarked, and then he asked, "What's the seventh rule on the rules most important list?"

The list flashed in his mind's eye and Tommy answered, "No wave riding in the castle."

"And, just now, weren't you attempting to wave ride down this hallway?" Whitelace asked.

"No sir," Tommy replied. "We were just walking quickly."

"Is that true, Woden?" he asked turning his attention to Michael.

"Yes," Michael answered.

"Yes, what," Whitelace asked.

"Huh," Michael replied with some confusion.

"What's the first rule," Whitelace asked Michael firmly.

David G. Groesbeck

"The first rule," he said as he mentally checked the list, "is that students are to address all superiors by title or with a Sir or Ma'am."

"So?" Whitelace prodded.

"So? Oh. Sir, yes sir," Michael said finally getting the point.

"You know, it's not good enough to just know the rules," Whitelace admonished, "you also have to follow them."

"Yes *sir*," Michael responded emphasizing the sir.

"That's better," Whitelace replied. "Now what's this I hear that you think you're brave enough to race with the big boys?"

"Race? Uh, sir," Michael stammered. "I don't know what you're talking about, uh, sir."

"I'm talking about wave racing," Whitelace said forcefully. "I hear you think you're good enough to make the team."

"Honestly, sir, I don't know what you're talking about," Michael pleaded.

"I heard you were showing off in front of the whole school yesterday."

"I just had an accident, that's all, sir, just an accident."

"Well we'll see," Whitelace said looking Michael right in the eye. "Team tryouts are tomorrow afternoon. However, if I were you, I wouldn't bother showing up; and that goes for you too, Travail." Tommy was bent over picking up his books and papers.

"Yes, sir," Tommy stood up and answered. "Can we go now?" he asked as he put his things into his back-pack.

"I suppose so," Whitelace answered. "You'll be seeing me again soon enough."

Tommy and Michael turned and headed down the hall. Carla was waiting for them when they arrived at the Main Hall. She had saved seats for them next to her. They sat down and, while they ate, they told her about the incident with Whitelace.

Chapter Fifteen

The First Day of Classes

They finished their meal and the three of them refreshed their Duplicato charm. They left the Main Hall and went into the Grand Foyer to check the Castle Directory. Many of their classmates were already there and Abigale had just finished checking the directory. With Abigale in the lead, they all went to their first class.

Professor Grumble stood behind her desk as the kids began arriving at the classroom. "Welcome to Political and Social Magic," she said as the kids entered the room. "Sit wherever you like."

Rectangular tables had been set up rather than individual desks. Each table had three chairs facing the front of the room. Abigale sat herself in the centermost chair at the centermost table located at the front of the room. Carla wanted to sit at one of the front tables and the boys wanted to sit at one of the back tables. After a little discussion, Carla agreed to sit at one of the back tables, but only after the boys promised to behave. Everyone settled into a chair and the room fell quite. Professor Grumble was an elderly witch with a round, full, friendly face. She was slightly over weight, but her robes disguised most of it. Although she was a little shorter than average, her straight and proper posture made her appear taller than she actually was. She had gray hair, large eyes and wore wire-framed glasses. Her voice was slightly high pitched, but it had a dignified firmness to it.

"In this class," the Professor began, "you will learn to distinguish quickly between a purely social situation, a social situation with political overtones and a purely political situation. Can anyone tell me why this is important?" Carla and Abigale both raised their hands. The Professor called upon Abigale.

"Abigale Antwerp," Abigale said as she rose from her seat. "We need to know whether a situation is social or political so that we can use the appropriate magic."

"That's correct," the Professor said. "In this class, you will learn to perform the magic that is used in social situations as well as the magic you will need in the political environment. Eventually, we will compare the two for their similarities and differences. Much of what you learn your first year will be basic in nature, but over the next three years, you will learn more sophisticated and complex magic. I urge you not to get impatient for the more complex magic. A solid foundation in the basics is very important since so much of the more complex magic has a piece of basic magic at its core. In this first semester, we will devote our time to the magic we use in our homes, which brings me to your first homework assignment. Before our next class, please read chapter one of your text. We will discuss it in our next session and begin learning some of the magic it contains."

"Now that you know a little about this class," the Professor continued, "I'd like to learn a little about each of you. So, beginning with this first table on my right, I'd like each of you to stand up, introduce yourself and tell us a little about yourself." The Professor pointed to the first student, a brown haired girl that Tommy and Michael hadn't yet met.

"My name is Bridgette Wildvine," the brown haired girl said, "and I come from the Blue River Valley. I enjoy late night scary stories and exploring the unknown. My favorite subject is History. When I graduate from the Queen's Academy, I would like to travel to the outermost Realms of Home as an Ambassador for the Queen." She sat down and the boy next to her stood up. It was Ronald Lockhard.

"My name is Ronald Lockhard," he started. "I come from the Lost Woods area of Charlotte's Village. My favorite subjects are Science and Mathematics. I have a keen interest in magically enchanted mechanical devices and hope to someday work for the Department of All Things Magical." Ronald sat down and the next student stood up.

The Life and Times of Tommy Travail

Tommy pulled out a sheet of paper and wrote a note for Michael. His note advised Michael that they should be as truthful as possible without revealing anything that might raise questions. Michael read the note and nodded his head in agreement. The remaining students, in turn, stood up and told something about their self. When the last student had finished, the Professor said that they had done well; she reminded them of their reading assignment and excused them. Tommy stood up quickly, took Carla by the arm and assisted her out of her chair.

"What's your hurry?" Carla asked.

"The Castle Directory is just outside the door. If we hurry, we can beat Abigale. I think you should lead us to our next class." Still holding on to her arm, he ushered her out the door to the directory. Carla studied the directory as the kids began filing out of the classroom. Carla nodded to Tommy just as Abigale arrived.

"I got it," Carla said to Abigale. "Come on we can walk together." Tommy nodded to Carla, and with a hand motion, he indicated that she and Abigale should go on ahead.

The two girls started and the group followed. Tommy and Michael fell in at the back of the group. Tommy touched his temple with his wand to refresh the Duplicato charm. He nudged Michael with his elbow. When Michael saw what he was doing, he did the same. Their next class was Historical Magic with Professor Pastorie. The group rounded a corner and approached a staircase. Reginald Whitelace was standing in a corner near the staircase. As the group neared the staircase, Whitelace raised his hand and stopped the group. Tommy and Michael had been joking around and not paying attention, so they were surprised when the group came to a halt. When they saw Whitelace, their heads dropped and their shoulders slumped.

"Who goes there," Whitelace said in a standard military challenge.

"I'm Carla Crosswell," Carla said, "and this is the Queen's Class."

"The Queen's Class?" Whitelace questioned with as bit of surprise in his voice. "That's a pretty lofty name you've given yourselves. Well, Queen's Class, what's the password?"

Everyone was suddenly confused. No one had heard of a password. They all looked around at one another for an answer, but everyone had the same questioning look on their face, including Abigale. So everyone was surprised when Carla said, "Allioposa," with a flat surety in her voice.

Whitelace's eyes widened and then narrowed as he stared at Carla. Everyone else was also staring at Carla. "Well," Whitelace started and then paused as he stared at Carla a little more intensely. "It would seem that you are correct. You may pass for now, all of you, except Travail and Woden that is."

The entire group, who were still staring at Carla, now turned to find Tommy and Michael. Carla took Abigale's arm and began to lead the group down the stairs. Tommy, who had not paid much attention to the many paintings around the castle, found himself staring at a painting on the wall next to him. Although he had been paying attention to the exchange between Whitelace and Carla, the painting had caught his eye. It was a painting of King Richard seated on his throne with his wife, who was now Queen Lucinda, standing next to his right side. Another figure had once been painted standing to the left side of the King; however, someone had painted over the figure. Tommy could still see the outline of figure as the newer paint over the older paint had left a ridge line. Tommy surmised that this must have been the Queen's son who had gone crazy and killed himself.

Michael looked at Tommy. Tommy was still examining the painting. Michael nudged him with his elbow. Tommy looked at Michael and he looked at Whitelace. Tommy turned his eyes toward Whitelace. The last of the group had gone down the stairs and a gap of several feet now existed between the boys and Whitelace. Whitelace was motioning them to come forward by curling his right index finger. Together, Tommy and Michael approached Whitelace.

"Yes, sir," Tommy said.

Whitelace was holding an elaborately engraved gold pocket watch. It had a face cover, which was open exposing several different watch faces. As the boys approached, Whitelace raised his left hand and turned his gaze from the boys to the watch. He stood there staring at his watch for several moments. It seemed to the boys that it was taking him forever to say or do something. Finally, Whitelace turned his head and icy stare back to the boys.

"See this watch," he started, "my father gave it to me as a gift when I was accepted into the Queen's Academy. It's self-synchronizing. This outer dial automatically sets itself to the exact local time, and it's precise to the second. Right now, it reads Castle Time." He paused briefly and then went on. "So, you two rule breakers have attended your first class. How many demerits did you earn?"

"None, sir," Tommy replied after a slight hesitation, but the expression on his face revealed to Whitelace that Tommy was not familiar with demerits.

"It would appear that you have not completely read your Rules and Code of Conduct Manual," Whitelace observed. "If you had, you'd know that getting six demerits during any semester will earn you a letter of reprimand from the Head Mistress, and a copy of it goes into your permanent file. Getting ten demerits in any semester will get you a disciplinary conference with the Head Mistress and, the best one, getting thirteen demerits in a semester is grounds for dismissal. It is very fortunate for you two losers that Prefects cannot issue demerits; otherwise, you'd be on your way out of here by now. It's too bad you didn't rack up a couple of demerits in your first class, because you both are about to get one."

"Why?" Tommy protested, "we haven't caused any trouble and we have been obeying the rules."

"I doubt you two know the rules," Whitelace said firmly. "What's the ninth rule most important?"

"Students are not to be late for class," Tommy replied after scanning the Duplicato list in his mind.

"And the punishment for being late to class is one demerit," Whitelace added as he turned his head slightly and looked at his watch. "My watch tells me that in one minute and ten seconds you both will earn your first demerit."

"That's not fair," Tommy protested again, "you've been holding us here."

"Fine," Whitelace replied. "You can stand here and we can debate the point, or you can try to make it to class. Which will it be?"

Tommy and Michael didn't hesitate. They immediately turned and headed down the stairs. When they got to the bottom of the stairs, Tommy started looking for a Castle Directory. Neither he nor Michael knew where the classroom was located. Tommy spotted a directory not too far from the bottom of the stairs and ran to it. He studied it for a moment, but he couldn't spot Professor Pastorie's classroom. Tommy suddenly got an idea. He didn't know if it would work, but he thought it was worth a try.

"Castle," he said. "This is Tommy Travail of the Queen's Class; please show me the fastest route to Professor Pastorie's class."

The Castle immediately responded. A piercing thin red line flashed across all four displays. It was quite confusing. The line seemed to squiggle all over the place. The only thing that Tommy could decipher for sure was that there was a doorway on the other side of a protruding wall just three meters to their right. It appeared from the Directory that once they made it through that door, the following corridor would eventually end in Professor Pastorie's classroom. Tommy pointed in the direction of the protruding wall and set off at a quick pace. Michael had to do a short running step to catch up with Tommy. They rounded the wall, but there was no doorway. Instead, there was another wall with a painting hanging on it.

"I don't understand," Tommy said. "I was sure…"

As the boys approached the painting, the painting swung back revealing a circular opening. A short puff of air popped out, ruffling their hair and blowing their robes about. It appeared to be a tube of some sort. It was just large enough to accommodate one person lying down. "I think we got to jump in," Tommy said. "What do you think?"

"I say we go for it," Michael replied.

Tommy didn't hesitate. He rose up as much as possible and dove into the tube head first. Michael grabbed the top edge of the tube with his fingertips, magically popped himself up and slipped into the tube feet first. In an instant, they were falling. It was similar to the water slides they had gone down back home, however, they were not sliding on water; they were riding on a cushion of air. There was a slight glow of light around them. They went down, around to the right, then around to the left. They went up slightly before dropping back down again. It was hard to tell how fast they were going, but they knew they were going really fast. They swished back and forth through a set of gentle curves, followed by a series of quick rises and drops. They went through a falling spiral. As they went around and around the spiral, they became somewhat dizzy and disorientated. The tube straightened out and began to level off some. To Tommy's horror, he could see the tube was coming to a dead end. Although he had slowed some, he was still going too fast to hit head first. He raised his arms and braced for impact. However, what appeared to be a dead end was actually the backside of another painting. Just before Tommy collided with the backside of the painting, it swung open. Tommy suddenly felt as if he was passing through a soft billowy cloud of feathers. His speed slowed almost to a stop as he exited the tube. He came out of the tube and softly fell to the floor in a pronounced belly flop. He quickly rolled to his side to make way for Michael. Michael came out of the tube and, before he realized he could have landed on his feet, landed with a soft poof on his butt.

The boys stood up. They were in the back of Professor Pastorie's classroom. All of their fellow classmates had taken their seats, but they had all turned around and were now looking at Tommy and Michael. Carla was near them. She was sitting at a table with two empty chairs. Professor Pastorie was standing behind his desk in the front of the classroom. Professor Pastorie was a middle aged man with dark straight hair and brown eyes. He had a pair of reading glasses set near the end of his somewhat pointed nose. And, to Tommy and Michael's surprise, he was smiling.

"Are we late?" Tommy asked slightly out of breath.

Professor Pastorie pointed toward the doorway. Above the doorway was a clock. Tommy and Michael turned to the clock as the second hand clicked to thirteen. "It appears that you are right on-time, and, History is about time and time makes History," the Professor said still smiling. "Please take your seats and we will begin."

Similar to Professor Grumble, Professor Pastorie gave them an overview of his class and followed it by having the students stand up and tell a little about themselves. When the last student finished speaking, the Professor told them to read the first chapter in their text before their next session. He asked Tommy and Michael to remain for a few minutes and then dismissed the class. Tommy and Michael met briefly with Professor Pastorie. Together they decided to hold their remedial History classes on the second and fourth school days each week, right after their last regular class. This worked well for everyone, as those were Tommy and Michael's short days, and the Professor had a free period at that time. The Professor said that the classes would be limited to a half hour each. He reminded them that the classes would continue until he decided they were ready to retake the test. He said the quicker they learned the material, the sooner they could end the classes. Tommy asked if they could cover King Oleander and the Tears of Damiana first. The Professor, knowing the subject had recently been in the news, was delighted with Tommy's request. He said that combining current events with ancient history was a good way to stimulate a lively discussion. The Professor told them to read chapters three and four in their History book before their first class the next afternoon.

The boys left the classroom and found Carla waiting for them. "That was quite an entrance," she said.

The boys smiled and, as they walked to the Main Hall for lunch, they told her what happened after she and the class left them with Whitelace. They arrived at the Main Hall and took seats.

"What was that password business?" Tommy asked Carla as their food began to appear. "I mean how'd you know?"

Carla smiled, but did not answer right away. She had been asked this question a dozen times or more since she led the class away from Whitelace. She took a couple of bites of her lunch.

"Aw, come on," Tommy said. "I've been dying to know."

"Well," she finally said, "the Rules and Code of Conduct Manual makes reference to 'other Academy traditions' without saying what those traditions are. So, I went to the library this morning before breakfast to see if I could find out what they are. One of the things I found out is that the Military School uses passwords; it's something that is ordinarily used only between the fifth and sixth year military students. I also found out that the current password is always posted in the Prefect office, so I went by there before coming to breakfast and got today's password."

"That was pretty sharp," Tommy complimented.

"Way to go," Michael added.

They had eaten most of their lunch when Abigale walked into the Main Hall. Neither Carla nor the boys had noticed that Abigale had

The Life and Times of Tommy Travail

not been in her usual seat at the front of the table. "I'll bet she was at the library," Tommy said after Abigale pasted by on her way to her seat.

"You just know it," Michael answered. "I'll bet she was in a tizzy. She didn't have a clue when Whitelace asked for the password. Did you tell her how you knew," he asked Carla.

"More or less," Carla replied, "but I didn't tell her everything." A broad grin spread across her face. The boys smiled back and Tommy gave her a wink.

They finished their meal a little early, so they decided to return to the Crow's Nest to freshen up before their afternoon classes. They opened the door when they got back to the Crow's Nest and entered the Community Room. The only one there was Mister Buttercup. He was lying on the floor in front of the fireplace. He raised his head and looked their way as they entered. He gave them a hello meow, set his head back down between his front paws and closed his eyes.

"Hi, Mister Buttercup," Tommy said, "Out all night catting around were ya?"

Mister Buttercup responded with a soft, muffled meow without raising his head or opening his eyes. Tommy reached down and scratched him behind his ears. Mister Buttercup purred softly.

The three of them agreed to meet back in the Community Room in fifteen minutes. Carla when up the stairs to the girls' bedroom and the boys went up to their bedroom. Michael went over to his bed and dropped his back-pack on the floor next to his trunk. He sat down on the edge of his bed and Tommy went to the bathroom to wash his hands and face. Tommy found the water cool and refreshing as he splashed it on his face. He dried his face and hands and returned to the bedroom area. Michael was lying on the bed staring at the ceiling.

"Whatcha thinking about?" Tommy asked.

"Oh," Michael responded, "I was thinking about how much I love it here, then I thought about Whitelace. We're gonna have a real problem with him. Got any ideas?"

"Not really," Tommy answered, "but we need to try our best to avoid him. I'm finding it harder and harder to control my temper."

"Me too," Michael affirmed.

"Come on. Let's go downstairs and see if Carla's ready," Tommy said. "We'll have to work this whole Whitelace thing out later. We can't take a chance on being late for class."

"Got you there," Michael said as he stood up and grabbed his back-pack.

They went back down to the Community Room. Carla had not yet come down, so the boys went and checked the Castle Directory. Two little figures appeared on the directory. They found Professor Krusher's classroom. It was on the ground floor at the rear of the castle, just inside from the Parade Grounds. Tommy reached out and touched Professor Krusher's classroom. A thin blue line appeared across the directory. A third little figure appeared on the directory as Carla approached.

"I was going to suggest that you boys always check the directory before we head off to class," Carla said, "after that incident with Whitelace and all. But, I see you guys have already thought of that."

"Well," Tommy said, "we were really just killing time, but you're right. I guess it's just something we're going to have to do."

Carla studied the directory for a few moments. When she was sure of their route, she opened the door and they headed out. They walked the length of one corridor to a flight of stairs and went down. Once they reached the bottom of the stairs, they turned right and went down another hallway.

"There's something I need to tell you about Professor Krusher," Carla said as they reached a corner. "Professor Krusher..." Carla stopped as they turned the corner. Whitelace was leaning against the wall some distance down the adjoining hallway. The three of them immediately stopped and turned around, but before they could make it back around the corner, Whitelace called to them.

"Travail, Woden and Crosswell," he said when he saw them turn around. "Come here."

They stopped, turned back around and walked to Whitelace. "Yes sir," the three of them said in unison.

Whitelace leaned forward and stared down at Carla for several moments before speaking. "Carla Crosswell," he finally said, "daughter of Master Wizard Abernathy Crosswell and Lady Witch

The Life and Times of Tommy Travail

Leila Crosswell, two of the Academy's finest. I am in total shock that you would take up with these two screw-ups. I'll bet your parents have no idea who you are spending your time with."

"As a matter of fact, sir, they do," Carla said as politely as she could.

Whitelace's eyes narrowed as he continued to stare at her. "Well, I don't imagine they're too happy about it. I know you're young, Miss Crosswell, but still; I mean, to be running around with the likes of these two, you should have more respect for your family. I think you should choose your friends more carefully."

Carla looked Whitelace directly in the eye, hesitated for a moment and then said, "I believe that everyone is *my* friend, including you Mister Whitelace. But, the friends I value the most are the ones that return my friendship." Carla remembered Tommy's firm conviction that Whitelace was in league with the Black Witch and added, "Perhaps it is you who should choose your friends more carefully."

Whitelace's eyes widened and he straightened up. He wanted to respond to her, but he couldn't. There was something about what she said and how she said it. He didn't know what it was, but there was something, and trying to figure it out would bug him for a long time. After a brief pause, he collected himself and turned his attention to Tommy and Michael. "How many demerits have you two earned so far? I know you have at least one apiece."

"Uh, we don't have any demerits, sir," Tommy answered.

Whitelace pursed his lips. His cheeks sunk in slightly and his nostrils flared. He raised his left eyebrow and lowered his right eyebrow. "What!" he exclaimed as his anger rose.

"We don't have any demerits, sir," Tommy answered again.

Whitelace looked the two boys over then said, "Don't tell me. Professor Pastorie excused first day tardiness."

"Something like that, sir," Tommy said thinking quickly, he wasn't going to tell Whitelace anything he didn't have to.

The whole encounter had not gone the way Whitelace thought it would. So, being a good military man, he decided to withdraw. He turned back to Carla and took out his pocket watch. He opened the lid and examined it. "Well, Miss Crosswell," he said, "I see you have just enough time to make your next class. You better get going, and take these two with you, I'm sick of looking at 'em."

Carla didn't wait for Whitelace to say another word. She grabbed Tommy by the arm and Tommy grabbed Michael by the arm. Carla set off down the remainder of the hallway with such force that she was practically dragging Tommy. Tommy let go of Michael, but Carla continued to pull Tommy along until they rounded the next corner. Once they got around the corner, Carla stopped and let go of Tommy. Tommy had the biggest smile across his face. He knew Carla Crosswell was indeed something special.

"What are you smiling about?" Carla asked tersely.

"Just two ordinary guys," Tommy responded, "and one very special girl, friends for life, right?"

Both Carla and Michael began to smile, and both responded with a firm, "Right."

They laughed and made fun of Whitelace as they headed toward Professor Krusher's Military History class, but underlying their fun was an unsettling feeling that things might get worse with Whitelace. They were almost to the classroom when they met up with a group of their fellow classmates. They joined the group, went the short ways to the classroom and went in. Tables and chairs were set up for the students just like the other classrooms. The Professor's desk was to their left. They went to their right and found a table at the back of the room. The wall directly across from the door was almost all windows, which gave the room a view of the entire Parade Grounds. In the far corner of that wall, at the back of the room, was a door that led out to the Parade Grounds.

Professor Krusher was at the front of his desk. He had his bottom against the front edge of the desk and was partially sitting on it. He was tall, physically fit and younger than the other Professors. He was about the same age that Tommy's father would have been. His black hair was closely cut and he had a long, but angular face. His dark eyebrows were almost straight, except for a small downturn on their outside ends. He had a friendly face. But, it was one of those faces that, when necessary, could quickly turn hard and stern. The Professor watched the students as they entered the classroom. When he saw Carla, he gave her a big smile and she smiled back at him. Tommy noticed this and thought it was unusual. Once everyone took a seat, Professor Krusher began. Unlike the other classes, he did not begin with a class overview. Instead, he began by having the students stand up and tell something about their self. Further, he asked that each student tell something different from what he or she had told in the previous classes.

Professor Krusher leaned against his desk until the last student finished. He then stood up straight and walked toward the windows. He had a slight, but very noticeable limp. Once he reached the window, he turned to the class and asked, "How many of you can wave ride?" Everybody raised their hand, except Bertram Buttwell, a small and frail looking boy. "Now," the Professor went on. "How many of you can wave ride using the foot method?" About half the class lowered their hands. Both Tommy and Michael kept their arms raised. "Okay," the Professor said as he walked back to his desk. "Do we have any fliers in the class?" Everyone who still had their hand in the air lowered it, except Carla. She lowered her arm some, but, for a moment, she held her hand just above shoulder height. The Professor looked at Carla, smiled and gave her the slightest nod. Carla lowered her hand the rest of the way and blushed slightly. Tommy and Michael, as well as most of the class, were looking at her. The expressions on the students' faces varied from surprise to envy. Tommy and Michael's faces were showing total shock.

The Professor quickly cleared his throat with an, "Uhm-uhm." All the students immediately turned their attention back to the Professor. "In this class," he began "*all* of you will learn to wave ride. Almost all of you will learn to wave ride using the foot method. And, if we're lucky, one or two of you will take the first steps in learning to fly." Oohs and Aahs spread across the classroom. The Professor paused briefly and then continued, "In our next class we will begin wave riding practice out on the Parade Grounds. Between now and then, I want you to read the first two chapters in your text. This will be the beginning of your training in Military Magic. In your first three years, you will learn many magical skills that have a Military application. You will learn how to defend yourself magically and how to use your wand as a weapon. If, after your first three years, you are accepted into the Military School, you will learn the advanced magic that will qualify you to serve as an

David G. Groesbeck

Officer in the Queen's Military. It is my sincerest hope that all of you will do well."

The Professor walked back to the windows and looked out across the Parade Grounds. After a moment, he turned around and said, "There is just one more thing before I let you go. As some of you may know, we will be holding tryouts for the Cross-Country Race Team tomorrow afternoon. As cross-country racing is difficult and somewhat risky, I don't generally recommend that first year students tryout for the Team. However, the tryouts are open to all students. If you think you might be interested, please stop by my desk on your way out and pick up a Racing Manual. If, after reading the manual, you feel that you have what it takes to be a racer, come on out to the Parade Grounds tomorrow afternoon and give it a go. That is all I have for today. If I don't see you on the Parade Grounds tomorrow, I'll see you the day after tomorrow for our next class session when we'll begin our wave riding training." The students started to get out of the seats. "Mister Woden," the Professor called to Michael, "please wait. I'd like to talk with you for a moment."

The students began filing out of the room. Some of the students stopped by the Professor's desk and picked up a racing manual. Carla told Michael that she and Tommy would wait for him in the hallway. Tommy stopped at the Professor's desk on their way out and picked up a Racing Manual, but Carla slapped his hand and he dropped it back on the desk. Before he could pick it up again, Carla grabbed his arm and ushered him out of the classroom. The Professor saw Carla knock the manual out of Tommy's hand, but didn't say anything. Michael picked up his pack-back and walked over to the Professor, who was still standing next to the windows.

"Michael Woden," he said, "reporting as requested."

Michael's formality brought a smile to the Professor's face. The Professor then told Michael that he had heard about his wave riding incident and asked him to consider trying out for the Race Team. The Professor said that he was the Coach of the Racing Team and that he'd like to see Michael at the tryouts. Michael was honest and told the Professor that he really wasn't a skilled wave rider, but that didn't deter the Professor. He said that, although riding skills were important, they could be learned. The Professor said he was much more interested in an individual's daring and courage. He told Michael that the tryouts would be held throughout the next afternoon, and invited Michael to come out to the Parade Grounds when he was finished with his last class. The Professor, with his slight limp, walked back to his desk. Michael followed. Once they reached the desk, Michael told the Professor that he would come to the tryouts, but he felt compelled to remind the Professor that he really wasn't that skilled. The Professor smiled and told Michael that he was pleased with his decision. Michael then told the Professor that Tommy might also be interested in trying out for the Team. That seemed to please the Professor and he extended his invitation to include Tommy as well. The Professor gave Michael two Racing Manuals, one for himself and one for Tommy.

Michael excused himself and went out into the hallway where Carla and Tommy were waiting. Carla was leaning against the hallway wall. She had her arms folded across her chest and a scowl on her face. Tommy was studying a nearby Castle Directory. Michael walked over to Tommy, gave him his copy of the Racing Manual and told him that the Professor had asked them both to tryout for the Cross-Country Race Team. Carla looked like she was about to explode.

"What did you tell him?" Carla asked curtly as she walked over to the boys.

"I told him I'd be there," Michael responded, "and that Tommy might also come."

"Humph," Carla grunted as she started down the hallway to their next class.

The boys followed her. "What was that all about?" Michael asked Tommy.

"Man, all she did was rag on me while you were talking to the Professor," Tommy answered.

"What about?" Michael asked.

"This whole cross-country racing thing," Tommy responded. "She says it's dangerous and she doesn't want either of us involved in it."

"What did you tell her?"

"I said I didn't think you were considering it, but if you decide you want to, that I would support you."

"Well I do want to go," Michael stated, "if for nothing else than to have a look."

"Sounds okay by me," Tommy said. "I'll go with you."

Carla was walking very quickly and the boys almost had to run to catch her. "Carla," Tommy called as he neared her. "Slow down. We've got to keep a lookout for Whitelace." Carla didn't say anything; however, she immediately slowed her pace. They walked in silence and kept a watchful eye for Whitelace.

They reached their next classroom with time to spare. A number of their classmates were out in the hallway talking and goofing off while they waited for the class to start. As Carla and the boys approached a voice from the classroom called out.

"Come on in boys and girls. It's about time to start class." The voice was that of Professor Colette Clearvoice. The sound of her voice was one of the most pleasant sounds that Tommy had ever heard. Her voice had such a range of qualities that it sounded as if it could have been made by a musical instrument. She, however, did not speak with a melody or in a musical way. She spoke each word smoothly and correctly, but the sound of her voice was unbelievably beautiful. It didn't matter what she said, just the sound of her voice was enough to induce a dream like state. However, her speech was not spoken in a dreamy way. Tommy had heard her voice before when she administered the 'Diction and Communication Skills' test. But, that had been their first test, and with all the tension and anxiety, he had been too nervous to appreciate the beauty of her voice.

Carla and the boys entered the classroom and headed to one of the back tables. The Professor walked over to the door to usher the remaining students into the room. She was slightly shorter than average. She wore a trim fitting set of robes that revealed a body size that was in perfect balance with her height. She had violet shoulder length hair and electric blue eyes. Her eyes, nose and mouth blended with the shape of her face in perfect harmony. She was as beautiful as her voice, and she was young. She was even younger than Professor Krusher.

The Professor closed the door once everyone had entered and walked to her desk. "Welcome to Vocalized Magic," she began. "This is the class where you will learn magic that is spoken. You will learn how to make magic with words, and, you will learn words that make magic. Among many other things, you will learn how to cast a spell and how to make an enchantment. It is all very exciting and I'm sure Vocalized Magic will quickly become your one of your favorite classes." Her excitement and sincerity showed on her face and in the warmth of her voice. A heightened level of excitement spread through the classroom. Everyone was suddenly invigorated and interested. This was the last class of the day and everyone had been getting a little tired, but the Professor had reenergized everybody.

The Professor went on and described what they could expect over the next three years. When she finished she had the class go through the routine of telling something about their self. Michael and Tommy began calling it 'Story Time'. When the last student finished, the Professor asked Abigale to see her after class, then she dismissed everyone. Everyone, except Abigale, left the room and gathered in the hallway. With Abigale missing, Carla took the lead.

Chapter Sixteen

A Drop of Truth and the Rules of Racing

Everybody wanted to go back to the Crow's Nest, so Carla checked a nearby directory and led the group off. The boys saw Carla touch her temple with her wand. Realizing she was refreshing her Duplicato charm, they did the same. They had gone quite a ways. As they were nearing the corner at the end of a long hallway, Whitelace came around the corner and headed right toward them. He motioned to the group to stop as he approached.

"Everyone, except Travail and Woden may pass," he said. Carla immediately led the class around the corner. In short order the class disappeared, leaving only Michael and Tommy.

"How many demerits," Whitelace asked as he stared down at the boys.

"None, sir," Tommy answered.

"How about you Woden," he asked, turning his attention to Michael.

"None either, ah sir," Michael responded.

Whitelace looked somewhat disappointed, but the expression on his face remained hard. "I hope you're getting the message that the two of you aren't wanted here. The Academy does not need your kind of riff-raff. Isn't there somewhere else you'd rather be?"

"It appears, Mister Whitelace, that this is where we must be," Tommy answered.

The Life and Times of Tommy Travail

"Are you getting smart with me," Whitelace responded as he leaned down so close that Tommy could feel the heat of his breath.

"No, sir," Tommy replied.

"Well, I'll tell you that your mere presence is an insult to everyone around you, especially young Miss Crosswell, and she would do well to shed herself of the two of you before something bad happens to her, if you get my meaning."

Threatening Carla pushed Tommy over the top. In the back of his mind, he had been thinking about this moment. He had thought about rule number two. It says that every Academy student shall honor, respect and protect every other student, past, present and future. Tommy had thought how he would challenge Whitelace to recite this rule and then show him how stupid he was because he apparently didn't understand the rule. That's what Tommy thought he'd do, but he couldn't contain himself and instead he said, "You know what? You're nothing but a mean, hard-hearted, stupid oaf, with bad breath… sir."

Whitelace straightened up and made the slightest smile. "You know that's so many rule violations that I'm not sure I can count them all. This kind of infraction certainly calls for a little disciplinary punishment. I would say," he pause briefly, then continued, "ten handwritten copies of 'The Rules Most Important' turned in by, say, mid-day tomorrow. Now get out of here before you two make me puke."

Tommy and Michael didn't hesitate. They headed the short ways to the end of the hallway, rounded the corner and almost ran over Carla. She had waited for them and she must have heard everything because she was furious. Her normally beautiful eyes were icy cold as she stared at Tommy.

"Come on, let's go," she said sharply as she tugged firmly on Tommy's robe sleeve. She had been angry before, but now she was doubly angry.

"Hey," Michael said. "What happened to the rest of the class?"

"I sent them on ahead with Bertram Buttwell in the lead," Carla snapped.

"Hey, way to go Bertie," Michael quipped.

Carla started in on Tommy. She said that he had done exactly what Whitelace wanted him to do. It gave him an excuse to dole out some punishment.

"But, but," Tommy protested. The harder he tried to think of a way to explain what he meant to do the more complicated it seemed. Carla wasn't giving him much of a chance to talk anyway, so he finally gave up. Besides, in his heart he knew she was right. He should have kept his mouth shut.

Once Tommy ceased his protests, Carla started in on them about the dangers of cross-country racing. Both Tommy and Michael were relieved when they reached the Crow's Nest and entered the Community Room. Since there were other students in the Community Room, Carla stopped her tirade. Bertram Buttwell had apparently gotten everyone back to the dormitory safely. They had two hours before dinner. Tommy said he wanted to start doing his lines and the three of them went into one of the study rooms. The room was empty. They sat down and Carla started again.

"I'm telling you," she said, "cross-country racing is dangerous. People get hurt all the time. People have even been killed. And what did Whitelace tell you two? Didn't he tell you not to show up?"

"Yes, Carla," Michael replied flatly, "but I don't care what he says, I was invited to the tryouts by the Coach and I'm going. Please, what do you say we put an end to this? Tommy and I are going and we'll find out for ourselves. If it's too tough and we can't make the team, well at least we'll have tried. Plus, I think it'll be fun." As soon as the 'fun' bit left his mouth, he regretted it.

"Fun," Carla exclaimed. "I told you it was dangerous. I..."

"Carla, please," Tommy interrupted. "We'll *all* go tomorrow and take a look. There's no harm in that. But for now, can we just drop it?"

"Oh, alright," Carla reluctantly agreed.

Tommy had quickly developed a plan to do his lines and he was anxious to implement it. If it worked, they would all learn the rules and he'd get the lines done quickly. Tommy and Michael had learned to copy each other's handwriting. It was a handy tool they developed for sharing homework.

"Michael," Tommy started. "I'll bet I can write these lines faster in my handwriting than you can write them in my handwriting. In fact, I bet I can write them faster than Carla can read them."

"Don't think so," Michael replied.

"I seriously doubt it," Carla added.

"Okay," Tommy said as he pulled out a couple of paper tablets and two pens. He took out his copy of 'The Rules Most Important' and gave it to Carla. "I have to do ten sets, but if Michael and I both do it, we'll only have to do five sets each. Carla you begin reading aloud. You must start slowly, but as you go, you can get faster with each different rule. After each set, the one that finishes first will get three points, the one that finishes second will get two points and the one that finishes last will get one point. And Carla, with the start of each new set you have to start over again slowly."

Carla began and the challenge was on.

Carla easily won the first set and Tommy finished second. Carla also won the second set, although not quite as easily as she had won the first. Michael finished second, but he and Tommy were very close. However, Tommy won the third set and Michael finished second. Carla was shocked. Then, Michael won the fourth set and Tommy finished second. Tommy knew Michael had caught on, but Carla was really confused. She thought for a few minutes before she started the fifth and final set. They were all tied with eight points each. Then it dawned on her. Tommy and Michael were combining the Duplicato trace in their memories with the actual memories they were accumulating. This caused a corresponding release of magic that they were using to guide their hands. Carla figured if two could play that game so could three. She started the final set. By the time they got to the last rule and finished, they were all going so fast that no one was sure who finished first. They all claimed the victory.

"I'm sure I won," Michael declared.

"Did not," Tommy responded.

"I'm sorry, but I know I won," Carla said with certainty.

"Did not," both Michael and Tommy replied in unison.

"Did so," Carla insisted, "and I would have won easily if you guys hadn't cheated."

"I wasn't cheating," Tommy said pleading innocence.

"Neither was I," Michael added.

"Were too," Carla said.

"Was not," Michael answered back.

They suddenly stopped and looked at each other. Although there hadn't been any doubt, they all knew from that moment on that Carla was truly one of them. Carla started to laugh and so did Michael and Tommy. They laughed until their stomachs hurt.

Tommy's plan had worked. They not only finished his lines, but in just under an hour, they had also learned 'The Rules Most Important'. Tommy put Michael's papers with his and put them in his back-pack. Since they still had nearly an hour before they had to leave for dinner, they decided to read some. Tommy chose his History book, Carla chose to read her Political and Social Magic text book and Michael chose to read the Racing Manual that Professor Krusher gave him. By the time they had to leave for dinner, Tommy had read both of the assigned chapters in his History book and Michael had gone through the Racing Manual a couple of times. Carla, as it turned out, was a speed reader and she had finished fully half of her text book. They gathered their things and took them to their bedrooms.

When they returned to the Community Room, there was a large group of their fellow classmates just preparing to leave for dinner, so they joined in. Abigale, of course, led the way. Carla walked with Abigale and the boys joined Jeremiah and Ronald at the back of the group. Tommy noticed that the group seemed a little different from what it had been earlier in the day when they were going from one class to another. He wasn't sure what it was, but there was a noticeable difference in the amount and general volume of the conversations. Once they reached the Main Hall and everyone took a seat, Tommy realized what was different. Many of the kids were sitting in different seats. This formed a number of new groups and pairings. Tommy guessed that this was the result of what had transpired in their classes. Now that everyone knew more about one another, many new friendships were being formed. Tommy started thinking about this and some of the other things that had happened. He remembered how they had to organize to find their dormitory the first time, and how they also had to organize to elect a Dormitory Leader. He began to see that all these things had been planned by the Academy. It was part of their training and education. They were learning all the time. Tommy was impressed and excited. These things had been interesting and well thought out. It made him wonder what else the Academy had in store for them.

The Life and Times of Tommy Travail

Tommy pointed this out to Carla and Michael as their food began to appear. They thought it was an intriguing observation and agreed with Tommy that those things must have been planned by the Academy. They wondered if any of the other things that had happened had also been planned by the Academy, but since nothing immediately came to anyone's mind, Michael changed the subject. He asked Carla and Tommy what they wanted to do after dinner. He wanted to suggest that they go to the outer castle grounds and practice the foot method, but he didn't want to get Carla started again on the dangers of cross-country racing, so he was shocked when she suggested that very thing.

The strange look on both Michael and Tommy's face asked the obvious question. "I still want to talk you out of this racing business," she began her response to the unspoken question, "but, I figure some practice can't hurt, plus, I can teach you a few things that might save your lives if you do persist with this foolishness. You know, Abigale told me that most kids don't even tryout for the team until their third year."

The boys didn't respond to Carla's last comment. They finished their meal and went out to the outer grounds. Michael and Tommy practiced for a bit while Carla gave them tips and advice. Once she was satisfied with their basic form, she taught them several new moves, some had been taught to her, and some she had invented herself. She taught them how to do a Flying Leap and showed them how to do a Skip. She told them that they couldn't wave ride over water. She said that they would only get a couple of meters and they would start to sink. She added that if they were going really fast, they could cross a slightly wider expanse of water, but they would still start to sink within three or four meters. She said that with a good jumping point, they could do a Flying Leap further than that. But, if they needed to cross a larger body of water, they could Skip. Carla told them that timing was critical in Skipping over water, but if they could avoid waves and keep their timing going, they could cross a whole lake.

Carla also taught the boys how to do the Wall Bounce, the Cushioned Landing and the Swoosh and Swirl, a kind of sliding turn. As she went from one move to another, she progressively gave them less time to practice each move. When the boys asked her to slow down, she refused. She had gotten herself a little panicky. The more she thought about the dangers involved in cross-country racing, the more frightened she became for the boys. She felt compelled to show them everything she knew about wave riding, but they were running out of time. It was getting late and they were going to have to return to the Crow's Next. However, by the time they did quit, Carla had showed them quite a few moves. The boys had not gotten very proficient with many of the moves, but at least they had an idea of how to do them.

When they returned to the Crow's Nest, they decided to go to their bedrooms and do some of their reading. All evening Michael had been anxious to tell Tommy what was in the Racing Manual, but he hadn't wanted to say anything in front of Carla. He knew she would start on them again. Tommy, on the other hand, wanted to talk about what he had read in his History book. Once they reached the top of the stairs into the bedroom, they both began talking simultaneously. They looked at each other and paused. Realizing that they both needed to know what the other had learned, they agreed that Tommy should read the Racing Manual and Michael should read the chapters in their History text. The boys went to their beds, laid down and read.

They were surprised how much of the information in the History book and the information in the Racing Manual related to one another. Their common connection was King Oleander, the son of King Andrew. When he was the young 'Prince' Oleander, his father ruled the Realm from Old Castle. As a young man, he began traveling around the King's Realm. Eventually, his travels led him beyond the furthermost reaches of the Realm and into many of the outer Realms of the endless Plane called Home. The last place he visited was the Realm of the Telesthesians. They were a race of seers. They had chronographic memories and could see through time. They remembered the past, present and the future. The future is not fixed, but as present events occur, they could see the future that results. Prince Oleander fell deeply in love with a young Telesthesian Princess named Damiana.

The Prince was preparing to ask Damiana to be his wife when a message came from his father. His father's message told him that war had broken out with the Kindlewalkers and he needed to return immediately. The Prince wanted to take Damiana with him, but he loved her too much to take her into the war zone. His heart was broken. It was worse for Damiana. She could see that if she went with the Prince, she would be killed. And, if the Prince left without her, she would never see him again. They spent their last day together as the Prince prepared to leave. In their final moments together, Damiana shed two tears, one from each eye. It was one of the most rarest of things. Only the greatest of emotions could cause a Telesthesian to shed a tear. After all, the future was always in their memory. As the tears dripped onto her cheeks, the Prince caught each one with the tip of his wand and placed it in one of two tiny glass bottles that he had magically created. Telesthesian legend held that if a Telesthesian teardrop was placed on the tongue and a question asked, a truth would be revealed. The Prince kissed Damiana softly, promised her he would never stop loving her and departed.

The Prince was horrified when he returned to the castle. It had been destroyed and his mother and father had been killed. Those that had survived the attacks had fled into the mountains south of Old Castle. The Prince went into the mountains and organized his people to fight the war. The people who had lived in other areas of the Realm also went into hiding, but they continued to do all they could to assist the Prince. The war went on for a number of years. The Prince established a complex array of hide outs, staging areas and travel routes. They utilized many of the caves in the mountains and, in some lower areas, even built tree top villages. The couriers and scouts that traveled across the mountains kept the Prince informed about the locations and movements of the Kindlewalkers. They also brought news from, and carried news to the other people of the Realm. This flow of information allowed the Prince to stay ahead of the Kindlewalkers and keep most of his people out of harms way. However, there were many skirmishes, and many were killed on both sides.

The war drew to a stalemate. Neither side was winning nor was either side losing. They just occasionally killed some of each other. Tiring of this senseless killing, the Prince sent a courier to the leader of the Kindlewalkers and invited him to a peace conference. The Leader of the Kindlewalkers had one of the ears of the courier cut off and sent him back to the Prince with the message that he would attend the peace conference. Legend says that, at the conference, the Prince showed the Leader of the Kindlewalkers one of the bottles that held one of Damiana's tears. After explaining what it was and what it would do, the Prince offered it to him. The Kindlewalker leader with suspicion and apprehension opened the bottle and let the teardrop fall onto his tongue. Almost silently, he murmured a question. No one heard what his question was, but as soon as he finished the question, he sat up very erect in his chair. His eyes became glassy for a moment and then, without saying a word, he stood up and left the meeting. His aides followed him. The next morning the Kindlewalkers were gone from the Realm. Every one of them had left. It is said that they moved to the furthest reaches of the Home Plane. They have never been seen or heard from since. The second Damiana tear has since become known as the 'Drop of Truth' but no one knows what ever became of it. The Prince became King and built Damiana's well and the New Castle. The King eventually married and fathered five children, but when he died of old age, he died with a broken heart.

The Introduction in the Racing Manual said that King Oleander created the Cross-Country Race shortly after moving into the New Castle. He created it to celebrate the bravery and courage of the couriers and scouts who had served so valiantly during the war. There have been many changes in Cross-Country Racing in the years since King Oleander created it. Originally, it was truly a Cross-Country Race. The Racers went from New Castle to Old Castle and back. Today the race is quite different. The modern race takes place on a closed course. It is a thirteen kilometer loop. Every Academy in the Realm fields a Cross-Country Race Team, and every Academy has its own course. Tommy took particular notice of this, he hadn't thought about there being other Academies in the Queen's Realm.

A Cross-Country Race Course has thirteen stages. Each stage has two routes; there is a route that contains a magically enhanced challenge and a no-challenge safe route. In each stage, the racer has the choice to take either the challenge route or the safe route. The safe route is always longer and more time consuming, but it still requires a modest amount of skill to complete. The challenge route is much more dangerous, but it is always shorter and faster. The Cross-Country Course at the Queen's Academy is called 'The Serpent's Spine'.

A Race Team consists of seven timed Racers and three Assassins. The competing Teams start onto the course in opposite directions from the Start/Finish Line. The Team Captain decides how many Racers go at any one time. All ten Team Members can start the Race together or they can be started one at a time or in groups. The three Assassins almost always enter the course first. They don't race for time; instead, they run interference for the timed Racers by clearing away as many of the magical enhancements as possible and impeding the progress of opposing Racers. Racers are individually timed, but their time doesn't begin until they enter the course. When a Racer makes one complete circuit of the Course and crosses the Start/Finish Line, he must turn around and head back out onto the Course in the opposite direction.

It generally doesn't take long before opposing Racers and opposing Assassins begin meeting on the Course. Racers, like Assassins, are allowed to interfere with the progress of an opponent. Blocking, tripping and holding are legal. The only weapon that can be used, however, is a wand, and a Pushback is the strongest magic that can be used on an opponent. Flying is not permitted and the Courses are magically enchanted to prevent magical flying. However, sailing, such as gliding from a high jump, is legal. In fact, since flying is magically blocked everywhere on the course, any aerial move that can be achieved is legal. The Racer that completes both circuits of the course in the shortest time wins the Race for his or her Team. Therefore, a Team can win with only one Racer completing the Race, providing it is the fastest time posted by either Team.

The Challenges that appear in each stage are duplicated so that a Racer will meet the same challenge in either direction, but generally, Racers going in opposite directions through a challenge will meet each other at least once. Challenges start as real terrain and then are magically enhanced. A Challenge might start out as a river crossing the course or a high cliff with a narrow ledge pathway, then, magical enhancements are added. Beasts, creatures or Kindlewalkers may be magically created to confront the Racers. There might be magical fire or a landslide of magical rocks and boulders. Magical enhancements can hurt racers, but only in a minimal way. Fire might smart and turn the Racers skin red, but wouldn't do any real damage. A shot from a

Kindlewalker's weapon might sting, but no more than being shot with a rubber band at close range.

All magically created creatures and warriors can be dispatched with a Pushback shot. In general, however, the bigger and stronger they are, the more shots it takes. Also, some creatures have shielding and may only be vulnerable in one spot. The magical enhancements present problems and complications, but the true danger is in the natural terrain of the course. Falling from a cliff or having a bad landing from a jump could result in real injury; as could running into a tree or falling into swift moving ice cold water.

Besides being removed from the race due to injury, both Assassins and timed Racers can be knocked out of the Race. Cross-Country Racing is a wave race, therefore a Competitor must strive to maintain his or her wave float at all times. If a Competitor is struck by *any* form of magic while in physical contact with the ground, the Competitor is deemed to have been captured or killed. A magically created glowing white 'X' appears on the Competitor's chest and back, and he or she must exit the course immediately.

The Racing Manual gave a detailed description of 'The Serpent's Spine' with diagrams and some examples of the possible magical enhancements. Magical Enhancements are changed from time to time creating new and interesting twists to the challenges. Tommy had been studying this part of the Manual for some time when Mister Buttercup jumped on his bed and walked right across Tommy's chest, crinkling the Manual slightly. Tommy tried to grab him, but he jumped off the bed and went to the window where he jumped up onto the window ledge and began to meow rather loudly. Tommy looked around and everyone else, including Michael, was asleep.

"Mister Buttercup," he called in a loud whisper, "You're going to wake everybody up." But, Mister Buttercup continued to meow. Tommy got out of bed and went to the window to quiet him. He reached down and began to stroking Mister Buttercup's back. He looked out the window to the courtyard below and once again saw the figure he believed to be Whitelace leaving the Castle and courtyard. Mister Buttercup settled down and Tommy returned to his bed, turning off his light on the way. He laid back and quickly fell asleep.

Chapter Seventeen

The Second Day of Classes

Tommy woke the next morning to the usual shaking of his bed. All the other boys were also just waking up. Tommy and Michael dressed quickly and used the bathroom to freshen up. Both boys were excited about the day. Tommy couldn't wait for the afternoon remedial History class with Professor Pastorie, and Michael couldn't wait for the afternoon Cross-Country tryouts. They went downstairs to the Community room and found Carla already there studying the Castle Directory. Tommy and Michael approached her.

"Good morning, Carla," Tommy greeted.

Carla smiled and greeted both boys with a good morning.

"Carla," Tommy said, "there are some things we need to talk about, so how about you let Abigale lead the group to breakfast and you hang back with us?"

Carla looked at Tommy with an inquisitive expression for a moment, and then agreed. Within a few minutes, almost everyone had gathered in the Community Room. Abigale went straight to the Castle Directory when she arrived. When she was sure everybody was ready to go, she opened the door and led the group out. Carla and the boys let everyone else go ahead and they followed at the back of the group.

"So what do you want to talk about," Carla asked as they started their walk to the Main Hall.

"Well, there are actually a couple of things," Tommy answered. "Yesterday in Professor Krusher's class, when he asked if anyone could fly, you kept your hand raised. Can you really fly, and how come you never told us? Plus, Professor Krusher seemed to know you, what's with that?"

"I told you guys about Professor Krusher yesterday," Carla replied.

"No, you didn't," Tommy said. "Do you remember her telling us about Professor Krusher?" Tommy asked Michael.

"Can't say that I do," Michael answered.

"Sure I did," Carla protested. "On our way to his class, I remember it was… Oh yeah, I remember now, I started to tell you just before we ran into Whitelace and I never did tell you. I'm sorry. Since I started to tell you when we were interrupted by Whitelace, I guess, it just left me with the memory that I told you."

"So," Michael inquired, "what is it that you thought you told us?"

"It's about Professor Krusher," Carla started.

"Duh," Tommy said, "we gathered that."

"Well," Carla continued while giving Tommy a disapproving look for his comment. "Professor Krusher is my Dad's best friend. They attended the Academy together. He's always been like an Uncle to me. I grew up calling him Uncle Ambrost."

"Wow," Tommy responded to her revelation. "That's pretty cool. You shouldn't have any problem passing his class."

"I don't think he'll show me any favoritism," Carla replied. "In fact, he might even be a little tougher on me."

"Yeah," Tommy agreed. "You're probably right. Adults are always trying to look out for what's best for us, or so they say. So, your dad and Professor Krusher attended the Academy together; and your Mom too?"

"Yep, they were all friends," Carla said as she smiled slightly. "I've heard a lot of tales of their adventures. They had great fun. My Dad and Uncle Ambrost were on the Race Te…" Carla stopped. The boys looked around; they mistakenly thought that Carla had seen Whitelace. But, she had really stopped because she hadn't meant to tell the boys that her dad was on the Cross-Country Race Team.

She hoped that they hadn't noticed what she had started to say. She wanted to change the subject.

"So what do you think we'll have for breakfast?" She suddenly blurted out. She knew it was pretty lame, but it was the first thing that came to her mind.

"What!" Tommy and Michael exclaimed at the same time, and Tommy continued, "I suppose we'll have what we have everyday, a little bit of everything."

The group started down the final curving staircase that would take them to the Grand Foyer. As Carla and the boys descended, the Grand Foyer came into view. When they got far enough down to see the doorway into the Main Hall, all three of them spotted Whitelace. He was standing next to the door.

"Good," Tommy said, "I was hoping we'd run into him."

"What!" Carla and Michael exclaimed at the same time. Michael and Carla looked at each other and gave one another a little snicker.

"You were hoping?" Michael asked.

"Yes," Tommy answered. "I want to turn in my lines." Tommy pulled his back-pack around, opened it and pulled out the handwritten pages.

They followed the group across the Foyer to the doorway. Almost everyone went through the door. To their surprise, Whitelace seemed to pay no attention to them. When Tommy got even with Whitelace, he stopped. Whitelace still hadn't noticed him.

"Excuse me," he finally said to Whitelace.

Whitelace looked down at him. "What do *you* want?"

"I've got my lines," Tommy answered.

"So?" Whitelace inquired.

"I want to turn them in, sir," Tommy answered.

"I don't want them," Whitelace responded. "They're to be turn into the Prefect's Office. And, they need to be turned in by, what was it, midmorning I believe, yes by midmorning."

"I believe it was midday, sir," Tommy corrected.

"No," Whitelace said firmly, "it was midmorning. I'm sure of it. Now get lost. I'm not much in the mood for putting up with your kind this morning."

Whitelace's last comment caused Tommy to take a closer look at him before he started to walk away. He noticed that dark shadows were beginning to appear below Whitelace's eyes and his whole face seemed to be a bit droopy. Tommy passed through the doorway where Carla and Michael were waiting for him.

"He looks a little peeked," Tommy said as they walked to their table. "I wonder if his late night work for the Black Witch is catching up with him."

Carla gave Tommy a dirty look. She was trying to convey to him that you just don't say those kinds of things where others can hear. Tommy got the message and changed what he was saying.

"Yesterday Whitelace told me that my lines had to be turned in by midday, now he says that they have to be turned in by midmorning, and they have to be turned into the Prefect's Office."

"So what," Carla responded. "They're done, so it's not a problem. We can go by the Prefect's Office after breakfast and you can turn them in."

"But it's not right," Tommy protested. "He can't just change things like that. It's not fair. What if they weren't done?"

"Well, I don't know," Carla said. "The way we finished them wasn't quite legal either." Tommy realized he was probably on the losing end of this discussion, so he shut up.

Their food began appearing on the table. "So," Michael said to Carla, "your dad and Professor Krusher were on the Race Team?"

Carla was just about to place a large scoop of scramble eggs onto her dish as Michael made his comment. It caught her by surprise and she accidently let the scoop of eggs plop onto her dish. They hit with a bit of a splash, scattering some scrambled eggs onto the table and the front of Carla's robes. Michael laughed slightly.

"You didn't think," Michael started.

"I don't want to talk about it," Carla interrupted, "not unless I can tell you everything and I don't want to talk about it here." Carla pulled out her wand and, turning it sideways, magically cleaned the eggs off her robes. "If we have time after we go to the Prefect's Office, we can go out to the courtyard and I'll tell you."

Carla wasn't very happy and the boys knew it was best to just shut up and enjoy their meal. They ate and talked a little about there first class, Professor Welkin's Science of Magic. When they finished, they left the Main Hall and checked the Castle Directory to find the best route to the Prefect's Office. The Office was neither far nor hard to find. Within a few minutes, they were at the door to the Prefect's Office. They entered and found a young man wearing Prefect Robes seated at a desk.

"Yes, what can I do for you?" the young man asked.

"I have these to turn in," Tommy said handing him the handwritten pages.

"Okay," he said as he took the papers. "You can go." Then the young man tossed the pages into the waste basket without even looking at them.

The three of them turned and left the office. They headed back the way they came and once they got far away enough not to be heard, Tommy said, "Well, what do make of that? He didn't even look at them."

"I wouldn't count on that happening every time," Carla remarked. "Next time they'll probably check them really close."

"You're probably right," Tommy agreed.

"Have we got time to go out to the courtyard?" Michael asked Carla.

Carla really didn't want to admit it, but she knew they had plenty of time before their first class. She hadn't thought about much of anything else since they left the Main Hall. "I believe so," she reluctantly answered him. By then they were back in the Grand Foyer.

They cut across the Foyer and went out the door to the courtyard. There were a few kids in the courtyard, but it wasn't hard for Carla to find a secluded spot. They sat down on the grass.

"There were four of them," Carla began. Tommy and Michael looked at each other curiously, but didn't say anything. "They all started at the Academy together. There were my mom and dad, Uncle Ambrost and the young Prince Stephen; you know, the one that went crazy and killed himself. They quickly became the best of friends. All four of them made the Race Team in their first year as alternates. By their second year, they were full fledged Racers. After their third year, Mom and Dad went to the Political School and Uncle Ambrost went to the Military School. Young Prince Stephen was exceptional and attended both the Political and Military Schools. He's the only one to ever do that. Over the years, they became four of the best Racers the Academy has ever had. They easily won every race in their final year. Dad, Uncle Ambrost and Prince Stephen were the Team's Assassins and Mom was the fastest timed Racer in the history of the Academy. She set many records."

"Wow," Michael interrupted. "You should be really proud."

"I am," Carla answered, "But, at the big Race at the end of their final year something happened. My dad, Uncle Ambrost and the Prince developed a spinning move in which they used Pushbacks and Comealongs on each other to increase their speed; when they were going fast enough, they would lock arms and start a spinning glide. This allowed them to fire the wands multiple times in every direction. If there was a high jump in a Stage, they found that they could make the same move as they jumped. This made it possible for them to go higher and farther than anyone ever had. They could spin high above a Stage and blast away at any opposing warrior or Racer."

"They had used it with great success during their last year. They called it the 'Cross Vailed Crusher' after themselves. In their last race, they executed this move from a high jump just as my Mom entered the Stage. The opposing Team had hidden their three Assassins and two additional Racers in the Stage. Once my Dad, Uncle Ambrost and the Prince reached their highest point, the opposing team members revealed themselves in a sneak attack and simultaneously fired at them. By a piece of bad luck, all five Pushback blows struck the Prince in the head and chest. Their combined force struck the Prince with such violence that it knocked him backwards so hard and so swiftly that he was unable to unlock his arm from my dad and Uncle Ambrost. His body flipped backwards, but his arm didn't. His arm broke in several places. My dad was still spinning towards the Prince as the Prince flipped backwards. The Prince's legs whipped backwards and the heel of one of his boots struck my dad in the head. It hit him in the right temple and above his ear. It struck him so hard that it peeled his scalp back, fractured his skull and knocked him unconscious. The Prince struggled to regain control as he fell back towards the ground. My Dad and Uncle Ambrost's arms had separated and my dad was falling back to the ground unconscious. Uncle Ambrost swooped down and grabbed my dad. He tried to cushion them before they hit the ground, but under the additional weight of my Dad and their excessive speed, he couldn't do much. He hit the ground with his left leg first and his knee exploded. The Prince regained some control before he hit the ground and was able to cushion his impact enough so that he didn't receive any additional significant injuries."

Tears had formed in Carla's eyes. Tommy put his arm around her shoulders to comfort her. "My dad was in a coma for weeks and weeks. They didn't know if he was going to live or die. My dad jokes about it today, but I don't see anything funny about it. He says that one incident knocked more sense into his head than any other thing in his life. But, it ended Uncle Ambrost's Military career. They've had to work on his knee several times over the years. And, it was sheer terror for my mom as she saw the whole thing happen."

Carla stopped. The boys didn't know what to say. After a long pause, Michael said, "Well, it mostly worked out all right. I mean, your dad has become the Wizard Master of Old Castle and Professor Krusher has become a Professor and the Coach of the Race Team." Carla frowned at him and he realized that might not have been the most comforting thing he could have said.

Tommy gave her a firm squeeze around her shoulders and said "Come on, let's go to class."

They got up, left the courtyard, entered the Grand Foyer and checked the Castle Directory. They located Professor Welkin's classroom and set off for their first class. Carla had a sullen expression on her face. She didn't quite appear to be sad, nor did she quite appear to be angry. It was a bit of a look of despair.

Tommy, hoping to cheer her up a little, said in a bright and cheerful way, "So you can fly, that must be pretty exciting. "

"Only once," Carla responded in a dry and somber tone, "and that ended badly too."

The last thing Tommy wanted to do was bring up more bad memories. "I'm sorry," he said. "We don't have to talk about that. Let's talk about something else. Like, like, what do you think our next class will be like?"

"No," Carla said. "I might as well tell you about my flying experience. It's just that, well, it's embarrassing. It was just a few weeks ago. I had finished my preschool and, since it was between school years here at the Academy, Uncle Ambrost, ah, that is Professor Krusher; I'm having a bit of a hard time remembering to call him Professor Krusher. I mean, like, he's been Uncle Ambrost to me my whole life, but I promised Mom and Dad I would call him Professor Krusher while I'm at the Academy."

Tommy started to smile. Carla was starting to get wound up. She was starting to tell the story like only Carla can tell a story.

"So, anyway, where was I," Carla continued. "Oh yes, Professor Krusher came to visit us. It was a gorgeous day. It was warm and about mid light wave. There was a slightly cool and refreshing breeze. Several white puffy clouds were set against the beautiful black sky. We were in the backyard. My mom and dad along with Unc... Professor Krusher were seated in lawn chairs around our outdoor table sharing a bottle of the Tinkleberry wine, and don't either of you go telling Professor Krusher that I told you he drinks the Tinkleberry wine."

"Come on, Carla," Michael said. "How would that ever come up in a conversation with a Professor?"

"Well, I don't know," Carla answered. "You just better not say anything to him."

"I promise, we won't," Michael pleaded holding his hands up in the air.

Carla's face was clearly beginning to brighten. Michael's antics of raising his hands actually caused her to crack the slightest of smiles, and she continued, "So anyway, Mom and Dad and Professor Krusher were seated next to the table. My mom had baked a large chocolate cake for the occasion with tons of chocolate frosting. I cut myself a piece of cake and sat down on the lawn behind them. I set my piece of cake on my lap and leaned back to watch the clouds. They looked so light and fluffy. I began imagining what it must be like to be a cloud and just float along, drifting from one place to another. I didn't realize it because I was looking up, but I had started to float off the ground. I must have risen two or three meters and I started to drift along. I gradually drifted over my parents and Uncle Ambrost. When my mom saw me, she screamed my name. Her scream broke my concentration and I immediately began to fall. I landed bottom first right on top of the chocolate cake."

A broad smile came across Carla's face and she continued. "The cake exploded, sending chocolate cake and frosting everywhere. It splattered Uncle Ambrost as well as my mom and dad. We were all covered in chocolate. Shortly after I landed on the cake, the piece of cake that had been on my lap followed me down and landed with a splat on top of my head." Although she would never admit it to the boys, she had cried when this had actually happened, but now it seemed kind of funny.

Carla laughed slightly. The boys had been doing everything they could not to laugh, but Carla's laugh set them off. All three of them laughed. They laughed the rest of the way to the classroom. They were the first to arrive at the classroom. Professor Welkin was seated at his desk making some notations on a sheet of paper. A medium sized caldron was in one front corner of his desk and a group of varying-sized bottles were in the other front corner. As they entered the room, he looked up and smiled, then returned to his notations. The classroom had raised tables, more like workbenches, with three stools next to each table. Carla and the boys selected one of the back tables, pulled up the stools, and sat down.

The rest of the class began filing into the room. Abigale was in the lead and she immediately headed for the front middle table. After it appeared that all of the kids had arrived, the Professor looked at his watch and then stood up. He was a middle aged man about average height and weight. His hair was neatly groomed and sandy colored. It was too long to be called short and too short to be called long. His eyebrows matched the color of his hair and they were slightly arched. His lips were thin and his nose was sharply ridged.

"Welcome to the Science of Magic.," he said. "You will find this one of your most fascinating and difficult classes. In this class, you will learn the science behind the magic. You'll learn how to make potions and elixirs. Not only will you will learn what works together and what doesn't, but, more importantly, you'll also learn *why* some things work together and some don't. You'll learn what magic is, how it is stored in both living and non-living things, and how we can tap that magic to do marvelous and wonderful things."

The Professor continued with his overview of the class for several minutes. When he finished, he had the class stand up one at a time and do the introduction thing that they had done in their previous classes. Without the Professor prompting them to, the kids were now telling different things about themselves. Of the many new things they learned about each other; they learned that potions and concoctions were of special interest to Bertram Buttwell, and that Bobby Drinkwater could see at times with his eyes closed. After the last student finished, the Professor gave them a reading assignment and dismissed them.

The class had ended early, but there wasn't enough extra time to do much, so the whole group decided to go on to the next classroom. They figured they could hang out in the hallway near the room until the class was ready to start. Abigale lead the way. Carla and the boys followed at the rear of the group. Carla was in a much better mood than she had been in earlier. The three of them kept a watchful eye out for Whitelace, but they made it all the way to the next room without any sight of him. Some of the kids went into the classroom, but Carla and the boys stayed out in the hall and entered into the general conversations with the other students. After a short while, Professor Lightwood called them into the room.

The room was quite different from the other rooms. There were no desks or tables for the students. There was only one chair in the room and it was behind the Professor's desk. Instead of tables and chairs, there were pillows of different sizes in a wide range of colors and designs scattered about the floor for the students to sit on. Everyone found a pillow and spot where they felt comfortable.

The Professor walked to the center of the room. She walked in a flowing kind of way with a balance and smoothness that made her seem to glide. She was a tall and slender woman with gray streaks in her black hair. She had an attractive face with dark black eyes and thin eyebrows. A few wrinkles near the corners of her eyes revealed that she was just past her middle years.

"I'm Professor Lightwood," she said, "and this is Magical Skills. While you're at the Academy, you will learn many different kinds of magic, but it is in this class that you will learn the *skills* necessary to perform that magic. Among other things, you will learn how to generate and control the specific magic you need. You will also learn the proper way to hold a wand. As you probably know by now, the manner in which you hold your wand can greatly influence the magic you do. And, you will learn the Art of magic. You can learn the mechanics of magic, but if you are to become great Witches and Wizards, you must learn the Art of magic. It will give your magic a flare and style. Also, if we are lucky, perhaps one of you will begin to show signs of being able to do magic with your hands rather than with a wand."

The Professor continued her overview and even discussed some of the things they could expect in their second and third years. When she finished, everyone expected to do the stand up and talk thing, however the Professor did something different. She said *she* would go around the room and tell each student their name and something about them. She said if she was wrong to say so, but as she went around the room, she got every name right and no one said she was wrong, although a number of the kids seemed to be uncomfortable with what she revealed.

When she got to Carla she said, "Carla Crosswell, a young girl who can fly, but is reluctant to admit it." She turned to Michael and said, "Michael Woden, a young boy who was very angry, but is now very happy." Then she stepped in front of Tommy. "Tommy," she said. She hesitated and the expression changed on her face, but for only the briefest of moments, then she continued, "Travail, a boy in search of a truth."

The class was awe struck and no one said a word. After she spoke to the last student, she walked over to her desk and started to dismiss the class, but then corrected herself and gave the students a reading assignment before letting them go. No one said a word. They all just got up and left the room, but once they got into the hallway, everyone erupted in conversation, except Carla, Michael and Tommy.

Clearly, Professor Lightwood had a magic that none of them were familiar with and it was disturbing. It was very unsettling to the boys because they could see that it bothered Carla. They had always counted on Carla knowing at least a little about everything, but her expression seemed to indicate that this was something new even to her. Abigale organized the class and they set off for the Main Hall and lunch.

Carla had been in deep thought. When they were almost to the Main Hall, she said, "She must be a Clairvoyant. They can sense things other people can't. They are very rare and are always enlisted into the Queen's Service. That's got to be it. She's a Clairvoyant, and that's not good. They are trained to sense secrets. We'll have to be careful around her."

The boys nodded in agreement, but because they had reached the Main Hall, there was no more discussion of it. Carla and the boys took their time eating lunch. While they ate, they engaged in conversation and general horseplay with the kids around them. By the time they finished, almost everyone else was done and ready to go to Professor Boardman's Abstract Magic class. For everyone except Michael and Tommy, Abstract Magic was the last class of the day. Tommy and Michael, of course, had remedial History after Abstract Magic.

Carla walked with Abigale and, as usual, the boys followed at the back of the group. The boys kept a constant watch out for Whitelace, but they made it all the way to there next classroom without any sign of him. Tommy was happy not to have another confrontation with him, but they hadn't seen him since breakfast, and that made Tommy a little uneasy. The group entered the classroom and, unlike Professor Lightwood's cushions on the floor arrangement, it had a table and chair set-up similar to the all the other classrooms. There were, however, three extra erasable writing boards in the room. They were filled with drawings, diagrams and formulas that were unlike anything Michael and Tommy had ever seen.

Professor Boardman was at one of the drawing boards. He was adding additional things to the board, which already looked filled to capacity. The Professor was undisturbed as the class entered and continued his work. The Professor was an odd looking fellow. He was shorter than average and somewhat overweight. He had a round plump face with big eyes and highly arched eyebrows. His ears stuck out slightly and he was bald down the center of his head with gray hair on the sides, which was slightly too long. His nose was large and round.

The students took seats and quieted down. After several minutes, the Professor turned around and almost looked surprised to see the students in their seats. "Oh, ah, welcome," he said. "Welcome to each

The Life and Times of Tommy Travail

of you. This is Abstract Magic and I'm Professor Boardman. In this class, you will study theoretical magic. We'll attempt to unveil some of the mystery of magic by exploring its unknown Realms. Much of the magic that we will talk about will never exist in practical form, but *some* of it will come into everyday use during your lifetime. As long as we study magic in the abstract, we will make new discoveries, which will lead us to a greater understanding of ourselves and the Realm and Plane we live in. One thing you will learn in this class is how to think in the abstract. And, I guarantee that this talent will come in handy once you enter your careers in the Political and Military Service of the Queen."

The Professor went on to discuss the current topics in Abstract Magic. In his enthusiasm, he had gone beyond the understanding of the students. Noticing the many confused looks on the faces of his students', he realized he had gone a bit too far. He abruptly stopped his discussion. After a moment, he said, "What I would like to do now is to get to know each of you a little bit." Tommy and Michael gave each other that, 'here we go again look', but the Professor had something else in mind.

"I am going to propose a question. When I point to you, I would like you to stand up, tell me your name and give me your answer to the question. Feel free to agree or disagree with what other students have said, but I want to hear *your* answer to the question. Does everyone understand?" There was a general affirmation and the Professor continued. "Okay, here we go. The question is; if you could see the magic, what would it look like?" The Professor then pointed to Abigale.

Abigale stood up and said, "Abigale Antwerp, and I think the magic would look like white silk sheets gently flowing in a light breeze."

"Very good," the Professor said and then pointed to Debbie Kaye Vantalkin.

Debbie Kaye blushed slightly as she stood up. "Debbie Kaye Vantalkin, I think it depends on whether you're talking about good magic or evil magic. I think that good magic is bright and cheery, while evil magic is dark and ugly."

The Professor then pointed to Debbie Kay Vantalkin. Debbie Kaye sat down and her twin sister stood up.

"Debbie Kay Vantalkin and I agree with my sister. I think good magic is warm and evil magic cold. I think good magic would be like a warm meadow pond with gentle waves rolling across its surface, where as evil magic is like a dark sea in a bad storm, with violent waves ripping its surface."

"Okay," the Professor said with a smile and then pointed to Ronald Lockhard.

"I disagree," he started, but then stopped. "Oops, sorry. Ronald Lockhard, and as I said, I disagree. I think all magic looks the same. I believe, it's what we create with the magic that makes it good or evil. I think magic would look like glowing energy, kind of like a white burning fire; and then when we take it and shape it, it would look more like a lighting bolt."

Ronald sat down and the Professor pointed to Tommy. Tommy had been giving the question some very serious thought. Ronald's comments made him think back to his first moments on the Home Plane. He recalled when he first opened his eyes and everything was topsy-turvy. He remembered seeing the faint blue gray streaks of light that shot across his field of view while his brain squished and tried to adjust. Tommy was sure that this was just an internal reaction, a result of what had happened to his body as he moved from his world to the Home Plane. It was kind of like seeing stars after being hit in the head. But, he thought it was as good of an explanation of what magic might look like as anything else he had heard.

"Tommy Travail," he said as he stood up. "I think that magic would look like millions and millions of faint tiny streaks of light going every which way. They would be everywhere and the whole thing would appear chaotic.

Tommy sat down and the Professor pointed to another student. The Professor appeared to be selecting students at random, but by the time they had finished, he had called on every student and had never called the same student twice.

"Well," the Professor said after the last student spoke. "This has been most interesting. I hope you all enjoyed it as much as I have." Several students nodded and a few voiced their agreement. "Please read the first chapter in your text before our next class," the Professor continued. "We are done for today. Have a pleasant afternoon and think a little about what we discussed today." The students began to rise from their seats. "Mister Travail," the Professor added, "I'd like to see you for a moment before you leave."

Carla, Tommy and Michael looked at each other with inquisitive looks. "Meet you in the hallway," Michael said, and he and Carla headed for the door.

Tommy walked up to the Professor desk. "Yes, sir," he said.

The Professor sat down in the chair behind his desk and looked up at Tommy. "I am curious about your answer to the question," he said. "Did you read that somewhere?"

"Uh, no sir. It's just something I made up," Tommy answered.

"I find your answer very interesting, especially the part about the magic being in chaos. You're the only one who suggested that. Did you know that modern Abstract Magicians now believe that magic is always in a state of chaos?"

"I had no idea," Tommy responded. "Like I said sir, it's just something I made up."

"Well I like your imagination young man," the Professor said. "I think I'm going to enjoy having you in my class."

"Thank you Professor," Tommy responded.

"Now run along," the Professor instructed, "and don't forget your reading assignment."

Tommy smiled and headed for the door. When he got out into the hallway, Michael was waiting for him, but Carla was gone. "Where's Carla?" he asked.

"Oh," Michael responded. "She figured that we had to go to remedial History, so she headed back to the Crow's Nest with the rest of the group. She said we should meet her back there after our class. So, what was that all about?" he asked pointing toward the classroom with his thumb.

"Oh, nothing," Tommy replied. "He just liked my answer to the question."

"I've checked the Castle Directory," Michael informed Tommy, "and we can go. I know the way."

Tommy felt he should also check the Directory, but he didn't want to make Michael think he was questioning his ability. So they headed off to their final class, keeping a lookout for Whitelace. They got to

Professor Pastorie's classroom without running into Whitelace. The Professor was waiting for them when they reached the classroom door.

"Come on in, boys, and take a seat," the Professor said. They did as the Professor instructed except, instead of sitting at the back of the room as they normally did, they sat at the front center table.

Tommy was excited. He had waited all day to discuss King Oleander with the Professor. Michael, on the other hand, was interested, but he was much more interested in getting this class over with so he could go to the Cross-Country tryouts.

"Well," the Professor began, "have you learned anything about King Oleander?"

"Yes, sir," Tommy answered, "and I have some questions."

"Such as?" the Professor encouraged.

"Uh, like, why didn't the Prince return to the Realm of the Telesthesians to get Damiana after the war with the Kindlewalkers ended?"

"Oh, very good question," the Professor replied. "It shows that you not only read your assignment, but have given it some thought. To answer your question, you must understand that the Telesthesian Realm is a hidden Realm in the most distant reaches of the known Plane. Once the Prince became King, it would have been inappropriate for him to undertake such a long and dangerous journey. Over the years, the King sent many Emissaries to find and bring Damiana back to him, but none of them ever returned."

"Do you think the Prince ever considered staying with Damiana and not returning to fight the war with the Kindlewalkers?" Michael suddenly asked.

"With what we know of the King's character and his commitment to his people, I doubt it," the Professor answered.

"Professor," Tommy inquired, "do you think that the second Damiana Tear still exists?"

"Ah, that raises another interesting question," the Professor responded. "Do you think that Damiana's Tears ever actually existed?"

"Our History book says they did," Tommy answered.

"Oh, did it? Or, did it just tell the Legend of Damiana's Tears?" the Professor asked.

"I'm not sure," Tommy answered. "I thought it did, but now I'm not sure."

"Good," the Professor said to both Tommy and Michael's surprise. "The study of History is about determining what is true and what is not. Therefore, it should be no surprise that some Historians have challenged the existence of Damiana's Tears. They suggest that the whole story was created to add mystery to the King's political solution to the war. Some Historians have even gone so far as to suggest that Damiana herself never existed."

"But, Professor," Michael interjected, "what about Damiana's Well and her statue? Don't they prove she really existed?"

"No, I wouldn't say they prove she existed," the Professor answered. "A proof is something that is quite rare in History. History is the story of the past and, unfortunately, the story that gets told is entirely dependent upon the notions of the one who tells it. As a result, we find truths, as well as lies, in all Histories. The job of the historian, therefore, becomes the focused separation of the truth from the untruth, and discovering a proof is something that is very rare, yes, very rare indeed. Now, in the absence of a proof, we have to assess all the available information and hope that it leads us to a truth."

"So, Professor," Tommy inquired, "are you saying that the story of Damiana may be just a fairy tale?"

"A fairy tale," the Professor asked with a smile. "That's an interesting way to put it. But, to answer your question, no I'm not saying that at all. I believe that the collection of evidence, including the well with her statue, indicates that she did exist. I just want you to be aware that what we accept as truth can change as we gather information."

"What about Damiana's Tears and the Drop of Truth?" Tommy asked. "Does the information we have support their existence?"

"The historical information on that is much weaker than it is for Damiana herself. But, most main stream historians believe that they did exist. Of course, should someone ever discover the whereabouts of the Drop of Truth, then we may have one of those rare proofs that I was discussing."

Tommy had given the Drop of Truth a lot of thought throughout the day and he wasn't interested in it as a historical proof. If he ever got his hands on the Drop of Truth, he would use it to discover the fate of his parents. "Professor," he inquired, "what do you think ever happened to the Drop of Truth?"

"Ah," the Professor said, "there are a lot of theories about that. Some say that King Oleander may have used it on his death bed, and others say that the Royal family has it, but there isn't much evidence to support either of those theories. The King returned to the mountains south of Old Castle many times during his lifetime. The mountains had been his home for many years during the Kindlewalker war. After the war ended and he became King, the mountains became his retreat. He used to go there to rest and revitalize himself. No one knew those mountains as well as the King. He knew all of the secret and hidden places. Because of this and other anecdotal evidence, many historians believe that the King may have hidden the Drop of Truth somewhere in the mountains. Years ago, a notable Wizard Historian named Winston Wandermost claimed to have seen some scrolls that said the Drop of Truth is in a cave surrounded by something called the Pit of Perpetual Pain. However, Wandermost refused to say where or how he had seen the scrolls. The whole story would have been totally discounted if it had not been told by such a reputable historian."

"Professor," Tommy inquired, "the scrolls that were recently stolen from the Ministry of All Things Magic, do you think they could have been the same ones that Wizard Wandermost claimed to have seen?"

"You must remember," the Professor advised, "that the Ministry has retracted its statement and now says that nothing was taken. But whether or not they were taken, it's interesting to note that the Ministry may have some scrolls concerning Damiana's Tears. I wasn't aware that the Ministry had any such scrolls. They may be a new find. And, they may or may not be the same scrolls that Wandermost claimed to have seen. But in reality, they could contain anything. They could indeed contain clues about the location of the Drop of Truth, but they could just as well contain evidence that Damiana's Tears never really existed at all."

"But Professor," Michael cut in, "if the scrolls only contained historical information, why would anyone try to steal them?"

"That's a good point," the Professor said, "It would make more sense if they contained something highly valuable, such as clues to the location of the Drop of Truth."

Tommy had a sudden thought. "I'll bet," he said, "that the Black Witch is behind it. After all, she is hiding out in the mountains south of Old Castle. She's probably using the same routes and hiding places that King Oleander used. Boy, I bet she'd give anything to find the Drop of Truth."

"That, Tommy, is a good observation," the Professor seemed to confirm. "If the Drop is hidden in the mountains, no one but those in league with the Black Witch would be able to look for it. The Queen's military, of course, could, but if the Black Witch knew what they were looking for, she would go all out to stop them. There would be major battles and I don't think that would go well for either side. However, should either side ever come into the possession of the Drop of Truth… well, I guess that would eventually become a future History."

The Professor paused and smiled. "You boys have done well today. We have traveled a long ways today. The next time we meet, I want us to discuss King Erlin, so read chapters one and two in your History text. Now run along. I think someone is waiting for you."

The boys looked toward the door and saw Carla standing in the hallway. The boys thanked the Professor for the interesting class and headed out into the hallway.

Chapter Eighteen

The Hazards of Cross-Country Racing

Tommy and Michael stepped out into the hallway where Carla was waiting. "I thought we were supposed to meet you at the Crow's Nest," Tommy stated in an inquiring way.

"You were," Carla answered. "But it was getting late and I was worrying that maybe you guys had gotten caught up with Whitelace or something."

Neither of the boys had noticed the time, but now that Carla was telling them they were late, Michael started to get anxious. "Man," he exclaimed. "I hope we haven't missed the tryouts."

Carla frowned. "You guys still want to do this, even after what I told you about my dad?"

"Come on, Carla," Michael grimaced. "Let's not start that again. We'll be careful. I promise." Michael took Carla by the arm and walked with her to the nearest Castle Directory. "Please understand, it's something that I just have to do."

The three of them found the best route to the Parade Grounds and started off, keeping an ever watchful eye out for Whitelace. They wound their way around the Castle and eventually exited out a door that opened to the Parade Grounds. They hadn't seen any sign of Whitelace. The Parade Grounds were the size of three or four soccer fields and looked very much like a sporting field. It was wide open and flat with tightly mown grass. The edge of a forest lined the entire far side of the field. The forest was thick with the exception of two wide gaps in the trees near each end of the field. When they stepped out the door onto the Parade Grounds, they saw three individuals standing in the middle of the grass field. The tallest of the three appeared to be Professor Krusher, but they couldn't tell who the other two were as they had their backs turned to them. Carla and the boys walked out to the center of the field. Once they got close enough, they recognized the other two figures as Jay-Jay and Bertram Buttwell.

"What ya say Jay-jay and hey Bert, how's it going?" Michael greeted once he saw who they were, and they all greeted each other.

"Say Bertram," Tommy inquired. "I thought you couldn't wave ride?"

"I can't," he answered. "I thought I'd come out and see if I could learn something."

The Professor hadn't paid any attention to them as he had his attention focused on a magic mirror he was holding. He was using it to watch the progress of racers on the course. Finally, the Professor looked up. He smiled when he saw Michael and Tommy, but his expression changed when he saw Carla. "Carla, er, Miss Crosswell," he corrected himself. This slip of the tongue brought a broad smile to Carla's face. "I'm surprised to see you here."

"I'm not here to tryout," Carla responded. "I'm just here to keep an eye on these two." She pointed to Michael and Tommy with her thumb.

"Very well," the Professor said. "I was just about to give Mister Jetfoot here instructions for his first lap. Now that you boys are here, the three of you can go together. You are to stay on the safe route at all times. It is very important that you follow this rule. You must never take a challenge route without getting permission first. Do you understand?" The three boys nodded. "The first laps you will take are to familiarize yourself with the course. Once you complete the course, you will reverse directions and wave ride the course in the opposite direction. These laps aren't timed, so there's no need to hurry. Take your time and do your best to learn the course."

The five students were facing the Professor. They were so focused on what he was saying, that none of them noticed the tall figure that glided up behind them on a soft wave ride. "Oh, there you are," the

Professor said looking over the heads of the students. He looked back down at the students and asked, "Have you met our Team Captain, Reginald Whitelace?" Everyone turned around. Carla and the boys were horror struck.

Whitelace gave Michael and Tommy a nasty look. "I know these three," he said indicating Carla and the boys, "but, I've never met these two."

The Professor introduced Jay-Jay and Bertram and explained that Carla and Bertram were just observers. The Professor told Whitelace that there were two racers on the course finishing a Counter Clockwise lap. He said that they should be coming out the C.C. exit at any moment and, once they did, he was going to send Tommy, Michael and Jay-Jay out on their practice laps. Whitelace acknowledged the Professor's decision, but suggested that he be allowed to run an inspection lap before anyone one else got onto the course. The Professor agreed, saying that since so many racers had been on the course already, a safety inspection would be in order. Whitelace said he was going to the C.C. exit and when the two racers came out, he'd enter the course there on a Clockwise rotation.

Whitelace turned to glide his way to the C.C. exit, but before he did, he gave Tommy and Michael a somewhat twisted look. The boys didn't quite know what to make of it. Just about the time Whitelace reached the gap in the forest line near the end of the field, two racers popped out from the gap at full speed. They both made sharp left turns in unison. Their seemingly effortless moves where quite something to see. They headed in the groups direction, but in route, they made several fishtailing S turns before they slid to an abrupt stop directly in front of an approving Professor Krusher. Whitelace, in the meantime, entered the course.

One of the racers was a girl and the other was a boy. The Professor introduced them as Adriana Stormwell and Roland Wannamaker. He said that they were both fourth year Political students, but that they had both made the Race Team in their second year. He congratulated the pair and then dismissed them for the rest of the day.

The Professor continued their preride instructions while they waited for Whitelace. He told the boys that, as they exited one stage and entered the next, the path route would become one. It would remain one until a fork appeared in the pathway. At the fork, there will be a sign with two arrows on it. The red arrow will point in the direction of the challenge route and the yellow arrow will point to the longer, but safer route. He reminded them that they were to follow the yellow arrows at all times. The Professor then told them that, when they exited the course for the first time, they were to take a lap around the spot where they now stood before reentering the course on their return lap. He told them that, in an actual race, the Start/Finish Pole would be standing were they now stood. He explained that in an actual race the racers have to lap the pole before returning to the course for their return lap. He said that the field that makes up the Parade Grounds is often the site of the biggest battles between competing racers. He finished by telling them that they would start with a Clockwise lap.

Whitelace appeared though the gap in the trees at the opposite end of the field just as the Professor concluded his instructions. Whitelace had a satisfied, somewhat confident, look on his face. Everyone, including the Professor, took this to mean that the course was okay to ride. However, Whitelace's confidence came from another source. He was sure that no one saw the little flick he gave his wand as he passed a challenge sign a few stages back. Whitelace glided up and told the Professor the course was fit to ride. The Professor then told the boys they could begin, but not before reminding them to follow the yellow arrows.

The three boys popped up on their waves and started their ride towards the appropriate gap in the trees. Whitelace followed suit. Once he got along side of Tommy, he said in a very low tone, "This one's especially for you Travail." Then he abruptly turned and sped away.

The three boys entered the course at a slow and reasonable pace as the Professor had instructed. They encountered a variety of terrain that tested their wave riding skills, but nothing really difficult. They ran across several series of closely arranged bumps and winding curves. There were steep inclines that slowed their progress, which were often followed by equally steep, but very fast, declines. The boys followed all the yellow signs and, to their surprise, found themselves exiting out of the gap in the trees and onto the Parade Grounds. They had been enjoying themselves so much that they hadn't realized how far they had gone. The three of them turned and headed for their lap around the area where the Professor, Carla and Bertram were waiting.

The Professor nodded his approval as the boys passed. Carla gave the boys a hopeful look and Bertram watched them with envy. The boys made the lap around them and headed back to the gap in the trees. As they reentered the course, the Professor opened his magic mirror and invited Carla and Bertram to watch the boys' progress with him.

They watched as the boys successfully navigated the first and second stage. The boys exited the second stage and entered the third stage. After a short distance, the pathway split. Tommy and Michael checked the challenge sign as they approached, the red arrow pointed to the left and the yellow arrow pointed to the right. But, Jay-Jay saw something different. He saw the yellow arrow pointing to the left and the red arrow pointing to the right. Tommy and Michael veered to the right while Jay-Jay veered to the left. By the time they had noticed that Jay-Jay had gone the other way, he was disappearing from sight. They both thought Jay-Jay was making a terrible mistake by taking a challenge route. But, almost immediately, they realized they were on the challenge route, not Jay-Jay.

The ground quickly fell away and they found themselves on an extremely steep slope. Their speed increased immensely. They could see in the distance that the slope curved upwards near the bottom to form a jump point. They pointed their wands at the ground in front of them and performed Pushbacks. But, the slope was too steep for a Pushback to stop them. They could see a stand of trees below and beyond the jump point. Both boys realized that they had made a mistake in trying to stop themselves. The Pushbacks had only slowed their speed, now it appeared that they weren't going to have enough speed when they hit the jump point to clear all the trees and reach the landing area. They turned their wands around behind them and started a series of Pushbacks in the hopes of increasing their speed.

Their speed did increase some, but by the time they hit the jump point, they still didn't know if they were going fast enough. They crouched down with their knees flexed and jumped as hard as they could just as they hit the end of the jump point. Shoulder to shoulder, they launched themselves high into the air. They made it over a jagged rocky area immediately below the jump point and cleared the first of the trees. For a moment, it appeared that they were going to clear all the trees, but they were losing momentum. As they lost their momentum, they began to lose their altitude, and then they saw it. One last large tree remained and they were headed directly toward it. They tried several different things to change their line of flight, but none of them worked. At the last moment, Tommy turned to Michael and gave him a mighty shove on his shoulder. It sent Michael tumbling out of control, but set him on a course to miss the tree. Tommy, however, hit the tree head on at full force. The impact knocked him unconscious and he began to fall through the tree. He crashed though the branches, which cut and scratched him everywhere. He continued to fall until his body finally hit the ground with a thud.

Michael struggled to regain control. He managed to correct himself some before he collided with the ground. He tumbled and skidded for several meters. He wasn't significantly hurt, although he had reinjured his shoulder. He was very dizzy and couldn't get to his feet. He looked back and saw Tommy lying on the ground and he wasn't moving. Michael was lying on his stomach and began to crawl towards Tommy.

Back at the Parade Grounds the Professor, Carla and Bertram watched in horror as the events unfolded on the Professor's magic mirror. Carla cried out. The Professor closed the magic mirror and put it in his pocket. He popped up on a wave and sped off in the direction of the gap in the trees where Michael and Tommy had entered the course. Carla also popped up on a wave and set off after the Professor. The Professor was quite a ways ahead of Carla and entered the course well before her. Carla entered the course and saw the Professor ahead of her. Where the pathway divided, the Professor took the safe route, but when Carla reached the same point, she took the challenge route.

The path Carla was on suddenly ended with the sharp edged cliff. It dropped down some five meters to the ground below. Carla sailed over the edge of the cliff and used her magic to take her to a soft landing while still maintaining her speed. The open expanse of land ahead led directly to a wide body of water. Carla used her wand to boost her speed and headed directly to the water's edge. Once she got to the water, she sailed out above the water and began a skip. Unexpectedly, sharp spikes of ice began popping up through the surface of the water. As each one popped up in front of her, she used her skills and wand to adjust her course without loosing the rhythm of her skip. She made it all the way across the water and skipped up onto the land where she instantly began pushing up her speed. She followed the path a short ways, exited the first stage and entered the second stage. She was quite a ways ahead of the Professor now.

When she reached the second stage challenge sign, she again took the challenge route. She had gathered substantial speed when the pathway abruptly led her onto a narrow ledge. She was in a narrow gorge with high walls on both sides. It was all black below her. She couldn't tell how high she was above the bottom of the gorge, but in its blackness, it appeared bottomless. She was on a ledge that stuck out of the wall on the right side of the gorge. It was only wide enough for her right foot. She sped down the ledge on one foot with the jagged walls occasionally brushing her right shoulder. The depths of the gorge were on her left side. She looked and saw that the ledge ended several meters ahead. She looked across the gorge to the opposite wall and saw that the ledge picked up on that side where it ended on her side. Just as she got to the end of the ledge, she did a mighty Wall Bounce and jumped across the gorge to the other side, landing on her left foot. As she sped along, she could see that this ledge also ended and she was going to have to make another Wall Bounce jump across the gorge. She made that jump across the gorge and several more before the last ledge led her back on to the pathway. She followed the pathway and exited stage two and entered stage three.

Once again, she chose the challenge route. Tommy and Michael had crashed on this challenge. She hit the steep down slope and pushed her speed as much as she could. She hit the jump point and pushed off. She was easily clearing the trees. As she approached the last tree, she looked down and saw Michael still crawling on his stomach towards Tommy. He had almost reached Tommy as she passed overhead. She had too much speed and almost overshot the landing area, but she brought herself to a safe, cushioned landing. She was still carrying a great deal of speed, but she didn't hesitate. She

The Life and Times of Tommy Travail

did a full speed hook turn and reversed her direction. She spotted the boys and set her course in their direction. Within moments, she came to a stop next to the two boys.

"Are you hurt?" she asked Michael.

"I think I'm all right," he answered as he tried to get to his feet. The dizziness had passed and he stood up okay.

Carla bent down and gently brushed Tommy's forehead. He was still unconscious. She checked to see if he had a pulse and he did. She saw that he was breathing, but it was soft and shallow. "Everything is going to be all right," she said softly in his ear. The Professor is on his way." She pulled out her handkerchief and gently blotted the blood from the many cuts and scratches on his face. Tommy opened his eyes a tiny bit and smiled slightly when saw Carla's face.

The Professor arrived and immediately turned his wand sideways and scanned Tommy from head to toe. "Thank goodness," he said, "nothing's broken." The Professor then turned his wand and pointed it at Tommy. He said some magic words and Tommy disappeared.

Carla's eyes opened wide in surprise and Michael's jaw dropped. "What happed to Tommy?" Carla excitedly asked. "Where'd he go?"

The Professor smiled and said, "He gone to the Infirmary. Since your dad and I had our accident, the course has been magically enhanced to allow for an instant transport of an injured racer directly to the Infirmary. But, it has its side effects. I'm sorry about this, Mister Woden, but I'm going to have to send you as well. We'll see you back at the Infirmary." The Professor pointed his wand at Michael, repeated the magic words and Michael disappeared. The Professor and Carla headed back to the Parade Grounds.

The experience of being transported to the Infirmary was a familiar one for Tommy and Michael. They squished and stretched exactly the same way they had when they originally transported from Earth to the Home Plane. In an instant, they found themselves on their sides curled up on a bed in the Infirmary. Tommy opened his eyes and, for a moment, saw the shooting thin blue streaks going every direction. Then his stomach started. By that time, Medical Wizard Healsau was standing next to Tommy and handed him a medium sized bucket. Tommy knew immediately what it was for. He took the bucket just as his lunch came up. With a grunt and a roar, it came up and splattered against the bottom of the bucket. In the meantime, Medical Wizard Healsau turned around and handed Michael a bucket. Michael was just coming to and, in a moment, he was repeating what Tommy had just done.

Medical Wizard Healsau gave the boys a potion that settled their stomachs and then he went to work on their wounds. He checked Tommy for a concussion and then patched up his cuts and scratches. He was working on Michael's shoulder when Professor Krusher came in. He had Carla, Jay-Jay and Bertram with him. No one said anything until the Medical Wizard finished his work.

"How are they?" the Professor asked the Medical Wizard.

"Oh, they'll be fine," Medical Wizard Healsau said. "They should rest here for a while just to make sure neither of them goes goofy, but they'll be okay. They're young and these two are pretty tough."

"And," the Professor added, "from what I just saw out there, they're pretty brave too, even if they are disobedient. This one hit a tree head on to save that one, and that one crawled almost three hundred meters to help this one."

Carla was a mix of emotions. She was concerned about the boys' well-being, but she was very angry that they would take a challenge route. On the other hand, she was very proud of their behavior and conduct during and through a disaster. She walked over to the space between the boys' beds. She stood there and just looked at them for a moment, and then she shook her head just slightly. With a slight smile and a quiver in her voice, she spoke, "Friends for life, right?"

Tommy and Michael both smiled and responded, "Right!"

The Professor stepped up and addressed the boys. "I'm proud of your actions out there boys, but I'm very disappointed in you two. I'm disappointed that you would take a challenge route after my repeated warnings not to."

"But Professor," Michael responded. "The sign… We followed the yellow arrow."

"Is that so?" the Professor questioned. "If that's so, how come you wound up on a challenge route?"

"It's true Professor," Tommy protested. "The yellow arrow pointed to the right and we went right, honest."

The Professor pointed to Jay-Jay and motioned him to come forward. Once Jay-Jay got to the foot of Tommy's bed, the Professor asked him what he saw.

"I'm sorry guys," Jay-Jay began, "but I saw the yellow arrow pointing to the left and I went left."

"Okay," the Professor said. "We might be able to see exactly what happened." The Professor pulled out his magic mirror and opened it. "We can replay the incident and, if we're lucky, we might be able to see the sign."

The Professor tapped the mirror with his wand and the replay began with the boys entering the first stage. The Professor tapped the mirror twice more and it began with the boys entering the third stage. It was a distant image, but they could see the sign ahead of the boys. The arrows appeared to point the red arrow to the right and the yellow arrow to the left just as Jay-Jay had said. The picture zoomed in some as the boys neared the sign. As the boys approached the sign, the arrows began to flicker and, as impossible as it seemed, both arrows began showing both red and yellow at the same time. At that point, the picture showed Tommy and Michael veering to the right while Jay-Jay swerved to the left.

"Well," the Professor said. "I'm sorry boys. It appears that you were both right. It looks like we had a magical glitch. It happens sometimes, but it doesn't generally result in this kind of disaster. I'm sorry it happened and I think it would only be fair to give the three of you another chance to tryout for the Team. Once you're healed, we'll schedule something."

Tommy looked at Michael and Michael nodded. "I think we better wait until next year before we try again," Tommy said. "I think Michael and I need a little more experience." Jay-Jay agreed that he should also wait another year.

"Well," the Professor responded, "it'll be my pleasure and I look forward to it."

It was music to Carla's ears. She wouldn't have to worry about them wave racing again, at least for another year. She was glowing when the Professor turned to her.

"And you, Miss Crosswell," he said to her. "You can join the Team right now if you wish."

Carla blushed, and then made a stern face. "You know how I feel about Cross-Country Racing, Professor."

"I know," the Professor said with a smile. "I just thought I'd make the offer."

The Professor turned back to the boys. "You boys take care of yourselves and I'll see you in our next class, if I don't see you sooner."

The Professor turned to direct Carla, Jay-Jay and Bertram to leave with him. Tommy motioned for Carla to come closer. Carla leaned toward Tommy before she turned to leave.

"It was Whitelace," he whispered to her. Her eyes opened wide and she straightened up. "We'll see you all back at the Crow's Nest before dinner," he said loudly. Carla nodded and turned around. Jay-Jay and Bertram, who hadn't said anything, waved and turned to leave.

"Hey, Bertie," Michael called out. Bertram turned back around. "Thanks for coming. We really appreciate it."

A big smile spread across Bertram's face and he stood up a little straighter. "You bet guys, see you later." He turned and they left the room.

Chapter Nineteen

New Castle Town

Over the next few days, the boys healed. They attended their classes and seemed to be doing very well. Their reputations for courage under fire spread wildly about the Academy. Although Tommy and Michael thought it was pretty cool, they really did try to play it down, which of course, seemed to encourage more of it. Carla's reputation as a skilled racer also spread about the Academy along with stories about the courage and heroism she showed while trying to help Tommy and Michael.

    Carla and the boys continued to have occasional run-ins with Whitelace, and he was always his usual nasty self. He ridiculed their performance on the Cross-Country Course and made fun of what he called their stupidity. Michael, and especially Tommy, wanted to accuse him of causing their accident, but they had learned not to mess with him. However, Tommy knew he wasn't done with Whitelace, not by any means. Tommy was watching Whitelace and making some plans.

    They began adjusting to their new life at the Academy. In fact, all the students were adjusting to their new lives at the Academy. The kids in the Queen's Class were becoming more like family than just classmates. Tommy had given the second Rule Most Important a lot of thought. That's the rule that says that the students will honor, respect and protect all other Academy students, past, present and future. As the students grew closer, this rule began to mean much more to all of them.

Their first week of classes ended and they began their first no-class day. At breakfast, Misty Firefist invited Carla and the boys to go with her and Kristy Firefist to New Castle Town. Misty told them she had cracked her message mirror earlier in the week, so she and Kristy were going to Kristy's Dad's magic mirror shop to get a new one. She said they were going to spend the morning doing homework and then go to New Castle after lunch. Carla and the boys accepted her invitation, providing they got enough of their homework done. If they got enough done to go, Carla thought Tommy and Michael should also buy message mirrors so they could communicate when they were apart.

Most of the students returned to the Crow's Nest after breakfast, however, some went to the library and some went out to the courtyard to study. The morning hours went by quickly. By lunch time, Carla and the boys were satisfied with the amount of homework they had finished and felt comfortable accompanying Misty and Kristy to New Castle. Carla and the boys met up with Misty and Kristy in the Main Hall. When they finished lunch, the five of them headed off for New Castle Town.

They took the side road so it didn't take very long to get into New Castle. New Castle Town was a busy center of commerce when the Royal Family lived in the Castle, but now it was predominately a residential community. The buildings and houses had a more modern appearance than those in Cantwell, but they showed their age. In the center of the town, the two main streets crossed. At one time, the stores and shops that lined the streets carried the finest and rarest items in the realm, but now most of them just carried everyday goods.

Kristy and Misty led the way as they neared the center of town. Tommy and Michael were taking in the sights and sounds of the town and almost missed seeing Kristy, Misty and Carla turn and enter a store. The store had large display windows on each side of the entrance. The displays were filled with all manner of mirrors from tiny and plain ones to full length mirrors with elaborate gold and silver scroll work. A sign above the entrance identified the name of the store as 'Images'. Tommy and Michael took a few minutes to look at the

The Life and Times of Tommy Travail

mirrors on display before entering the store. Light and images were reflected over and over again from mirror to mirror. The whole effect was mesmerizing and hypnotic.

Tommy opened the entrance door and he and Michael entered the store. The hypnotic effect was significantly greater inside the store. The store had numerous display tables full of mirrors of various sizes and shapes. The walls were covered with larger mirrors. Tommy examined the store for a mirror like the one that had transported them to the Home Plane, but he didn't see anything like it. The three girls were standing at the front counter talking to a tall red haired man. When the boys caught up to the girls, Kristy introduced the man as her father, Wizard Padraig Firefist.

Tommy asked what all of the mirrors did and Wizard Firefist explained that most of the mirrors had not yet been magically enhanced. He said that they were made in such a way that they would accept all kinds of enchantments, but each mirror would only accept one enchantment. Most of the time the witch or wizard that purchased the mirror would put their own enchantment on the mirror. However, the store could pre-enchant any mirror for an additional charge. Some mirrors, like message mirrors were pre-enchanted at the factory.

Misty told her Uncle that she needed a new message mirror and he directed her to a display table that held nothing but message mirrors. All five of them went over to the display and examined the various message mirrors. Michael and Tommy each selected a medium size fold up mirror and Misty chose a slightly larger non-folding mirror. After they paid for their mirrors, Kristy said she wanted to stay and talk with her father for a while. She suggested that the rest of them take in the town and visit some of the other shops and stores. Everyone liked the idea, especially when Misty said there was an exquisite sweet shop just down the street. They decided to meet Kristy back at her dad's store when they were finished.

Misty, Carla and the boys left the store and headed for the sweet shop. On their way, they passed by the curiosity shop that Jingleshangles had mentioned. Tommy recognized the name, Things Mostly Curious. He told his companions that he wanted to visit the shop after they were finished at the sweet shop. They arrived at the sweet shop and Misty was right. The sweet shop had everything that

David G. Groesbeck

was sweet, from extra rich chocolates to ice cream sodas. One side of the shop had a long snack bar with stools where they served many different flavors of soft and hard ice cream as well as several different kinds of soft drinks. The four of them took seats. A tall teenage non-magical boy with freckles and a white hat stood behind the snack bar.

The four of them took seats at the snack bar and the tall boy took their order. Misty ordered a chocolate fudge sundae and Carla ordered a double scoop cone of All Nut soft ice cream dipped in hard shell chocolate. Tommy ordered a Roddenberry root, root beer ice cream float and Michael ordered a frozen Sarsaparilla. They had a good time while they ate and drank their treats. Michael and Tommy were feeling so good that they even cracked a couple of jokes about their misfortune at the Cross-Country tryouts. This concerned Carla slightly because she didn't want the boys to take the seriousness of what had happened too lightly. But, it made her feel good to see that they were getting over the whole incident.

They finished up at the snack bar and browsed around the shop. Each of them bought a bag of chocolates, caramels and Chewy Chew Chews. They left the shop and headed back the direction they had come. Tommy had forgotten about the curiosity shop until he saw the sign in the front window. He pointed it out and they all went into the shop. It was packed with all manner of things. There were shelves and tables with gadgets and devices. Half of one wall was filled with used wands, some were in need of repair and others looked like new. Mr. Keepers, the non-magical shop owner, had just finished collecting money from a customer at the back counter. He looked up as the kids came in and gave Misty a little wave and a smile. He was a short overweight man with a round face and at the tip of a noticeably red nose, sat a pair of thin reading glasses. He wore a brown suit coat and a checkered vest. He had a pocket watch in one of his vest pockets, which was connected to the other vest pocket with a gold chain fob. Under his breath, Michael asked Carla why his nose was so red and Carla guessed that it was from a bit too much of the Tinkleberry wine.

The kids spread out and began to look over the many items on display. There was a hand carved Narco tusk hanging from the ceiling.

It was some three meters long. Along side of it, hung a real dragon's skull with its massive and sharply pointed teeth fully exposed. Michael found his way to a display case full of time pieces. It contained hour glasses, wrist watches and a variety of pocket watches. Since his twelve hour watch was no good in a land of thirteen hour days, he wanted to get himself a new one. While Michael was examining the time pieces, Tommy came across a table covered with old mechanical devices. There were so many items that they were stacked on top of one another.

Tommy was fascinated with the many odd looking gadgets. He picked up a couple of them and tried to imagine what they did. He turned to find Mr. Keepers and saw that he was showing Michael a watch, so he turned back to the table and picked up another contraption. When he did, it exposed something that he recognized. He couldn't believe it at first. He moved the other devices out of the way and picked it up. It looked almost identical to the mechanism he had played with so often on his grandfather's desk. He examined it closely and there was no doubt in his mind, it was exactly like the one his grandfather had on his desk, except it was in better condition. The finish on the metal was brighter and there wasn't any rust. He peered inside and saw three shiny surfaces just like his grandfather's device. Tommy set the machine back on the table and hurriedly went over to the display case where Mr. Keepers was still showing Michael time pieces.

Michael was leaning over the display case with his head down examining a wrist watch. He caught Tommy's approach out of the corner of his eye, but he didn't look up. He continued to study the watch. "Hey, Tommy," he said, "I think I'll buy this watch. It's really cool. It's loaded with dials and buttons. Mr. Keeper doesn't…"

"You gotta see what I found," Tommy interrupted. "Sorry, didn't mean to cut you off, well, I guess I did, but you gotta see this."

Michael looked up and could see the bright-eyed excitement on Tommy face. "What is itm Tommy Boy?" he asked. "What's got you so excited?"

"Mister Keepers, can you tell me about this thing," Tommy asked turning his attention away from Michael for a moment.

"What thing would that be, young man?" Mr. Keepers inquired.

"Over on this table," Tommy answered as he took a hold of Michael's arm and set off in the direction of the table. Michael quickly set the watch down and Mr. Keepers followed.

"What do you think?" Tommy asked when they got to the table.

"About what," Michael asked back. All he saw was a table full of odd looking mechanisms.

"About this," Tommy answered as he reached down and touched the device.

"What about it?" Michael asked.

"Don't you recognize it?" Tommy suggested. "It's just like the one on my grandfather's desk."

The expression slowly changed on Michael's face as he recognized the object. He eyes grew even larger as the meaning of it began to set in.

"Mister Keepers," Tommy asked, "can you tell me what this is?"

"I believe," Mr. Keepers started then paused as he took a closer look, "Yes," he continued. "The man that sold that to me said it was a very old message mirror, maybe one of the first message mirrors ever made."

"How does it work," Tommy inquired.

"That I wouldn't know," Mr. Keepers answered. "As I just told your friend, being a non-magical, I don't know how any of this magical stuff works. I leave it up to the Witch or Wizard that's interested in something to make it work."

"How much do you want for it?" Tommy asked a bit too excitedly.

"That'd be one drop of Silv... ah, Gold," Mr. Keeper stuttered.

"That's a bit expensive," Tommy replied realizing that his excitement just caused the price to go up.

"Well, lad," Mr. Keepers replied. "That is quite a valuable antique you know. Things like that don't come along everyday."

"Mister Keepers," Tommy said questioningly. "If it's so valuable, how come it was buried under all this other junk? Come on, what's your best price?"

"You wouldn't happen to have a spot of the Tinkleberry wine on you, would you," Mr. Keepers asked and then answered himself as

The Life and Times of Tommy Travail

Tommy shook his head, "No, didn't think so, too young and all. Okay how about one drop of silver?"

"I'll tell you what," Tommy suggested as he reached into his pocket and withdrew four remaining drops of metal from his pocket. He opened his hand slightly to see what he had without letting Mr. Keepers see what he had. He saw that he had one drop of gold, one drop of silver and two drops of tin. "I'll give you one drop of silver and two drops of tin for this thing and that watch Michael was looking at." Michael's eyes widened again.

"Oh, I don't know," Mr. Keepers hesitated. "That's a pretty fine watch."

"Now wait a minute," Michael said. "When we were over at the counter, you told me you didn't even know if that watch worked. And, beside I didn't even try it on. I might not like it once I try it on." But, Tommy knew how much Michael really wanted that watch.

"Come on, Mister Keepers," Tommy interjected. "One drop of silver and two drops of tin, that's all we have," Tommy lied.

"Well... Okay," Mr. Keepers finally agreed. "You boys drive a hard bargain," he added as he picked up the device. He then walked over to the displace case, picked up the watch and went to the back counter. The boys followed. He reached under the counter, pulled out a box large enough to hold the antique message mirror, and placed it inside. He handed Michael the watch and said, "That's two pieces of silver and one of tin."

"I don't think so," Misty said. She and Carla had walked up behind the boys. "I'm sure I heard you agree to one drop of silver and two drops of tin."

"Oh, oh," Mr. Keepers stuttered. His face started to turn as red as his nose. "I suppose you did. Ah, yes, yes. I believe it was as you said Miss Firefist, one piece of silver and two of tin."

Tommy handed Mr. Keepers the three drops of metal. He had already slipped the drop of gold back into his pocket. Tommy picked up the box and slipped it under his arm. He and Michael thanked Mr. Keepers and the four of them left the shop.

"Pretty slick, Tommy Boy," Michael said once they were back outside. "Thanks for the watch. You know, he told me, just before you interrupted us, that he wanted two pieces of silver for this watch."

235

Michael slipped the watch onto his wrist as Tommy and the girls watched. To everyone's surprise, the watch lit up, the dials began turning and the bezel spun.

"Wow," Carla said. "What does it do?"

"Don't know," Michael answered. "It's gonna take some time to figure everything out, but it certainly does a lot more than just tell the time."

"Okay," Misty said, "does your watch tell us if we have enough time to make another stop?"

Michael looked at his watch and was surprised to see a single word illuminated across its face. It said, "Yes."

"Uh," Michael grunted, "it appears we do."

"Good," Misty said, "I want to go to Witch Wicker's and buy a crystal necklace. We'll have to cross the street. It's down an alley on the other side of the street."

Misty and Carla walked side-by-side and the boys followed behind also walking side- by-side. Michael wasn't paying much attention to where they were going as he kept studying his watch. Four dials were now appearing on his watch. The main dial, on the top part of the watch face, gave the current time. The other three, on the bottom half of the watch face, were giving an elapsed time. A tiny label appeared above each one. The first one said, 'Past'; the middle one said, 'Present'; and the third one said, 'Future'. Below each elapsed time dial another message appeared. Under the one labeled Past, it said, "Things Mostly Curious" and the elapsed time dial showed twenty eight minutes and forty seconds. Under the dial labeled 'Present' it said, "Main Street" and the elapsed time dial was showing six minutes and seventeen seconds. Finally, under the dial labeled 'Future' it said, "Witch Wicker's" and the dial was showing twenty minutes and eleven seconds.

The girls reached the alley and turned down it. Michael was so engrossed in his watch that if Tommy hadn't grabbed his arm, he would have walked right past the alley. There was only one shop in the alley. A sign protruded out above the doorway. It said, "Witch Wicker's Magical Crystals and Candles." The girls entered the door and the boys followed.

The shop had crystals hanging everywhere that glittered and glistened in the light. There were many display cases also containing crystals in numerous sizes and shapes. On a table next to the door, a tall four sided crystal stood nearly a meter in height. In the center of the crystal was a white unicorn standing on its hind legs. Tommy looked at the unicorn and jumped slightly when it turned its head, looked at Tommy and flicked its mane back. Candles were also placed everywhere. The candles varied in size from little stubby ones to large ones that were taller than the kids were. Some of them were plain while others had intricate designs and ribbon-like features. The whole shop was filled with a blend of many different aromas.

The girls headed for a display case containing crystal necklaces and the boys headed for a very large crystal ball in the center of the room. The crystal was so large that it sat in its own cradle on the floor and the top of it was still above Michael's head. A large price tag at its base set the crystal's price at a whopping 10,000 drops of gold. All the way around the crystal ball, there were signs that said, "Warning: Gaze into this Crystal Ball at Your Own Risk."

Tommy and Michael looked at the crystal ball and felt themselves being pulled into it. They felt as if they were falling towards the center of it as images flashed by. The images were coming and going so fast that they couldn't make sense of them.

"Hey you two," Carla called. "Are you ready to go?"

"What," Tommy asked as he regained his senses. "We just got here."

"I don't think so," Carla responded. "Misty's already bought her necklace and we're ready to go."

Tommy reached over and tugged at Michael's arm. "Huh," Michael grunted.

"Time to go," Tommy said.

"But we just got here," Michael objected.

"I don't think so," Tommy replied.

Michael looked at his watch and saw that almost twenty minutes had gone by since they entered the shop. "Wow," he exclaimed. "That was weird."

"Yeah," Tommy replied, and they headed for the girls who were waiting at the door.

"Did you see…," Tommy started to ask Carla.

"Third year," Carla responded, interrupting him.

"What?" Tommy asked with a look of confusion on his face.

"Third year," Carla repeated. "Crystal balls can be perilous. That's why we don't study them until our third year."

"Oh," Tommy said. "I can see why."

They met Kristy at her dad's shop and headed back to the Castle. When they got back to the Castle, they had just enough time to go to the Crow's Nest and put their things away before departing for dinner. After storing their things in their bedrooms, they met up with some of their other classmates in the Community Room and headed to the Main Hall for dinner.

"Do you think you can make that message mirror thing work?" Michael asked Tommy while they followed the group to the Main Hall. "I mean, you never figured out the one on your grandfather's desk."

"I don't know," Tommy answered, "probably not, but I'll bet Ronald Lockhard can. I'm going to ask him to take a look at it."

"Good idea," Michael agreed.

They went on Whitelace watch and didn't say any more until they got to the Main Hall. When they entered the Main Hall, they spotted Whitelace seated at the Military table with the rest of his classmates. Tommy found Ronald and told him about the antique message mirror. Ronald, with his interest in enchanted devices, was very curious about the thing, so when Tommy asked him if he'd examine it, Ronald said he'd be happy to take a look at it right after dinner. Once everyone was seated, food began to appear.

Chapter Twenty

The Plan

Carla and the boys ate a hearty meal and finished ahead of everyone else. They decided not to wait for the rest of their classmates. However, if they had seen Whitelace leave ahead of them, they would have waited. Tommy told Ronald that he'd see him back at the Crow's Nest and they left the Main Hall. Whitelace was waiting for them when they enter the Grand Foyer.

It turned out to be a very bad encounter. Whitelace accused Tommy of cheating on his school work and, when he saw Michael's new watch, he accused Michael of stealing it. The discussion got very heated and loud. Ronald along with some of the other kids came into the Grand Foyer from the Main Hall and, although they watched what was going on, no one dared get close to them. It ended with Whitelace giving Tommy and Michael lines. When Carla protested, he gave her lines as well. By the time it was over, almost the entire Queen's Class had gathered in the Grand Foyer along with several kids from other Classes.

Carla and the boys returned to the Crow's Nest with their classmates. By now, everyone had gotten used to these assaults on Carla and the boys and, although they didn't like it, there didn't seem to be anything anyone could do about it. No one even asked questions anymore, they just took it as part of their daily routine.

David G. Groesbeck

Tommy, Michael and Ronald went to their bedroom area. Tommy got the antique message mirror out of his trunk and gave it to Ronald.

"See if you can figure out how to make this thing work," Tommy said to Ronald as he handed it to him. "My grandfather has one just like it and I'd like to try to send him a message with it."

"Wow," Ronald said. "I haven't ever seen anything quite like this. It's really old. This is gonna take some time to figure this out. Can I hang on to it for a while?

"Sure," Tommy answered. "Take all the time you need, but the sooner you figure it out the better."

"Well, I can't promise anything, but I'll give it my best shot," Ronald replied.

Tommy and Michael left Ronald with the device and headed back down to the Community Room. They had agreed to meet Carla there and do Whitelace's lines. Carla was waiting for them when they got there. They chose a Study Room and took seats at an empty table. Tommy sat on one side of the table and Carla and Michael sat across from him. They got out their notebooks and started writing copies of The Rules Most Important.

Tommy finished the first rule and started on the second rule, but almost immediately, he stopped. "This is the rule I'm having the most trouble with," he suddenly said.

"Huh," Michael and Carla said at the same time.

"This second rule," Tommy replied.

"You're having a difficult time writing it?" Carla questioned with considerable confusion on her face.

"No," Tommy answered, "I'm having a difficult time following it. It says we're supposed to honor, respect and protect all other Academy students, past, present and future. And, I have come up with a plan to deal with Whitelace, but if I'm right, I might have to violate this rule."

"Well," Michael said with increased interest, "I wouldn't have any problem violating this rule when it comes to Whitelace, and you shouldn't either."

"Yes, you would if you knew how bad it could hurt him," Tommy replied. "This could result in more than just simple payback, it could ruin his life."

"I don't think we want to get into that kind of thing," Carla immediately interjected.

"It'd serve him right," Michael said emphatically. "Tell me your plan."

"I think we should drop this whole thing right now," Carla said. "I don't think anything good is going to come from this kind of talk."

"I disagree," Michael said. "I think we should hear Tommy's plan before we make any decisions."

"I agree with Michael," Tommy asserted. "I think we should discuss it."

"Well I don't," Carla continued to protest.

"Listen," Tommy pleaded, "if it turns out to be a bad idea then we can drop it, but I really would like to get your feelings on this. I'm not sure what's right and what isn't, and I especially would like to hear what you think, Carla."

"Well okay," Carla acquiesced, "but I'm still not sure we should even talk about this kind of stuff."

Tommy leaned forward so he could speak in softer tones. Carla and Michael followed suit. "I think that Whitelace is working for the Black Witch." Tommy began. "Every evening or two, he slips out of the Castle after hours. I think he goes somewhere to meet with another spy for the Black Witch or to do some of her evil work. So I was thinking, if I follow him some night, I might be able to get some kind of evidence that he is working for the Black Witch."

"And then what?" Carla inquired.

"Well that's where I have a problem," Tommy answered. "If I turn that evidence into the authorities, then all kinds of bad things could happen to him. He might even be arrested."

"So where's the problem?" Michael asked with a wry smile.

"Rule number two," Tommy answered.

"I still don't see where there's a problem," Michael repeated.

"I do," said Carla. "What if there are other things involved?"

"Like what?" Michael asked.

"Like, what if he's being forced to help the Black Witch?" Carla replied. "What if he doesn't have any choice?"

"Well, I think that would be for the authorities to sort out," Michael responded. "And, I don't think it's a violation of rule number two either. If he's working for the Black Witch, I think we have higher duty to report him, and if he's being forced to do it, we should still report him so he can get help."

"You might be right," Carla seemingly agreed, "but what if he's doing something completely innocent, like taking care of a sick relative or something?"

"Well then we wouldn't have anything to report," Michael shot back, "so no harm, no foul."

"But," Carla countered, "you're forgetting something. In order to follow Whitelace, we'd have to violate another rule. We'd have to be outside of the Crow's Nest after hours. I don't know how many demerits we'd get for that, but I'll bet it's a bunch. And, if it turns out that Whitelace is doing something perfectly innocent, then we'd be taking that risk for nothing."

"Wait a minute," Tommy cut in. "What's with this *we* stuff? I wouldn't think of asking you guys to take such a risk. But I think its worth the risk, so I'm willing to break rule... rule... rule number... six," Tommy stuttered as he tried to remember the correct rule number.

"Hold on, Tommy Boy," Michael interjected.

And, at the same time, Carla said, "Now you wait a minute." Carla raised her index finger in Michael's direction indicating she'd like to speak first. Michael obliged and Carla when on. Speaking directly to Tommy she said, "I'm confused. You say you're reluctant to violate rule number two, but you seem perfectly willing to break rule six."

"It's different," Tommy explained. "If I break rule number two and some really bad stuff happens to Whitelace, he's the one that ends up paying the price for my actions. However, if I get caught breaking rule number six, then I, and I alone, pay the penalty."

"Let's make something clear," Michael interrupted. "If you go after Whitelace, I'm going with you. I don't care about rule six or rule two when it comes to that monster. I've had about all I can take from him and if he pays the price for our breaking the rules, so much the better.

And, if he is in league with the Black Witch, I don't think it's a violation of rule two. I think it's our duty to turn him in."

Carla desperately wanted to disagree with the boys, but she knew them well enough to be able to tell when they were going to do something whether she agreed with them or not. So she thought she would take a different approach, and she said, "I'm not saying I agree with you, but how would you carry out this plan?" Carla was hoping that she could find some flaw in Tommy's plan that would make it unworkable.

"I don't know," Tommy said to Carla's surprise.

"See," she said thinking quickly, "you don't even know what you'd do. I don't call that a plan."

"But, I do have some ideas," Tommy replied to Carla's disappointment. "Like I said earlier, every evening or two, Whitelace slips off. From what I can tell, he doesn't go every night, but he never misses more than one night in a row. So, I was planning on watching him and, if he doesn't go one night, then the next night I'd wait for him and follow him when he leaves the Castle."

"Where would you wait for him?" Carla asked, "and how would you get there?"

"Well, that's the part I don't know," Tommy answered. "Maybe I could go out to the outer gardens after dinner and just not come back to the Crow's Nest. I could wait there until Whitelace shows up."

"What if Whitelace doesn't show up," Carla questioned. "You'd be running the risk of getting caught outside after hours for nothing."

"Say, I have an idea," Michael suddenly said. "We could ask the Castle Directory if there's a quick route from the Crow's Nest to the inner courtyard. The last time we did that, we got a heck of a ride to Professor Pastorie's classroom."

"That's a great idea," Tommy agreed. "If there is a short cut, then I wouldn't have to leave the Crow's Nest at all until I was sure that Whitelace was on the move."

"Hey," Michael said with a frown on his face, "that's *we* wouldn't have to leave the Crow's Nest. I'm serious about this. If you go, I go as well."

"Okay," Tommy responded. "You've made your point. We go after Whitelace together. Check and see if there's anyone in the Community Room. If no one's there, we can ask the Directory now."

Michael got up, walked to the door and peered out. He then returned to the table. He didn't sit down, but rather he leaned over and said, "The only one out there is Ronald and he's all engrossed in that message device you gave him. I don't think he'll pay any attention to what we're doing."

"Good," Tommy said as he stood up. "Let's go see what the Castle Directory has to say."

Carla reluctantly followed the boys into the next room. When they got there, Ronald looked up and upon seeing Tommy, he smiled and said, "This is quite a machine."

"Have you figured anything out?" Tommy asked.

"A couple of things," Ronald answered, "but I'm still quite a ways from making it work."

"Well, keep it up," Tommy encouraged. "I'm sure if anyone can figure it out, it's you." Ronald beamed with pride and returned his attention to the antique device.

Tommy walked over to the Directory with Michael and Carla along side. Tommy spoke to the directory in soft tones. "Castle, this is Tommy Travail of the Queen's Class. Please show me the quickest route to the inner courtyard from here."

Nothing happened. Tommy turned to Michael and Carla with a look of disappointment on his face. Michael was also frowning, but Tommy could see just the slightest bit of a smile on Carla's face. He turned his attention back to the directory just in time to see it light up with thin blue lines. He and Michael smiled and Carla frowned slightly. They all took a moment to study the Directory. Then, with confusion on their faces, they looked at one another. They turned around to have a look. The directory was showing a route out the window behind them.

"Is this some kind of joke?" Michael asked. "Are we supposed to jump out the window? We'd get killed. It's got to be 30 meters to the ground."

"I don't think it's that far," Carla said shaking her head. "But, I agree with you, it's certainly too high to jump."

"I want to take a look," Michael said as he walked over to the window. He opened the window when he got there and stuck his head out. "Uh oh," he said.

Carla and Tommy also stuck their heads out the window. "Uh oh is right," Tommy exclaimed.

What they saw was a line of bricks that protruded out of the side of the tower. The bricks weren't much wider than a foot width. They were connected in a smooth way and spiraled down and around the outside of the tower. "You can't walk down that," Tommy said with disappointment. "It's far too narrow and too steep"

"I don't think you're supposed to walk down it," Carla said. "I think you're supposed to do a single foot wave ride down it."

"How scary is that," Michael exclaimed.

"Pretty scary," Carla responded, "and plenty dangerous." Carla knew she could do it, but she doubted the boys could.

"If we did manage to get down, how'd we get back up," Tommy asked.

"Coming up would be a lot easier than going down," Carla explained. "To come back up, you'd be pushing all the way, but going down would require you to brake all the way and that'd be a lot harder."

Michael's burning desire to deal with Whitelace overrode any good judgment he had. "Scary or not, I want to give it a try," he said and, in his usual charge right in way, he crawled out onto the window ledge.

Carla gasped and almost fainted. Tommy grabbed his arm and tried to pull him back in, but Michael just pulled away from him. In an instant, Michael was up on a single foot wave. He pulled out his wand, pointed it at the sloping bricks, and gave himself the slightest push off. He began to slide down the spiraling bricks. About halfway down he was going too fast and lost his balance. He started to fall outward. Suddenly, with the most gentlest softness, the Castle magically pulled him back to the wall. The sudden shot of fear he felt began to subside as he realized the Castle wouldn't let him fall. With a surge of bravado, he sailed the rest of the way down.

Michael hit the ground and looked up. "Come on, Tommy Boy," he called up to the two heads sticking out the window. "Give it a try, the Castle won't let you fall."

Against Carla's protests, Tommy crawled out the window and repeated what Michael had done. However, the Castle had to prevent Tommy from falling four times on his way down. Carla took a deep breath of relief as Tommy slid from the brick work to the ground.

Both boys looked up at Carla. "It's your turn," Michael called to her.

Against her better judgment, she crawled out of the window and did as the boys had done. The Castle didn't have to catch her at all on her way down. She slid off the brick work and came to a stop next to Michael. She doubled up her fist and hit Michael in his upper arm as hard as she could. Michael instantly found out that she could punch really hard.

"Ow!" Michael hollered. "That really hurt."

"It was supposed to hurt," Carla replied. "Don't ever do anything like that again!"

"Well," Michael pleaded. "We had to find out if we could do it, didn't we?"

"Not by risking your life, we didn't," Carla shot back.

"You have to admit, it wasn't the brightest thing you've ever done," Tommy added.

"Alright, alright," Michael conceded. "I get the point. Let's just say that I had a feeling that everything was going to be okay."

Carla tightened her lips and scowled at Michael. In a tender way, Michael smiled back at her. He knew that her anger was a reflection of her true concern for him, and it felt good to have someone, besides Tommy, who was sincerely concerned about his well being.

"Shall we try to go back up?" Michael asked cautiously.

"I'll go first," Carla said to Michael and Tommy's surprise. "That way I can check and make sure that the Castle will also protect us going up as well as coming down." Without waiting for a reply, Carla popped up on a single foot wave and launched herself back up onto the spiraling line of brickwork. A couple of times as she spiraled upward, she intentionally leaned outward. Each time the Castle gently pulled her back. When she reached the top, she crawled back into the window and motioned to the boys to come on up.

Tommy went next and Michael came last. Once they were back inside the Community Room, they closed the window and headed back to the Study Room. As they went past Ronald, he looked up from the antique device, smiled, and then returned his attention back to the device. He apparently hadn't noticed anything that they had done.

All three of them seemed to be on the same track once they entered the Study Room. They took their seats and returned to their lines. They scribbled out the lines as fast as they could without saying much of anything. They all needed some time to think about what they had discussed and what had just happened.

Carla finished first. She took out one of her text books and thumbed through it. She really wasn't paying any attention to what she was doing. She was in deep thought about the possible consequences of what the boys were planning and she was trying to decide if she should go along with it. By the time Tommy and Michael finished their lines, she had made up her mind. She decided that she would continue to object to the whole plan, but if the boys decided to go through with it, she would go with them.

"I still think this whole thing is a bad idea," Carla commented as the boys put their notebooks back into their back-packs.

"Listen, Carla," Tommy replied, "we simply have to do something about Whitelace. Even if he is not spying for the Black Witch, maybe we can discover something that will get him off our backs. He's become too much of an interference. I need to do some things to try to find my parents and constantly having to watch out for him makes it much more difficult. I think we need to do this."

"I agree with Tommy," Michael added in support. "I think we should start watching for him tonight and as soon as he shows up we should follow him, whether that's tonight, tomorrow or whenever."

Then Tommy said something that shocked everyone, including himself. "We won't do it," he said, "if Carla doesn't agree it's the right thing to do."

"What!" Carla and Michael exclaimed simultaneously.

"Two ordinary guys and one special girl," Tommy responded. "Friends for life, right?"

"Right," both Carla and Michael answered.

"Then Carla's got as much say in what we do as any of us. And let's face it Michael, she's more level headed than either of us."

"Well, you're probably right there, Tommy Boy," Michael agreed. "And, you're certainly right that Carla should have as much say in what we do. We are a team and we shouldn't do anything that we don't all agree on. Now, Carla, what do I have to say to convince you that we should do this?"

Carla was taken back. She hadn't figured on this. She thought she'd be able to continue to protest right up to the time the boys did it anyway. It made her feel good to know that she was truly accepted as an equal, but now she realized it came with a responsibility that she hadn't thought of previously. She couldn't make this decision based solely on her personal feelings. She had to think about what was best for everyone. Tommy did need to find out about his parents; Whitelace was costing them a lot of wasted time; Whitelace was not only being disruptive to the three of them, he was disrupting the entire Queen's Class; and, it was important to know if Whitelace was working for the Black Witch or not.

"I'll tell you what," she said, but she really wasn't sure what she was going to say. "I, ah, well okay. I'll go along with the plan to follow Whitelace, but we only go when we're sure that no one will see us leave the Crow's Next. Abigale is nice and all, but she's a good leader, and if she finds out we left the Crow's Nest after hours, she'd be duty bound to report us."

"That sounds fair to me," Tommy said.

"Me too," Michael added.

They made their plans. Carla and the boys would watch for Whitelace out of their bedroom windows. If he showed, and they could leave their bedrooms without being seen, they would meet in the Community Room. If there was no one in the Community Room, they'd make their exit out the window. They returned to their homework without much else being said about the matter. When they felt they had done enough homework for one evening, they wished one another goodnight, and went to their bedrooms.

They watched for Whitelace until it was quite late, but he never appeared. They attended classes the next day and that evening they watched for Whitelace again. This time Whitelace did show up, but Carla never came to the Community Room. She told the boys the next day that Abigail was sitting up late on her bed doing some of her homework. It wasn't until the fourth evening of the school week before everything worked out. The Professors had worked them pretty hard through the week and, on that evening, everyone went to bed early, everyone except Carla and the boys. When Whitelace appeared in the courtyard, Carla and the boys easily slipped down the stairs to the Community Room. Since no one was in the room, they immediately went to the window and opened it. They almost gave themselves away as Whitelace had not yet left the courtyard. The noise of the window opening caused him to pause and look around. Fortunately, he never thought to look up. After a brief look around the courtyard, he left through the big arch. Michael jumped out onto the window ledge and went down first. Tommy didn't wait until Michael reached the ground. He followed Michael out the window almost as soon as Michael pushed off. Carla followed Tommy the same way. One at a time they slid off the brickwork into the courtyard.

They went as quickly as they could to the edge of the big arch and peered around the corner. They could see the backside of Whitelace. He was doing a soft wave ride down the center walkway of the outer gardens. He was three quarters of the way to the road. Carla and the boys popped up on a wave and slipped off into the gardens. They took a zigzag course using the trees and flowers as cover. They had to move quickly as they couldn't afford to loose sight of Whitelace. This forced them to take a few chances of being spotted, however it was the only way they could stay close enough to see him.

Whitelace reached the road and turned in the direction that led to Cantwell and, ultimately to Old Castle. Carla and the boys turned in the same direction when they reached the roadway, however they didn't get onto the road itself. They kept to the side of the road and tried to stay in the shadows as much as possible. They eventually reached the outer edge of Cantwell where Whitelace turned and went through one of the gaps between the buildings that led into the park. They approached the area cautiously and, when they were sure they wouldn't be seen, Carla and the boys entered the park. The park was empty and dark. The only light came from Damiana's well which glowed continuously.

They couldn't spot Whitelace at first. They dropped down off their waves. Even though they had broken a few rules, they felt there was no sense in breaking them even further by wave riding in the park. With great care, they moved around the park looking for Whitelace. They suspected that he had gone to the well, but since they couldn't immediately see him, they had to move cautiously. They finally got into a position where they could see the well and, as they had expected, they saw Whitelace. He was standing out on the pulpit and had his wand out. Carla and the boys snuck up as close as they thought they could without being caught. They could see most of what he was doing. He had his wand pointed toward Damiana's statue and fired three of the PUH type shots that are used in the Square Table pool game. In the brick wall behind Damiana's statue were the three large marble inserts with their engraved starbursts. There was one on each side of her and the third was above her head. The first shot Whitelace fired struck a brick located below the marble insert on Damiana's right. The second one struck a brick immediately below the marble insert on Damiana's left. When the third shot struck a brick just below the marble insert above Damiana's head, all three inserts dropped from sight and revealed a mirror behind each one.

Whitelace then fired two bright green bolts of magic at the center mirror. He immediately followed that with three at the mirror to his left, two at the mirror to his right and finally one again at the center mirror. The green bolts of magic bounced from mirror to mirror multiplying into an astonishing display of magical light. The bolts began to form a line and spin in a circle around the well opening. The line then dropped into the well and spiraled down along the wall until it was out of sight.

Carla and the boys were amazed. They looked at one another with wide eyes and nodded their heads to show that amazement. Whitelace leaned forward to the low brick wall that defined the outer edges of the pulpit and picked up a small notepad. He made a couple of short notes and set it back down. He stood up and once again fired magical shots at the mirrors, but this time with a different number of shots at each mirror. The result was very similar to the first attempt. It ended with the line of green light pulses spiraling down the well.

Whitelace repeated the process several times. He varied the number of shots he took at each mirror, but he never changed the order of his shots. Each time the results were as dazzling as the first time. However, it was clear they weren't doing what he wanted them to do.

The whole thing seemed strangely familiar to Tommy, but it wasn't until Whitelace made his final attempt for the evening that he realized what it was. He got really excited when it came to him and he suddenly found himself desperately hoping Whitelace would quit for the evening. Tommy was extremely relieved when Whitelace finally turned and stepped out of the pulpit. When Whitelace stepped out of the pulpit area, the marble inserts popped up and once again covered the mirrors. Whitelace closed the pulpit gate and tapped the lock with his wand. He took a brief look around and then headed down one of the paths that would take him out of the park.

Chapter Twenty-One

The Depths of the Well

Carla and Michael stood up to follow Whitelace as he left the park, but Tommy grabbed their arms and pulled them back down. Michael started to object, but Tommy covered his mouth with his hand.

"Let him go," he whispered in Michael's ear.

Tommy waited until he was sure Whitelace had left the park, then he stood up and said, "I know what he's doing and I think I know how to do it. If I'm right, he was close, I mean really close. If he had tried a couple of more combinations, he'd probably have gotten it." Carla and Michael didn't have the slightest idea what Tommy was talking about and their faces were showing it. Recognizing this, Tommy grabbed Carla and Michael by the arm and helped them to their feet. "Come on," he said. "I'll show you."

Tommy led the way and they went to the edge of the well. "What was he trying to do?" Carla asked.

"He was trying to get into the well," Tommy answered.

"Why the heck would he do that?" Michael inquired.

"I think he's looking for the Drop of Truth," Tommy replied.

"Oh come on," Michael grumbled. "Professor Pastorie says that's hidden in a cave or something up in the mountains."

"I don't think so," Tommy said with some conviction. "I think the Old King hid it right here, right below his beloved Damiana."

"What makes you think Whitelace is looking for the Drop of Truth," Carla asked.

"Because," Tommy answered, "he got the Drop of Truth scrolls from that Skeezicks guy. You know, the one who stole the scrolls from the Ministry of All Things Magic. It's like I said, I think he's working for the Black Witch and he's trying to get the Drop of Truth for her."

"I don't know about that," Carla responded, "but maybe."

"Come on," Tommy said, "follow me." He jumped over the wrought iron fence and followed the edge of the well to the wall behind Damiana's statue. "We have to find which bricks Whitelace hit to open the mirrors." Tommy squinted his eyes and examined the embossed coat of arms on the bricks below the nearest marble insert. He reached through the collar of his robes and pulled out his medallion. After looking at it very closely, he reexamined the bricks. "Just as I thought," he said. "Let's go and look on the other side." Before Carla or Michael could question him, he was off to the other side of the well. By the time Michael and Carla caught up with him, he was already examining the bricks below the marble insert on that side. "Yep," he said. "It's the same and, if I could see the bricks below the one above Damiana head well enough, I'll bet I would find another one."

"What are you talking about?" Michael asked a bit impatiently.

"Look at my medallion," Tommy said flashing his medallion in front of Michael's face. "See that coat of arms? If you look close enough you'll see a brick that's embossed with exactly the same one and there's one just like it on the other side of the well."

"Hey," Carla said. "I thought each one of the bricks was embossed with a different coat of arms."

"Apparently not every brick," Tommy replied. "Let's go around and get out on the pulpit and see if we can open the mirrors."

They went around the well to the pulpit area. Carla touched the lock with the tip of her wand and unlocked the gate. The three of them stepped out onto the pulpit. It gave them an eerie feeling. It was as if they were floating out above the mouth of the well with its great black depths below them. Directly across from them hung Damiana's statue, also suspended over the open mouth of the well. Tommy took out his wand and fired three PUH shots at the bricks below each of the marble inserts. Nothing happened. Since he couldn't see which of the top bricks was the right one, he had to try several times before he hit the right one and the marble inserts slid out of sight.

"Carla," Tommy said once the mirrors were exposed, "if this works you can go back to the castle if you want. You don't have to be party to this."

"What!" she cried out. "Why would I want to do that?"

"Because," Tommy answered, "if this does lead to the Drop of Truth, I plan on using it. If I get my hands on the Drop of Truth, I going to drop it on my tongue and ask that the fate of my parents be revealed to me. I know it's a Treasure of the Realm and maybe it would be best if you weren't part of it being destroyed."

"You got to be kidding," Carla said. "I wouldn't miss this for anything. I want to help you find out about your parents. And besides, if you use the Drop of Truth than neither the Black Witch nor the Queen gets it, and that's probably best for everyone."

"I was hoping you'd feel that way," Tommy said. "I just wanted you to know that you could back out without any hard feelings."

Carla tilted her head slightly to one side and looked at Tommy and Michael. "Friends for life, right?" she asked."

"Right," both Tommy and Michael replied.

"Friends for life," Tommy added with conviction.

"But," Carla asked Tommy, "what makes you think you can make this work when obviously Whitelace hasn't been able to?"

"I think I know the code," Tommy answered. "It's maybe the oldest code of all. I think King Oleander used the ancient code that was used to transport people from our world to the Home Plane. It's the same one we used to get here. It's three, two, three and then one. Whitelace was getting really close."

The pulpit area was a little crowded with all three of them standing out on it. As a result, none of them noticed Whitelace's notebook lying on the ground next to the low brick wall that bordered the pulpit. Whitelace was almost a quarter of the way back to the castle when he noticed it was missing. He was angry with himself for having lost it, but he knew he had no choice; he had to go back and find it. He turned around and slowly headed back to Cantwell and the park. He searched the road as he went.

"What kind of magic do you think Whitelace was using," Tommy asked Carla.

"From the green light," Carla began, "I'd say it was some type of Emeralda light charm, maybe a Go Getter or a Serpent's Back. But, no, I don't think so. Those two aren't often used in short bursts, their more like streams of magic. Say," she said with a sudden burst of inspiration, "I'll bet he was using a Tap Setter. It's an Emeralda light charm and it's always used in short bursts. It's the kind of magic you'd use to empower something else. I'll bet that's what it was, it was a Tap Setter."

"Super," Tommy exclaimed. "Can you teach it to me?"

"Sorry," Carla replied with a sad expression on her face. "That's pretty advanced magic. It takes a lot of control, and you haven't yet learned that kind of control."

"Can you do it?" Tommy inquired.

"I don't think I know the right recipe. I'm sure I read it in one of my mom or dad's books, but I've read a lot of magical recipes and I can't remember them all, and even if I could, I'm not sure I'm good enough to perform it."

"Is there any other magic that you do know that might do the same thing?" Tommy asked.

"I know the Flash Blast. It's not an Emeralda charm so the light isn't green. It's actually an icy blue white. But, it is a light charm that energizes, and it can be used in short bursts. I used to use it to animate my dolls and other toys. You want me to give it a try?"

"You bet," Tommy answered firmly. "The code is three blasts at the center mirror followed by two blasts at the left mirror, then three more at the mirror on the right before one final blast at the center mirror. Have you got that?"

"Not a problem," Carla responded, "three, two, three and one."

"Whenever you're ready, go for it girl," Tommy encouraged.

Carla moved up between the two boys, pointed her wand at the center mirror and began firing icy blue white pulses of magic. Whitelace slid into the park and continued his wave ride up the pathway. He was watching the ground in search of his notebook and hadn't paid any attention to the well. When he finally looked up, it was just in time to see Carla fire her last shot at the mirrors. He stopped immediately. He was well within the sight of them, but being the good Military student that he was, he instantly cast a camouflage spell on himself. As long as he didn't move, he would appear to be invisible. He would continue to appear invisible even if he moved, but watery lines would show around his silhouette. If someone was to be looking directly at him when he moved, his outline could be spotted.

Carla's pulses of blue, white light reflected from mirror to mirror and multiplied as they went. The light pluses began to line up and swirl around the well opening just as Whitelace's green ones had. Suddenly, the line of them headed right toward Carla and the boys. They ducked and the line of magical pulses struck the low brick wall just to their right. A section of the wall disappeared and the line of magical light slithered along side of the well's wall. It spiraled downward counterclockwise, touching bricks as it went. As the pulses touched each brick, the brick moved out slightly from the wall. By the time the line of light pulses had spiraled all the way to the bottom, a line of smoothly connecting bricks had moved out from the wall slightly wider than a foot width. It spiraled downward similar to the brickwork that went down and around the Crow's Nest tower, except this was on an inner, rather than an outer, wall. The walls of the well also began to glow as the line of magical pulses descended.

The interior of the well was now lit it all the way to the bottom. The three of them peered over and looked. The well was very deep, but they could see the glittering surface of the water at the bottom.

"I'll go first," Carla suddenly said to Tommy and Michael's surprise. "We can't expect the well to protect us the way the Castle did back at the tower. If I go first, I can test it. If I run into any problems, I'm pretty sure I could turn around and come back up."

"I don't think this will be quite as difficult as the tower," Tommy said. "The forces as we spiral down will help us stay against the wall."

"That might be true," Carla agreed. "But, we'll have to be careful not to bump the wall too hard. That could knock you off balance and it's a long way down." She moved to the opening created by the now missing section of the low brick wall and popped up on a single foot wave. "Wish me luck," she said as she started a very slow wave ride to the first protruding brick.

"Just be careful," Tommy replied. "We know you can do it.

Carla pointed her wand out in front of her and started her descent. She controlled her speed well and glided around and down slowly. On her way, she tested to see if the well would catch her if she began to fall and it would not. When she reached the bottom of the well, she slid off the line of bricks onto a raised ledge that circled the well about three feet wide. It was also made of bricks and its surface was about a half of a foot about the surface of the water that filled the bottom of the well. There were two arched openings about three feet wide and three feet high. They were on opposite sides of the well. A stream of water a few inches deep flowed silently out of one of the openings. It ran through a trench in the ledge into the large pool of water that filled the bottom of the well. Similarly, water flowed out from the large pool through the other arched opening. The water was crystal clear. What appeared from the pulpit to be the glittering of the water's surface turned out to be the glittering of the numerous pieces of precious metals that covered the bottom of the well about a foot below the water's surface.

Carla looked up. She could just barely see the two shadowy figures of Michael and Tommy. "The well won't protect you," she called out. "But, it's not as steep as the tower so you can control your speed better. I think you can make it okay."

That's all Michael was waiting for. He immediately popped up on a single foot wave, glided over to the protruding bricks and, in a moment, he was spiraling down the well. Tommy watched Michael until he saw him land safely at the bottom, then he followed. Tommy had a couple of narrow escapes, but he too landed safely at the bottom.

Whitelace made a dash for the well as soon as Tommy dropped out of sight. He glided right out onto the pulpit. Maintaining his camouflage, he cautiously peered over the edge just in time to see Tommy make his last few spiraling loops. He wanted to see and hear as much as possible, so he gradually leaned as far forward as he could. Although it was a long ways to the bottom, he could see and hear well enough to get the general idea of what was going on.

Tommy took a few moments once he arrived at the bottom to take it all in as Michael and Carla had before him.

"Now what?" Michael asked. "Do ya think we're supposed to go down one of those waterways?" He pointed to one of the arched openings.

"Your guess is as good as mine," Tommy replied. "Let's take a look."

The three of them walked around the ledge to the nearest opening. It was the one that was bringing the water into the well. Carla knelt down and lit the end of her wand with bright directional light.

"Eugh," she said as she looked down the opening. "I don't think we're supposed to go down there. It doesn't look very inviting. In fact, oh, oh, I think I see some eyes looking back at us. I think we better move back."

"Let me have a look," Michael said as he bent down and looked over Carla's shoulder. "Uh oh, I think you're right." He grabbed Carla by the shoulder and gently pulled Carla and himself away from the opening. He had to push Tommy back as he went. "We definitely aren't going down there," he said emphatically.

"Maybe we should check the other opening," Tommy suggested.

"Be my guest," Michael replied. "But if it's anything like this one, you better be careful because it looks like something's living in this one."

Tommy went around the well until he got to the other opening. He lit the end of his wand and carefully looked into the opening. After a few moments, he slowly backed away and stood up. He looked over to Michael and Carla and shook his head. "I don't think we want to go in this one either," he said as he started back towards them. As he passed by one of the protruding bricks, he paused and examined the coat of arms embossed in it. His medallion was still hanging loosely outside of his robes. He grasped it with one hand and examined it, then looked back at the brick. He looked at the next protruding brick and once again looked back at his medallion. He then quickly scanned all the nearby protruding bricks. "Just as I suspected," he commented, "They all match my medallion." He completed his walk back to Michael and Carla.

"I have an idea," he said as he reached the pair. "We have to examine the walls and see if there are any more bricks that match my medallion. Here, study this and we'll have a look." He held out his medallion towards Michael and Carla as far as his necklace would allow.

"This will take forever," Michael complained. "The differences in the coats of arms are so minuscule that we'd be here a week examining bricks."

"I have an idea," Carla spoke up. "We can do the Duplicato charm, but when you conjure up my Mother's recipe add a thimble of the Tinkleberry wine and a chip of crystal. It'll make the image in your mind translucent and, when you scan the bricks, a match will cause the brick to light up in your mind's eye."

They all did as Carla suggested and began scanning the walls. They spread out and each covered a different section of the wall. In a couple of minutes, Carla found the first one. Tommy told her to mark the spot and continue scanning.

"I found another one," Michael called out.

"Me too," Tommy added. "Mark the spot."

They scanned the wall from where the bricks met the ledge to just above their heads. Anything above that was too high for them to make out the details of the embossing. When they finished, they had found four in all.

"Okay, now what do we do?" Michael inquired.

"I think we have to hit them with PUHs," Tommy explained. "You know, like I did up at the top to reveal the mirrors. But they're so far apart that I don't think I can spot them all from one place."

"I can circle them with magic light," Carla informed them. "It won't last real long, but probably long enough to hit them all."

"Do it," Tommy directed.

They moved as a group. As they identified the correct bricks, Carla placed a lighted circle around them with her wand. Once all four bricks were highlighted, Tommy took his wand and hit the one nearest him with a PUH. The brick slipped back and recessed itself about three inches, but immediately it began slowly moving back out. By the time he aimed and fired at the second brick, the first brick had fully returned to its original position. He proceeded and fired shots at the third and fourth bricks. They all receded upon impact, but they all had also returned to their original positions. And, nothing happened.

"I think you might have to hit them all simultaneously," Carla guessed.

"How can I do that?" Tommy asked with some confusion.

"We could each take a brick," Michael suggested.

"Yeah, but we'd still be one short," Tommy replied. "You'd think that this would be designed to be accomplished by a single person."

"A skilled wizard could do it," Carla answered. "First, he'd probably have two wands and secondly, he'd do a Double Double charm."

"Can you do a Double Double?" Tommy asked Carla.

"Yes," she answered, "but there are a couple of problems. First, you need two wands to do a Double Double."

"Here take mine'" Michael interrupted as he extended his wand in Carla's direction.

"No," she said to Michael. "Since the bricks are not directly across from one another and they're not even at the same height, it would require extreme accuracy. I'm afraid I'm not that good with my right hand."

Tommy suddenly realized, now that she had mentioned it, that Carla almost always used her left hand to control her wand, and now that he thought about it, she also wrote with her left hand. She was a lefty. Tommy thought it was strange that he had never noticed it before.

Whitelace stepped on his notebook and, as a reflex, he rose up and leaned back to see what he had stepped on. Spotting his notebook, he bent down, picked it up and put it in his pocket. Tommy had been looking up at the spiraling brickwork at the time Whitelace moved. "Hey," he said softly. "I thought I saw something move at the top of the well." Everyone looked up and carefully watched the opening at the top of the well. Whitelace, realizing his mistake, didn't immediately look back over the edge of the pulpit. After watching the top of the well for a couple of minutes and not seeing anything, they returned to their task.

The light circles around the correct bricks started to fade. Carla walked around the ledge and re-circled them before they went out. She talked as she walked. "I can do a single Double," she said, "if you two can hit the other two bricks at the same time…"

"I think we can do that," Michael said confidently.

"Yeah, I think so," Tommy agreed. "You'll just have to do a countdown so we can time our shots with yours."

"Okay," Carla said, "let's get into position. I'll try to hit those two bricks." She pointed at the two she had selected. "Tommy you go for that one," she continued as she pointed at another brick, "and

Michael you go for that one." She pointed at the remaining brick. "I'll countdown from three and, when I say 'Now', fire at your brick." Once they were in position, Carla began her countdown. She began to twirl her wand in her fingers. She looked back and forth between the two bricks she had to hit. "Three," she began, "two, one,... Now!"

The three of them fired simultaneously. Two light flashes came out of Carla's wand and went in opposite directions. They struck Carla's targets just as Michael and Tommy's shots hit their targets. All four bricks slid back and stayed back. There was a loud rumbling and the bottom six feet of the well's walls began to rotate. The walls rotated, but the ledge they stood on did not. The arched opening rotated with the walls. As they moved, they exposed yet another layer of bricks and closed off the water flow. The walls continued to rotate until they had rotated ninety degrees and then they stopped. One opening now just showed a face of bricks, but the other opening opened to a very short hallway. At the far end of the hallway, the kids could see the top of a curving staircase going downward.

They ducked down and stepped through the small arched opening into the short hallway. They could faintly hear the rushing of water. They approached the top of the staircase and the rushing noise got a little louder.

"I guess we go down," Tommy said, and he led the way down the staircase. The further they went down the staircase, the louder the rushing noise became.

Whitelace had carefully peered back over the edge of the pulpit when he heard Carla begin her countdown. He saw the bottom walls rotate and he watched as the kids exited the well through the small opening. However, he also saw something that made him panic. When the bottom of the well wall had rotated, the spiraling line of protruding bricks separated at the point where the moving bricks met the stationary ones. It created a gap. Almost instantly, the protruding bricks began to recede and the light in the well began to dim. He didn't have time to consider his options. If he was going to follow the kids, he had to act fast. So he popped up on a single foot wave, slid out onto the ever narrowing line of bricks and began his descent.

Whitelace got about two-thirds of the way down before the bricks would no longer support him. He lost his balance and fell. It was almost totally dark by then. There was only a tiny bit of light that crept in through the small arched opening at the bottom. He jerked his wand around to try to cushion his fall with a spell, but it slipped out of his hand. He fell spread eagle and hit the surface of the shallow water. The blow almost knocked him out. He was stunned and wasn't sure how severely he was injured, but he was in a lot of pain. He rolled over in the shallow water and laid there with just his face sticking out above the surface. His left cheek began to swell and his left eye began to blacken. A small amount of blood trickled from his nose. The cool water seemed to soothe his pain. Although he was hurt, he was lucky. If he had landed feet or head first, he would have sustained significantly more injuries. It may have even killed him.

Tommy, Carla and Michael were almost at the bottom of the stairway when Whitelace hit the water. The sound of rushing water near the bottom of the stairs was loud enough to cover up the sound of Whitelace's impact. When they reached the bottom of the stairs, they exited the stairway though a regular sized doorway. The sight in front of them was a bit overwhelming at first. They were standing in a large room that was longer than it was wide. At the far end of the room, there was a waterfall coming out of a large wide opening near the ceiling. The water fell into a wide trench at their level that ran the full length of the room. The water flowed down the trench and exited the room at the opposite end through an opening at floor level. Just above this opening was another opening. A line of large wire mesh trays came out of the opening and floated above the trench. They were tightly connected and extended the length of the trench. They exited the room by going through the water as it fell from the upper opening at the far end. The trays weren't moving, but it was clear that they were designed to move. A very large round funnel shape extended down from the ceiling. The bottom of the funnel was capped and it ended several feet above one of the trays.

Carla and the boys were standing on a walkway that ran along side of the trench. The walkway continued past the side of the waterfall into a hallway at the far end. There were three levers on the wall along the walkway. The kids took the time to examine them. They were labeled. One said, "Open Door and Cut-off Water Flow." It was in the up position. The second lever said, "Start Conveyor." It was in the down position. The third lever said, "Open and Close Shoot." It was also in the down position.

"I think I know what this does," Michael said. "We're below the bottom of the well and if I flip this second and third lever, I think we can turn it on." Before Carla or Tommy could stop him, he reached out and flipped the second and third levers into the up position.

The trays began moving, clinking and clanging as they went. They traveled from the near end and went through the waterfall at the far end. The cap on the bottom of the funnel shape began to open. Water and precious metals began to fall out. The metals were collected in the trays as they passed under the funnel and the water passed through the trays into the trench. This added to the noise already filling the room. Carla and the boys followed the first loaded tray as it moved along the length of the room until it went under the waterfall. They paused and watched several trays pass under the waterfall.

Up above, in the well, Whitelace was still laying in the water when he felt the precious metals begin to move underneath him. He fought through his pain and stood up. He began frantically looking for his wand. He knew he would be at a distinct disadvantage without his wand. Plus, his camouflage spell had been broken when he had dropped his wand. The pieces of precious metals were moving below his feet and he was sinking. By the time he found the wand, the ledge was out of reach and he was being sucked down. It was as if he was being flushed down a giant toilet; and he couldn't stop it. He used his wand to restore his camouflage spell.

Down below the well, the trays continued to move along as they were filled with precious metals. Finally, the last thing to come out of the funnel was Whitelace. He came out with a final gush of water. He fell to the tray below and landed with a smash and a groan. There was too much noise for the kids to hear him. He realized that it might not be a very good thing to remain on the tray, so, despite his pain, he forced himself off the tray and onto the walkway. The kids were just the length of the room away from him. Although he was wet, cold and full of pain, he stood perfectly still so that he wouldn't give himself away.

Michael looked back at the funnel and when he saw that nothing more was coming out of the funnel, he looked at the levers. It was just in time to see the third lever return itself to the down position. Michael looked back at the funnel and saw the cap at its bottom begin to close. "Hey," he said, "look at this. It's automatic." Carla and Tommy turned and looked in the direction Michael was facing. They had no idea they were looking right at Whitelace. "Look," Michael continued. "When the metals stopped coming, the lever flipped itself down and the cap closed on the funnel. Just then, the first lever flipped into the down position. There was a large rumble as the bottom part of the well began to rotate. It closed the little upper arched opening and restored the water flow into the well. Although they could barely hear it above the noise in the room, they could feel it. "If we're going to follow this," Michael continued, "we better get a move on before the last tray passes and the whole thing shuts down."

Carla and Tommy agreed. They followed the walkway past the waterfall and into the hallway. Although they were in a hallway, there were large openings in the wall on one side that allowed them to view the trays as they came out from the waterfall. As the trays emerged from the waterfall, they were shocked to see that the precious metals had been cleaned and separated by type. Where a pile of mixed metals and debris had once been, there were now several long piles. Each pile contained only one kind of metal. There was more gold than any other metal. But, there was also a lot of silver along with many other types of metals, including copper, tin and some the kids didn't recognize.

They continued to follow the trays as they moved along. The trays next went through a translucent barrier. "That's magic," Carla said, "and it's really powerful magic." They moved along so they could see the trays emerge from the other side of the barrier. As the trays came out of the magic, the metals were no longer in piles. The metals were now formed into small bricks. They were all the same size and shape regardless of what type of metal they were and they were all embossed with the same coat of arms that was on Tommy's medallion. The trays moved along to the end wall where they passed through a narrow horizontal slot just wide and tall enough to allow the trays with their bricks of metals to pass through.

Chapter Twenty-Two

The Room of Destiny

Carla and the boys couldn't go any further. The hallway ended at that point with a large iron reinforced wooden door. The door was closed and it had no door knob or key hole. Michael started to move towards the door like he was going to try to push it open, but Carla grabbed his arm and pulled him back. "Always beware of a door that has no door knob or key hole," Carla said firmly. "Generally speaking, they can only be opened by a charm, and if you try the wrong thing, they can be very dangerous. Let's think about this first."

The kids were now as far away from Whitelace as they could get. It was a lot cooler down there than it had been in the well. Whitelace was still soaking wet and the coolness made him begin to shiver. He knew that his involuntary movements could cause his silhouette to appear around his camouflaged body. He had to use his wand to dry himself off magically. He knew that this might increase his chances of being discovered, but this looked like the best opportunity to dry himself. As the kids studied the door, Whitelace turned his wand sideways and passed it from his head to his toes. He did it a second time. The first time he dried himself and the second time he warmed himself. Still hurting quite a bit, but feeling better now that he was warm and dry, he stood still once again and watched as Carla and the boys tried to deal with the door.

"Where do you think that door leads to?" Michael asked as they moved back a little.

"I'll bet it leads all the way back to the Castle," Tommy answered, "probably right to the Treasury Room."

"That'd be a good place to keep the Drop of Truth." Michael stated. "That old King Oleander was a pretty cleaver guy," Michael went on. "He found a way to tax some people without them even knowing they were being taxed."

"Maybe too cleaver," Carla said with a scowl on her face. "I have always been proud of the 'well' suffix that was added to our family name, but now… I mean, it seems that maybe the King had everybody that worked on the well add that suffix to their name just so he could keep track of everyone who knew what was really going on down here. I'll bet he made them swear an oath of secrecy. I wonder how many of them wound up in his dungeon because they said a little too much."

Carla was getting a bit distracted and Tommy recognized it. "So you think that this door can only be opened with a charm?" he asked her.

"That'd be my guess," she answered flatly. Her mind was still somewhere else.

"Come on, Carla, get with it," Tommy said sharply. "We can think about the meaning of all this later, but for now, we need to keep moving."

Carla shook her head as if to clear her mind. "Okay, okay," she said. "The door needs a charm. Nope, don't think we can do it."

"Don't you know any charms that'll open a door?" Tommy asked.

"Sure," Carla replied, "but it's a general kind of charm. You know, the kind of thing that you'd use if a door was stuck or its latch was broken.

"Try it anyway," Michael ordered.

Carla didn't like the way Michael ordered her. She gave him a dirty look and Michael got the message.

"Sorry," he said. "I think this thing's getting to us all a little bit. What I should have done is ask if you thought it was worth a try."

"Yeah, it has been a bit tense," Carla agreed. "I think I know what will help a little." She reached under her robes and pulled out a medium sized white paper bag. She opened the top of the bag and offered it to Tommy and Michael. The boys knew immediately it was

The Life and Times of Tommy Travail

Chewy Chew Chews. The bag was full to the brim with them. The boys took several of them and popped them into their mouths. Carla did the same and put the bag away.

Tommy started to say something, but with a mouthful of Chewy Chew Chews, all he could do was mumble. Michael tried to make a comment about Tommy's inability to talk, but all he could do was mumble. Carla snickered and tried to make fun of the boys, but she couldn't talk either. Big smiles spread across their faces and they all started to laugh. They each put a hand over their mouth to prevent themselves from spitting out their Chewy Chew Chews. They laughed anyway. Drool, spit and the Chewy Chew Chews juice dribbled from they hands, but they continued to laugh. It took a few minutes and several attempts for them to regain their composure, but they certainly felt better.

Whitelace watched enviously. His whole body ached, and at that given moment, he would have traded his prized pocket watch for just a couple of those Chewy Chew Chews. "Clever girl," he thought.

Carla took out her wand and cleaned the boys off once they settled down and Tommy did the same for her. "Okay," she said, "back to the door. I can try my charm on it, but like I said, it's a general charm and I'm sure this door is going to require a specific charm, a very specific charm. So to be on the safe side, let's back up a little more. You never know how these things will react."

They backed up a little. The boys stood on each side of Carla, but slightly behind her. Carla took out her wand and pointed it at the door. She began moving the tip of her wand in circles and then she said, "Open door, open wide; I desire the other side; whether fast or slow; the other side you must show." She had drawn her wand into tighter and tighter circles as she spoke and, as she finished her charm, she thrust her wand slightly towards the door.

The door reacted immediately, but not in the way they had hoped. The door folded itself, bringing its top and bottom together to form a giant mouth. It sprouted huge sharply pointed teeth and began wildly snapping at them. Carla and the boys jumped back. The door continued its snapping so they continued to back up. They eventually moved back far enough to satisfy the door. The door stopped its snapping, its teeth disappeared and it unfolded itself.

"Told ya," Carla said.

"Maybe we could try blasting it," Michael suggested. "Between the three of us maybe we could hit it hard enough to knock it open."

"I don't think so," Carla replied. "It'd probably just absorb our magic and get stronger."

Tommy leaned against the wall and dropped his head slightly in deep thought. He reached up with his hand and rubbed his mouth and chin to help with his concentration. As he rubbed the corner of his mouth, he tasted a little of the sticky Chewy Chew Chews juice. He licked his lips and an idea began to form. "I think I got it," he said. "But, it'll be risky."

"So what else is new," Michael quipped. "Everything we've done so far has been risky. What's the plan?"

"Carla needs to hit the door again with her charm. When the door goes berserk, I'll get as close as I can and then I'll throw Carla's bag of Chewy Chew Chews into its mouth. If we're lucky, it'll get all gummed up just like we did. When its teeth are stuck together, we can try to slip under the bottom half of the door."

"That just might work," Michael said in agreement. "The door's wide enough that Carla could go first and then you and I can go side by side right after her."

"Yes, it just might work," Carla added. "We could do a tumble and roll or a belly slide. I think I might be able to do a belly sliding wave ride."

Whitelace realized that their plan might work. If he was going to follow them, he knew he had to get real close to them. It was the only way that he might have enough time to also slip under the door before it freed its teeth. He was still in a lot of pain, but while their attention was once again focused on the door, he began to move slowly towards them. Tommy turned around at one point and looked over his shoulder. Whitelace froze. After a moment, Tommy turned back around. Whitelace began moving again. He continued until he was right behind them. He got so near them that he had to soften his breathing.

"I think you and I should try to tumble and roll," Tommy said to Michael. We know we can do that."

"I agree," Michael affirmed. "But maybe we should keep a couple of the Chewy Chew Chews for ourselves, in case we need them later. This might get really exhausting before we're finished."

"Not a problem," Carla cut in. "I also brought the bag of chocolates."

"That'll work," Tommy declared.

The thought of a bag of all healing, energy restoring, melt in your mouth chocolates was more than Whitelace could handle and he began to drool. Unfortunately, he was to0 close to them to move, so he had to let the drool run down his chin.

"There's just one more thing," Tommy added, turning his attention to Michael. "What does your watch say?"

"You wanna know what time it is?" Michael asked with a goofy look on his face.

"No," Tommy answered. "Where does it say you are at the present time?"

"Oh, oh yeah," Michael said looking at his watch. "It says we're in the Precious Metals Inspection Hall."

"And what does it say about the past and future," Tommy asked.

"It says that we were in the Precious Metals Collection Room and that we'll next be in the Room of Destiny."

"The Room of Destiny," Tommy pondered aloud. "Well that's a good sign," he said encouragingly. "It sounds like we make it."

A broad smile spread across Michael's face. "This is going to be a snap," he said with some certainty.

"Maybe, but maybe not," Carla said seriously, "we still have to be careful and do this right. It wouldn't be too cool if that thing bit you in half and only half of you made it into the room."

The smile disappeared from Michael's face.

Carla and the boys decided how close they could get and still be out of the range of the snapping door. Carla took out the bag of Chewy Chew Chews and gave it to Tommy. Carla got between and slightly ahead of the two boys. Carla pointed her wand at the door and said her charm. Just as before, the door folded itself, grew teeth and began viciously snapping at them. Even though they were out of the range of the door, they still leaned way back as it began snapping. Tommy waited until its massive mouth was wide open and then he tossed the bag of Chewy Chew Chews into it. He hung onto the bottom of the bag just slightly, allowing the contents of the bag to spread out across much of the now closing mouth. The snapping of the door began to slow. Each succeeding bite became smaller until after a final bite, its teeth became locked together in a mass of gooey sticky Chewy Chew Chews. It shook violently as it tried in vain to open it jaws.

Tommy tucked his medallion back under his robes and gave Carla a little push in the small of her back. She took one step and jumped head first into a sliding belly wave ride. She slipped under the open bottom of the doorway without any problem. Tommy and Michael looked a one another, touched hands and then, in unison, did a tumble and roll under the struggling jaws of the door. Whitelace waited for a brief moment for Tommy and Michael to clear the doorway, then, through his pain, he leaped forward head first and did a belly ride just as Carla had done.

Whitelace came to a stop right at the heels of the now standing Tommy and Michael. Unfortunately, he came to a stop just about an inch too short of completely clearing the doorway. Just as he came to a stop, the door freed it jaws and with a loud bang, its top and bottom halves slammed back into their normal positions. The toe of Whitelace's right boot had not cleared the doorframe. When the bottom half of the door slammed closed, it came down on the tip of his boot and smashed his toes. Lighting bolts of pain shot up his leg. He held his breath and gritted his teeth. He fought with everything he had to prevent himself from screaming in pain. Although his toes were going to be extremely bruised, he was fortunate. The door had a slight gap between its bottom edge and the floor. If the door had come all the way down to the ground, it may have severed his toes all together.

They were in a large circular room. Through two narrow slots in the curving wall to their left, they could see the still moving trays. These trays were empty, as the ones loaded with the precious metals had long since gone ahead. Across the room and slightly to their right, were three doors. In the center of the room, a round flat disk, about three feet in diameter, was set into the floor and its surface was about six inches above the floor.

Carla and the boys looked at one another with wry smiles. They had made it. Their exhilaration, though, quickly turned to curiosity and consternation. After all they had just done, they were now facing three doors. They were all wondering the same thing and together they took a step towards the doors to see if they had doorknobs or keyholes.

"I think I'll change my surname back to Cross and drop the well altogether," Carla suddenly said to Tommy and Michael's surprise. "I used to be so proud of that part of my name, now it offends me."

"I think your wrong Carla," Tommy advised. "The fact that your ancestor was part of building the well, as everyone else knows it, is indeed something to be proud of. But, the fact that your ancestor was part of building all this," Tommy spread his arms showing that he meant everything they had seen so far. "Well, it's really something special, something to be really proud of. And, who cares what that old King was doing anyway. Cross*well* is a fine family name that says your family goes back to the earliest times of the Realm. Your family name is also well known for the other fine accomplishments that your family has made. Look how well respected your parents are. Nope, I'd be proud if I were you, not offended."

Whitelace slowly stood up as they talked. He took a step back being careful not to put any weight on his smashed toes.

Carla smiled broadly. Tommy's pep talk was just what she needed. "You know," she said, "you're right. Thanks."

They took another step, and as soon as they did, a plume of purple smoke started to come out of the center of the round disk. It grew larger and larger. It began to swirl. Around and about it went as it grew. Gradually, it began to take form. It started as the outline of a large overweight man.

"It's a Whisper," Carla said.

"What's a Whisper," Michael whispered, not being sure what she meant.

"The aberration in front of us," Carla answered. "It's called a Whisper; it's a likeness of the witch or wizard that created it. It contains images and sometimes, the memories of its creator. Whispers can be very interactive if they are created by a first rate witch or wizard."

The purple smoke continued to add greater and greater definition to the large man it was creating. The purple smoke was consumed by the figure it was creating until all the smoke was gone. In its place stood a slightly larger than real life elderly man in purple robes and a pointed purple hat with a white fuzzy ball at the end. The top half of the hat flopped to one side. Long white hair stuck out around all sides of the hat. The figure was standing with his back to Carla and the boys.

"Greetings adventurer," the figure started, but then stopped, looked back and forth, and then turned around. Now that they could see his face, they knew immediately he was King Oleander. They recognized him from his many portraits around the Castle. However, this King Oleander looked different. He didn't have the stern fearsome look that the King in the portraits had. He looked older and friendlier. He had a full white beard, slightly red cheeks and a pair of narrow rectangular glasses sitting on the end of his prominent nose.

A smile lightened his face and a twinkle came to his eyes as he saw Carla and the boys. "Oh, oh my," he said upon seeing them. "We have more than one adventurer and young ones at that. Well, greetings young adventurers you have found your way to the Room of Destiny. Shortly you will make a decision that will forever shape the rest of your lives. Before you, there are three doors. You must choose one and only one. Once you have chosen and gone through a door, you can not turn back and return to this room."

"Now," the Whisper image of King Oleander continued. "The door on the left is the Door of Wealth. If you go through this door and survive, you'll be wealthier than you can imagine, but you'll never be able to return to this place, nor will you have any memory of it. For you, it will no longer exist and the well will no longer open for you. The center door is the Door of Life. This door leads directly to the surface, where you can live out the rest of your lives as you see fit. However, like the other doors, the path carries a Forget Forever charm. Once you reach the surface, you will not remember anything about this place. But, if life should lead you back to this place, you will once again be able to choose a door. The final door, the door on the right, is the Door of Knowledge. If you go through this door and survive, you will gain the truth you seek, but like the Door of Wealth, you will not remember this place and you will never be able to return here. It will no longer exist for you."

"Your Majesty, ah, Mister King, sir," Michael stuttered. "May I ask a question?"

"Certainly," the King answered with a smile.

"What do you mean, if we go through a door and *survive*," Michael asked.

"The reward you seek is not easily obtained," the King replied with a much more serious look on his face. "Beyond the Doors of Wealth and Knowledge lay journeys that will test your skills, cunning and worthiness, make a mistake and you'll likely die. For adventurers as young as you, I think the choice is clear. You should choose the center door, the Door of Life. If life does bring you back when you are older, you will stand a much better chance of being successful with either of the other two doors. Yes, I think your choice is clear," the King added in a very fatherly way. "You are much too young."

"But, Your Majesty," Carla cautiously disagreed. "I'll bet you were no older than us when you began your adventures around the Realm and Home Plane."

"Ah, this is true," the King answered honesty, "but times were different back then. Things have changed."

"Things may not have changed as much as you think," Carla continued to disagree with great care. "But, for the sake of this boy, we must choose the Door of Knowledge. He seeks to know the fate of his missing parents. He can not begin his life until he knows the answer to this question."

"That is a noble quest," the King responded, "and you have just passed your first worthiness test. However, I still believe the center door is the correct choice for you. Are you sure you're all well enough to continue your quest?"

"Yes, sir, Your Majesty," Tommy answered for Carla, Michael and himself. "We might be a bit messed up from our journey so far, but we're all okay."

"Are you sure," the King persisted.

Whitelace realized that the King's Whisper was looking past Carla and the boys and looking directly at him and he was quite a sight. His cheek was swollen, he had a black eye, there was a smudge of dried blood under his nose, a patch of dried drool stuck to his chin and he was standing on one foot to keep the weight off his smashed toes. It was clear that the King could see past his camouflage and was waiting for his reply. Whitelace nodded his head to affirm that he was all right.

Just as Whitelace nodded, Carla said, "I'm sure we're all fit enough to continue our journey."

The King seeing Whitelace's nod and hearing Carla answer squinted his eyes and frowned slightly. "Well, if you're sure," the King said acceptingly and Whitelace nodded again. "Very well then, you make your selection by going through the door of your choice."

Carla and the boys started to walk towards the Door of Knowledge. It took them closer to the King. Once they were along side the King's Whisper, Tommy stopped and turned towards him. "I have one final question," he said. "Why did you have everyone who worked on the well add the suffix of 'well' to their surnames?" Tommy's medallion began to feel warm against his chest.

The King was taken back for a moment. The question surprised him and he felt something unexpected. "I feel the Purple about you," the King said with a somber look on his face. "Are you a young Prince?"

"No," Tommy answered immediately. "I'm just an ordinary guy, about as ordinary as they come."

"I see," remarked the King, "and what is your name?"

"Tommy Travail," Tommy answered.

"So you're of the Tra and of the Vail. That is most interesting. As interesting as the question you ask, it led me to believe that you had a 'well' suffix on *your* name."

"I ask for a friend," Tommy clarified.

"Uhm," the King began. "Well, I did it as a reward for those who worked so hard to construct this place. I did it so all would know and acknowledge those who were here."

"So you didn't do it to keep track of those who knew what was down here?" Tommy asked.

"Oh, goodness, no," the King replied with a surprised look on his face. "There was no need for anything like that. Everyone who worked down here agreed that their lives would be better and safer if they didn't know what was down here. So, to the man, everyone who worked on this project exited through the Door of Life when it was completed. The Forget Forever charm erased all their memory of what was down here. Because of the 'well' suffix, almost everyone one who worked here led successful and productive lives."

"If no one knew about this place, then how did you expect anyone to find it?" Tommy asked. "Or, was it your intent that no one would ever find this place?"

"My, no," the King said. "Quite the opposite, I hoped those with great need would seek this place. It is designed to test and reward those individuals that demonstrate the characteristics of those who served with me in the Kindlewalker war. That's why I hid three scrolls around the Realm that give clues to the location of this place. I don't suppose you know how many of them have been found?"

"I don't have any idea," Tommy answered.

The King looked questioningly at Michael and Carla, but they just shook their heads indicating that they didn't know either. As the King started to look toward Whitelace, he noticed that Whitelace was holding up two fingers. "Oh, okay," the King said. "I was curious. The first of the two that preceded you indicated that only one scroll had been discovered and he had been the one that discovered it. The second one said that she only knew of one scroll. She said she saw it at the excavation site of an ancient estate, but shortly after seeing it, it went missing. The scrolls have a Get Lost spell on them. If they are left unattended for too long, they will get lost until they are found again."

"Did I understand you to say that two people have come here before us?" Tommy questioned.

"Yes," answered the King. "The first was very, very long ago. He was a middle aged wizard and he chose the Door of Wealth. But unfortunately, he didn't fare too well and died during his journey. The second was not too long ago. She was a dark witch who said she was in search of a Prince. She chose the Door of Knowledge…"

The King paused, so Tommy asked, "What became of her?"

"I can't say for certain," the King said with doubt in his voice. "She disappeared somewhere along her journey. However, I suspect she also died and we just haven't found her remains."

"I wouldn't be so sure of that," Tommy pondered. "She may have found another way out of here. She may, in fact, be the Black Witch who now resides in your mountains south of Old Castle."

"Indeed," the King quipped with a surprised look on his face. "That's very interesting, very interesting indeed. You have impressed me with your questions and insights. You have earned a second worthiness point. You will need three proofs of worthiness in order to pass by Dragona. If you have passed a third test of worthiness by the time you reach her, she will let you pass. If you haven't, she will challenge you and if she doesn't like your answers, she might even eat you."

The King motioned for Tommy to come closer. Tommy stepped forward. He was standing right next to the King. His medallion was now very hot. He shrugged his shoulders slightly to move it off his chest a little. The King's Whisper bent forward and whispered in his ear.

"Young Prince," the King's Whisper began. "I believe your quest is greater and more important than either of us realize, so I'm going to give you two riddles that will help you on your way. First, remember this: Three is One, One is Two, and Two is Three. This can greatly reduce the length of your journey. Secondly, remember: Where there is a bridge, no bridge exists; and, where there is no bridge, a bridge exists. Will you remember this young Prince?"

"Yes, Your Majesty," Tommy whispered, "but I assure you I am no Prince. I'm just an ordinary guy." By now, Tommy was sure his medallion was falsely leading the King to believe he was a Prince.

The King whispered one last bit of advice. "Be mindful of your shadow," he said and then he straightened up to his full height. He smiled and then his face turned serious. "Now it is time for you to confirm your decision by stepping through the door of your choice. Remember, it is not too late to choose the Door of Life."

"Thank you, Your Majesty," Tommy said to the King. He turned and looked at Carla and Michael. He was going to offer them one last chance to leave him and go through the Door of Life. His intention was written across his face.

"Don't you dare ask that question, Tommy Travail," Carla said sternly. "We go where you go," she confirmed, speaking for Michael and herself.

Tommy nodded, turned and started toward the Door of Knowledge. When he stepped in front of the door, it opened.

"Fare-thee-well, young Prince," the King said.

Tommy turned back towards the King for the briefest of moments, tilted his head slightly as if to say, "I'm not a Prince," and then stepped through the doorway. Michael and Carla followed.

Whitelace moved forward as soon as the three of them stepped through the doorway. He moved with a substantial limp as he tried to keep his weight off his injured toes. He hesitated at the Door of Wealth, and then moved on. He hesitated a bit longer at the Door of Life, and then moved towards the Door of Knowledge. He looked over to the King, and the King smiled. Whitelace turned back to the doorway and stepped through it.

Chapter Twenty-Three

The Cavern of Contemplation

Carla and the boys found themselves in a tunnel cut out of stone. As they walked, Tommy reached under his robes and pulled out his medallion. He let it fall to his chest outside of his robes. It had gotten so hot while he talked with the King's Whisper, that it had burned him slightly. They proceeded cautiously watching for hidden traps and pitfalls. "Thank you," Carla suddenly said to Tommy.

"For what?" Tommy asked with surprise.

With all that had just transpired, Tommy may have forgotten, but Carla hadn't. It was too important to her. "For asking the King about the 'well' suffix," she replied with a broad smile. "It makes all the difference."

"Not a problem," Tommy responded. "You had a right to know the truth."

They walked a ways further and, after rounding a corner, they entered a large cavern. Across the cavern, three tunnels led out. To their right was a large closed door. The door was bolted, chained and sealed with no visible door knob or key hole. They walked closer to the door. Once they got close enough, they could see that, in the center of the door, there was a large recessed impression of the King's coat of arms. The impression was circular and had lines cut through it that divided it into thirds.

"I don't think this door requires a charm," Carla said. "I think it requires something to be placed into that impression. I think that whatever it is, it kinda acts like a key."

"I believe you're correct," Tommy confirmed. Michael also confirmed his agreement with a nod. "It looks like it comes in three pieces," Tommy continued. "And guess what, there are three tunnels that lead out of here. Anyone want to bet that each one leads to a piece of the key?"

"I don't think that there's any doubt," Michael said with certainty. "What do you think we should do? Maybe we should split up and each of us take a tunnel. If we find a piece of the key we can come back here."

"Hold on," Carla objected. "My grandmother says that people in difficult situations or facing trouble should always stick together."

"But," Michael responded, "it is sometimes a good military tactic to divide up."

"I don't care," Carla said forcefully, "I trust the wisdom of my grandmother, and I say we stick together. She said that there is a special strength that comes from staying together."

"I agree with Carla," Tommy intervened. "I think we must stick together."

"Okay," Michael conceded. "I was just trying to point out our options. To tell you the truth, I'd feel a whole lot better if we did stick together. So I guess we just need to decide which tunnel we explore first."

"I don't care," Tommy responded. "Pick one."

Carla pointed to the tunnel that was all the way to the left.

"Okay," Tommy said. "Let's go."

They crossed the cavern and entered the tunnel. It was similar to the tunnel that had taken them to the cavern. They had gone a ways when the light in the tunnel suddenly disappeared and all went black. Carla and the boys froze. Carla lit the tip of her wand and cast some light around them. Tommy and Michael also lit their wands. Although they should have been making plenty of light to light up the tunnel, the darkness was so black that it ate their light. It took all they had and still they only made enough light to encompass themselves in a ball of soft yellow radiance. They crept along, moving in the shortest of increments, not knowing what was in front or around them. It took a long time, but they moved a considerable distance. However, their ball of light had been getting smaller and smaller. They could no longer see their feet.

Carla had been thinking about her grandmother. "Say," she suddenly said. Her suddenness startled Tommy and Michael and they both jumped slightly. "I have an idea. Let's try putting our wand tips together."

She raised her wand out in front of her. Michael and Tommy touched the tips of their wands to the tip of Carla's. Suddenly all the light returned to the tunnel. They blinked their eyes until they adjusted to the brightness of the light. However, once they regained the sight, they grabbed onto one another. They were standing on a narrowing strip of floor. On both sides of them, the floor disappeared into the blackness. The narrow piece of walkway they were standing on was just about to make a sharp jog. If they had gone another step or two in the darkness, they would have fallen into the abyss that was now around them. They followed the ever narrowing walkway with their eyes and could see that it ended in a cove that had all of its floor. In the center of the cove was a pedestal that held a sparkling object.

"I think I can wave ride the rest of the way," Carla said. "Down there near the end, when it gets real narrow, I'm sure I can single foot it the rest of the way. You guys can wait here, but be ready to come after me if something starts to go wrong."

"Are you sure you want to do this?" Tommy asked.

Carla didn't answer, she just gave him that, 'I said it, so I must have meant it' look.

Tommy nodded and Carla set off. She popped up onto a wave, negotiated the jog and moved well at first, but she slowed as the walkway narrowed. When the walkway became too narrow for both of her feet, she raised her right foot and glided the rest of the way to the cove.

"She's not just left handed," Tommy thought, "she's left footed too."

Carla stayed up on her wave and glided to the pedestal. She examined the object on it. It was a pie shaped section of the King's coat of arms. It was jewel encrusted and inlayed with gold. Carla

The Life and Times of Tommy Travail

passed her wand over the object to test it for hidden magic. When she didn't get any response, she leaned forward and picked up the object. It was warm to the touch, and for some odd reason, it felt good in her hands. She turned around and glided back to the narrow end of the walkway. She raised her right foot again and slid out onto the walkway. She carefully maneuvered her way back to the boys.

Tommy and Michael congratulated her. She was all smiles. "Wait until you feel this thing. It's incredible," she said with wide eyes.

"Just hang on to it for now," Tommy instructed. "At least until we get back to the point where the floor is whole again." Carla nodded and they cautiously headed back in the direction they came. Carla hung onto the object all the way back to the cavern.

Whitelace was happy to see their return. He had started to follow them, but stopped when everything went black. He decided that he would wait in the cavern while they explored the two remaining tunnels. His injured toes made it difficult for him to get around and he would benefit greatly from the rest. However, he wasn't sure what he would do if they failed to return.

Carla took the object over to the door. After examining the object and the door, she determined where the piece fit and placed it in the recessed impression. "Shall we try the center tunnel," she asked as she turned around and walked towards the boys.

"Might as well," Michael said with a little uncertainty in his voice. "It appears that one is probably just as dangerous as the other."

"What does your watch say?" Tommy asked as the three of them walked to the entrance of the center tunnel.

"Uh," Michael started as he raised his wrist to view his watch, "it says we're in The Cavern of Contemplation, and in the past, we were in The Tunnel of the Lost. It says that we will next be in The Tunnel of Doubts."

"The Tunnel of the Lost," Carla said while she gave it some thought. "I think I get it," she abruptly pronounced.

"What's that," Tommy inquired.

"The Tunnel of the Lost," she repeated. "It's meaning."

"I didn't know it had a meaning," Michael interrupted.

"I think it does," Carla responded. "I think it means: 'You must come out of the darkness to see the light.'"

"Wow," Tommy said. "That's pretty deep Carla. Do you really think? I mean, it does raise some questions, but don't you think that's a bit esoteric?"

"Maybe," Carla responded. "But, I think carrying that key piece and this cavern has had an effect on me."

"Well, we are in The Cavern of Contemplation," Michael interjected. "So maybe that's what we're supposed to do; think about what we're doing."

"Could be," Tommy seemingly agreed. "However, we better move on and see what this next tunnel has in store for us."

Carla and Michael agreed with a head nod and the three of them entered the tunnel. The tunnel was well lit. It was dead straight. It stretched out before them as far as they could see. Cautiously, they started out. They went slowly at first, but the further they went, the faster their pace became. The tunnel never seemed to change. They had gone quite a ways and still the tunnel stretched out in front of them as far as they could see. Tommy suddenly stopped and turned around. They had gone so far that the tunnel behind them now stretched out behind them as far as he could see. Michael and Carla both turned around to see what Tommy was looking at.

"What is it?" Carla asked.

"Oh, nothing," Tommy answered with a slightly puzzled look on his face. "It just seems that we're not making any progress. We've picked up our pace quite a bit, and yet we seem to be no closer to the end than when we started. But yet, when we look back, it appears that we've traveled a considerable distance."

"What do you suggest?" Michael inquired.

"I guess we should just continue," Tommy answered. "How do you feel?" he asked Carla.

"I agree," Carla said. "I don't think there's any point in turning around."

"Yeah," Michael said, agreeing with Carla. "I don't see any reason to turn around, at least not yet." And with that, they continued.

They had traveled a ways further, when all of a sudden the tunnel began to move. They all stopped. The tunnel began to turn from end to end. It continued until it had rotated a full hundred and eighty degrees.

"What the heck!" Michael exclaimed. "What was that?"

"The tunnel's turned," Carla answered, "and now we're facing the way we came."

"Are we," Tommy said questioning Carla's assessment. "Or is our objective still in ahead of us?"

"Oh…, I hadn't thought of that," Carla said with doubt in her voice.

"The question is," Tommy continued, "do we now continue in this direction or, since the tunnel has turned end for end, do we turn around and head in the opposite direction?"

"Your guess is as good as mine," Michael answered.

"I think we should continue in the direction we're facing," Tommy concluded. "Regardless of what the tunnel does, I think we should continue to move forward. What do you think?"

"Like I said, your guess is good as mine," Michael repeated.

"I'll go along with that," Carla agreed. "At least, if we have to back track, we'll have an idea of which way we came."

They continued for a ways when once again the tunnel shook and began to rotate. This time, however, the tunnel did not completely rotate from end to end. This time it rotated only ninety degrees. They all stopped and looked at one another with perplexed expressions on they faces.

"I still think we should continue in the same direction," Tommy reaffirmed.

Both Carla and Michael agreed with a nod, so they continued. They went a bit further when the tunnel shook and rotated again. This time it rotated two hundred and seventy degrees. They stopped when the tunnel began to rotate, but as soon as it stopped, they continued without any discussion. However, as they went, they could, for the first time, see that the light at the end of the tunnel was getting nearer. They all noticed it at about the same time and automatically quickened their pace. The light got brighter the closer they got. Their pace had increased to a trot. In a relatively short time, they had reached the end of the tunnel and exited it at almost an all out run. Their excitement only lasted for a second. When they looked around, they found themselves back in The Cavern of Contemplation. Their faces sagged and they shoulders slumped.

David G. Groesbeck

"Oh man," Michael exclaimed loudly. "That was a waste of time and effort."

"What did we do wrong?" Carla asked. "Maybe we should have turned around when the tunnel rotated."

"Maybe," Tommy replied, "but this is going to require some thinking before we attempt it again." He went over to a large rock and sat down, leaned forward, rested his elbows on his knees and cradled his chin in his hands.

Whitelace had stretched out on a rock in the back of the cavern and had actually fallen asleep while the kids were in the tunnel. The commotion of their return woke him up and he slowly rose up so he could see and hear them. He started to laugh to himself as he realized they had failed. But, his glee quickly turned to concern as he realized his fate was also dependent on their success.

Tommy sat on the rock for awhile deep in thought. Carla took out her bag of chocolates, took one out for herself and passed the bag to Michael. He took one and handed the bag to Tommy. Tommy took one and set the bag on the rock next to him. Eventually, he took his wand and began making marks on the ground between his feet with its tip. "I think I've got it," he finally declared. "If the Tunnel makes the same rotations, I'm pretty sure I can get us to the other end. But this time, I think we should wave ride it. There doesn't seem to be any dangers in the tunnel and, if we wave ride it, we can move much further with much less effort."

"And we'll be a lot quicker," Carla added.

"I'm ready when you guys are," Michael quipped.

The three of them headed for the tunnel entrance and went in. Whitelace was watching as they entered the tunnel when his eye caught Carla's bag of chocolates still sitting on the rock. Once he was sure they were out of sight, he limped his way over to the bag. He picked it up and could see that it was nearly full. He started to take one out of the bag when his conscience kicked in. He realized that what he was about to do was stealing. He hesitated for a moment. He came up with a few flimsy excuses to justify his action but ultimately, right or wrong, he decided that his immediate need was sufficient reason. He took one out of the bag and popped it into his mouth. It melted in his mouth with a rich smoothness of sweet chocolate flavor.

He took his time and savored every delicious and healing moment. It really didn't heal his injuries so much as it relieved and soothed his pain somewhat. He reached in the bag and once again hesitated for a moment, but then continued and removed another piece. He put it in his mouth and set the bag back on the rock. He really didn't like taking what wasn't his, so he decided that a minimum of two would be needed to sooth his pain some and restore his energy, so he limited himself to just two. "Any more than that," he thought, "would be wrong." He returned to his place at the back of the cavern and waited for the kids to return.

Whitelace didn't have to wait very long. Since the kids were wave riding this time, they traveled the tunnel much quicker. However, the tunnel did not rotate in the same sequence that it had the first time as Tommy had hoped. After a short while, they found themselves once again exiting the tunnel back into The Cavern of Contemplation.

"Well, Tommy Boy, so much for that idea," Michael jabbed.

"Give me a minute," Tommy responded. "I think I'm on the right track. I just need to modify my plan to deal with random rotations of the tunnel. It'll just take a minute." He walked back to the rock that he was sitting in earlier. Carla's bag of chocolates was still sitting on the rock. He bent over and picked it up. Peered inside and took out another piece. He gave the bag to Carla and knelt down to view his earlier markings. He drew several more lines and this time he scratched out a formula. "That's it," he finally said with a tone of confidence. "Let's go." He got up and headed for the tunnel entrance. Carla and Michael followed without any questions.

They popped up on their waves and slid into the tunnel. As on the previous two occasions, after they had traveled a considerable distance, the tunnel rotated. This time, however, Tommy stopped, determined the degrees of rotation and calculated which direction they should go. Tommy made his determination and they proceeded. They continued doing this through several rotations of the tunnel. They began to become discouraged, but they persisted until finally, after one rotation they could see the light at the end of the tunnel becoming larger. They knew this indicated that they were near the end. They didn't get as excited as they did the previous two times. Their hope was high, but so was their fear that that they would once again exit the tunnel into The Cavern of Contemplation. Their anticipation increased the closer they got to the end.

They finally reached the opening of the tunnel and slid out. They looked at one another and began to laugh and cheer. They were standing in a large alcove and in the middle of the alcove was a pedestal with a glimmering key piece sitting on top of it. Michael glided over to the pedestal and picked up the key piece. Just like the other piece had with Carla, this piece felt warm in Michael's hand and it felt unusually pleasurable to hold onto.

"Hey," Carla said harshly. "You should have checked that for hidden magic before you picked it up."

"Sorry," Michael said sheepishly. "I didn't think. But, it doesn't appear that there was any."

"Luckily," was Carla's single word response.

"Let's go," Tommy directed.

They turned and reentered the tunnel. Tommy followed his formula as the tunnel went through its rotations. After a modest amount of time, they found themselves gliding back into The Cavern of Contemplation. Michael walked over to the big sealed door, determined its proper position and placed the key piece in the recessed circle in the door.

Michael turned around and faced Carla and Tommy. His eyes widened and his face brightened. "I think I got it," he said with the look of discovery on his face. "If Carla's right and these tunnels do have a meaning, I know what this one means."

"Okay," Tommy said obligingly. "What is it?"

"Well," Michael started. "That was The Tunnel of Doubts, right? And, what I think the whole thing meant was that: first, there is doubt, doubt leads to questions, questions lead to answers and answers lead to solutions."

"Hey, that's pretty good," Carla affirmed. "That works."

"I don't know about you two," Tommy said discouragingly. "I think you're both stretching things a bit."

"Say what you like," Michael said with some confidence, "but I agree with Carla. Carrying that key piece has an effect on you, and this room, well; it just seems to do something to you."

"Okay," Tommy agreed, but the tone of his voice seemed to indicate that he really didn't care about it one way of the other. "Where does your watch say we'll be next?" he asked Michael.

Michael looked at his watch and read it aloud, "The Tunnel of Fore and After Thought."

"If you two are ready," Tommy suggested, "I think we should go."

Carla and Michael nodded and the three of them went to the entrance of the third and final tunnel. "Here we go," Michael announced and led the way into the tunnel.

They went a short ways and the tunnel began to expand. It grew wider and wider the further they went until they found themselves in a long wide tunnel. Their progress was halted when they approached a recessed area in the floor that stretched all the way from one side wall to the other. The floor was recessed some ten feet. The recessed area extended nearly a hundred feet before it abruptly rose back to their level on the other side. A series of floating square platforms zigzagged their way from one end of the recessed area to the other. Some of the platforms were black while others were white and they appeared to be floating in mid air without any supports. They were at the same height level as the walkway the kids were standing on. The ceiling of the tunnel continued to be low until shortly before the recessed area when it shot straight up several feet to form a vey high ceiling above the recessed area.

Carla and the boys approached the edge of the recess and looked across the recessed area to where it ended. They could see a small alcove where a pedestal stood holding the third and final key piece.

"There it is," Carla shouted with excitement as she pointed across the recess.

"It looks like all we have to do is cross over and get it," Michael said with a margin of confidence.

"Somehow I don't think it's going to be that easy," Tommy said with a little sarcasm.

They peered over the edge and looked down to the floor of the recessed area. The floor was done in a black and white checker board pattern and it was not level. It tilted from the far end towards the end were the kids stood. It also was not flat. It had numerous high and low areas that rolled softly into rounded peaks and valleys.

"Well," Michael said. "We might as well give it a try."

Both Carla and Tommy wanted to object, but neither of them could think of a good reason, so they just nodded and Michael took a step out onto the first platform. When nothing happened, Carla and Tommy followed him. The platforms had a small space between each other, so Michael made a small jump and moved to the second platform. As soon as Michael jumped, the platform that Carla and Tommy were still standing on began to wobble. It required them both to jump quickly and together to avoid falling off.

"Maybe we should jump to the next platform at the same time," Tommy suggested. "There's enough room for the three of us to go together."

Carla and Michael agreed and together they jumped to the third platform. There, they made a mistake and looked down. The rising and falling of the checkerboard floor below was dizzying. In a moment, it became extremely difficult to determine whether they were looking at the next platform or an aberration of the black and white squares of the floor below. Suddenly, the platform began to wobble and, before they could decide which way to jump, the platform tilted sharply and dumped the three of them off.

They fell the ten feet or so to the floor below. They expected a hard landing, but instead they found the floor soft and pillow like, but it was extremely slippery. In fact, it was friction free. They could not stand up nor stop their downward slide. They slid up, down and around the peaks and valleys of the floor towards their starting end. Once they reached the end wall, they were funneled into an opening that carried them into a shoot. They slid up and around.

A trap door opened in the walkway floor near where they started. The end of the trap door nearest the edge of the recess opened while the other end remained hinged to the floor. One by one, they slid out of the trap door and came to rest at the upper edge of the recessed area. They were pretty close to where they had taken their initial step out onto the first platform.

"Wow," Michael said. "That was a blast."

"You know it," Tommy agreed.

"However, we're no nearer our objective," Carla seemed to scold, but the big smile and twinkle in her eye showed that she had enjoyed it as well.

Tommy thought for a bit and then said, "Okay, look I don't see why we all have to try to cross this. Only one of us has to get to the other side to retrieve the key piece.

"What do you have in mind," Michael asked.

"If I try to cross this alone, you two can stay here and, if I become confused, you can spot for me. I can keep trying to get across until I get tried, then one of you can go. Sooner or later, one of us will make it."

"It sounds like a good plan to me," Carla said. "Michael and I can move out to the sides and, between the three of us, we should be able to determine the correct next move."

"I'll get on the first platform and face the other end. I will have to go forward, either to my left, straight forward or to my right. You guys spot the real location of the next platform and tell me which way to go."

Carla and Michael agreed. They separated and moved all the way to each of the side walls. Tommy stepped up on the first platform and faced forward. Carla and Michael both said, "Right." Tommy moved slightly to his right and took a small diagonal jump. He successfully landed in the middle of the next platform. He continued to look directly towards the far end and took extra precautions so that he didn't accidently look down. Carla and Michael called out, "Straight." Tommy jumped forward and landed in the middle of the third square. "Left," Carla and Michael called out. Tommy turned slightly to his left and jumped diagonally, but as soon as he landed, it wobbled and swiftly tilted. Instantly, Tommy found himself falling to the floor below.

Carla and Michael watched Tommy slide across the floor below them. They watched as he was funneled into the opening and in a moment, the trap door opened and Tommy slid out to the edge of the recess. After some discussion, Tommy tried again. This time he only got to the third platform before he was thrown off. On the third attempt, he was thrown off the second platform.

"Maybe I'm not doing something right," Tommy said with exasperation in his voice. "I'll give it one more try. If I don't make it, then one of you can give it a go."

Tommy moved out onto the first platform, this time he got to the fourth platform before it began to wobble. Before he fell, he turned around and faced Carla and Michael. He shrugged his shoulders and threw up his hands as if to say, "I give up." As he began to fall, he saw something he had never seen before. He started waving his arms wildly. He continued waving his arms as he slid across the floor. With his arms still waving, he was eventually funneled into the opening. By the time he popped out of the shoot, he was so excited he could hardly talk.

"I saw something," Tommy said trying to catch his breath. "Come, look!" Tommy stepped to the edge of the recess, turned around and pointed up.

Carla and Michael quickly came over to see what he was pointing at. They looked up and, on the face of the wall that was created as the low ceiling changed to a high ceiling, were four square inlayed bricks. Three of the bricks were arranged in a row side by side. The fourth brick was centered just below the middle of the three bricks above it. The bricks were the same brownish gray that they had seen elsewhere in the well complex and they were embossed with King Oleander's coat of arms.

"When I started to fall," Tommy explained, "that brick on the top left was white in color, now it's brown like the others. I think that might show us the way. Let's give this another try."

Carla and Michael readily agreed. All three of them were excited. Tommy stepped out on the first platform. He quickly turned around and looked up to the bricks. The single brick in the second row turned blue. Tommy was surprised to see that the brick turned blue rather than white, but in the first row of bricks, the brick on the right had turned black. By now, he knew that the second platform was black in color, so at least that seemed to make some sense. He turned slightly to his right and made his diagonal jump. He landed safely on the second platform and once again turned to view the bricks. The bottom brick remained blue, but now the center brick in the top row was black. Tommy turned around and looked down just enough to see that the platform in front of him was also black, so he jumped forward. He once again landed safely. He quickly looked around to the bricks and saw that the left brick on the top row had turned white. He looked back towards the next platform and, out of the corner of his eye, he could see that it was white. He turned slightly to his left and made his leap. As soon as he landed, the platform wobbled and suddenly tilted. Once again, Tommy found himself falling to the floor below. After a few moments, Tommy popped out of the trap door and slid to the edge of the recess.

"Shoot," Tommy exclaimed when he came to a stop. "I thought we had it that time."

"You want one of us to give it a go," Michael inquired.

"No," Tommy answered. "I'll try it a couple of more times. But…, you know, I'm getting thirsty."

"Not a problem," Carla said in her self assured way. "She reached under her robes into her carry all bag. She fiddled with it for a few moments and then pulled out a bottle of Roddenberry root, root beer.

"Wow," Tommy said. "I didn't even know they put that in bottles. Where did you get that?"

"Oh I have my ways," Carla responded wryly. She touched the bottle with the tip of her wand and chilled it. She opened it and handed it to Tommy.

Tommy took a good swallow. It was perfectly satisfying. He took a second drink and passed the bottle to Michael. Michael took a couple of drinks and handed it back to Carla. She took a drink, replaced the cap and put it back in her bag.

"Okay," Tommy declared. "I'm ready to go back at it." He got onto the first platform and they tried again.

It took several more unsuccessful attempts before Tommy realized that the color of the bricks had nothing to do with the color of the platforms. Instead, he started to believe that the color of the bricks indicated whether a given platform was safe or not. It took a couple of more tries before he completely solved the puzzle.

"Okay," Tommy said as he popped out of the trap door after his most recent failure. "Here it is. When I step out on the first platform, the brick representing the next platform will turn black or white. If it is black, then it is safe to jump. If it is white, the platform is unstable and unsafe. However, if I wait long enough, the brick will eventually turn black indicating that the platform is safe. But, as soon as the next platform becomes safe, the platform I'm standing on becomes unsafe and I must immediately jump. If I hesitate even for just for a moment, it will tilt and I'll be thrown off."

"That's the way I'm reading it," Michael confirmed.

"Yeah, I agree," Carla added.

They tried one more time and Tommy almost got to the other side before he was dumped. Between his nerves and the excitement of getting so near the other side, he hesitated for a moment too long before making a jump and quickly found himself falling to the floor once again. His next attempt, however, was successful. He took great pride as he stepped off the last platform and into the alcove. There it was right in front of him, the third and final key piece. He started to reach for it.

"Make sure you check it for hidden magic first," Carla hollered across to Tommy.

Tommy stopped and turned around. "How do I do that?" he hollered back.

"Wave your wand over it," Carla replied. "If there's something there, you'll know it."

Tommy did as Carla instructed and nothing happened, so he picked up the key piece. He found it warm to the touch as Carla and Michael had with the other two pieces. He also began to understand what Carla and Michael had been talking about as he noticed how comfortable and satisfying it was to have it in his hand. Tommy turned and went to the edge of the recess.

"I'm not going to try to make it back on the platforms," Tommy called to Carla and Michael. "There's no sense to it," and he jump over the edge into the recessed area. He slid across the floor in one final ride. He was funneled into the opening and popped out of the trap door right next to Carla and Michael's feet. He had a big smile on his face and when he looked up at his companions, they were also smiling.

Michael stretched out his hand and helped Tommy to his feet. "Way to go, Tommy Boy," he said as he patted Tommy on the back.

"That," Carla said, "was a toughie."

They turned and headed back the way they came with their arms around one another's shoulders and smiles on their faces. They didn't have to travel far before they exited the tunnel back into The Cavern of Contemplation.

Whitelace was dozing lightly, but heard their arrival. He slowly sat up and, although they had been gone a long time, he instantly knew by their jovial nature that they had been successful.

Tommy walked over to the sealed door followed closely by Carla and Michael. Tommy raised the final key piece up. Just as he was about to put it in place, he felt something on its reverse side. He pulled the piece back and turned it over. He found a small number three engraved near one edge. "Michael," he suddenly said, "I'm going to hold this piece up near the spot in the door where it goes, when I do, tell me what your watch says for the future."

Tommy held the piece near the recessed area in the door and Michael looked at his watch. "It says we'll be on the Long Road of Experience."

Tommy pulled the piece back near his chest. "And now, what does it say," he asked.

"It went blank," Michael answered.

"What is it?" Carla asked. "What's going on?"

"It's something the King told me," Tommy replied. "I think we have to remove these other two pieces, but to be on the safe side, I think each of you should remove the piece you placed."

"Are you sure that's a good idea?" Carla questioned.

"I'm pretty sure we have to," Tommy answered.

"Well, okay," Carla agreed, "But maybe Michael should remove his first since it was placed last."

"I don't think that'll matter," Tommy advised, "but why don't you go first Michael, just to be on the safe side."

Michael removed his piece without any problems, so Carla removed her piece as well; also without any problems.

"Turn them over and see if you can find a number," Tommy instructed. They did as he asked. Carla found a number two and Michael found a number one. "Okay," Tommy continued. "Let's set them on the floor in the order they were in the door. They assembled the King's coat of arms on the floor. "The King told me a riddle that he said would shorten our journey. He said to remember that; Three is One, One is Two, and Two is Three. Now, if we make a mark to indicate what number is on the back of each piece, we should be able to rearrange the pieces according to the riddle." They quickly rearranged the pieces. "Now, let's install them in the recess in this order. Carla you go first." Carla placed her piece into the door and Michael did the same. Tommy held his piece up near its proper position, but did not push it into the recess. "Okay, Michael," he said. "What does your watch say now about the future?"

"Wow," Michael said with genuine surprise. "Now it says that we'll be on the Shortcut to Dragona's Dungeon."

"That's it," Tommy declared and he inserted the final piece. The reassembled King's coat of arms instantly began to glow and Tommy's medallion became very warm. Although his medallion was still hanging outside of his robes, it became so warm that he could feel it through his clothing.

They hadn't realized it, but they were standing on a trap door. The front edge of the trap door, the edge nearest the sealed door, dropped down while the back edge remained hinged at floor level. It created a slide and all three of them fell on their butts and slid down through the opening.

Whitelace stood up immediately and as fast as he could run with his sore toes, he ran to where the kids had been standing. When he looked down the trap door was starting to close, so without hesitation he jumped onto the still sloping floor area feet first. His body went through the opening, but by the time his head was clearing the ever narrowing opening, it was a bit too tight and he banged his forehead hard against the floor edge as he passed. He saw sparkling lights as the blow almost knocked him unconscious. A big knot quickly began to form on his forehead.

Chapter Twenty-Four

Dragona and the Pit of Perpetual Pain

Carla and the boys let out squeals of delight as they slid down the slippery slope of the slide. They went down, rounded several curves, when up a gentle slope and then dropped down sharply before they finally slid out of the shoot onto a large rectangular stone floor. All three of them quickly got to their feet and stepped forward. They were standing on a balcony like structure that was several feet higher than the main floor below them. Next to them was a large arched entrance door. In front of them stretched a long wide staircase that went to the main floor below. They were in a very large cavern type structure that had been roughly cut out of some type of shiny black stone. It had a domed roof, that was several meters above the main floor. The entire cavern was lit by flaming torches that sat in sconces around the walls. A large round chandelier hung from the domed ceiling. It had over a hundred small flaming torches on it that flickered light about the room. The flickering light from all the torches in the cavern danced across the roughly cut surfaces of the shiny black stone of the walls. It was dazzling to see, it made the whole room appear to be moving.

    The far wall of the cavern was rounded outwardly. On the main floor, just in front of the center of the outwardly curving wall, lay a giant dragon. She was lying with her head down and facing directly towards the bottom of the staircase. She was magnificent and fearsome in appearance. Her body was covered with blackish blue-green scales.

Two rows of curved, sharp, pointed, bone-like structures went down her back on each side of her spine. She had a long and massive tail that ended with a pair of the sharp and pointed bone like structures. She had four legs. Her hind legs were much more massive than her front legs. Her front legs were smaller and more like arms, which were perfectly suited for grabbing and clawing. All four of her feet ended with four razor-sharp, pointed claws. Halfway up her front fore legs, she had a pair of sharply pointed dew claws that could snag any prey that tried to escape from her grasp. She had a pair of large black wings that were partially folded back along side of her body. Her head was massive with a large wide mouth. Her mouth was full of large pointed teeth. A longer pair of fang-like teeth protruded from her upper jaw that met a similar pair of larger teeth, which protruded from her lower jaw. She had two large, oval nostrils and large, yellow eyes with black, vertical slits as pupils.

Carla and the boys stood at the top edge of the staircase and took in the amazing sight in front of them. The dragon suddenly flared her nostrils and snorted. She raised her head and stared at the three figures standing at the top of the stairs. "Huhh," she exhaled and a small burst of flames came out of her mouth followed by a long red and forked serpent's tongue. Her tongue whipped in the air for a moment before she drew it back into her mouth. "I see you have finally arrived," she said in low and slow feminine voice.

"Wow," Michael said abruptly "a real live, talking dragon."

"Dragons can't talk," Carla corrected.

"That one just did," Michael shot back.

"Real dragons can't talk silly boy," Carla scoffed. "She must be a magical re-creation."

"Oh," Michael said, "that makes me feel better."

"Don't get me wrong," Carla advised. "She's probably every bit as dangerous as a real dragon, maybe even more so."

"Well that makes me feel much better," Michael teased.

"That's Dragona," Tommy interjected. "The King warned us about her. She's going to demand that we show three proofs of worthiness. If we can't, she'll challenge us."

"Do we have three?" Michael asked.

"Don't know," Tommy answered. "I know we got two, but I have no idea if we've earned a third."

"Come travelers," Dragona said and a puff of smoke came out of her nostrils. "Come and stand before me."

"I'm not going down there," Michael declared.

"We don't have any choice," Tommy countered. "It's the only way to get past her." He grabbed Michael's arm and took the first step down the stairs. Michael grabbed Carla's arm and the three started down the long staircase. The further they descended the stairs, the larger Dragona appeared. She had looked large from the height and distance of the balcony, but as they took their last step off the staircase, they realized how truly huge she was. Her mouth was large enough to snatch one of them up and swallow him, or her, whole. They were still some ten or twelve feet from her.

She lowered her head slightly and took a slow and serious look at them. "Come closer," she ordered. She spit her tongue out for a moment and then continued, "so I can see you better."

Carla and the boys slowly moved closer. They cut the distance between them and Dragona in half. Suddenly, she dropped her head and put her face right in from of them. It took the kids' breath away for a moment. She turned her head slightly and with one of her big, yellow eyes, she looked them over. Her breath was unbearably hot.

She raised her head back up and spoke. "I have received only two proofs of worthiness. How dare you come before me without three proofs of merit? Maybe I should just eat you now and get it over with."

"No, please, Your, ah, Mightiness," Michael suddenly pleaded. "You don't want to eat us."

"And, why don't I?" asked Dragona.

"'Cause, 'cause," Michael struggled for an answer. "Because, we're no good to anyone if we've been eaten." Tommy looked at Michael with that, 'that's the lamest thing I've ever heard' look.

"Please, you gotta give us a chance," Tommy interjected before Dragona could react to Michael's idiotic comment.

"And, why should I do that?" Dragona inquired.

"Well, ah...," Tommy stumbled trying not to give an idiotic answer of his own.

"Because we took the shortcut," Carla suddenly said when she saw Tommy struggling. "It's likely that we missed the other opportunities to prove our worthiness."

"You took the shortcut," Dragona asked with some surprise. "That was pretty cleaver of you to figure that out."

"Ah, well," Tommy said reluctantly. "The King did help."

"Oh, did he?" Dragona said somewhat rhetorically. "That's interesting. Why would the old man do that?"

"He said our quest might be important," Tommy answered.

"Humm," Dragona said as she pondered the situation. "Okay, then, I'll ask you the 'standard' question for those who take the shortcut."

"There's a 'standard' question?" Michael asked Tommy under his breath. Tommy poked Michael with his elbow.

"What's that?" Dragona asked.

"Nothing, Your Mightiness," Michael answered. "The 'standard' question, you were going to ask us the 'standard' question."

'Yes, yes," Dragona mused. "Miss this question and Dragona will have a tasty treat this day."

Whitelace had slid out of the shortcut just after the kids had stepped to top edge of the staircase. While Carla and the boys were descending the staircase, he had worked his way to the top step. He was now sitting on the top step watching the events below.

"Okay," Dragona said, "here's your question. What was the meaning of the three tunnels that led from The Cavern of Contemplation?"

Carla leaned forward and turned her head to look at Tommy. She gave him that, 'I told you that was important' look. Tommy began to panic. A thought or two had come to his mind when he had returned to The Cavern of Contemplation with the key piece, but he had been so caught up in the whole shortcut thing that he just kept pushing it out of his mind. "What was it," he thought over and over in his mind.

"Well," Dragona said, "what is your answer? I'm getting hungry."

Carla took the initiative and spoke up "The first tunnel," she said, "The Tunnel of the Lost, it meant that you must come out of the darkness to see the light."

"Huggh," Dragona grunted and a puff of smoke came out of her nostrils. "And...," she inquired.

Tommy continued to scramble through his thoughts. "Back," he thought. "It had something to do with back."

"The second tunnel," Michael continued with the answer, "The Tunnel of Doubts, well, that meant that: first there is doubt, doubt leads to questions, questions lead to answers and answers lead to solutions."

"Huggh," Dragona grunted again and another puff of smoke came out of her nostrils. "And...," she inquired once more.

Tommy was on the spot. Carla, Michael and Dragona were looking at Tommy for an answer. "Ah, er," Tommy stuttered softly. "Ah, the third tunnel, The Tunnel of Fore and After Thought." When he said the name of the tunnel, it came to him. However, since he hadn't had the opportunity to discuss it with Carla and Michael, he remained quite unsure of himself. His lack of confidence caused him to speak in very soft tones, just above a whisper. "The meaning of the third tunnel," he continued, "was that, in order to learn and move forward, we sometimes have to look back." Dragona didn't say anything. She just slowly blinked her big eyes closed and then opened them just as slowly. She lowered her head all the way down and rested her massive jaws on the ground. She closed her eyes and raised a portion of her large tail, which exposed a small open doorway.

Tommy spotted the doorway and didn't hesitate. He grabbed Michael's arm, Michael grabbed Carla's arm and, as swiftly as they could, they took off for the opening. As soon as the three of them passed through the door, Dragona dropped her tail, once again blocking the doorway. The three of them turned around when they heard her tail drop. The doorway was now fully blocked with a section of Dragona's blackish blue-green scales.

Whitelace had stood up when the kids bolted for the open doorway, but they were through the doorway and Dragona dropped her tail before he could get halfway down the staircase. Dragona raised her head and ordered him to come before her. His camouflage apparently didn't work on her any better than it had worked on the King. Whitelace considered running, but there was nowhere to go, so he slowly descended the stairs and stood before her just as the kids had moments before. Whitelace knew he was going to be in trouble if she asked him the same 'standard' question that she had asked the kids. Although he had heard Carla and Michael's explanation of the meaning of the tunnels, both here and in The Cavern of Contemplation, he hadn't been able to hear Tommy's answer because he had spoken so softly. All Whitelace heard was something, something "look back."

Dragona did eventually ask Whitelace the 'standard' question and when it came to the third tunnel, Whitelace said, "The meaning of the final tunnel is; never look back."

Dragona reared up and came snapping down on Whitelace with the intent of snatching him up in one tasty morsel. Despite his pain, Whitelace was able to move quick enough to avoid becoming a snack for Dragona. A major battle began between a determined dragon and a highly proficient military student and wizard.

Carla and the boys found themselves standing in a large circular room roughly twenty meters across. The whole thing was the inside of a large dome. The walls not only curved around, but they also curved upward. A walkway four feet wide went around the outer walls. It ringed the entire circumference of the domed room. A large depression filled the rest of the room. It was like the depression a giant donut might leave. The depression was bowl like, except in the center, a pillar of rock protruded up to the level of the walkway. It had a flat top area and in the middle of that, there was a pedestal where a tiny bottle sat emitting a bright white light. The depression that surrounded the pillar of rock was filled with a moving mass of black smoke. It filled the depression like water, except that it was constantly moving and swirling. It was black and nasty looking. It was the Pit of Perpetual Pain.

A bridge made of planks floated in the air just above the whirling black mass and extended from the walkway out to the rock pillar. The start of the bridge was directly across the walkway from the door, so when the kids entered the room it was right in front of them.

Tommy and Michael spotted the tiny bottle at the same time. Michael took a quick step towards the bridge, but Tommy grabbed his arm and stopped him.

"Come on, Tommy Boy," Michael objected. "There it is. The thing we've been looking for. Come on, let's find out about your parents."

"No," Tommy said firmly. "I think it's a trap." That stopped Michael immediately.

"If Professor Pastorie is right," Tommy concluded, "we're looking at the Pit of Perpetual Pain and I don't think any of us what to fall in there."

"Uh, no," was Michael's short answer.

"Plus, there's a second riddle that the King told me. It didn't make much sense before, but it does now. The king said, 'Where there is a bridge, no bridge exists; and, where there is no bridge, a bridge exists.' I'm pretty sure he was referring to this bridge."

Carla quickly agreed. "We need a way to test the bridge. See if you can find something to toss out onto the bridge." They all looked around, but there wasn't a single thing, not a single pebble or grain of sand.

Tommy realized it was useless to look any further, so he paused and gave it some thought. "I've got it," he said after a few moments. "Carla, give me your bag of chocolates."

Carla and Michael instantly knew what he had in mind and the chocolates would work as well as anything. Carla got out the bag of chocolates and gave it to Tommy. Tommy opened the bag, took out one piece of chocolate, and tossed it out onto the bridge, only it didn't land on the bridge. It passed right through the planks and into the black mass below. The chocolate sizzled as it entered the blackness.

"It's an aberration," Carla declared. "We can see it, but it really doesn't exist."

"Well that solves the first part of the riddle," Tommy said with a serious, but oddly satisfied look on his face. "Now, let's find the bridge that really exists."

"I've been thinking about that," Carla advised, "and I have an idea."

"Sure," Tommy encouraged. "Let's hear it."

"If we're careful," she began, "we can run the tips of our wands around the top edge of the pit while we walk around it. If the real bridge looks anything like the false bridge, we should be able to feel the first plank."

Tommy and Michael agreed it was an excellent idea and the three of them set out to do it. Carla and Tommy set out clockwise from their position and Michael set out counter clockwise. They met back up on the other side of the room where Carla and Michael believe they touched a plank. Tommy took out a piece of chocolate and tossed it where they believed the bridge to be. The piece carried out, then down. Suddenly, in what appeared to be mid air, it bounced. It bounced three times before it came to rest. It seemed to be just floating in the air. Tommy took a small handful of the chocolates and tossed them out. They did the same thing the first piece had done, but now there were enough of them to define the outline of the bridge. Tommy took a second handful and tossed them out, but shorter this time. He took out a third handful and tossed them out, but this time he threw them out further. Chocolates now stretched nearly the full length of the bridge.

"I'm pretty sure I can get out there now," Tommy said with some excitement. His excitement had been building ever since he first saw the tiny bottle containing the Drop of Truth. He was just moments away from finding out about his parents. His heart was racing and he had to try to slow himself down. He still had to make what was a potentially dangerous crossing of the bridge. "I'm going to give it a try," he declared.

"Okay," Carla said, "but listen to me. There could be holes or missing planks, so take tiny steps and don't put any weight on your foot until you are sure that you're firmly on a plank."

"Got ya," Tommy confirmed.

"Go get 'em, Tommy Boy," Michael encouraged. "Just be careful."

Tommy slowly and cautiously stepped out onto the bridge. In tiny amounts, he steadyily worked his way to the other side without any mishaps. He found himself standing on the rock pillar with the pedestal holding the Drop right in front of him. The tiny bottle shined with such bright light that Tommy could hardly look directly at it. He started towards the bottle when Carla called out.

"Check it for hidden magic first," she hollered.

Tommy stopped and raised his wand, then moved forward. When he was close enough, he passed his wand over the pedestal and the Drop. He felt nothing, so he gently picked up the bottle. There it was in front of him. He was holding in his hand the answers to the questions that had troubled him ever since his parents went missing; it was over five years now. Tommy raised the bottle to remove the stopper.

Suddenly, an enormous roar came from the direction of Dragona's dungeon. It was so loud that it shook the entire domed room. While Carla and the boys had been exploring the domed room, Whitelace had been engaged in a battle for his life. When Dragona roared, she lifted her tail slightly and Whitelace slipped into the domed room. He was no longer projecting his camouflage and he was a pitiful sight. His cheek was still swollen and his black eye was now a deep purple. The large knot on his forehead had also turned a deep purple. There were still traces of dried blood under his nose and a speck of dried drool was still clinging to his chin. But now, there was a slash across the bridge of his nose that was slowly dripping blood. His robes were torn to shreds. It had numerous long slices in it where Dragona had slashed at him. Many of the slices revealed Whitelace's bare skin where bleeding cuts and gashes could be seen. He was now dragging his foot with the damaged toes. The false bridge stretched out between Whitelace and Tommy.

"Stop," Whitelace shouted. "That's my property. It belongs to me."

"I wondered when you were going to make your presence known," Tommy answered back.

"You never knew I was here," Whitelace said boastfully.

"Oh, didn't I," Tommy said back smartly. "I was pretty sure I saw you while we were still in the well, and then again in the Precious Metals Collection Room. When the King told me to be mindful of my shadow, I was sure he was talking about you. And, do you think it was an accident that I left the bag of chocolates on the rock in The Cavern of Contemplation? So you see, Mister Whitelace, I've known you were following us all along."

"Well, maybe," Whitelace replied. "But, that doesn't mean anything. You are holding my property and I want it."

"So you can give it to the Black Witch," Tommy accused.

"The Black Witch? Ha," Whitelace said. "Do you think I want that for the Black Witch? You gotta be kidding."

"You paid that Skeezicks guy to steal the scrolls from the Queen's Ministry," Tommy continued to accuse.

"I didn't pay him to steal the scrolls," Whitelace said in is own defense. "I told the no-good-for-nothing that I'd pay him for any information he could get for me about Damiana's Tears or the Drop of Truth. I didn't know the idiot was going to steal them. I didn't even know that the scrolls were stolen until I read it in the newspaper."

"If you're not trying to find the Drop of Truth for the Black Witch, then why are you so interested in it?" Tommy asked.

"I'm on a mission," Whitelace answered.

"For who?" Tommy asked continuing his challenge.

"I don't think that's any of your business," Whitelace said firmly.

"Since I have the Drop of Truth, I believe it is my business," Tommy countered, and then added, "Be as secretive as you wish, but you won't get any cooperation from me so long as I believe you're working for the Black Witch."

"I am *not* working for the Black Witch," Whitelace said indignantly. "I..., well..., okay I'll tell you. I'm on a mission for the Head Mistress. She told me I was to find out everything I could about the location of the Drop. In fact, she's the one that suggested I contact Skeezicks for possible leads. I'm not sure, but I think she was hoping to give the Drop to the Queen as a gift."

Carla and Michael had been standing directly across the room from Whitelace when he slipped in past Dragona's tail. Being good tacticians, they separated and slowly moved in opposite directions around the room until they were halfway to Whitelace. They were now even with Tommy and spread as far apart as possible. Although they were closer to Whitelace, they now presented three widely separate targets. However, they all knew that they didn't stand a chance against him. He was a well trained sixth year Military student plus, on his own, he had just beaten, or at least gotten past, a very fearsome dragon.

Whitelace took a step towards the bridge. Tommy raised his hand in an attempt to stop him. Unfortunately, he had the Drop of Truth in one hand and his wand in the other, and not thinking, he raised the hand with his wand in it. Whitelace thought Tommy was going to fire magic at him and he instinctively drew quick aim and fired a bolt at Tommy's hand. The bolt contained powerfully strong magic. Whitelace's magic was supercharged because of his battle with Dragona. When the magic struck Tommy's hand, it instantly broke two of his fingers and sent his wand flying out and into the Pit. Tommy howled in pain.

When his wand entered the black rolling mass, it exploded with a loud boom that shook the entire room. Whitelace took the opportunity of the distraction and charged towards Tommy.

"Whitelace, no, the brid…," Tommy screamed in an attempt to stop him. But before Tommy could get out the word 'bridge', Whitelace stepped on what he thought was the first plank of the bridge, but since the plank didn't really exist, he tumbled into the Pit of Perpetual Pain.

Whitelace began to scream as soon as he touched the blackness. They were deep loud terrifying screams that spoke of horrible pain. He disappeared into the blackness, but, although they were muffled some, his screams continued. Carla and Michael ran the rest of the way around the room to the point where Whitelace had entered the blackness, but there was no sign of him, just his muffled blood curdling screams.

The instant Whitelace had started to scream, the words of rule number two flashed across Tommy's mind; 'Every Academy student shall honor, respect and protect every other student, past, present and future'. Tommy couldn't shake the words from his mind. He thought about all the trouble Whitelace had caused and what a problem he'd been, but that rule number two wouldn't leave his mind. Finally, he came to a realization. Once he did, his path was clear, as he now understood that Rule number two was not a Rule; it was a Code of Conduct, a Code of Honor. It didn't matter whether Whitelace deserved rescue or not, he was Honor bound to do all he could to save him. Although he desperately wanted to know about his parents, it would have to be at another time and another place. Because of his broken fingers, Tommy couldn't remove the tiny bottle's stopper with his hand, so he raised the bottle to his mouth and pulled the stopper with his teeth. He then let the brilliant silvery drop fall from the bottle onto his tongue and asked, "What must I do to save my fellow schoolmate?"

The answer was in his mind in an instant. Although he didn't want to accept it, he knew it was the truth. It was the truest thing that had ever been in his mind. It raised doubt and fear, but it was the truth, and he knew what he must do.

Tommy looked up at Carla and Michael. He knew this might be the last time he ever saw them, so he said to them loud and clear, "Hey, just two ordinary guys and one special girl, friends for life, right?"

"Right," Carla and Michael said simultaneously, and to their horror, Tommy jumped into the Pit.

Tommy's medallion immediately began to shine a brilliant white light as it hung loosely outside of his robes. As he entered the black darkness of the swirling mass, the light from the medallion formed a protective bubble around him. The bubble was large enough to accommodate two or more people. As soon as Tommy realized that he was not dead or screaming in pain, he began to move in the direction of Whitelace's screams.

Carla and Michael saw the bubble form around Tommy. They watched as he moved toward Whitelace's last known location. They wanted to help, but there was nothing they could do.

Tommy crossed the Pit. At one point, he came across the skeleton of some unfortunate animal that had accidently found its way into the Pit. The bones still quivered, yielding to the pain. Tommy found Whitelace curled up in a ball screaming in agony. Tommy quickly encompassed his body with the protective bubble. Whitelace's screams soon turned to moans. Tommy grabbed Whitelace and began to pull him along. It was exceptionally difficult as Whitelace was a large lad. It was further complicated because Tommy could hardly use the hand with the broken fingers.

"Meow," Tommy heard. "meow." Tommy would recognize that voice anywhere. It was Mister Buttercup, and he was trying to lead him to safety.

"I hear ya," Tommy called out. "Keep talking, I'm coming."

"Meow," Mister Buttercup called, and Tommy moved in the direction of the sound.

Mister Buttercup continued to meow and Tommy continued to move in his direction. Tommy eventually reached the high rounded wall at the edge of the Pit. As his bubble cleared the blackness away from the wall, Tommy saw Mister Buttercup. He was inside a large opening. The opening was sealed from the blackness by a magical barrier. As Tommy's protective bubble covered the opening, Mister Buttercup stepped through the magical barrier into Tommy's protective bubble and then turned around and stepped out of the bubble and back through the magical barrier into the opening.

"I get it Mister Buttercup," Tommy said. "You're trying to show me that we can pass through the barrier even if the blackness can't." Tommy pulled himself and Whitelace through the barrier and into the opening. They were in a long cave like tunnel. "I got to go back for Carla and Michael," Tommy said to Mister Buttercup. "Watch Whitelace. I'll be right back." Tommy passed through the protective barrier and his bubble returned. By that time, Carla and Michael had moved around the pit to where Tommy had entered the tunnel.

Tommy spotted them and called out, "You have to trust me, but one at a time, you must jump into the Pit. You must try to jump right into the bubble around me. There's a way out down here."

Michael looked at Carla and Carla looked back. "He must save you first," Michael said. "Neither he nor I could live with ourselves if something happen to you. Take your time and make an accurate jump."

Carla reluctantly agreed, took a good look at Tommy and his bubble, and made her leap. She successfully landed inside Tommy's bubble, but knocked him down in the process.

"Well thank you very much," Tommy said with a smile as he sat on his butt. "You certainly know how to make an entrance." Tommy stood up, put his arm around Carla's shoulder and escorted her to the barrier and the tunnel opening. "Step right through it," he instructed and gave Carla a slight push.

Carla stepped into the tunnel, said hello to Mister Buttercup and immediately turned her attention to helping Whitelace. He was in bad shape. Whitelace was only semiconscious and wasn't able to do anything for himself. Tommy returned to retrieve Michael.

Carla jumped when she heard Michel scream out in pain, but in a moment, he and Tommy entered the tunnel through the barrier. "What happened?" she asked right away.

"Oh, no big deal," Tommy answered. "Michael just missed the bubble a little."

"Oh yeah," Michael responded. "It's easy for you to say that it was no big deal, it wasn't your butt that got fried by the blackness," and then he smiled. It made both Carla and Tommy smile too. But, their smiles turned to looks of extreme concern as they looked at Whitelace.

"We got to get him to the infirmary," Carla explained, "and the sooner the better."

"I think this tunnel will take us back to the Castle," Tommy said. "Come on Mister Buttercup, lead the way." He reached down and gave Mister Buttercup a 'thank you' scratch behind his ears.

Carla and the boys did everything they could to lift, carry, and drag Whitelace gently back to the Castle. Mister Buttercup led the way. They followed Mister Buttercup for a ways until they came upon a three way fork in the tunnel. At this point, the character of the tunnel changed in appearance. It was clear to everyone that they had entered the lower levels of the castle. Mister Buttercup took the tunnel that went to the right and the kids followed. After a short distance, the tunnel ended with what appeared to be a door. However, the bottom of the door was about two feet above the floor. When Mister Buttercup reached the door, he rose up on his hind legs, pushed the door open with his front paws and jumped through the opening.

Carla and the boys struggled to get Whitelace over the raised lower door seal. They tried to be as gentle as possible, but Whitelace was still out of it. He moaned as the kids pulled and tugged him over the raised seal. Once they were past the door, they realized why it had a raised seal. It really wasn't a door as such. It was a life sized portrait of King Oleander. It was hung by hinges on its side so it would swing open. The kids knew instantly where they were. They were on the first staircase balcony above the Grand Foyer.

Chapter Twenty-Five

Friends, Family, and a Few Things Most Familiar

The early morning light was beginning to fill the Grand Foyer. Two Prefects were standing duty near the entrance doors to the Main Hall. They were preparing for the arrival of the students who would soon be coming down for breakfast. Carla and the boys were surprised to see that it was already morning. Carla ran to the staircase in search of help. Halfway down the stairs, she spotted the Prefects.

"Hey, Sir Prefects," Carla called. "We need some help up here. There's been an accident."

The two Prefects immediately headed for Carla. Carla, in turn, headed back up the stairs to the balcony. Tommy and Michael were sitting on the floor next to Whitelace when Carla returned. The first Prefect to reach them was Gottfried Titlemost, Whitelace's chief rival in the race to be chosen for the Queen's Guard.

"What's happed here?" Gottfried asked, and then seeing that it was Whitelace who was curled up on the floor, he exclaimed, "Oh my, Reggie. What's happened to you man?" Whitelace just moaned.

"He fell," Tommy said.

The second Prefect arrived. "It's Reginald," Gottfried said to him. "We've got to get him to the infirmary. I'll take him. You go get Professor Krusher and tell him that Reginald has been hurt, and then notify the Head Mistress that there's been an accident which has resulted in injuries." The second Prefect said okay and left immediately.

Gottfried took out his wand and placed a charm on Whitelace. "It'll make him lighter and protect him," he said in answer to the puzzled looks on the kids' faces. Gottfried then picked up Whitelace ever so gently and carried him to the infirmary.

The kids followed. "Make him lighter," Michael asked in a rhetorical way. "Why didn't you think of that, Carla?" he asked in a joking kind of way. "That sure would have made getting him here a whole lot easier."

"Don't know the magic," Carla said flatly. She then smiled and said, "But you can bet I'm going to learn it, especially with you two around."

They arrived at the Infirmary and Gottfried laid Whitelace on one of the empty beds. Medical Wizard Healsau came out of his office when he heard their noisy arrival.

"What's going on?" he asked as he approached. When he saw Whitelace, he moved to the side of the bed quickly and began to examine him.

Just as the Medical Wizard began his work, Professor Krusher entered the room, followed shortly thereafter by the Head Mistress. The Professor questioned Gottfried for a moment and then dismissed him to return to his duties.

"What has happened, Ambrost?" the Head Mistress inquired as she entered.

"I don't really know, Griselda. I just got here myself, but it seems that Reginald has taken a bit of a fall"

"A fall didn't cause these injuries," Medical Wizard Healsau said. "Can anyone tell me what actually happened to him?"

"He fell into the Pit of Perpetual Pain," Tommy answered.

"What," the Head Mistress, Professor Krusher and the Medical Wizard all exclaimed at once.

"He fell into the Pit of Perpetual Pain," Carla repeated for Tommy. "And, Tommy saved him," she added.

Everyone looked at Tommy and for the first time the Medical Wizard noticed Tommy's broken fingers.

"Oh, I see you are also injured," the Medical Wizard said. "Is anyone else injured?"

"Just Michael's bum," Tommy answered with a smile. "It got fried a bit in the Pit." Michael gave Tommy a dirty look. He didn't want anybody examining his bottom.

Two of the Medical Wizards assistants came in. The Medical Wizard set them to work on Tommy and Michael's injuries and turned his attention back to Whitelace.

"Is he going to be alright," Professor Krusher asked the Medical Wizard.

"I think so," he answered as he worked, "but it's going to take him some time to heal. I don't think there's any residual magic and, although the injuries look bad, I don't think they go too deep, they should heal. But, I can't say for sure. The Pit of Perpetual Pain, I thought that was just a myth."

"I, as well," the Professor concurred.

The Head Mistress and the Professor talked privately for a few minutes and then the Head Mistress left. The Professor told Carla and the boys that they were to rest there at the Infirmary for the day and that they were not to discuss what had happened with anybody. Carla protested being confined to the Infirmary because she wasn't injured. However, Professor Krusher made it clear that she had no other choice. Carla acquiesced. They all took beds, the Professor left and, in no time at all, they fell asleep.

They were awakened by one of the Assistants in the late afternoon. Once they were awake, a dinner meal appeared on trays next to their beds. They were starved and couldn't wait to get something to eat. However, just as they were about to take their first bites, Medical Wizard Healsau came out of his office and approached their beds.

"How's Whitelace?" Tommy asked once the Medical Wizard was alongside his bed.

"Oh, I think he's going to be alright," the Medical Wizard answered. "He's been in and out of consciousness a couple of times and his mind seems to be okay. Listen, I have a message for the three of you," he added. "You are to meet with the Head Mistress in her office as soon as you've finished eating." The Medical Wizard then smiled kindly and returned to his office.

Just a moment before, they were ready to eat just as fast as they could, but now the sooner they finished, the sooner they had to face the Head Mistress. They began to eat their meal, but not quite as heartily as they had previous thought they would.

"Do you think we're going to get expelled?" Michael asked without directing his question to either Carla or Tommy in particular.

"I would say that there's a pretty good chance," Tommy responded.

Carla laughed. "Expelled?" she asked. "Are you kidding? We'll be lucky if we're not thrown in the Queen's Dungeon."

"What do you think we should tell the Head Mistress?" Michael asked.

"I think we should tell the truth," Tommy answered.

"I agree," Carla added. "We may have broken a few rules, but I don't think we should disgrace ourselves by lying about it."

The boys agreed. Tommy suggested that Carla tell the story when the Head Mistress asks them what happened. That made Carla smile slightly. She had mixed emotions. She loved to tell a good tale, but it looked like this one was going to have an unhappy ending. They finished their meal and set off for the Head Mistress's Office.

They found her office and the door was closed. They knocked and the Head Mistress's voice from inside told them to enter. She had them sit down in three chairs that were placed close together in front of her desk. Once they were seated, she asked them to explain what had happened. Carla, in her usual elaborate way, began to tell the story. Tommy and Michael sat with somber looks on their faces and didn't say anything. But, nobody can tell a story quite like Carla and a couple of times she made the boys smile. This brought disparaging looks from the Head Mistress and the boys returned the somber expressions to their faces. It took her a while to tell the whole story, but eventually she finished when she told the Head Mistress how they crawled out onto the Grand Foyer balcony through the painting.

The Head Mistress sat and stared at them for a few minutes after Carla had finished. "First," she finally said, "all three of you will be excused from classes tomorrow."

"Are we being suspended?" Tommy asked.

"No," the Head Mistress answered. "But, the day after tomorrow is a regular no class day and I think it would be less disruptive to the classrooms if you three weren't there for a day or two. You will, however, be responsible to contact your Professors and gather your homework assignments. Now, secondly, the three of you are never to speak of this incident again, to no one at any time. Do I make myself clear?"

All three of them nodded, but Tommy asked, "But, Head Mistress, what do we say when the other kids ask us what happened?"

"You'll tell them that you saw Mr. Whitelace fall and when you tried to help him you also got hurt, and nothing more," the Head Mistress answered. "This whole thing could ruin Mr. Whitelace's chances of being selected to the Queen's Guard. It might even ruin his entire career if the whole story ever got out, and we don't want that, do we?" All three of them shook their heads. "Okay then," the Head Mistress continued. "You are excused from classes tomorrow, but you'll be expected to return to your classes the first of next week."

"Head Mistress Ma'am," Carla asked. "If I'm going to be off for two days, can I return home? I think I'd like to talk with my parents."

"I think that might be a good idea, young lady," the Head Mistress answered.

This caught Tommy and Michael by surprise, but Tommy elbowed Carla and she got the message. "Oh," she said, "and could Tommy and Michael come along and serve as my escorts?"

The Head Mistress thought for a moment and then answered. "Yes, in fact, it might be best if all three of you were gone for a couple of days until things settle down. You can leave tomorrow, but you must be back by the following evening, before curfew, understand?"

They nodded and then Carla asked, "Can I tell my parents the whole story?"

"Yes, that'll be okay. They'll hear about it sooner or later from Professor Krusher and I guess it's best they hear it from you first. You tell them what you just told me, and also, be sure to tell them what I've told *you*. They'll know how to handle it."

Head Mistress then excused them, but on their way out, she gave them another warning about keeping the story to themselves. Carla and the boys were ecstatic as they left the Head Mistress's office. Not only weren't they going to be thrown into the Queen's Dungeon, they weren't even going to be expelled, and to make it a little nicer; they were going to get an extra day off school.

They left the Head Mistress's office and headed to the Crow's Nest. On their way, they discussed their plans for the next day. Carla said she wanted to go to the library in the morning and Tommy said that he needed to replace his wand. So it was decided that Carla would go to the library in the morning, and then afterwards she would see all the Professors and get their homework assignments. While she was doing that, Tommy and Michael would go to the curiosity shop in New Castle Town and get Tommy a new wand. That way, they wouldn't have to stop at Cantwell on their way to Old Castle. And, that suited them all just fine, as none of them were too interested in getting anywhere near Damiana's well at the moment.

There were a number of kids in the Community Room when they got back to the Crow's nest. They were bombarded with questions as soon as they arrived and they did as the Head Mistress had instructed. They told everyone that Whitelace had tripped and fallen, and that they just happened to be there when it happened. That seemed to satisfy almost everybody, but there were a few suspicious looks.

Ronald Lockhard came down the stairs from the boys' bedroom and got really excited when he saw Tommy. He came down the remaining stairs in a hurry and went directly to Tommy.

"It was just an accident," Tommy started before Ronald could say anything.

"What?" Ronald asked with a little surprise. "Oh, oh yes, I thought it was something like that. But, I've got some exciting news. I know how it works."

"How what works?" Tommy asked.

"The antique message mirror, I know how to make it work."

"Really," Tommy said in surprise. In all that had happened, he'd forgotten about the device.

"Yeah," Ronald replied. "Come on upstairs and I'll show you."

Tommy and Michael excused themselves and followed Ronald up to the boys' bedroom. Carla also excused herself and went up to the girls' bedroom. As soon as the three boys got to the bedroom, Ronald rushed over and took the device from his bed.

"See," he said excitedly, "it takes a wand to power it. You write a message on a piece of paper and put it on the platter. Then you insert a wand right here." He pointed to a small opening on the lower front face of the device that was just big enough for the business end of a wand. "The wand," he continued, "collects ambient magic and charges the device. The roller comes out, copies the message, and then sends it off. The message will contain a sufficient magical charge to activate the device on the receiving end and, if there's a piece of paper on the platter of the receiving device, it will print the message. If there's no paper in the receiving device, it will hold the message until someone puts a piece of paper on it, or the magic runs out. If it has a wand in it, it will hold the message indefinitely."

"Wow," Tommy said. "I don't know how to thank you. This means a lot to me and I know it will mean a lot to my grandfather."

"Hey," Ronald said. "It was a lot of fun. The pleasure was all mine."

"Just the same," Tommy continued. "If there's anything I can do for you, you just let me know."

"Okay… Oh, yes," Ronald said in after thought, "there is one other thing. The device seems to contain some kind of translation component to it. Does your grandfather by chance speak a different language?"

"Well, yeah sorta," Tommy answered.

"Well, that's cool," Ronald replied, "because I think this thing will translate the message for him. Oh yes, that reminds me, don't forget to put an address on the message you write and indicate the language you'd like it translated into."

"Thanks again," Tommy said.

"Anytime," Ronald replied as he headed back to the stairwell and the Community Room.

"Hey, that's great, Tommy Boy," Michael said. "Looks like you got a message to write. While you do that, I'm going to lie down for a bit. My butt is still a little sore."

"Yeah," Tommy agreed. "My fingers are still really sore, but I think I can still write out a message. But, I'm going to need to borrow your wand to send the message."

"Here," Michael said as he pulled out his wand and gave it to Tommy. "Leave it in that machine all night if you want."

The boys went to their own beds. Tommy spent considerable time thinking about what to write. Michael, however, fell asleep almost immediately. Tommy decided to keep his message as brief as possible in the hopes that the whole message would be transferred correctly. He took out a pen and a sheet of paper and wrote:

To: Professor Layton Galloway
　　The University of Brookfield
　　The Museum Curator's Office
　　Planet Earth
Earth language

From: Tommy Travail
　　The Crow's Nest at the Queen's Academy
　　In the New Castle on the Home Plane
Written in the Home Plane language

Dear Grandfather,

Michael and I are all right. You'll be happy to know that we are in school. I haven't found out anything about Mom and Dad. I will let you know as soon as I do.

To make the device work and send a message, write a message on a piece of paper, put it on the platter and insert the wand in its proper slot on the front face. You'll be able to figure out where it goes. Don't forget to address it and put the translation languages on it.

I Love You Very Much,
Tommy

Tommy put the message on the platter of the device and inserted Michael's wand. The machine began to hum a little and it glowed slightly. The roller came out, rolled over the message, and then retracted. The machine continued to glow and hum for a few moments and then it seemed to shut itself off. Tommy removed the message and inserted a blank piece of paper. He left Michael's wand in it just as Michael had suggested. He put the device on his night stand, turned off the light, got back into his bed and fell asleep.

Tommy awoke the next morning and as soon as he got out of bed, he checked the device. He was disappointed to see that the piece of paper was still blank, but he wasn't surprised. He didn't know how the times of his two worlds compared and he didn't know how long it might take the message to get to Earth. He was disappointed, but hopeful.

Tommy and Michael met up with Carla in the Community Room and they went to breakfast. After breakfast, they went to the Infirmary to check on Whitelace. They spotted Whitelace as soon as they entered the Infirmary. He was partially sitting up in his bed on the other side of the room. He looked bad, but nowhere near as bad as he had the day before. Medical Wizard Healsau had done a lot in healing his injuries, but he looked weak and tired. Although he was awake, he hadn't noticed them until they were halfway to his bed. When he saw them, his eyes got very large and a peculiar look spread across his face. Carla and the boys immediately stopped when they saw the expression on his face. They suddenly realized that they just might be the last people that he'd want to see. They were just about to turn around and leave, when another unusual expression came across Whitelace's face, he smiled. It was a frail smile because of his over all weakness, but it was a warm smile. Carla and the boys had never before seen him truly smile. Whitelace weakly raised one hand and motioned with two fingers for them to come closer.

"How are you doing, Mister Whitelace, sir?" Tommy asked once they were along side of his bed.

"They tell me I'm going to be alright," Whitelace answered in a soft grumbly kind of voice. His many screams of pain had extremely stressed his vocal cords. They could see that it was difficult for him to talk. "It's just going to take a while for me to get my strength back," he continued, "but I'm glad you came by. I want to apologize to the three of you. I was wrong about you. You are three of the brightest, bravest and most honorable people I know. I would be proud to fight along side of you three, any time, any where."

Carla and the boys were stunned for a moment and didn't know what to say. Finally, Carla spoke first. "Well, I don't think we know what to say. That isn't quite what we were expecting to hear. Your apology is certainly accepted and your kind words are appreciated. Despite what some others might have thought," Carla took a quick look at Tommy and Michael, "deep down inside I always thought there was a good and decent person in you, and you have just proven me right. Your record proves you are one of the brightest and best ever to attend the Academy. I am proud to have you as a fellow schoolmate, and I too would be proud to fight along side of you."

"Here here," Tommy said. "I'll go along with that."

"Me too," added Michael.

All four of them smiled. It may just have been the smile on his face, but Whitelace was suddenly looking a little better.

"Well," Tommy said, "we do have to go. We're headed back to Old Castle for a couple of days. I hope when we get back at the first of the week that you're back on duty. The Castle isn't the same without you looking after things." Tommy smiled wryly. "We'll check in with you when we return and see how everything's going."

"Yeah," Michael agreed. "You need to get better, the first Cross-Country race will be coming up soon and the team needs you."

"Oh, Mister Whitelace, sir" Tommy said. "There's one more thing. We've had a talk with the Head Mistress and I can assure you that we will do as she says."

"Thanks," Whitelace said as the kids started to turn and leave. "By the way," he added, "my friends don't call me Mister Whitelace, sir; they call me Reggie." He gave them a wink with his blackened eye, winced slightly, and then smiled.

They all smiled. Carla and the boys gave him a little hand wave good-bye and they left. They split up once they left the Infirmary. Carla headed for the library and the boys headed for New Castle Town.

The boys went directly to the curiosity shop when they arrived in New Castle Town. They entered the shop and Tommy went to the wall that displayed the used wands. He examined the wands as he moved along the wall. There were hundreds of them on display. He really didn't have any idea of what he was looking for, so he just looked. There were long ones and short ones, thin ones and fat ones, light ones and heavy ones, but nothing was catching his eye until he saw something familiar. He immediately took the wand off the wall display. He examined it closely and his first impression had been correct. It was exactly like the wand that he had found in his grandfather's office. The two wands could have been twins. In their short time on the Home Plane, Tommy had never seen two wands alike. It felt good as he held the wand in his hand. It felt familiar. It felt comfortable. It reminded Tommy of the feeling that he had gotten when he carried the key piece back from The Tunnel of Fore and After Thought.

Mr. Keepers, the non-magical shop owner, came over to Tommy. "Find something you like there laddie," he asked.

"Maybe," Tommy answered coyly. He had played this game once before with Mr. Keepers. "How long's this old thing been lying around?"

"Oh it's been here a while," Mr. Keeps answered, "but that doesn't make any difference, it's still a fine piece, just hasn't found the right owner yet."

"How much?" Tommy asked.

"Uh, well, I think that goes for one drop of sil… er ah, gold, yes that's it one drop of gold."

Tommy almost bit his tongue trying to keep himself from laughing. "Where did you get this wand?" Tommy asked fighting back his chuckle.

"I got it where I get all this stuff," Mr. Keepers answered smugly. "I bought it from somebody."

"But who'd you buy it from?" Tommy continued to press.

"Oh, I'd have to think about that for a while." Mr. Keeper replied. "I buy so much stuff you know."

"Well," Tommy began. "I'll give you one drop of silver for it and maybe a bit more if you can tell me who you got it from."

"Let's go over to the counter and I'll see if I can find any record of where I got it," Mr. Keepers said and headed off to the main counter.

Tommy followed along. When he got to the counter, he reached in his pocket for his last drop of gold. If he couldn't make a deal for one drop of gold or less, he was going to have to go to the bank, or possibly, borrow it from Michael if he had any money left. Tommy had been carrying his Euro in his pocket all this time. Even when he changed clothes, he made sure he put the Euro in his pocket. He could no longer read the words on it. The characters just seemed to appear as squiggly lines, just as his medallion and his father's journal did back on Earth. Tommy had just gotten used to it being there. It was always like a little reminder of home.

Tommy may have gotten too used to it being there. As he pulled the drop of gold out of his pocket, the Euro also came out and dropped to the floor. Tommy bent down, picked it up, and set it on the counter.

Mr. Keepers had pulled out a ledger and was looking through it. He looked up at one point and when he did, he spotted the Euro.

"I got something just like that," Mr. Keeper exclaimed. He reached in a drawer, pulled out a Euro, and set it on the counter. "See," he said. "It's got those same funny squiggly looking lines on it. The guy I got it from said it had magic in it."

Tommy looked at it. Just like it was with his Euro, he was unable to read it, but there was no doubt that it was a Euro. Tommy didn't know if the wand belonged to his mother or father, but he knew the Euro had to belong to one of them. His parents, as far as he knew, were the only people who could have come to the Home Plane from Earth since the Euro was created. "Where'd you get this?" Tommy asked.

"I got it from, hey wait a minute," Mr. Keepers hesitated. "I got it from the same guy I got that wand from. I remember now. He's that ruffian that was in the papers here not too long ago. It was something about some missing scrolls."

"Skeezicks," Tommy declared.

"Yes, that's the guy," Mr. Keepers confirmed, "Barnabas Skeezicks."

"I'll tell you what," Tommy said. "I'll give you one drop of gold for the wand and this note." He took his drop of gold and set it in the middle of the counter top.

Mr. Keepers wanted to refuse the offer, but he couldn't take his eyes off the drop of gold. Finally, he swiped his hand across the counter top and snatched up the piece of gold. "Deal," was all he said.

Tommy smiled, picked up the two Euros and put them in his pocket. He slipped his new wand up under his sleeve and turned to locate Michael. He started towards Michael and then turned back around. "Say, Mister Keepers, do you remember that antique message mirror you sold me a few days ago."

"Sure," Mr. Keepers replied.

"You didn't by chance get that from Skeezicks as well, did you?" Tommy asked.

"You know," Mr. Keepers replied thoughtfully, "now that you mention it, I may have. I can't say for sure, but it really seems to me that I did get it from him."

Tommy thanked Mr. Keepers, collected Michael up, and they left the shop. It was now clear to Tommy that, sooner or later, he was going to have to track down this Skeezicks character. They went to the sweet shop before they left town and loaded up on Chocolates and Chewy Chew Chews.

Carla and the boys all got back to the Crow's nest about the same time. They went and had a quick lunch and then returned to the Crow's Nest. When they got back, they went to their bedrooms to gather their things before leaving for Old Castle. Tommy checked the antique message mirror, but the piece of paper was still blank, which discouraged him some. Once they gathered their stuff and packed their back-packs, the boys met Carla and they left the Castle.

The boys were much more skilled wave riders now and they moved along quickly. They completed the first half of their journey before they took a break. At their current pace, they would arrive in Old Castle around dinner time. Carla and the boys sat on the ground under a large tree and shared some Chewy Chew Chews.

Carla had been anxious all day to talk about her trip to the library. "The reason I went to the library today," she began, talking directly to Tommy, "was because of something King Oleander said to you when you told him your name. He said, 'So you're of the Tra and of the Vail.' That got me thinking. So when I got to the library this morning, the first thing I did was to check and see if there were any references to Travail, but unfortunately there wasn't any. I then checked to see if there was anything on the Tra. It took quite a bit of research and a bit of good luck to find anything. It seems the Queen had all references to the Tra asterisked."

"Asterisked?" Tommy asked inquisitively.

"Yes," Carla answered. "It seems that the Queen has ordered that all references to the Tra be removed. In every text where the Tra had been mentioned, there is now an asterisk, and the information has been removed. If you check the asterisk, it says, 'Removed by order of the Queen.' However, I got lucky when I happened to find an old Travel Bulletin. It must have been overlooked by the Queen's Guard."

"The Travel Bulletin," Carla continued, "doesn't go into too many details, so I'm guessing at some of this. But, it seems that the Tra was a Noble group that, for some reason, went to the outer edge of the Realm and set up their own Kingdom. It appears to have been a very successful and prosperous Kingdom. When King Oleander was young and on his travels, he probably visited there. Anyway, sometime after King Oleander became King, the Tra people were betrayed by their own Queen. Well, she wasn't really their Queen; a Succulant killed the real Queen and took over her identity."

"A Succulant, what's that?" Tommy asked.

"It's a very rare and yet very powerful beast of a creature," Carla answered seriously. "It has the power to transform itself into the image of other living thing. As it grows, it works to accumulate as many living things around it as it can. As it ages, it begins to draw its life force from those living things. It can live for a very long time if it has enough victims. Just as it dies, it spits out a rat like creature that will eventually grow into another Succulant."

"So the Queen of the Tra was replaced by a Succulant," Tommy stated in an inquiring way.

"Yes," Carla replied. "Like I said, a Succulant killed the Queen and took her place. It appears that the Succulant eventually sucked the life force out of the Tra people. By the time the Travel Bulletin was issued, the Succulant and the Tra people had completely vanished. Their Kingdom remains empty to this day and no one dares to go there. In fact, that is why the Travel Bulletin was issued. It was to warn travelers to stay away from the area."

"But," Tommy interrupted, "isn't it possible that some of the Tra survived?"

"Yes, it's possible," Carla answered.

"So, if any of them did survive, then one of them could have been my dad's ancestor."

"Yes," Carla confirmed, "and there's something else I want you to think about."

"What's that," Tommy asked.

"It's the 'vail' part of your name," Carla continued. "Vail is the Family name of the Royal Family. King Richard was a Vail. They have all been Vails going all the way back to Erlin's time. So, it is possible that you are indeed of two Royal bloods, the Tra and the Vail. Maybe you really are a Prince."

"Somehow I doubt it," Tommy responded flatly. "I mean, it might be fun to think about it, but I'm pretty sure old King Oleander was feeling the magic of my medallion and that led him to some false conclusions. But, it could be that I'm somehow related to the Tra people. I think that's a good lead and we can work on that. We can ask Professor Pastorie about them."

"I don't think so," Carla interjected. "If the subject of the Tra has been asterisked by the Queen, he'll be forbidden to talk about them. I think it's best to keep him out of it. I believe if we're going to find out more about the Tra, we'll have to get into the Great Library at the Newest Castle. It's run by the Ministry of All Things Magic. I seriously doubt that anything in their restricted section would ever be asterisked, so if there's anything left to be found on the Tra that's where it would be." Carla paused for a moment and then continued, "And, I don't think you should be so quick to dismiss the 'vail' part of your name either. I think we should look into that too."

"You're right, of course," Tommy conceded. "We must look into anything that might reveal something about my parents. Which reminds me, being that we'll be so close, I want to go to the Old Castle. I have a couple of ideas and there's a theory I want to test."

"Sure," Carla responded. "We could go tomorrow morning."

"Thanks, Carla," Tommy said looking deeply into her eyes. "Thanks for caring enough to do all of this for me. In fact, thanks for *everything* you've done for both me and Michael."

"Not a problem," Carla said with a smile.

Tommy stood up and extended his hand to assist Carla. Michael, who had been listening intensely, but hadn't said anything, also stood up. Once the three of them were on their feet, they popped up on their waves and continued on their journey. As they expected, they arrived at Carla's house just in time for dinner. Carla had sent her parents a message on her message mirror telling them they were coming. Carla's parents greeted them with concerned looks, but welcomed them with true warmth and friendliness. They invited them to come and eat, and eat they did. The trip had made them hungry and Lady Witch Crosswell made the most delicious food. When they finished, Carla explained that she and the boys wanted to go on an early morning wave ride to the Old Castle and back. Carla's dad approved. The boys knew that Carla wanted to talk with her parents in private, so Tommy and Michael excused themselves and retired to the guest bedroom.

The next morning Carla and the boys got up early, but not as early as Carla's parents had. Carla's dad had already eaten and gone off for the day, and her mom was busy preparing breakfast for Carla and the boys when they came down. Carla's mom gave them a warm good-morning greeting and set their breakfast out on the table. She asked the boys how they were feeling. She asked Tommy how his fingers were doing and asked Michael how his bottom side was coming along. When she asked that, Michael's face turned as red as Mr. Keepers nose. He mumbled something about it being just fine and Carla and Tommy laughed.

They set off for the Old Castle when they finished eating. Carla told her mom that they would be back for lunch. She also told her that they were going to have to leave after lunch for their return trip to the New Castle and the Academy. They popped up on their waves and rode down the old road to the Old Castle. As they approached the old burnt out structure, they recalled their first meeting and the boys first day on the Home Plane. So much had happened in such a short time, it seemed like a lifetime ago.

They glided up to the old fountain where Tommy and Michael first appeared. "I've been doing some thinking about this," Tommy began. "This is where we arrived. We can compare this to the University Museum and the breezeway that connects the Museum to my grandfather's house. My dad seems to have first appeared on that breezeway. If his appearance there can be related to our appearance here, we might be able to determine where the Magic Mirror that transported my dad to Earth is located."

Tommy and Michael made a few calculations and paced a few things off. Having done so, they found themselves standing in the middle of the old burnt out Castle. "If we're right," Tommy said, "the Mirror Room should be just below us. Let's look around and see if we can find a way to get to the Castle's lower levels."

It took some time, but Carla uncovered a hidden door with stairs that led downward. They lit their wands and proceeded down the dark staircase. At the bottom of the stairs, they entered a labyrinth of catacombs. It took quite a while, but with some good calculations, a little guesswork, and a bit of luck, they found themselves standing in front of a door that Tommy was sure led into the Magic Mirror Room. The lock on the door was broken and Tommy pushed it open. They entered the room. The room was filled with the same glowing light that had filled the Mirror Room below the Museum. The room was, in fact, identical to the room below the Museum in every way, except the Mirror was gone. It appeared that someone else had beaten them there and had taken the Magic Mirror. Tommy was devastated. Since there was no longer any reason for them to stay there, they returned to Carla's house.

Carla's mom was just setting lunch out for them when they returned. They had just missed Carla's dad. He had been there, but he had just left. "What's the matter?" Carla's mom asked when she saw the gloomy looks on their faces. "Didn't you enjoy your trip to the Old Castle?"

"Oh, we enjoyed it," Carla answered. "We just expected to run across some interesting things on our way, and we didn't."

"Well, that's too bad," her mom consoled, "I hope you'll enjoy your lunch."

They did enjoy their lunch. Afterwards, the boys thanked Lady Witch Leila and apologized for not getting much of a chance to visit with the Master Wizard. She said she would pass their apologies along to him. Carla gave her mom a big hug and a kiss and they left for their return to the Academy.

The trip back to the Academy was a somber one. Tommy couldn't get over the missing Mirror. They arrived back at the Crow's Nest and headed to their bedrooms to drop off their stuff. They agreed to meet back in the Community Room.

Tommy went over to his bed and tossed his back-pack on it. He looked over to the antique message mirror and the piece of paper on the platter had writing on it. Tommy's emotions soared as he picked up the message and read it. It said, "Dear Tommy, I am so very happy to hear that you and Michael are all right. And, I'm very pleased to hear you two are in school. I was preparing to set out on a rescue mission, but if you're okay, I guess I can cancel it. I'm sorry you haven't been able to find out anything about your mom and dad. If you do find out anything, let me know. However, this message contraption is very old and doesn't seem to work very well. I don't know how long it will last, so I suggest that we keep our communications to a minimum. But, do keep me informed and let me know if there is anything I can do. I Love You Very Much Too, Grandpa."

Tommy was exploding with emotion. He called Michael over and showed him the letter. Even though Michael said he would never go back, the letter from home also filled him with joy and excitement. Enthusiastically, they ran to the stairs to go down and show it to Carla. Halfway down the stairs, they ran into Ronald Lockhard, who was on his way up.

"It works," Tommy said as soon as he saw Ronald. "I sent a message to my grandfather and he just sent one back. Thanks a million. You're the best."

"That's super," Ronald said as he beamed with pride. "I'm glad I could help." Ronald then continued on his way up and the boys continued on their way down.

Tommy spotted Carla and showed her the message. Although she didn't know Tommy's grandfather, it made her happy to see Tommy and Michael in such high spirits. They decided to go into one of the Study Rooms and start on their homework, but Tommy and Michael had to return to their bedroom and get their books first. Carla went on ahead to the Study Room as she already had her books.

Tommy put the letter from his grandfather in his trunk and got out his books. Michael got his books as well and they returned to the Study Room. They took seats across from Carla and started in on their studies. After a while, Tommy paused in a mood of reflection.

"You know what," he said out of no where, "when old King Oleander said that Dragona would eat us if she didn't like our answers, I thought he was kidding. But as it turns out, he wasn't kidding, he wasn't kidding at all."

"No, he definitely wasn't kidding," Michael added.

"Well, I tell you," Tommy continued. "The next time we're in a situation like that and someone tells me a dragon is going to eat me, I'll believe him."

"The *next* time, what do you mean, the *next* time!" Carla exclaimed with a scowl on her face, but the expression on her face quickly turned into a whimsical smile. "Now listen to me Mister 'of the Tra and of the Vail', don't you go off and start thinking you're some kind of Prince or something, and that you can get away with that kind of stuff anytime you want."

"Well, I certainly don't think I'm a Prince," Tommy said with a smile on his face, "but I do think I'm special."

"What," Michael said with a dumb look on his face.

"That's right," Tommy continued. "I think we're both special. I mean, we *were* just two ordinary guys until we happened to meet one extraordinary girl. As a result of that chance meeting we all became friends, friends for life, right?"

"Right," Carla and Michael answered together.

"So," Tommy went on, "I come to realize just how special we are to have a friend like her. The point is that; her friendship makes us special."

"I whole heartedly agree with you," Michael responded. "We must be very special to have her as our friend, and I must say, the whole Home Plane is lucky that we do."

Carla's face turned red with modest embarrassment and Tommy gave Michael an inquiring look, as he didn't quite follow Michael's last comment.

"Well, stop and think about it," Michael said in response to the expression on Tommy's face. "We've caused a considerable amount of trouble since we've been here. Just think how much more trouble we might have caused if we didn't have Carla looking after us."

All three of them paused and thought about it for a moment. It didn't take long before they had formed images of the additional havoc and chaos the boys may have caused if they hadn't had Carla's guidance. Realizing the scary truth that the boys could have caused even more trouble and mayhem struck them as frightening and funny all at the same time. They started to laugh. They laughed and laughed, they laughed until tears dropped from their cheeks.

THE END

"Meow"

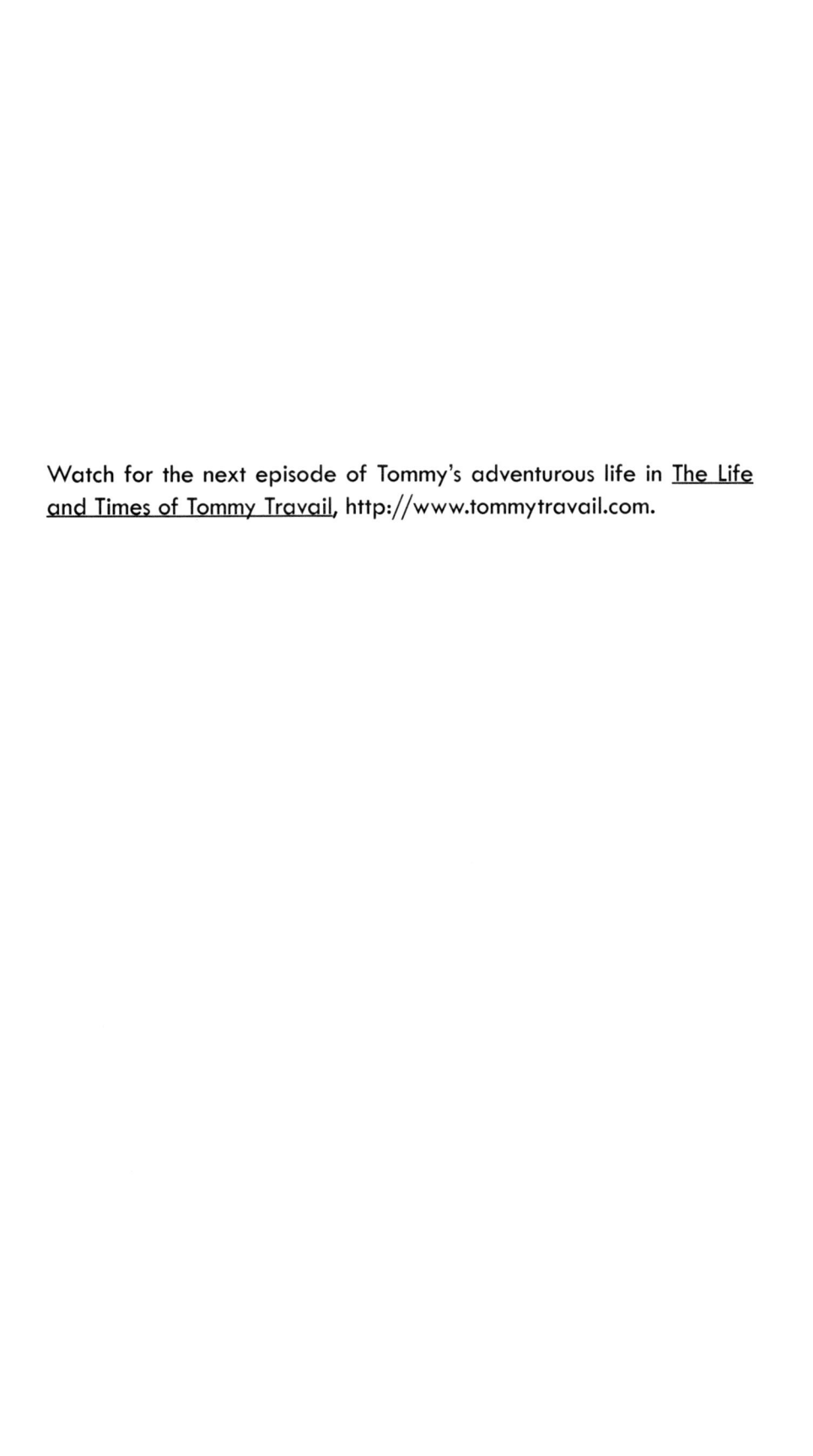

Watch for the next episode of Tommy's adventurous life in The Life and Times of Tommy Travail, http://www.tommytravail.com.

CPSIA information can be obtained at www.ICGtesting.com
Printed in the USA
BVOW070613011111

274930BV00003B/3/P